THE CURE

FOR

DROWNING

THE CURE

FOR

DROWNING

LOGHAN PAYLOR

RANDOM HOUSE CANADA

PUBLISHED BY RANDOM HOUSE CANADA

Copyright © 2024 Loghan Paylor

www.penguinrandomhouse.ca

Random House Canada and colophon are registered trademarks.

Library and Archives Canada Cataloguing in Publication

Title: The cure for drowning / Loghan Paylor.
Names: Paylor, Loghan, author.
Identifiers: Canadiana (print) 2023046713X | Canadiana (ebook) 20230467148 |
ISBN 9781039006454 (softcover) | ISBN 9781039006461 (EPUB)
Subjects: LCGFT: Novels.
Classification: LCC PS8631.A95 C87 2024 | DDC C813/.6-dc23

Text design: Jennifer Griffiths
Cover design: Jennifer Griffiths
Cover illustration: Jennifer Griffiths

Printed in Canada

10 9 8 7 6 5 4 3 2 1

For all of us who came before,
    no matter how we knew ourselves and our desires,

    and for Michael, always.

& I will name my hunger a blessing,
loving it as I love all other animals.

"NOVEMBER," KEATON ST. JAMES

JANUARY 1931

IT WAS A BITTER AFTERNOON, DURING ONE OF THE WORST winters the province had ever seen. A ten-year-old girl walked into the forest with her two brothers and didn't come out again.

The youngest, Jep, remembered they were looking for cranberries, drawn over the snowy fields and across the river into the wetlands and forest on the other side. He blamed the oldest, Landon, for getting them lost. Landon always reminded Jep that there were no cranberries to be found in January. That they had been seeking beech nuts, buried deep under the snow. Six-year-old Jep had been told to stay home but followed his siblings anyway.

The three of them had trod a large, meandering loop of the forest without finding a single cranberry or beechnut. Kathleen wanted to press on, up into the pine forest on the ridge, but it was too far for the smallest feet in their party, so Landon turned them homeward, unsure of his way among the snow-buried trails. After, he would claim it was Jep's fault they ended up at that part of the river at all.

Neither disputes that it was a late winter afternoon, with blank, heavy clouds overhead. Three children walked among evergreens so dark they seemed black, the snowscape slowly turning blue-grey as the light slanted. Twelve-year-old Landon in the lead, his hat frosted like a birthday cake. Kathleen, ten, in the middle, glaring at the back of his head. Behind them, jumping from one boot hollow to the next, came Jep, bundled in his oversized coat and scarf. Unseen eyes watched their progress with silent, patient interest.

They emerged from the woods on the ridge that swept up from the river and stopped. They could see the farm where it lay a few miles ahead, skirted on three sides by fields marked with fletchings of trees and fences. The river traced the foot of the ridge for several miles, then ran down to join the Grand River and finally empty into Lake Erie.

Kathleen started whistling. A long gust of wind shook the branches of the trees behind them, the evergreens adding their hissing chorus, until the children were surrounded by the sounds of rushing water, the creak and groan of branches rubbing together.

"Stop that," Landon snapped. "You'll call them up."

"No, I won't," Kathleen said, but she fell silent and tucked her face back into her scarf. The wind died away. Sparkling lights flickered at the edge of their vision, dancing along the snow. A trick of the fading winter light, the children thought.

Below their feet, the ridge plunged straight down to the bank for half a mile in either direction, cut by a narrow gully that was a creek in warmer seasons. The downed ash tree they had used to cross the water hours earlier lay several miles northwest. It would be dark by the time they reached it again. To the left, the river was wider and deeper, the ice hidden under a blanket of pristine snow. To the right, it narrowed and broke into shallow rapids, the current moving too quickly to be caught by the frost.

"We'll cross there," Landon said, pointing to a place just above the rapids where the ice was solid and impressions of animal tracks marred the snow. Without waiting for a reply, he plunged down, breaking a path for the others to follow.

When they reached the bank, Landon stepped out first, sliding his boots one at a time through the snow. Kathleen took Jep's hand and towed him along in her wake. To their right, the ice fell away, revealing the rushing, blue-black water of the rapids. As Landon pulled ahead, moving quickly towards the opposite bank, Jep tugged free of Kathleen and hurried after him.

Kathleen placed her feet hesitantly, arms windmilling for balance when her boot slid on the hidden ice. When the boys reached the other side, they waited for their sister impatiently, cold and hungry and eager to be home. Landon tucked in Jep's scarf, brushed the snow from his hat. Darkness rushed up the valley, the very last of the light dying in the northwest. Purple-blue shadows slithered across the snow to lick their boots.

"Kath, come on!" Landon called. But Kathleen had stopped in the middle of the river, staring at the gap in the ice where the rapids rushed. As they watched, she took two steps towards the open water. As though she were hypnotized, Jep would say later.

"Kitty?" Jep started towards the river's edge, but Landon grabbed the back of his coat.

She took another step and paused, her head cocked, eyes on the open water. "Can't you hear it?" Kathleen's voice was barely a whisper above the wind over snow. "Someone's calling me."

"That was us," Landon yelled.

"No, there's a light, somewhere under . . ." She shuffled a few more steps. The ice groaned. Landon shoved Jep farther up the bank, telling him to stay put, and started towards his sister.

He remembered later that her face was lit with a faint green-blue glow. Jep claimed that the footprints they'd made on the ice also shone with the same light, like a reflection of the dusk sky. Except the clouds hung low and there was no light anywhere.

Kathleen took another step towards the water, her eyes following something under the ice.

"No!" Landon's voice cut through the darkness. "Look at me, Kitty. At me."

His sister startled, as though just realizing where she was. The ice creaked beneath the children's feet. On the bank, Jep started to cry.

"Don't move, Kitty," Landon said. "Stay exactly as you are." He began edging forward. Snot dripped from Kathleen's nose. She wiped it with her mitten. A few more steps and he would be within reach.

A blue-green light under the ice drifted towards the centre of the river. Kathleen followed it with her eyes, and then turned, lifting a boot.

A sharp crack. Landon's shout. The ice broke and Kathleen plunged into cold black water.

Somehow Landon managed to carry her body two miles uphill across the fields and back to the farmhouse. By the time he stumbled up the back steps, Jep, half-dead on his feet, trailing him, it was full dark and pelting sleet had started to fall, coating the trees and the fence rails and the steps in cruel ice. The door opened, spilling orange kerosene light onto their faces, the warmth of the kitchen hitting them like a wall. Their sister's small body slid to the floorboards. Jep's tears had long since frozen into icy tracks down his cheeks.

Their mother refused to believe Kathleen was dead. She stripped the girl of her frozen clothes and wrapped her in a dozen quilts, sent her husband, Dermot, out to the woodshed to fetch logs to build up the fire. She heated bricks and shoved them between the blankets, wiped Kathleen's pale, grey face with a cloth she dipped into hot water. Pried open her lips to spoon tea into her mouth, which trickled out again. The girl remained frozen, her flesh as unyielding as a tree limb. Long after Jep had crept upstairs to bed, and Landon had drunk his weight in hot tea and felt fiery, agonizing feeling return to his fingers and toes, Caroline sat by Kathleen, her daughter's limp hand clasped in hers, muttering every prayer she knew.

That night, the sleet gave way to the worst blizzard in a century, which pounded the walls of the farmhouse. After midnight, with her daughter still pale and lifeless, Caroline began the older prayers, her Gaelic whispers filling in the silence between the cracks and hisses from the wood stove. Just before dawn, when the wind eased and stars showed through the break in the cloud cover, she went out to the barn with the axe and gathered a newborn lamb from its place among the flock and carried it out into the frozen field, glittering and white in the palest of predawn light. The scattering of blood across the snow was a constellation all its own.

Red broth painted her daughter's lips with a facsimile of life. Red, too, was the sliver of heart-flesh Caroline slipped between her teeth and onto her tongue. When the two boys and Dermot stepped heavily into the kitchen that morning, the dead girl opened her eyes and smiled at her father.

Landon claimed later that she was never dead, only in a false sleep brought on by cold water. That she was saved by his mother's tireless efforts to rewarm her. Jep believed that she was dead for certain, that no one could have survived that freezing water, let alone the hour it took to carry her home. Dermot said it was a miracle from God. Whenever Caroline was asked how her daughter had survived, she looked away out the nearest window with a thin, brittle smile and did not answer.

However it happened, as Jep went out to feed the sheep and found one less lamb among the flock, and as Dermot took Landon out to the barn and switched his legs for carelessness, their sister who had been dead sat at the kitchen table and drank another cup of her mother's red broth.

For three days, she didn't speak, alternating between sleeping and staring at the pale sunlight on the wall. Her family had to teach her again how to hold a spoon, how to turn the pages of a book, and how to fumble a button through a buttonhole. She wouldn't speak, merely watched them all with large hazel eyes. It was Jep who took to calling her Kit, since the innocence of a kitty didn't seem to fit her anymore.

By the time the snow thawed in the spring, Kit could run and laugh and wrestle with Landon and Jep as well as any other child. If reading sometimes came slow where before it had been quick, or a distaste for sweets was now replaced with a desire to lick honey straight from the jar, or if a shadowed look sometimes passed over Kit's face like a cloud across the sun, these were but small changes to accept in the wake of a miracle. To see their dead child running, whole and alive, in the sunlit fields, was a thing Dermot and Caroline never questioned too closely.

Kit seemed to remember nothing from before that winter day. And in all the years that came after, no one heard Kit whistle again, not even in summer under a high noon sun.

PART ONE

APRIL 1939

KIT

THE FIVE O'CLOCK PASSENGER TRAIN FROM TORONTO only came through on Fridays, and it wasn't always easy to steal away from my chores in time to meet it. As the sun began to draw lower, I took my chance, riding out of the gate on the pretense of tracking a fox to its den. The vixen easily gave me the slip, as I expected, but she'd led me across the road and along the river. Soon, I was down the valley and three fields over, where the train whistled in the distance.

I put my heels to my horse and we began our headlong rush to the tracks. The game was to race the train to the far end of the fields, catching it before it disappeared into the trees and out onto the narrow railway bridge over the river. Between the uneven ground, the gopher holes, and the cedar-rail fences, it was an incredibly foolish game, but my horse, Rat, and I had been playing it since he was a half-broke yearling and I was barely tall enough to reach his withers. We had never managed to win, and yet I hoped that one day we would, and some small part of me would be caught by the train and carried away, flying out across the country to the farthest ends of the continent. I would be able to close my eyes and be any-where but here with just a wish.

The train whistled, and I took it as a challenge. Rat jumped the first fence with a practised surge of muscles, me floating on his back like a dandelion wisp. He got his hooves under him and we pushed forward, gaining on the train a little at a time. The second fence appeared in the distance, a little taller and with a top rail grown rickety from the number of times we'd clipped it on the way over.

The passenger cars seemed motionless alongside us, as though the train and the horse and I were standing still while the landscape rushed past beneath us. In one window, I saw the watery smudge of brown and grey that was my reflection. In the centre of it was a face pressed against the glass. I caught the impression of dark hair under a hat, wide, intelligent eyes—not frightened, but curious—a mouth hidden in the reflection of the field. Her hand, instinctively rising up towards the window.

REBEKAH

Our journey was like a series of images in a silent film. Small, anonymous creeks, nameless forests and fields broken with fence lines. A herd of cows, their heads bowed near a barrel trough beside a barn. Grass still tipped white and grey from the winter. A flock of geese rising into a ragged vee, skimming overhead and out of my sight. The sun stretching fingers across the landscape, flashing between the trees. The faintest touch of gold on the waters of a flooded valley as we screeched past.

My mother was asleep with her hands tucked inside her muff, her face slack beneath her hat. My father frowned slightly at his newspaper, glimpses of the landscape reflected in his glasses.

I set down my pen. I had already written two letters to Madeleine and yet it still seemed impossible that I would not see her tomorrow, with her dimpled smile and the crush of her curls against my cheek as we kissed hello. Even less could I comprehend the distance that now separated us. My thoughts ran in the tempo of the train, jolting along the tracks that cut through the landscape like shears.

It would have been possible to make the journey from Montreal in a single day, but for the sake of Maman's health, we had travelled only as far as Toronto and spent the night at the Royal York Hotel. It was nowhere near as grand as the Windsor, but comfortable enough for one night's stay. Maman had even admired the crystal chandelier in the lobby, though only after we were settled in our rooms, for fear the English would overhear us and think she was impressed.

During an early dinner in the dining room, the waiter's smile stiffened at my father's German accent. We were surrounded now by flat English vowels and guttural g's. All my life I had swum freely between languages: French with my friends, my maternal grandparents, and throughout the city; German reserved for studies with my father; and English for school language lessons and a handful of my father's colleagues. English had been easily tamed during my lessons in the chilly upper classroom overlooking the *parc*. Here, though, it was a swirl of sounds that flew past almost too quick to catch. My mother spoke quietly and only to us, darting glances at anyone who came near our table, and my allegiance to Quebec was evident with every syllable that dropped from my lips. Even my father, accustomed as he was to speaking with his anglophone patients, had stumbled while placing his order.

I picked up my pen, determined to finish my letter, but I couldn't bring myself to write more about our journey. Madeleine and I had only spoken about my leaving in the most abstract terms. She said she was excited for me, as though this was not an exile but an expedition into the unknown. It seemed impossible that I would never again sit beside her in the upper classroom at Sacré-Coeur, our elbows jostling for space on our shared desk. The edges of my vision blurred and I wrenched my thoughts away.

The train whistled long and loud as it slowed to take a wide curve. I could see the engine ahead, smoke curling along its back like a mane. I had imagined a jaunty little steam engine like something from a picture book, but this was a black, brutal machine. A hawk wheeled overhead, so high that even the noisy passage of the train did not shake it from where it stood pinned against the clouds.

The landscape abruptly fell into a long, rolling field. In the distance, a flicker of movement. A dark smudge that grew and resolved itself into a horse and a rider. The train continued to bank right, then straightened. The horse followed, curving into a smooth parallel with the tracks. I looked around me, as though there was someone I should alert about this runaway horse.

But when the rider drew alongside, I saw he was not in danger at all. Crouched low in the saddle, he was racing the train. I leaned closer to the glass, wishing the horse wings, thrilled by the chase.

The train whistled again, and I pressed my face against the window as they ran straight at a fence, the horse leaping up and over in a smooth, powerful movement, the rider seeming to float, shirt billowing. As the horse pulled out of the landing, stretching his neck and regaining speed, the rider noticed me. Two straight eyebrows lifted in surprise. The sun on my cheek where it slanted through the window, the horses' hooves churning against the grass, the rider's brown hair gleaming in the same sunlight.

Then the horse veered away from the train, dropping speed, and I sailed onwards, craning my neck to look back.

The mayor was waiting to greet us at the station. As a young porter with spots on his face wrestled our cases into a motor car, I let my mother fuss with my hat and tidy my hair.

The mayor was a short man with a red complexion, who pumped my father's hand enthusiastically. "Dr. Kromer! A pleasure to meet you at last. And your family!"

My father was wearing the expression he reserved for patients: keen interest overlayed with professional detachment.

"Mayor Gorseman, may I introduce my wife, Mad—Missus Régine Kromer, and my daughter, Miss Rebekah Kromer." Maman offered her hand and Mr. Gorseman shook it nearly as heartily as he had my father's. I nodded politely, keeping both gloved hands wrapped firmly around the handle of my suitcase. I had refused to let the porter take it, for fear that he would scratch the new leather or jostle the books I had carefully packed inside.

"Good, good," the mayor said. "Please, climb in, I'll take you to the house."

After he tipped the porter, my father got into the front seat, while Maman and I squeezed into the back next to our cases. I was surprised when Mr. Gorseman himself took the wheel.

As the car came to life with a jittering, snorting start, he shouted over the noise of the engine, "A beauty, isn't she? I got her off a man in Orangeville just last month!"

We pulled away from the station and down the road, an altogether more jarring ride than the easy swaying of the train. The town of Harrichford was smaller even than I'd imagined, and lower to the ground. Shop fronts with striped awnings squatted next to brick houses. Without the soaring cathedrals and stone buildings of Montreal, the sky here seemed overwhelming.

"That's the grocer's," Mr. Gorseman shouted over his shoulder. "Post and telegraph office in there as well. Beside him is the chemist and local vet." The noise of the motor carried away most of what the mayor was saying, but my father nodded.

There were only a few people on the single main street and a handful of parked cars. We overtook a wagon pulled by large, placid horses, their feet as big as dinner plates. When another motor car passed us, Mr. Gorseman cheerfully tooted his horn and the driver tooted back. We drove by several churches, and each seemed as tiny as the china models my grand-mère set up each Christmas in her parlour.

At last, having shown us every building in Harrichford, Mr. Gorseman drove out of the village along a narrow road with fields and farmhouses on either side.

"This is the quickest way to your new place," he said, his thick hands gripping the steering wheel. "But don't follow it all the way or your feet will get wet!" He laughed heartily at his own joke, then explained. "Head far enough and you get to Kincardine, on the shore of Lake Huron. I'm going to take Milly—that's my wife— to the beach there this summer. Have ourselves a picnic."

He turned right onto a dirt road that brought us down into a river valley. Huge trees nearly touched overhead, forming a tunnel. The river twinned the road for a half mile before crossing under us as we rumbled over a small bridge. Then it vanished into the forest.

Mr. Gorseman turned into a lane that led to a two-storey house made of yellow brick with a front verandah and tall, rectangular second-floor windows above the door. It reminded me of nothing so much as a great staring face, its wooden mouth set in a yawn.

My father's shiny black motor car sat in the turnabout out front, having been shipped down last week on a freight train.

The mayor pulled to a stop and heaved himself out of the driver's seat to open the door for Maman and me. "I had some boys come round last week and trim the trees and turn over the gardens for you," he said to Maman, but she was fussing with her coat and did not answer. The flower gardens looked as though no one had taken so much as a rake to them in a decade, but everyone knew the English had different standards.

"*Tout sera parfait*," I said, taking Maman's arm, and I gave him my best smile, the one Sister Anise told me to reserve only for God and special occasions.

The mayor helped my father unload our cases from the car onto the drive, and then hovered, clearly wishing to leave, but not wanting to cause offence.

I extended my hand. "*Merci, monsieur*, for showing us the village."

He shook it gently, and then offered a firm grip to my father. "It's the least I can do. Doctor, I can't tell you how glad we are you've come to us, but now I'll let you get your family settled. Why don't you come round the municipal offices, say, eight o'clock? I'll take you into Orangeville and introduce you to everyone at the hospital."

It took my father a moment to parse Mr. Gorseman's English, but then he broke into a professional smile. "Tomorrow at eight, yes. Thank you."

The mayor got into his car and reversed down the lane, honking twice at the end of the drive before he disappeared down the road in a cloud of sputtering exhaust. In the silence that followed, I picked up my suitcase and followed my parents through the front door.

The house was full of evening sunlight and dust. Our house in the city had held the perpetual scent of flowers and wool rugs, with a lingering trace of antiseptic from my father's office on the ground floor. This yellow house smelled like grass and wood and water.

Our belongings had already arrived, and our furniture and carpets and trunks of clothes and my father's crates of books dominated the space, seeming to take up far more room than they ever had at home. My father had studied a blueprint of the house in advance and had taken great pains to dictate to the movers where each piece of furniture was to go. Though my mother had protested, Papa had decided that the downstairs front room was to be a reception area for patients and not for our use. Maman had reluctantly agreed that the spare bedroom upstairs would become the family parlour, with the second-best sofa and her china ornaments and anything else my father deemed unsuitable for his office. I had my own small room, at the back of the house on the second floor, and a view of the river.

Maman became animated. Hanging her coat and hat in the front hallway closet, she busied herself with unpacking the kitchen. My father retired to his new office and shut the door. I could hear him stacking his heavy medical volumes on the bookshelves.

I hung my own coat in the closet, dropped my bags in my room and reluctantly went to assist my mother. Together, we unearthed dozens of plates, teacups, bowls and flatware from their nests of newspaper inside the crates.

"*Ces brutes maladroites*," my mother muttered darkly, holding up a sugar bowl cracked in two. I made a sympathetic noise.

For supper we ate beef sandwiches, pickles and cheese that Cherise had packed for us only yesterday morning. We ate our supper standing, my mother contemplating the painted walls and murmuring to herself about papering. After we were done eating, I went out the back door and sat down on the steps overlooking the garden. It was even more overgrown than the front yard. A ragged lawn hemmed in by forest ran down to a fence draped with brambles and vines. Beyond that, I could see the last colours of the sunset glinting on water between blades of tall marsh grass and the branches of small trees. I heard the evening songs of more birds than I could recognize, the air filled with the smell of spring.

"*Pour l'amour de Dieu!*"

My mother's cry brought both my father and I running up the stairs and into the sitting room. She was on the floor, cradling the little china bisque doll that had sat on her vanity for as long as I could remember. The face was cracked, one cheek caved in completely. My mother sat tracing the remaining features of the face with one fingertip, tears on her cheeks.

"*Je l'ai emballée si soigneusement.*" She *had* wrapped her doll carefully—I'd had to run to find her more tissue paper.

My father studied Maman in confusion for a moment, and then at a gesture from me, went over and kissed the top of her head. "I will get you a new one, *ma femme chérie*, don't fret."

My mother cried harder. Papa, looking not a little annoyed, sighed and went back downstairs.

I wrapped my arms around Maman and let her rest her head on my shoulder as she gave way to all the upset our dislocation had caused her. My mother had a sensitive constitution and regularly fell prey to various headaches, digestive troubles, swooning weaknesses and other such maladies. When she felt well enough, she kept a tight circle, visiting with her parents or childhood friends, and hosting my father's colleagues for dinner once or twice a year.

On rare days, she awoke flush with health and would undertake herculean tasks with a vigorous, inexhaustible energy as though to make up for lost time. The day after my seventeenth birthday, she decided that I required a new wardrobe fit for a young woman in society and dragged me into every department store along St. Catherine Street in the space of a single morning. There had been a day last summer when she had my father's chauffeur drive us to Verdun, and we kicked off our shoes and waded in the St. Lawrence River, shrieking at the cold. She bought us ice creams and we sat with our bare feet in the sand, laughing at the gulls who circled us, begging. On those days, she was generous and funny, more vividly alive than anyone I'd ever known.

But those moments were inevitably followed by weeks of low spirits, when she couldn't bring herself to leave the house, or even get out of bed. After school, I would sit with her and read aloud from whichever novel I was devouring, while Cherise brought her cups of weak tea and small treats from the kitchen to tempt her appetite. Often, I was the only one who could coax her into bathing or coming downstairs to sit near the front window in the sunshine. Papa worried about her and I never doubted that he cared for her, but he had a physician's disposition and lacked the patience to be at her bedside. And so it fell to me.

I had known, from the moment my father announced at the dinner table that he'd been offered a new position in Ontario, that the move wouldn't be easy. But there had been no chance that he would turn down the opportunity to build his own practice away from the resentments and politics of Montreal, no matter what it cost Maman to move away from her parents and the neighbourhood she had lived in her whole life, first as Régine Beauxdons and then as the esteemed Mrs. Kromer.

After a while, she freed herself from my arms, dried her face and went to get ready for bed. I gathered up the doll and carried it quietly to my room. A few days with the evidence out of sight and perhaps Maman would forget the whole incident.

I unpacked my books and toiletries and hung my clothes in the armoire. Everything looked strange in this new room. Some part of me remained hopeful that this move was only temporary—that after our little adventure in the countryside, we would be back in Montreal by Christmas.

The light had faded completely by the time I heard my father come upstairs. His footsteps turned into the master bedroom and then the click of the door shutting echoed through the house. The house felt too silent, with no Cherise singing to herself in the kitchen, no Monsieur Caneau with his clippers in the front garden, no Jeremy to bring the car and answer the door and assist my father with the thousand little tasks of a medical practice.

I climbed into bed and opened my copy of *Kitty Foyle*, Christopher Morley's latest novel. The book had arrived just before we left, a neatly wrapped parcel decorated with New York stamps. It smelled of new paper and glue, and I spent a long moment admiring the drawing on the jacket before cracking it open. I started to read but found my eyelids falling almost immediately. I lay back, the book sliding onto the coverlet. The bed swayed as though I was still on the train, getting carried away faster and faster, my compartment door locked and no one around to hear my cries for help.

KIT

I came out of the chill morning air into a barn warm with the heavy breath of animals. In his stall beside Big Pete and Daisy,

Rat looked up from his breakfast long enough to assess my pockets with one sleepy eye.

"Jep?" I called. No reply.

I climbed up into the hayloft. The sparrows were small shadows huddled in the eaves. Through the open loft door, there was only the faintest touch of light on the eastern edge of the sky. We'd had an early spring—several weeks already without frost—but still my breath clouded in the air as I pitched hay into the sheep paddock below.

I clambered back down the ladder. "Jep? You here yet?"

The sheep milled reluctantly until I heaved open the door at the far end of the stable and shoved the matriarch with my hip to send all three dozen of them outside.

I found my brother with our milk cow, sitting on a milking stool, his hand idle, his head against Maeve's warm flank.

"Jep."

He looked up with a sleepy smile of such innocent happiness that I found myself forgiving him instantly. My mother often accused me of being a lazy daydreamer, but Jep was worse. Ask him to fetch eggs from the henhouse and he would be gone an hour, requiring Landon or me to chase after him, only to find him sitting on the roof, staring into space. I may have had a fiery imagination, prone to seeing an ocean in any creek, but my younger brother lived half his life in fairyland. Ask him to hold one end of a board you were nailing, and he'd get distracted by a bird flying overhead and let it slip.

Jep was too tender-hearted for hunting, had no head for cards nor reflexes for jacks, and no interest in machines. He liked animals and went soft-hearted over anything small or injured—my father credited Jep with saving no less than a dozen winter lambs

over the years. Though he had some trouble with people, crea-
tures flocked to his side. My mother often called him her little
St. Francis, earning an indulgent smile from my father. It was easy
to love Jep, even on mornings when he left me with more than half
the chores.

"Get that milk inside and go slop the pigs," I said.

Jep gave Maeve an affectionate pat, collected the milk pail and
ambled out the door, the milk only sloshing a little.

Rat thumped a hoof against his stall door and cribbed his head
side to side, earning his full name of Rattle-Tattle once again. He
wanted to be out, and I was running behind. I turned him, the other
horses and Maeve into the field, then cleaned the stalls and refilled
the water troughs. I let the chickens out of the coop, and while
they pecked in the yard, I hunted on my hands and knees for eggs,
my coat pulled over my nose against the reek of their shit. Finding
half a dozen, I gathered them in my shirttail and carried them to
the house across a yard grown brighter and pale in the dawn light.

My mother was in the kitchen, her back to me as I kicked off
my boots at the door. I gently laid the eggs in a bowl on the table.
The kettle was boiling.

"I'll get more water," I said.

"I sent Jep."

I sat down on the kitchen chair closest to the stove and thawed
my fingers. My hands still ached from nailing in the new roof shingles last week.

"Did you bring the eggs?"

"Yes."

"Is the milk strained?"

I got up from the chair and fetched the jug and the metal strainer
and carefully poured the milk through to sift out any dirt or hay.

"Mr. Scarletti, the science teacher, thinks we should be boiling milk to make it clean," I said. "Like some man named Pasteur recommended."

My mother snorted, busy cracking eggs into a skillet. "More likely to curdle and spoil."

"He says it makes it safer to drink." I set the jug on the table and eyed the chair near the stove.

"Ruins the taste and cooks all the goodness out of it." The hiss of frying eggs underscored her words. "You've been drinking our milk straight from the cow your whole life and look at you. Never a day sick. That teacher is talking nonsense."

As she reached for the saltshaker, she caught sight of me standing idle in the middle of the kitchen.

"Go help your brother with the pump. I'll need that water sometime before next year."

I sighed, grabbed the empty milk pail and went to stuff my feet back into their boots.

By the time we got back, Jep holding the door open for me as I staggered into the kitchen under the weight of two water buckets, the sun was fully up, bringing colour and noise to the world and Landon and my father to the breakfast table. Jep took the seat near the stove as I poured water into the cistern. Landon was seated next to my father, already piling biscuits and sausages onto his plate.

"Someone's taken the Petersons' place," Landon said. "They arrived yesterday."

"What one is that?" Jep already had butter smeared on his chin.

"The old yellow brick house off the main line, beside the river," my father answered, without looking up from his newspaper.

Landon picked up the thread. "Damp, shady kind of place. Widow Peterson lived there after her husband passed, and then she passed too—must be empty nearly a year now."

I remembered the widow's funeral, a humble affair in the Church of England on the other side of the railway tracks. A frosty day in mid-January, the ground too frozen to dig a grave. Landon had told me they'd send her body to the morgue in Orangeville, to sit on ice until spring. The thought of her frozen eyes still haunted me. Mrs. Peterson had been a Protestant, which meant she was going to hell, at least according to our priest, Father Bradley. So maybe she was better cold than burning.

I shook the thought away. Landon was still talking about the new arrivals. "The truck was piled with furniture, crates and trunks, and rolled-up carpets. And they also delivered a motor car, black and shiny like anything."

"I bet it's a foreign prince and his family in hiding, the last of their line and fleeing to Canada to escape execution," Jep said, licking a dribble of jam off his wrist.

Landon shot him a look. "Don't be stupid."

"Maybe he's a politician," I said. "Disgraced in Ottawa and forced to retire to the country to avoid a scandal."

My father looked up from his newspaper. "If it's that bastard Bennett, I'll have him run out of this town before you can say—"

My mother reached for the teapot. "Princes and politicians, such imaginations! It's only the new town doctor." Four heads swivelled in her direction. She took a long sip of tea, clearly enjoying the momentary silence. "I had it yesterday from Mrs. Crochett, who had it from Sally at the telegraph office. Ever since Dr. Samuels got promoted off to surgery in Toronto, the mayor's been advertising for a new doctor and now he's found one."

"Where are they from?" I asked at the same moment Landon said, "Who is it?"

"Some German and his French wife and their daughter, from Montreal. Sally's cousin Tom loaded their cases into the mayor's car at the station. He said they were awfully well-to-do, fur-trimmed coats and all the rest."

My father snorted, returning to his paper. "The last thing we need in this town is another damn foreigner. Can't expect anything of quality from them. Is his medical degree even real?"

I stopped listening. The widow's one daughter now lived in Boston, and the yellow house had stood empty since the funeral, the windows shuttered and the lawns growing wild with dande-lions and goldenrod. I rode past it often enough on Rat, a short-cut on my way to town. The only time I'd dared peek through the ground-floor windows, I'd seen nothing but empty floorboards and faded wallpaper.

I had hoped that it would be bought by a retired army colo-nel, a hero of the Great War, or perhaps a lady author like Miss Montgomery. But a doctor, and a foreign one? That was almost as good.

My mother's empty teacup landed in its saucer, the signal for the real work of the day to begin.

That afternoon, my father determined that the spring grass was already strong enough to move the flock to the summer pasture. I went out to the paddock beside the barn with a light heart. We'd sheared the sheep last month—a dirty, exhausting day I dreaded every year. Since then, the flock had been kept in the stable or cor-ralled in the paddock, eating the last of our hay supply and impa-tient for warmer weather.

It took all of us, the horses and the dogs included. My father rode Big Pete, our draft horse, while Landon rode Daisy, the white-spotted cart horse. I was on Rat, of course, and Jep and my mother were on foot. Our sheepdogs, Gordie and George, were wild, eager to be working the flock again.

It took forever to get everyone organized in the yard. The sheep were slow and stubborn after a winter close to home, the lambs zipping around their legs. My mother went first, leading the matri-arch on a thick rope to set the pace, while Landon and I rode on either side of the flock and my father at the rear, the dogs skim-ming the edges to nip at any stragglers. Jep ran ahead to open gates.

We took them across the road and along a track past Mrs. Crochett's place, headed for the pasture my father rented from a family in town, which lay east of our farm in a small valley. The sun was bright without being hot and the ground was dry under Rat's hooves.

I'd never got the hang of whistling, so Landon was the one who commanded the dogs, sending them zipping left and right like gusts of wind eager to do their god's bidding. The sheep flowed like a woolly river across the road and up the track, the dogs bark-ing and snapping at any who tried to jump out of line.

The track led up over a small rise, the forest close on either side, before sloping down into the valley fields where the grass was thick and green. Landon and I kept an eye out for stragglers. Last year half the flock had turned away from us and ended up in the woods.

It felt delicious to be out in the sun and the wind, after a long, cold winter. The sheep bunched together and then strung out, bleating and bumping into each other as the dogs herded them towards the field. As we came over the hill and they saw open ground, a few of them broke off from the flock. Landon spurred Daisy into a trot to overtake them, neatly guiding the strays back into the mass of wool and legs. I kept a tight rein on Rat as he pranced, wanting to surge after Daisy.

The bush to my right was mostly thorn and crabapple trees, with a few ash and yellow birch trunks swaying above them. The strong spring sunshine had coaxed the undergrowth into a tangle of dogwood and blackberry shoots. I could hear the trickle of the creek—the same one that ran down into the valley and across the pasture. The sunlight filtering through the canopy picked out a dozen wavering shades of green but didn't reach the shadowed and damp forest floor.

The sound of a branch breaking made me rein my horse to a stop. I peered into the trees, shading my eyes to see into the gloom. My father rode past me, escorting the last sheep downhill towards the pasture gate.

A shape flickered in my vision, deeper in the forest. It was low to the ground, slinking along the creek. I coaxed Rat forward with my knees so I could get a better look. We'd had so much trouble with coyotes last summer that Landon, my father and I had taken shifts guarding the flock overnight with the shotgun. Odd to see one alone, though there were always stories about rabid coyotes who had lost all natural caution.

I pressed Rat another few steps forward until we were standing under the eaves of the trees. The shape was gone, and the forest was silent except for the sound of water trickling in the creek. Then another sound grew in my awareness, too sustained to be a growl, more like a cat's purr. It resolved into a chorus of voices, low and indistinct, the syllables running together. The occasional whisper rose higher than the rest so that I could almost understand what it was saying, then faded. I raised myself in the stirrups, straining to pick out the words from the trickling noise of the creek.

Then something moved sharply in the undergrowth, crashing through the bushes, straight for me. I flinched, throwing up my hands to cover my head just as Rat spooked. I felt a sickening lurch as my horse shied, then took off down the track towards the valley, with me nearly out of the saddle and struggling to regain my seat.

Ahead of us, my family was herding the sheep through the pasture gate. Half the flock was already in the field with my mother and the dogs, as my father and Landon urged the rest on. Jep was balanced on the gate, his feet on the third rail, counting the sheep as they squeezed past.

Rat pounded down the track towards them. I'd dropped the reins in my panic and leaned to try to grab for his bridle, hoping to turn his head, but couldn't reach it or secure the flailing reins.

The sheep spotted us first and panicked, stampeding the gate. Landon was too slow in whistling for the dogs, and my father too far back. Jep flung an arm around the gatepost as the sheep hit the fence like a wave, knocking rails to the ground, the posts shuddering from the impact. As the heavy gate swung all the way open to slam against the fence rails, Jep yelped in pain. His feet slipped off the rail and he hung for a second, crushed between the post and the gate, and then he slid down into the grass and lay still, his arm at a sickening angle.

My mother plunged into the flock, staggering side to side as she fought her way towards her youngest. My father charged forward on Pete, sending sheep sprinting in all directions into the pasture. Rat finally came to a heaving stop, and I tumbled off him and ran.

Jep, pale and sweaty, was breathing in quick, nervous gasps, like a rabbit caught in a snare, my mother crouched at his side.

"Mary, Mother of Jesus, what were you thinking, you stupid girl?" My mother seemed caught between the desire to hug Jep and slap me. I stayed out of arm's reach just in case.

"I saw something in the forest! It came right at us, and then Rat spooked—"

"All of that over a grouse?"

"It wasn't a grouse! I heard this strange sound, and there was something else, like a shadow, or a—"

"There was nothing else, Kathleen! Stop lying and own up to the foolishness that almost got your brother killed."

My father was still astride Pete, keeping the sheep back from the gate as Landon slid off Daisy and to the ground.

My mother pointed at him. "Landon, go home and get the wagon—"

"No time." My father cut her off. "Landon, you'll take Pete and get your brother to that new doctor, right quick, you hear?"

"Yes, sir."

My father dismounted and held out the reins to Landon.

My tongue unfroze. "I'm the better rider," I said. "Let me take him—"

"You've done enough," my father growled.

"I'll be careful—"

"That's enough, Kathleen," my mother said, stroking Jep's forehead as he whimpered. Without looking at me, she added, "Your father and I will get the rest of the flock into the field."

"But you'll need at least three—"

"No, you take that fool pony of yours and go back to the house and get something on the table for dinner."

"I can help—"

"For once in your life, you'll do as you're told!"

———

Feeling useless I stood next to Big Pete and tightened the girth, then held Landon's stirrup as he swung up on the big animal. My mother wrapped Jep up in my father's flannel shirt, so that his wounded arm was held tight across his chest, then she and Pa lifted him up in front of Landon. She wouldn't let me touch him.

"Go quick but not stupid," my mother said. "If there's any need, you telephone from the doctor's to Mrs. Crochett and she'll bring the message to us."

Landon nodded, already nudging Big Pete into a walk. I called after him, "You'll get there faster if you go over the west fields and through the forest to the ford."

Landon glanced back at me. "The road is safer," he said, and then turned Pete up the track.

REBEKAH

"And lastly, every morning and evening before you go home, you must empty the kitchen waste into the barrel out in the . . ." My mother searched for the word in English. She failed to find it and settled for gesturing vaguely towards the backyard.

The young woman, Maria, stood in front of her, her face a blank stone of courtesy. Papa had hired her, sight unseen, on a recommendation from the mayor. My mother had been furious when Maria turned up on our doorstep at seven this morning, but my father had mildly observed that it wouldn't be easy to find help in a village this small. Then he had ducked past us and out to the car, quick as a cat, leaving Maman, Maria and I staring at each other in the front hall.

Maman had given our new maid a tour of the house as though
it were a grand chalet, instead of a two-storey country home with
only three occupants. But as she explained Maria's duties, her language skills were fraying at the same rate as her temper.

"I'm sure the job will be much like the ones you are used to,"
I said, stepping in when I saw Maman's eyes begin to tighten.

Maria shrugged. "I've never been anybody's servant, but I cook
and clean well enough for my pa and my brothers. I reckon washing one set of knickers is much like another."

Eyeing the twitching vein in my mother's neck, I said, "Why
don't you begin by washing the china we've unpacked, and then
put it away in the upper cupboard."

Maria sighed and tramped towards the kitchen while I led
Maman to the stairs. My father called them spells—moments
when she would fly into a towering rage or collapse into incon-
solable tears over a dropped teaspoon. Any change to her routines
made her especially susceptible. My father and I had shielded her
as best we could during the journey, but I knew better than to
think we could escape an upset forever.

"Maman? Shall I make you some tea?"

"That girl should do it. Isn't that why your father hired her?"

"I'm happy to—I know just how you like it."

Maman winced at the sound of china being rattled into
the sink.

I pressed on. "Why don't I read to you in the parlour? Or we
could unpack the rest of your clothes?"

She took a breath, as though surfacing from underwater. "No,
thank you, *chérie*. I am feeling a little tired. Perhaps I will lie down."

She drifted up the stairs and I heard the master bedroom door
shut. Splashing and mutinous muttering came from the kitchen.

I missed my dear Cherise, with her bright smile, her little jokes and her cheerful singing as she went about the chores, her voice so sweet and fine it made even my father smile. I hadn't cried when she left us for her new place—a young family in Côte-des-Neiges, under the shadow of the half-built basilica—because no one cried over a servant, but I wanted to cry now.

I went into my father's office. In this new yellow house, the heavy walnut desk ate up much of the space. Normally, I would have been at school at this hour, but here the day unrolled like an uncut bolt of cloth, too tightly woven to find even a single loose thread to grasp. Still, I had promised my grand-mère Beauxdons a letter as soon as we arrived, and this was a quiet place to sit and write. I could give it to Maria to drop at the post office on her way home this evening.

I had managed two dozen lines when there was a tremendous noise outside. I hopped up and went to the window to see two figures thundering up the lane on a big black horse. Hooves slid on gravel and moments later a fist pounded on the front door.

I froze, unsure whether to rouse Maman or to handle this myself. I went out into the hall just as Maria opened the front door.

A young man's voice, stressed and out of breath: "The doctor. I need to see the doctor!"

"He's not here," Maria said. Over her shoulder, I could see that the older of the two was supporting the other.

"My brother—when will the doctor be back?"

"What is the trouble?" I said, pushing past Maria. The taller of the two had chestnut hair and a shirt damp under the arms from straining to hold up a heavier-set younger boy with lighter hair and a rounder face. The boy was deathly pale.

"My brother fell, and his arm—it's hurt. Where's the doctor?"

I swallowed. "I will send for him. *Entrez*, please." Maria was forced to give way as the two boys stumbled through the front door. I guided them to the sturdy little settee across from Papa's desk. The younger boy sat with a slight gasp, his arm held tightly to his chest by a crude sling made out of a shirt.

"Maria, telephone the mayor's office and tell them that Dr. Kromer is needed at home immediately." She stared at me. "*Maintenant, s'il vous plaît.*"

She turned and headed down the hallway towards the telephone.

The boy moaned and slumped against the cushions. His brother sat on the barest edge of the settee, legs taut under him as though to spring up at any moment.

"The doctor?"

"He is coming. Please, Mister—?"

"McNair. Landon McNair. This is Jep."

I crouched in front of Jep, who was carefully unwrapping his arm.

"He fell off a gate and his arm got caught," Landon said. I had to bend my ear to parse Landon's flat vowels, so unlike the crisp speech of my English teacher at Sacré-Coeur.

"You fell, Jep?"

"Yes, ma'am."

His left arm was limp and swollen, the fingers puffy sausages. Both of them were staring at me. I inhaled to calm myself. I had watched my father examine injuries—some bleeding, some not—with gentle fingers. I didn't know how long it would take for Papa to get here and this boy needed help.

I took Jep's arm in my palms, thinking of the soothing way my father kept asking questions during examinations.

"Nothing else hurts?" I asked, running my fingers gently down his forearm.

"Just a few bruises, nothing serious," Landon said, hovering at my shoulder.

"And your *tête*, Jep—your head—did you hit it when you fell?"

"No, ma'am, I don't think so."

I studied Jep's eyes. They were clear, pupils a regular size in their green pools. There was redness under the lower lashes where he had been crying.

I touched the arm gently where the skin was puffiest. No bones peeking through, thank God. I doubted my stomach could have handled it. "Can you feel this?"

Jep winced and nodded, holding his breath. I withdrew the pressure and touched a forefinger against the tips of each finger of his left hand. "And this?"

"I can't feel the smallest ones, no."

Landon crouched next to me on the floor, one hand squeezing Jep's knee in reassurance. The sleeve of his shirt brushed my elbow, and I could smell horse and sweat and sun-bleached cotton in the air between us.

"Any history of illness in your family?"

Jep squinted in thought. "Our Ma's mother went out with heart trouble—"

He was interrupted by the roar of a motor and the crunch of gravel as my father's car pulled into the drive. I was on my feet in an instant, suddenly conscious of how close the three of us were.

I was at the open door before Papa reached the top step.

"*Qu'est-ce qui se passe?*" he asked me.

I gave him a quick, calm report as he handed his hat to Maria. He strode into the study, and I followed at his heel. Landon came forward, all the concern and anxiety I had managed to allay back on his face.

"I'm Dr. Kromer. What seems to have happened?"

Landon introduced himself and his brother, then repeated the story, a little more coherently this time. My father listened as he moved Jep's arm gently one way and another, heedless of the boy's gasps of pain. He repeated my gesture of touching Jep's fingers, as well as squeezing the arm in multiple places, along with a dozen other things I hadn't known to do. At last, he stood back from the settee and went to the cupboard at the side of the room to withdraw what he needed.

"The arm is broken and the shoulder dislocated. I will need to realign the shoulder joint, then reset and splint the arm. Rebekah, please make Mr. McNair comfortable while I tend to his brother."

I opened the door to the hallway, motioning for Landon to step through first. He hesitated, but at Jep's small nod he relented. I followed him, closing the door firmly behind us.

Alone with me in the corridor, Landon seemed suddenly conscious of his dirty, bedraggled state, and shifted from foot to foot on the carpet. His pants were slightly too short for his legs, his boots patched in several places.

"May I offer you some tea?"

A cry of pain came from the study, and Landon turned towards the door. I reached for his sleeve but stopped short.

"Please, do not worry. My father is very good."

"Your father? Oh, of course." He smiled for the first time since they'd arrived. "You're the French girl everyone's talking about."

"What do you mean?"

"My neighbour's cousin carried your bags at the station. If the entire county didn't know you were here before the car turned off Main Street, they would have by this morning."

"Oh."

"I won't trouble you for tea, but I'd appreciate some water for my horse. We had a hard ride over here."

I sent Maria to fetch a bucket while I followed Landon outside. A few moments later, she came staggering out, the water sloshing on her skirt. She dropped the bucket without a word at the top of the steps and disappeared. As Landon carried the pail to the horse, a thought that had been niggling at me came into the light.

"I saw you yesterday."

Startled, he looked back at me.

"Out in the field near the train tracks." Although this horse was not the same as the one he'd been riding.

"That wasn't me. I'm not much of a rider. I've been saving up for one of those." He nodded at my father's car.

"You're a fan of motor cars?"

"Only the fast ones. Someday, I'll own my own and I'll just slide into the seat and go where I please."

The horse had guzzled the pailful. Landon set the empty bucket back on the top step. Then he leaned on the railing, looking up at me. "When I have my car, you name the day and I'll take you anywhere you want to go."

"Montreal."

"Montreal, Chicago, Pacific Ocean—lady's choice."

I smiled. Now that his brother was in expert hands, Landon had relaxed. He was nothing like the boys I had known at home, in their proper school jackets, slicked hair and spectacles.

The tanned arm he braced on the railing was pleasantly muscled. Madeleine and I had sometimes wandered the shops downtown, giggling at the young clerks who fumbled to package our purchases and blushed when we spoke to them. Looking at him now, I couldn't imagine Landon blushing.

I smiled at him. "Has your family always lived—"

The front door opened, and my father led Jep out onto the porch, his arm and shoulder neatly wrapped with a splint and a sling. The tartan shirt was draped over his shoulders like a cape.

"Now, young man," my father said to Jep, "absolutely no lifting or pulling of any kind. I shall be most displeased if I see you back here before it's time to remove the splint."

"Yes, sir," Jep said.

My father addressed Landon. "I've given him some morphine for the pain, so he may be a little tired for the rest of the day." He looked at the horse. "You and your brother rode here?"

Landon flushed a little. "It was the fastest way."

"Allow me to drive your brother home," Papa said. "He can't risk another fall."

Landon protested for the sake of politeness, but soon Jep was bundled into the front seat. My father glanced at me from the driver's side. "Rebekah, write up the case notes and update the inventory." I caught approval in the tiny smile that tugged at the corner of his mouth.

As the car disappeared up the road, Landon unhitched the horse. I stayed on the verandah, looking down at him.

"You make a good doctor's assistant," Landon said, reins looped in one hand. With his dark eyebrows and shirtsleeves rolled to the elbow, he reminded me a little of Tyrone Power in *Jesse James*. Madeleine and I had gone to see it at the York back in February.

"I'm just glad your brother is all right."

He nodded and swung himself up into the saddle. "We're both grateful for the care you and your father gave him, Miss Kromer. I'm sure we'll meet again."

I nodded. At the end of the drive, he raised a hand and then turned to follow the car.

I found Maria in the front hallway, scrubbing dirty footprints from the carpet and floor. "Trust those McNairs to make a mess," she muttered.

"I think we can forgive a little mud under the circumstances," I said.

She paused to look up at me. "You're new here, miss. But you should know that whole family is nothing but trouble. You best stay clear."

KIT

When Jep arrived home in the doctor's car, I was still confined to the kitchen, peeling potatoes for dinner. I watched the car pull up beside the house like a scene in a silent film. My mother, hurrying to the car. My father, shaking the doctor's hand once, twice. Jep, looking small and pale under my father's flannel shirt, the dogs twining around his legs. His arm splinted and wrapped in a white bandage and tucked neatly in a sling. I nicked my knuckle with the peeler and cursed, putting the finger between my lips.

At last, the doctor's car pulled away and my parents brought Jep inside. I put the potatoes on to boil and sliced pork while they settled him into a chair beside the fireplace in the front room and wrapped him in a quilt. My mother made him milky tea and brought out the last pieces of Christmas candy. My father hovered in the hallway between the kitchen and the living room, looking as though he would like to be doing something but he wasn't sure what.

"The doctor's a very decent man," he said at last. "Wouldn't hear a word about settling up until he knew Jep was mending well. Truly decent."

This was a far cry from his opinion at breakfast, but I knew better than to point that out. My father went out to check the sheep, while my lopsided dinner rolls rose in a pan near the stove. When Landon arrived home half an hour later, my mother sent me outside with a mug of tea for him and, with a sigh, took over the dinner preparation.

As Landon slid out of the saddle in the yard, he said, "I watered him before I left and walked him all the way home. I'm not stupid." He led Big Pete to the trough.

"I wasn't—"

"Yes, you were. I know better than to run a horse four miles there and back again."

I said nothing more, just handed Landon the mug and began untacking Pete. My brother took a gulp, then stood looking into the distance for a long moment.

"You ought to be more careful," he said finally.

I paused, the heavy saddle and blanket in my arms. "I was being careful! There was something in the forest—"

"Not because of what happened with Jep," my brother said. "Although that was stupid, and you know it."

"Rat spooked—"

"Yesterday you told Pa you were going to track a fox."

"And I did."

"Then why did someone just ask me if I'd enjoyed my ride beside the rail tracks, three miles farther on?"

The saddle grew heavier. "I don't know."

"Jesus, Kathleen, you're not a child anymore! You can't go galloping around the countryside!"

I glared at him. "What I did had nothing to do with what happened to Jep."

"When I brought Jep in, Maria Sevlich looked at me like I was dirt under her shoe."

"That Prod cow has never liked us."

"But people talk, Kathleen, especially about a girl tearing around the countryside in boy's clothes when she should be home doing her chores."

"I pull my weight. Whatever I do in my own time is none of your business or anyone else's!"

I hefted the saddle higher and stalked to the barn, where I dumped it onto the rack, throwing the blanket over it.

When I returned, Landon had disappeared, leaving Big Pete standing. I growled under my breath and made sure the horse was brushed and fed and given an extra apple for his hard work. I did the evening chores alone. By the time I finished milking Maeve, my father had returned from the fields, and everyone else was sitting down to the dinner I had made.

That evening, we all gathered in the living room around the fire. My mother said she was too tired for her usual darning and sat with a cup of tea next to Jep. Landon was on a chair by the door, cleaning and polishing his boots. My father brought down his pipe from the mantelpiece and had a smoke—a rare treat for him.

I tried to concentrate on my comic, but my eyes glazed over the first page.

"I guess no playing for a while," Jep said at last. He was staring at his fiddle on the sideboard. I felt another stab of guilt. He loved playing in the evenings, out on the porch in good weather, around the fire in bad. He'd only mastered a handful of tunes, but I still loved listening to him.

"Pa, tell us the story," Jep said.

Landon groaned. "Not again. We agreed—Christmas and Easter only."

"Please," Jep begged.

My father sighed. "All right, son, we'll make an exception."

I dropped my comic and came to sit on the floor near Jep's chair as Landon made a disgusted noise and returned to cleaning his boots.

My father cleared his throat. "Your great-great-grandfather Corin McNair lived on the edge of a small village in Ireland. By day, he fished the seas and by night he slept near his fire. Season after season, year after year, he lived alone, speaking to few and knowing none."

He took a long draw of his pipe, sighing out the smoke. "One day, a terrible storm drove up along the coast, bringing rain and wind and waves higher than a man's head.

"Corin stayed safe within his hut, whittling driftwood while the wind moaned like a living thing, rattling the walls. A keen, piercing cry split the air as thunder cracked over the cliffs. He shivered, said two Hail Marys and went to bed.

"The storm had blown over by the next morning, and so, as usual, Corin walked down to the shore and prepared to launch his boat."

"And then what happened?" Jep asked. I could practically hear Landon roll his eyes behind me.

"He heard a cry."

"What did he find?" Jep knew perfectly well how the story went, but he loved the ritual questions.

"He found a seal.

"The cry came again, drawing him towards a massive tree, uprooted and washed up on the shore. Trapped beneath it, as I've said, was a seal. Its fur was dark grey slate, lighter where the salt water had dried. Corin looked down, silently weighing the beast. Its meat could feed him for a month and the hide could easily provide him with a new pair of boots.

"The seal looked up at him. Its eyes were brown, like the heart of an oak, their expression soft as fresh earth. Its flank heaved with the effort of every breath."

Jep's voice again. "But he didn't kill it, did he?"

"Corin began to dig. As the sun rose and the mist burned off the water, he was able to ease the seal out from under the trunk."

"More fool him," Landon scoffed. "If he'd killed it when he had the chance, we'd have turned out better."

"Hush," my mother said.

My father carried on as if he hadn't heard. "The tide had turned. Corin looked to his boat, already bobbing dangerously in the shallows. He went to rescue his craft, cursing the seal to whatever god would take it. When he came back, the seal was gone."

I knew the rest of the tale as well as anyone else. The seal swam far out into the waves and dove deep, the salt ocean washing her wounds clean. Her family greeted her with cries of joy, amazed to see her alive. In the days that followed, as she and her sisters hunted the shallower waters of the cove, she dwelt upon the face of the man who had looked upon her with compassion.

Night after night, she kept vigil as the orange glow of a cottage window shone out over the waves, overcome with longing for this man-creature, with his deft hands and sea-grey eyes.

At last the selkie could resist no longer. She dove to the bottom of the cove, pulled off her sealskin, gathered up handfuls of dark sea mud and fashioned herself a woman's body. Two supple arms, two round thighs. A proud nose, delicate ears. Two fistfuls of mud became full breasts, ten pebbles her toes, strands of kelp her hair. Using a driftwood twig, she carved two eyes, two nostrils and the secret cleft between her legs. When she had finished, she admired her reflection in the underside of the sea surface and was satisfied.

At dawn, she walked onto the shore, with her hair long and tangled and eyes as black as sea pebbles, a bundle of fur under her arm. When he saw her, Corin was afraid and reached for the fish knife in his belt, but she spoke to him in a strange tongue as she came close, then combed two fingers through his hair, and Corin's heart broke open with loneliness and desire. He took her into his home and gave her bread and stew, which she ate, and clothes, which she wore. For most of that day and into the night, he sat and spoke to her of all the things his heart had ached to say to someone for many years. She listened and grew to love him more.

When he had finished with words, she drew him down to the sleeping pallet. Every place his mouth touched turned her skin warm and every place he traced with his fingers shone with life and soul. The selkie threw her head back in ecstasy and forgot the wild pleasures of riding the waves, forgot the caress of the north wind and the taste of salt. Drunk on the scent of this man's skin, she did not hear the lamenting of her kin, leaping and crying in the cove. That night she slept, cradled not by kelp, but by Corin's arms.

He named his wife Siobhan, and he taught her to draw sweet water from the spring, to pound wheat into flour and to sweep the floor of the cottage. She learned quickly, watching him with her sloe eyes and furtive smile. The only thing she would not touch was the hearth fire. She shrieked when he showed her how to strike sparks from a flint and shuddered to watch him place logs on the hearth.

Some nights, when seals came calling and barking into the cove, she went down to the water, frowning as if recalling a dream. Corin quickly pulled her away from the shore, telling her about his plans for a new house, a new boat. She smiled and grew happy again.

The old sealskin sat in the corner behind the door, forgotten. When it began to stink and his wife complained, Corin hid it in the roof thatch and no more was said about it.

My father said, "Within a year, Siobhan bore him a son."

"And they were happy," Jep added. Landon snorted.

"Yes, they were," my father said. "Until several years later, when a damp rain blew across the sea and the roof began to leak.

"Their young son pointed to something dark peeking through the thatch. When Siobhan reached to touch it, she remembered her true nature."

She pulled the sealskin from where it had been hidden and ran down to the beach, stripping off her clothing as she went, leaving a trail of cotton dress and wool shawl and underthings on the sand behind her. She wrapped herself in the sealskin and plunged into the waves, as her son toddled after her. By the tideline, he waited for his mother to surface, and waited, until finally a dark shape broke the water, with dripping whiskers and eyes as dark as the ocean depths. The seal gave a barking cry, once, twice, and then vanished again into the waves.

Corin returned from fishing to find his son hungry, his hearth cold and his wife gone. He thought of her dark, beautiful eyes, of the long hours he had spent in peril on the waves to see her fed and clothed, and his heart cracked. He took his crying son, leapt into his skiff and rowed out onto the sea, calling Siobhan's name. Silence. He lifted his son in his arms and cried that he would drown him unless his seal wife returned. For long minutes, only waves lashed the hull. Corin tightened his jaw and threw his child over the side.

The boat rocked in silence and Corin's eyes blurred with tears. Then a blunt nose pushed the child to the surface. Corin threw his net and caught them both, dragging his son and his wife into the boat. While the boy cowered, she writhed and flung herself desperately towards the water. Corin seized his club and drove down. The seal slumped against the struts and the skin unwrapped to reveal Siobhan, limp but still breathing. Wrapping an arm around his shivering son, Corin steered his boat back to shore.

There he pulled the sealskin out from under Siobhan's body and tossed it aside. Then he dragged her up the beach by her hair and across the threshold into their house, locking her inside. Corin built a fire to warm his son, and when it was as tall as a man and twice as wide, burning hot enough to curl the edge of the thatch, Corin took the sealskin and threw it into the flames. Within the house, Siobhan screamed. The skin smouldered, then began to burn, giving off a greasy smoke that clung to the roof of his mouth. In the house, his wife's cries gave way to sobbing and then to silence.

Siobhan became a sullen, quiet woman who sat for hours staring out at the sea like one who is dead but has gone on living. She stayed with him another three years. Then one day, Corin found her drowned body on the rocks, washed clean and wrapped in kelp.

Corin took his son by the hand, walked to the nearest port and bought passage on a boat to the New World. He moved as far from the ocean as his money would carry him, which turned out to be a landlocked plot of forest in Harrichford County. Corin became a farmer, and eventually married a fully human woman of Scottish stock who bore him five more children. Three of his children survived to adulthood, including Corin's eldest son—the one his mother saved from drowning—who inherited both the farm and a deathly fear of water.

"And our family has lived here ever since," my father finished, tapping his pipe on the fireside to empty the ashes into the hearth.

"It doesn't make any sense," I said, as I always did. "How could she drown? She was a water spirit."

"That's how the story goes," Landon said, who had at last stopped polishing his boots to listen.

"Kelpies can drown," said Jep.

"No, they drown people," I said. "How could a creature that lives in the water drown?"

"She was in human form—" Landon began.

"That's all there is to the story," my father said.

"But why did—"

"The fences in the summer pasture need to be walked. Kathleen, you will see to it tomorrow after church."

I looked at my father, then nodded silently.

"I just checked them—" Landon began.

"To bed, all of you." My father's voice was sharp with exhaustion. "Jep, especially, needs his rest."

We went. Landon paused by my door, as though to say something to me, but it was Jep who patted my elbow before moving past us and awkwardly climbing the attic ladder, hanging on with one hand.

I had use of the tiny second upstairs bedroom, while my brothers shared the attic. Landon's bed sat behind a curtain made from an old blanket, and Jep's mattress was raised up on four wooden grocery crates that held all his treasures. On the coldest winter nights, the two of them slept on the kitchen floor beside the stove, piled in a heap of quilts, the dogs snoring gently at their backs. As a child, I had pleaded to be allowed to sleep under the eaves with them, but now we were older, I had come to appreciate my privacy.

I lay in my bed and listened to the murmur of my parent's voices through the stovepipe that ran up from the kitchen and through my room to the roof.

"I just don't know what to do with her, Dermot. My mother called her fey-touched."

"Your mother said the same thing about Jep."

"It marks them differently. Jep is quiet, loving. Kathleen is a liar and a troublemaker, sent to punish me for my sins—"

"What sins are those, my love?"

My mother's response was indistinct, but I heard my father chuckle.

"She's wild, I'll grant you, but give her time, Caroline. I recall a similar hot-headed young woman, oh, about twenty years ago, and she turned out all right in the end."

My mother's sigh was so deep it carried through the stovepipe.

"Did you see that get-up she was wearing today? If anyone had seen her, I would have died of shame."

"Trousers are better for riding," my father muttered. "You know they are. And you're the one who taught her to ride."

The creak of a chair. I could picture my father placing an arm around her shoulders. "One arm safely mended today is plenty of blessings."

I pulled the quilt over my head and thought about the part of the story my father hadn't told that night.

The sea salt had entered my great-great-grandfather's blood when the selkie first grasped him between her thighs and bit his lip. Much as he feared the sea, its salt ran in the veins of their first-born son and all his descendants. The sweat that had dripped from my great-great-grandfather's brow on the dark earth as he cleared these fields had poisoned the soil. The harder he worked and the more he sweated, the less fertile his land became. While his neighbour's crops flourished, his harvests remained stunted, twisted, resembling the twisted fronds of seaweed and kelp.

Two generations survived on withered potatoes and stunted grains, until my grandfather had the sense to purchase some sheep and turn it all into pasture.

As a child I thought it was the selkie's blood that kept my family from prosperity, but our lands lay east of the escarpment and sloped downhill towards the river. The ridge kept the lower half of the fields in shadow, even on a summer's day, and every rainstorm washed another layer of precious topsoil down into the river. So perhaps I had no need to use tall tales to excuse my family's failings.

The next morning, I squeezed into a hideous black-and-red-checked dress that pinched my shoulders. Years of struggle had taught me that my mother could not be swayed from making me wear a dress to Sunday mass. She'd mostly given way to my argument that men's clothes were more practical for farm work, but on the matter of church, she would not budge.

I was not pretty in the way that girls are meant to be. My mother had dimples and small feet. I was as gangly as a half-grown turkey. My hair was straight and mouse brown, and no amount of rainwater rinses or brushing could make it glossy or thick. My breasts refused to grow at all, and my hip bones were forever hitting table corners and door frames. My mother despaired of ever marrying me to anyone.

I put on the only pair of shoes I owned that were fit for church and jammed a hat onto my head. Then I went down the stairs to join Landon on the porch. This one time, Jep had been permitted to stay home.

My eldest brother was wearing his best shirt and clean trousers. My mother was in her blue dress, her hair carefully curled and her hat pinned expertly on her head. She frowned as I appeared, reaching out to adjust my hat. Then she licked her thumb to smooth my eyebrows.

"You need to wear that hat more often. If you kept out of the sun, it would help your complexion—"

"Ma—"

She looked down at my sagging stockings and sighed.

"You know where the garters are. Do you need help putting them on?"

"I don't," I said, glancing at Landon. He was pointedly looking the other way, though I could see his shoulders shaking with suppressed laughter.

As I passed him on the way down the front steps to join our father in the lane, he murmured, "A pig in a dress is still a pig."

I grabbed the soft flesh of his inner elbow and twisted hard. He yelped and shoved me away.

"That's enough," my father said. "We're going to be late."

It was a two-mile walk to church, and the morning was bright and dewy, promising to heat up into a warm day. My parents walked ahead, with Landon just behind. I trailed at a distance, hating my shoes, hating my dress and hating everyone. Throughout the service, I kept my eyes down, mechanically standing and sitting, mouthing along to the hymns. I saw nothing of the congregation except for pairs of shoes passing at the end of our pew. I fled out the door the moment church was over, leaving my family to shake hands and exchange greetings with our neighbours. The sooner I reached home, the sooner I could shed these clothes and begin to breathe again.

REBEKAH

After mass, my father went out on a call, leaving a plate with toast crumbs and the dregs of his tea on the dining-room table. My mother got up from her chair and bustled into the kitchen to nag Maria to clear our breakfast things. I escaped to my father's empty office to continue reading *Kitty Foyle* and let myself fall into the world of hot asphalt and shady rooms that made up Morley's Philadelphia.

I could hear my mother's impatient footsteps ricocheting from one end of the house to the other, and I managed barely a dozen pages before she came into the office. She had changed into her yellow silk dress with pearl buttons. She had also rouged and put on a tasteful amount of lipstick, but makeup couldn't disguise the slightly brittle quality of her confidence.

"Rebekah, please freshen up. I need you to accompany me to lunch at the mayor's house."

My mother was typically anxious at the thought of meeting a new neighbour or even a clerk in a shop. Amelia Gorseman had trundled right up to us in the street this morning and shook her hand, exclaiming that she needed to come that very day to lunch with all the ladies the new doctor's wife needed to know.

"I would," I said, making a slight moue of disappointment, "but I've developed a headache."

My mother's demeanour changed instantly. She did not tolerate sulkiness, but illness she understood. She went to the kitchen to demand that Maria make me a cup of weak tea, then insisted that I put down my book and draw the curtains of the study against the brightness of the day. Finally, after I was reclined on the settee with a cup of tea at my elbow and an Aspirin to take if I worsened, my book safely out of reach on the shelf, she was convinced it was safe to leave me.

"Another time, *chérie*," she said, gently patting my cheek. "The ladies will be very disappointed, but I will make your excuses."

"Thank you, Maman." I tried my best to look wan but valiant.

A few moments later, the front door thudded shut. I tracked Maria's footsteps through the house, up and down the stairs to freshen the beds, out into the garden to empty the scraps, the clatter of dishes being stacked in the kitchen cupboards.

At last, I heard the rustle of a coat in the front hallway, then the door closed again. I went to the window to watch Maria tramping up the drive to spend her Sunday afternoon with her family.

The sun threw dappled shadows on the green lawn, and the sky seemed even bluer than before. I was finally alone.

I retrieved my hat and coat from the front closet, and I was through the kitchen and out the back door into the garden before I could think too hard about what I was doing.

KIT

It was a bright day, with a brisk wind blowing through the forest as I rode down the track to the valley pasture. The sky was brilliant blue, clouds sailing across it in puffy white squadrons. The tools in the saddlebags jingled with every step Rat took.

After church, I had changed into work clothes, flinging the dress into the farthest corner of my bedroom. Outside, I tacked up Rat and looped a roll of fence wire over the saddle horn. Wire cutters and pliers went into the saddlebags, along with an oatcake and some cheese I'd swiped from the lunch table.

When we reached the pasture, I unsaddled Rat and turned him loose with the sheep. The gate was in decent shape, in spite of yesterday's fiasco. I gave the anchor post a good kicking and found it solid enough. The hinges were intact and only the bottom rail had been knocked free of its wiring. I dug the tools out of the saddlebags, cut away the damaged wire, and began resetting the bottom rail.

It should have been Landon out here doing this miserable chore. Even though he was only fifteen months older, twenty and a quarter to my nineteen, he lorded it over me as though it were five years. My brother lived in the here and now, in the world of cars and chores and food on the table. He was easily satisfied by the smiles of pretty girls in town, hitching a ride to a picture once a month in

Orangeville, and bossing me and Jep around. I'd never heard him express a longing for adventure or show real imagination.

Satisfied that the gate was fixed, I slung the saddlebags over my shoulders and began the long hike around the inside perimeter of the cedar split fence. Every ten feet, I stopped to shake each set of standing posts and check that the rails were seated properly. I rewired the ones that felt loose and cleared away any climbing vines or brambles that threatened to overtake the fence. The sheep kept coming over to see what I was doing, shoving their faces under my arms and getting in the way of my pliers. It was boring, frustrating work—my least favourite type of chore—and I knew it was my father's way of punishing me.

As I braced a particularly rickety rail against the post with my shoulder while trying to hold the wire in place and use the pliers at the same time, I fumbled and then cursed as the pliers slipped from my sweaty fingers and dropped into the grass.

A shadow fell across me: Landon. He retrieved the pliers and fixed the wire into place with a deft twist. I wiped my hair out of my face as he surveyed my work with a critical eye.

"Come to gloat?" I said.

"Figured you could use a hand."

Sometimes he had his good points.

We walked the rest of the fence line in companionable silence. When we paused for repairs, I braced the rails while Landon wielded the pliers.

The sun was well overhead, even hot, by the time we circled back to the gate. As we flopped down in what little shade the fence provided, I dug the food out of the saddlebags to share with my brother.

"Thanks for the help," I said.

Landon shrugged. "It woulda taken you all day on your own."

I began to laugh, then realized he was serious. "No, it wouldn't."

My brother swallowed a last bite of oatcake. "Sure," he said in a mollifying tone.

I went and caught Rat, led him back to the fence and began resaddling him. Landon collected the tools and the wire.

"I pull my weight," I said, jerking on the girth.

Landon gave me a falsely patient look. "You know what your problem is, Kathleen? You never stop to think about what will happen later."

"That's not true."

"Someday you're going to have to grow up. I pity you because I don't think you're prepared for that."

I paused as the horse shifted under my tugging on the girth. I let go and vaulted onto his back, gathering the reins.

"Kath, where are you—?"

"It's my life. I don't need approval from anybody, especially you." I kicked Rat into a canter, leaving Landon standing with the saddlebags like so much luggage.

"Kathleen! Get back here! I'm not hauling this stuff home."

I urged Rat towards the fence, clearing it in a smooth jump. Landon's cursing faded into the background as we melted into the woods.

REBEKAH

The sunlight was warm against my cheek as I stepped over the stile at the bottom of the garden and onto the footpath by the river. The light bounced along the surface of the water and the tips of the rushes that grew along the edge. The air smelled fresh and sharp, the wind just slightly cool. The house was soon out of sight.

I followed the path until I came to a place where it widened and led down to the river's edge. The water was shallow here, a gentle rapids skimming over pebbles. On the other side the track continued up into the trees. I crouched among the rushes at the edge of the river, where the water stilled, took off my gloves and scooped a little into my palm to drink. It was much colder than it looked.

A bird swooped overhead, squawking a harsh alarm, followed by a great splashing from beyond the reeds. I froze. Cherise had warned me about all the wild animals that stalked the countryside. Then I heard laughter, and a voice said, "Quit it, you devil."

Another splash and then a shriek.

"Rat, you perverse excuse for an animal! I oughtta skin you and make something useful, like a rug."

I peeked through the reeds. A grey and brown horse stood in the shallows, reins trailing over its neck. A saddle lay abandoned on the opposite shore. Someone was standing on the other side of the horse, but I could only see his legs and boots. The horse snorted and pawed the water, creating another tremendous splash.

Another shriek and a giggle. The boy darted around the horse's head and that's when he caught sight of me.

His trousers were damp at the knees, and his shirt was off-white, a little too big around the shoulders, and translucent where the horse had splashed him. Sunlight caught the top of his head, turning the dark hair a brilliant gold-brown.

"Are you lost?" he called.

I stood up slowly. "No," I said, in the most confident voice I could muster.

The horse shoved him with its head and the boy nearly lost his footing. "You pig," he said, pushing the animal's neck.

He was the boy I'd seen from the train window, but he seemed younger. His nose was long, and the overlarge clothes hid slender limbs. He studied me just as curiously, taking in my slightly muddied shoes and the gloves I held in my left hand.

"I saw you from the train," I blurted.

He immediately looked wary. "No, you didn't."

"I've never seen someone do something so stupid. What were you thinking?"

"I wasn't."

I must have looked incredulous, because he shrugged.

"Don't you ever do things like that? Things that stop you from thinking, sweep you right out of your head?"

"No."

"Well, try it sometime."

I realized I needed to get home in case Maman returned early. I turned back the way I'd come.

"You visiting folks around here?" the boy called.

"No, I'm from—I live here now."

"You're in the Peterson house?"

I frowned, unsure.

"The big yellow house, just up the way?"

I nodded and a smile split his face. I felt my lips twitch in response. This was the first stranger who had smiled in my direction since our train had pulled away from Bonaventure Station. It warmed me as much as the sun on the back of my neck.

"You're the doctor's daughter." A statement, rather than a question. Landon had been right—everyone knew we were here.

"Yes, I'm Rebekah Kromer."

He waded across the ford, water rippling over the toes of his boots, and shook my hand. "I'm Kit, and this"—jerking his chin towards the horse—"is Rat."

"Kit, short for . . . ?"

"Just Kit," he said. The water rushed between us, inches from my shoes. Then he asked, "Do you like cats?"

The trees were taller on the other side of the river. I had paused to pull my shoes and stockings back over my numb, cold feet, and now we walked side by side under a leafy canopy, the horse trailing behind. Shade dappled in dark pools and brambles scraped my ankles. I had to walk fast to keep up with my new friend's quick stride.

Before long, we were climbing a long, sloping rise towards a handful of farm buildings. Two black-and-white dogs came bounding down the field towards us. Kit greeted them happily, sending them away before they reached me. Ahead, I could see the outline of the roof of the house, with smoke curling from the chimney, and a collection of outbuildings and paddocks. I expected Kit to lead me to the house, but instead he turned towards the largest barn, opening the paddock gate to let Rat and me through but closing it against the dogs.

The stable was dim, the air hazy with dust motes floating in rays of sunshine. Kit stripped the horse of his saddle with quick, nimble fingers while I wandered the length of the aisle, noting the rusting equipment, but also the clean stalls and the soft twitter of sparrows in the rafters. Kit sent the horse out into the paddock with a brisk slap to the rump. Then he was back at my side, tugging me towards a ladder in the far corner stall.

He went first, disappearing through a trap door in the ceiling. For a moment I wondered whether I should have followed a strange boy across the countryside for no more than a shared interest in cats, but I gathered my skirt and followed cautiously.

It was a hayloft. In books, they are hiding places for criminals or heroes on the run, or for clandestine meetings between lovers. This hayloft, however, appeared to be only for holding hay, with large bales stacked nearly to the ceiling. The doors were shut and the roof sealed tight against the damp, but the gaps between boards let in yellow bars of sunlight. Kit climbed up the bales in the back corner and disappeared, calling, "This way."

I followed, ignoring the scratch of hay against my knees and palms. I reached the top and peered down. Kit was sitting in a small depression in the hay, beside a mother cat with four tiny kittens. Kit gently picked up a grey bundle and held it up so I could see.

"Surprise," he said.

A lump formed in my throat. We had left my beloved old cat, Menuet, behind with my aunt, to live out the last of her days in comfort, but I still woke in the dark every night to reach for her soft fur. Kit mistook the look on my face, for he pulled the kitten back towards him. "You don't like it?"

I climbed down and settled myself in the hay beside him.

"I love it," I said, holding out my hands.

Kit grinned and handed me the tiny bundle of fur. The kitten yawned and then aimed fierce blue eyes up at me, minute claws clutching my thumb. Kit snuggled the remaining kittens in his lap, while the mother cat settled down for a nap.

"Harriet is the best mouser we've ever had, and her kittens are always strong and healthy," Kit said, then proceeded to give me the pedigree and life history of every cat in the neighbourhood. I wasn't really listening as I stroked the tiny head and ears, feeling the softest purr vibrate through my palm. I could already imagine him curled on my lap in the study and next to my pillow at night. For the first time in weeks, I felt calm and settled.

"Do you want him?" Kit asked.

"Yes, please." I snuggled the grey kitten close to my face.

Kit smiled, staring down at the kittens in his lap and then at me. "They'll be weaned in a few weeks. I could bring him to you then."

"I'd like that," I said. "Thank you."

We sat in silence for a moment, the hay muffling all sounds from outside, the kittens purring. In years to come, I would clutch that moment to my heart like a talisman, tracing every detail. The gold light pouring through the cracks between the barn boards, landing on Kit's hair like a beacon. The warm, close air of the loft, the rich smell of dried grasses and warm fur. Our knees just touching, our eyes on the kittens, but how aware I was of Kit's ribs rising and falling beneath the shirt, of the deft fingers delicately stroking the kittens' heads. Even then, I wanted the moment to last forever.

"Kathleen!" A voice from outside broke into our dusty sanctuary. I frowned, looking around for a sibling I hadn't yet met.

Kit started. "My mother," he grimaced, gently placing the kittens back in their nest and climbing to his—no, her—feet. I blinked. Now that I was looking carefully, it was clear. No Adam's apple, the voice not a high tenor but a girl's mellow alto. The slightly wider hips, the loose shirt.

"Kathleen!"

Kit flashed me an apologetic look, climbed out of the nest and started down the ladder. I followed.

A woman was standing in the aisle of the barn, the sleeves of her dress rolled to the elbows. She was half a head shorter than Kit, with a round face and Landon's dimples. Her reddish curly hair was haphazardly pinned up on the back of her head.

"There you are. I've been looking . . ." Her voice died away as I appeared on the ladder, and I could feel her eyes on me as I descended and brushed off my skirt.

Kit shuffled from one foot to the other. "Rebekah, this is my mother, Caroline McNair. Ma, this is—"

"The doctor's daughter. I understand I have you to thank for treating my son's arm."

"It was my father who did all the work, ma'am."

Mrs. McNair huffed, whether in polite disagreement or approval of my modesty, I couldn't tell. We followed her out of the dim barn and into the sunlight, which seemed all the brighter.

"The boys are just back from checking on the flock. They'll want to say thank you, I'm sure. Jep especially."

With the spell of the hayloft broken, I was suddenly aware of how much time had passed.

"Thank you, but my mother will be expecting me at home. I've already been out longer than I meant to be."

Mrs. McNair shot a slight frown in Kit's direction.

I grappled for politeness. "Another time, perhaps. I would be delighted to meet them both when I am less rushed."

"We won't keep you, then," Mrs. McNair said, already starting to turn away.

"I'll walk you back," Kit said. "Ma, I'll only be a little bit."

"You have chores, Kathleen," her mother said sternly. "I'm sure my husband would be glad to take you home, Miss Kromer, if you can wait a moment."

"That's very kind, but I would enjoy the walk," I said.

"I'll point you on your way," Kit said, stepping to my shoulder. She was just a little taller than me.

I turned to Mrs. McNair, inclined my head with a politeness Sister Anise would be proud of. "It was a pleasure to meet you, ma'am."

She nodded and headed for the house, one of the dogs shadowing her heels.

We walked up the lane to the road in silence.

"You thought I was Landon," Kit said.

"No! You're clearly not him, but I thought—"

"It's all right. My mother claims we looked like twins as kids— even she couldn't tell us apart. Which meant Landon spent half his childhood in dresses."

"He must have made a pretty girl."

Kit shrugged a shoulder, looking sideways at me. "Prettier than me, anyway."

"No, you're—" Words, normally so obedient, escaped me.

At the end of the lane, a weathered gate marked the entry to the road. Kit gestured to the right.

"Follow this to the first crossroad, then turn right. Walk on until you see the church, then turn right. A half mile down from there is the Peterson place. Though I suppose it's the Kromer place now."

"I suppose it is." I tucked my ungloved hands into my sleeves. The wind kicked up a puff of dust from the road and sent it whirling between our feet.

Kit said, "I guess I'll see you around, Rebekah." Then she turned and walked back towards the farmhouse, hands in her pockets.

The walk home took longer than I expected, and I was grateful to stumble at last into the cool front hallway. The house was still empty. I lay back down on the couch, my feigned headache from earlier now quite real, and fell into a half-doze.

When Maman returned a quarter of an hour later, bubbling with new energy and neighbourhood gossip from her long luncheon with the ladies, I was lying quietly on the settee, just as she had left me.

JUNE 1939

KIT

THE DAYS LENGTHENED AS SPRING MARCHED ON TOWARDS
summer. By the time the kittens were weaned, the hay had grown
to knee height and the river rushes were thrusting up between last
year's dead growth.

While we usually sold our barn kittens to a pet shop in
Orangeville, Harriet's litters were the exception, because they
shared her gifts as a mouser. I hadn't thought of that when I'd
shown the little grey one to Rebekah. I considered forgetting my
promise, but when I remembered how she had plunked herself
on a bale in her fine dress, never minding the dust or the bits of
hay, and held the kitten to her cheek, I found I couldn't.

Her kitten had grown into a feisty creature, forever wandering
to the edge of the hayloft and getting into trouble. It wouldn't be
too much of a stretch to claim he'd simply disappeared. Two days
after they were weaned, I waited until my father and Landon were
tangled in an argument over the newspaper at the breakfast table,
and stole out to the barn. I caught the kitten, wrapped him snug in

my shirt and was up on Rat and off through the back field before
anyone noticed I was missing.

It was a pleasant ride, with Rat content to be stretching his legs
in the sunshine and the kitten fast asleep next to my stomach. I
took my time, knowing that my return would bring punishment
and long hours of weeding. We forded the river and scrambled up
the far bank, the long grass swishing against the horse's legs as we
rode up towards the Kromers' back garden. I dismounted with care
and hitched Rat to a nearby apple tree.

I crossed the back lawn, my charge now awake and beginning
to wriggle, and went around to the front door. It wasn't until I
was thudding the large iron knocker that I wondered whether
Rebekah really wanted the kitten. Had she been humouring me?
Hard to tell given how polite she was, her accent giving each word
a musical charm.

The door opened and Maria's dour face appeared. She took me
in with a single, sneering glance.

"What do you want?"

"Is Rebekah here?"

Her eyes narrowed with mistrust. "What business is it of
yours?"

"I have a delivery for her."

"Delivering what?"

"It's a surprise."

"You should've come to the kitchen entrance." When I continued to stand there, she stuck out her hand. "Give it here. I'll take
it to her."

"No, it's not that kind of—"

"Maria, what is the matter?"

A quiet voice from the interior, yet it rang with authority and an accent I couldn't place. Maria half-turned, bobbing her head. "Nothing, sir. I'm dealing with it—"

"I'm here to see Rebekah," I said, a little more loudly than I'd intended.

The door opened wider, revealing a tall, light-haired man with a neat beard and high cheekbones. He was wearing pressed trousers and a white shirt cuffed at the wrists. I met his gaze squarely, clutching my own shirt front as the kitten began to mew in protest.

I'd seen Dr. Kromer the day he had brought Jep home. Up close, he was even more intimidating. "What business do you have with my daughter?"

"I have . . . a delivery," I said, unhooking tiny claws from my stomach.

"I told her all deliveries were to be at the kitchen door, sir, since I know you don't appreciate unnecessary interruptions." Maria enunciated the last part carefully, as though reciting a rule someone had drilled into her head.

I was starting to regret leaving the house this morning, let alone my rash promise to a stranger I'd met by the riverside. "Look, if I could just speak to—"

"Papa? What is going on?"

Footsteps in the hallway and then she was in the doorway, wearing a green dress, her dark hair neatly set.

"Kit, hello," Rebekah said, blinking in surprise.

I untangled the kitten from inside my shirt and held him up. Her eyes widened and she pushed past Maria.

"You brought him! I had been hoping—" She scooped the kitten out of my hands and held him to her shoulder, leaning her cheek into his fur. There was a dark smudge of ink on her jaw.

"One cat, as promised," I said, breathing in her happiness and excitement as a shield against Maria's glare and Dr. Kromer's cool gaze. Rebekah, oblivious, was now excitedly examining the kitten from ear to tail.

"You're such a handsome boy, aren't you? You're so big now. Look at those huge paws," she exclaimed, holding up one of his white-socked feet.

"What will you call him?" I asked, watching the kitten sniff her face delicately, then begin to wash her nose.

"Patroclus," she said immediately. I smiled. My old school-teacher had thought very highly of the Greeks and read us passages from the *Iliad* on rainy afternoons.

Dr. Kromer's voice broke into our exchange. "*Que faites-vous?*"

"A cat, Papa, for the house. They bring good luck."

"*Ta mère n'aimera pas* ça."

"*Maman a peur des souris qu'il y a dans le garde-manger. Patroclus sera le notre gardien de la maison.*"

I couldn't understand a word, but their body language was clear enough. Rebekah hadn't told her parents that the kitten was coming. Dr. Kromer regarded it for a long moment, then reached out a tentative hand. Patroclus sniffed his fingers and then gave a huge yawn. A smile cracked the corner of the doctor's mouth and softened his whole face, transforming him in an instant from stern physician to indulgent father.

"*Si maman est d'accord—*"

Rebekah's face split into a smile and she kissed her father on the cheek.

The doctor looked at me. "How much?"

"Oh, no, it's not—it's a gift. For your—for Rebekah."

The smile she beamed at me from the doorway was worth every scratch already beginning to sting on my stomach.

Dr. Kromer inclined his head. "Thank you, uh, Mister—?"

"Kit," I said. "McNair. Just Kit will do."

"Thank you, just Kit," he said and stepped back into the house. "Have a good day."

Rebekah looked up from the kitten. "Would you like to come in? For some tea? Or some lemonade?"

I hesitated. The day was already warm and lemonade was always good, but I could read Dr. Kromer's expression. It was not his invitation. "No, thank you. I should be getting home. My father will be needing me."

"Give my best to your parents," Dr. Kromer said. I had one last glimpse of Rebekah's face and then the door was shut in my face.

Rat was where I'd left him, restless and eating clover. We rode home slowly, stopping to splash in the river, where I stripped off my shirt and cleaned the little beads of blood from the kitten's scratches on my stomach.

When I got home, Landon was still sulking over his argument with my father and Jep was in a dirty mood, having neglected to close a gate and been sent to round up three escaped pigs. My mother took one look at me and ordered me upstairs to change into a dress and a sunhat, then outside to the garden to stake beans and hill potatoes. I was relieved that no one asked where I had been.

I said nothing of the kitten, even when Jep discovered him missing and spent half a day searching the barn and the other out-buildings. I should have felt guilty, watching Jep paw through the wood pile, but when I pictured Rebekah's cheek pressed against grey fur, it seemed worth all the trouble.

REBEKAH

The following week, I walked the two miles along the road to the McNair farm. Maman had thought I'd lost my mind when she found me in the kitchen, up to my elbows in flour and sugar as Maria hovered, looking on in disapproval. I explained to Maman, twice in French and then again in German, that I was making almond cakes for the family down the road, the one who had given me Patroclus. Since Kit had refused any money for the kitten, I felt it my duty to repay them in some way they would accept.

Maman pursed her lips, standing carefully away from the kitchen table to avoid getting the slightest stain on her dress.

"*C'est pour la charité? Pour la famille pauvre?*"

"They're not poor, exactly, just—I think they will like them."

"*Si c'est pour la charité, alors d'accord.*"

"It's not—" I said.

The kitchen door swung shut behind her. Maria pushed her sleeves to her elbows and stomped over to the sink to begin washing up the bowls and spoons I had dirtied.

"No one here needs your charity, let alone those McNairs," she said, cutlery clattering against the bottom of the sink.

"It's not charity. It's a payment."

Maria snorted. I rolled my eyes behind her back.

My arrival was punctuated by a chorus of barking as the same two dogs came galloping out towards the road. I told myself to continue walking as though the sight of them didn't send a shiver of fear down to my toes. They met me halfway up the lane, running in circles and shoving their heads under my elbow to sniff at the basket. I was afraid to push them away, but also feared for the safety of the *financiers*. So I stood, trapped, as the dogs circled me.

A whistle pierced the air. "Oi, George! Gordie!" A tall figure loped towards me from the porch. "Get on, get on!" The dogs obediently turned and ran off towards the barn. The young man came closer, halting a few feet from me, eyeing me suspiciously until his expression broke into a smile.

"I almost didn't recognize you under that thing." It took me a moment to realize he was referring to my hat. "It's Landon, from the other week."

"Yes, hello, Mr. McNair."

He laughed. "Mr. McNair's my father. It's Landon to you, Miss Kromer."

"Rebekah," I said. It had been several days since I'd spoken this much English. My head was already beginning to ache.

"Rebekah," he repeated, rolling the syllables like one would savour a lemon ice on a hot day. "It's a pretty name."

"Thank you."

"So what's in the basket, Little Red Riding Hood?"

"Pardon?"

"You never heard of Little Red and the big bad wolf?"

It took me a moment to realize he was referring to *Rotkäppchen*.

"Oh, yes. I'm bringing some cakes, for your—for Kit. As a thank you for the"—I couldn't think of the word fast enough—"small cat."

"For the small cat, huh?" He reached over and tugged aside the cloth on top of the basket, revealing the golden cakes inside. "Well, there's a mystery solved. Seems an awfully nice gift in return for such a runt of a kitten. For these, you could have had the big tom."

"I am happy with the one I have," I said, covering the cakes again.

"Come on, you better bring those inside."

As we walked down the lane, Landon told me the story of Little Red Riding Hood. I didn't have the heart to tell him how much more gruesome the Grimm brothers' version was.

The kitchen smelled like bacon fat and woodsmoke from the big black stove that squatted along one wall. Signs of family life covered every surface: a wrinkled newspaper on the table, a smeared butter dish with a collection of toast crumbs around the edges, a pair of socks hung to dry near the stove and a riding saddle dumped in the farthest corner, surrounded by cans of polish and dirty rags. Landon swept into the room ahead of me, putting my basket on the table on top of the newspapers.

"Kathleen, put the kettle on, will you?"

"Put it on yourself," came the sharp reply.

Kit was at the kitchen sink, elbow-deep in soapy water. Her back was to me, and for a moment I couldn't reconcile this figure in a cotton dress with the person who had shown up on my father's doorstep with my kitten.

Landon had moved to the bottom of the staircase. "Jep! I've got a surprise for you," he yelled, catching my eye and winking. "Kath, the kettle."

"You've got two hands," Kit snapped, reaching to pump more water into the sink.

"I'll do it," I said. A splash as Kit dropped the pan into the sink and spun around.

"Rebekah, I didn't . . . hello." She wiped her hands on the front of the dress. "I didn't know you were coming today."

Landon had already pulled aside the cloth on top of the basket and helped himself to one of my *financiers*. He leaned on the table, seeming to be fascinated with each bite of the cake.

"I would have called," I said, "only I knew you didn't have a telephone."

"Of course. Uh, why did you, I mean, why are you—?"

A thunder of footsteps on the stairs announced Jep's arrival in the kitchen. He skidded to a halt on socked feet, catching himself on a chair.

"Rebekah brought us a gift," Landon said, brushing crumbs from his hands. "As a thank you for, how did you put it? Oh, yes. For the small cat."

Kit paled, hands tightening on her skirt.

Jep looked among the three of us. "Hello," he said, coming around the table. "I remember you. You helped me when I broke my arm."

"Yes. Are you feeling better?"

He held up his arm and made a fist. "Your father checked me last week. I'm good as new."

"Jep, why don't you show Rebekah your treasures while we wait for tea?" Landon said, staring at Kit.

I hesitated, then saw how eagerly Jep looked at me.

"Do you want to see my room?" he said. Without waiting for a reply, he grabbed my elbow and began tugging me up the stairs. Behind us, I heard the slam of the kettle hitting the stovetop.

Jep led me along the second-floor hall and then up a ladder, less steep than the one to the hayloft in the barn. We emerged in an attic room that stretched nearly the length of the house, under a peaked roof that angled low on both sides. There were two windows, as small as portholes, and two beds at opposite ends of the attic. One was shrouded in a curtain that looked like it had been made of an old blanket, while the other was raised up on wooden crates, each crate on its side, like a shelf.

Jep dropped to his knees by this second bed and grinned up at me. "This one's mine."

The crates were filled with rocks, feathers, broken bits of coloured glass. I saw fossils and tin soldiers and a few carved wooden animals.

"It's very impressive," I said, straining my ears to see if I could hear anything from downstairs.

Jep handed me a goldfinch feather, yellow with a black tip as though it had been dipped in ink. He began rearranging a few of the pebbles. "They're always like that," he said quietly. "Don't worry about it."

I blushed. "I didn't mean to cause any fuss."

Jep took another feather from the crate and stuck it among the pebbles like a flag. He turned to look up at me. "Is it true you have the missing kitten? I've been so worried about him."

"I'm *désolée* that you've been worried," I said, then I told him about Patroclus—his meals in the kitchen, how he slept on my feet at night, his adventures in the garden—until Landon called us down for tea.

Mr. and Mrs. McNair arrived home from town to find the four of us taking tea on the porch. Mr. McNair shook my hand and introduced himself in a distracted way, as though my presence had woken him from deeper cares. Dermot McNair was a heavy-set man, with the wind-chapped skin of someone who spent most of his life outdoors. He was wearing worn but clean clothes, ironed fastidiously into submission. His hair, though combed back with Brylcreem, had come loose in a few slick curls. Caroline gave me a brisk nod of recognition and continued into the kitchen.

"How was the bank?" Landon asked, half rising from his seat on the steps.

"Never you mind," his father said, and vanished inside, his steps quiet for someone so big, as Jep asked that I describe what it was like to ride in a streetcar.

Soon, Mrs. McNair re-emerged to ask if I would stay to eat with them, given I'd brought such a fine treat, and I said yes.

In my house, dinner was a dignified and peaceful affair, eaten in small bites with the correct cutlery. Sometimes my parents quietly discussed the day's events, or my father gave his opinion on a column in the newspaper.

Dinner in the McNair house was nothing of the sort.

"He is the only thing standing between this country and disaster!" Landon shouted.

"Ralston is a restless idiot with an itchy trigger finger," his father thundered.

"Who else is going to stop those warmongering bastards?" Landon said, emphasizing his point with a gravy-covered fork.

"Language," Caroline said tartly, spreading butter on a piece of bread. "Rebekah, would you like more potatoes?" I took the dish she passed me, barely able to follow the verbal tennis match across the table. Beside me, Kit was quiet, a shadow of the person who had coaxed me to come see a kitten all those weeks ago.

At a stern look from Caroline, Dermot and his eldest son both subsided into silence.

Eventually, Dermot cleared his throat and asked, "So, Miss Kromer, what brought you by today?"

I fingered the cutlery. "Well, I thought I would—"

"She brought the cakes as a thank you," Landon said. He was meticulously wiping every drop of gravy and potato from his plate with a crust of bread.

Kit went still, as everyone looked at me.

"Yes, I wanted to thank you all for the, uh, the . . ." The word escaped me again. "The small cat. The grey one. He is very sweet."

Silence around the table.

Caroline rested her knife on the edge of her plate and looked at Kit. "You gave Rebekah the grey kitten?"

Kit stared at her plate.

"I'll bring him back. First thing tomorrow," I said. I would miss him fiercely, but in that moment I would have done anything to take the miserable look off Kit's face.

Landon looked as though he was about to speak again, but Dermot folded his hands and met my eyes. "Please, keep the cat, Miss Kromer. Making his daughter happy is the least I can do to repay your father."

Jep spoke into the silence that followed. "She named him Peony."

"Patroclus," I corrected, aware of Landon restlessly spooning more potatoes onto his plate as Kit remained unnaturally still.

"That's a funny name. Is he a saint?"

"Don't be stupid," Landon said. "He was a Roman poet. Wrote all those plays about boys killing their mothers and big, angry monsters."

I swallowed a smile. "Actually—"

"He was Achilles's companion," Kit said quietly. "When Patroclus died, Achilles went mad with grief and killed all the Trojans."

Landon snorted. "And how would you know anything about history?"

Kit glared at him, and for a moment, I feared they might leap at each other with knives drawn.

"Let's have some of those lovely cakes you brought us, Miss Kromer," Caroline said, standing up from the table and beginning to collect plates. I got up too, and together we cleared away the dishes and brought out the basket of *financiers* and another pot of tea. Kit didn't move to help, sitting mute and rebellious at the table, staring at nothing.

The almond cakes went well with the strong black tea and the tension soon eased. Jep and Landon fell to bickering over films, and whether Roy Rogers or Buster Crabbe would win in a gunfight. Under the cover of their argument, I leaned slightly towards Kit.

"I'm sorry I caused all this trouble."

Warm breath tickled the side of my neck. "It was worth it."

Then Jep was demanding to know if every house in Montreal served *financiers* after dinner.

I stayed far later than I intended. At the question of who would walk me home, both Kit and Landon leapt to their feet and then glared at each other. I stood between them, my hat and gloves in the emptied basket. As I opened my mouth to insist I could find my own way home, Dermot said, "You shouldn't be walking in the dark. I'll hitch up the cart and Landon'll take you."

I returned Landon's smile.

As I waited on the front porch, Jep came bounding down from the attic and pressed something into my palm. It was a small rock, with the impression of a fern along one side.

"For you," Jep said. "Can I come see Patroclus next week?"

"Jep, that's not polite," Caroline scolded, and gave me a grimace of apology.

"Of course, you may visit," I said.

Landon came driving around to the side of the house. He hopped down to help me up onto the wagon seat. After I said all my other goodbyes and promised to return soon, I looked around for Kit. She had vanished as quietly as a shadow.

Landon kept up a steady stream of chatter as we drove. It was early evening, the sky darkening to indigo. Small shapes darted and fluttered between the trees, their chirps grating my ears. I wondered what kind of birds they were.

"Bats," Landon said, then laughed at my expression.

I looked down at my gloves and discovered a button missing from the cuff of the right. I must have made a tsk of annoyance since Landon raised an eyebrow. I showed him the glove.

"You can have one of mine," he said, tugging a button on his shirt. "I will make a sacrifice to such a noble cause."

I laughed and swatted at his hand. "Don't—your mother will never forgive me for the extra work!"

Soon, I recognized the treeline around the yellow house. Landon slowed the horse to a halt and caught my hand. We had stopped just beyond the edge of the garden, the apple trees screening us from the windows.

"What my mother doesn't know won't hurt her," he said.

"I could never lie to your mother about anything. She's formidable."

He crooked one eyebrow. "Is that so?"

I nodded. He leaned in and kissed me, softly, his lips dry and warm against mine. His grip on my fingers didn't tighten. The air was cool between us as he withdrew, dropping my hand.

A heroine in a book would have slapped him, if for nothing other than show. But I was no heroine. I was merely a girl overwhelmed by sensation and worn out from thinking in two languages all evening.

I cleared my throat. "Good night, Mr. McNair. I can find my own way from here."

"I'm sure you can," he said, and he took me at my word, staying put as I climbed down with some difficulty from the cart. Once I was on the ground, he handed me the basket and tipped an imaginary hat. "Thank you, Miss Kromer."

"For the cakes?"

He smiled. "Those too."

I blushed as he turned the cart in a great circle in the road and started back the way we had come.

I stood for a few moments, watching the cart disappear into the twilight. I pulled on my gloves before walking up the drive to the door.

My father was reading in his study when I came in.

"Did you have a pleasant visit?" he asked, not looking up.

"Yes, lovely."

Something in my voice caused him to look up over the top of his book. "You didn't walk home on your own, did you?"

"No, Mr. McNair brought me back." The evasion slid out smoothly over the rapid beat of my heart.

My father nodded, attention already drifting back towards his page. I said good night and went upstairs.

Long after I had settled into bed, I felt the brush of Landon's lips against mine. It was nothing like I'd imagined a kiss with Madeleine would be—soft, intoxicating, our silent laughter behind the neglected shelves of the library. But, still, I had felt something.

JULY 1939

KIT

NOTHING MORE WAS SAID ABOUT THE GREY KITTEN. But after Rebekah's visit, my mother kept me inside, making meals, cleaning dishes, carding wool, washing clothes that dried in minutes on the fence line. Weeks vanished like sand through my fingers, and suddenly, it was high summer, cicadas droning in the ash trees and heat shimmering over the hayfields.

"It's too hot," Jep moaned, slouching in the shade of the porch. I looked up from shelling peas on the steps. My mother sat in a rocker nearby, the sock she'd been darning lying discarded on her knee as she fanned herself with a newspaper.

"There's nothing I can do about it, pet," she said. "Did you feed the pigs?"

"Yes," Jep said, sliding down and rolling over until he was face-down on the porch floorboards.

"Are the horses watered?"

"Yes." My brother let out a sigh as deep as the stupefying dullness that covered the whole earth.

Landon had gone to town with my father, where there was the possibility of ice cream and cold drinks, leaving me here on the porch with a bucket full of peas. Even breathing seemed to demand too much work, and my clothes stuck to my back.

The newspaper slapped against wood as my mother killed a fly. "All right, go on." I looked up. "The pair of you are as useless as a bottomless bucket. Get yourselves off to the river or to town, whichever."

I scrambled to my feet, dumping shelled pods. Jep was already at the bottom of the steps, practically vibrating with excitement.

"But you come back in a better mind, you hear? I'll have none of this sulking at dinner."

Jep bounced up the steps to kiss our mother on the cheek, and then he was off, ducking through sheets hung on the line and scattering chickens. I raced after him, down the back field towards the river.

Dragonflies skimmed the surface of the water as I waded onto the bank. It was heaven, with the cool water on my skin, and the sweet smell of summer hay in the air. After my dip, I stretched out on the grass, letting my clothing dry in the sun as the cicadas droned from high in the ash trees.

I rolled on my side and stared up into the branches. I'd been trapped in the house and garden too long. The forest had always been a living, breathing thing that spoke to me without words. A feather fallen across my path or a spray of red maple leaves would unerringly guide my steps. The slightest tickle of a breeze against my cheek would nudge me around obstacles that my brothers stumbled over. I was never lost, no matter how far I wandered.

I could tell which berries would give themselves to me willingly and which would cling to the stem, no matter how ripe they looked. I knew which tree limbs would snap under my weight as I climbed. I could find crayfish and trout lazing in the shadows of an oxbow when others returned empty-handed. The swallows gliding low over the water in the evening told me I would wake up to raindrops against my windowpane, no matter that the radio called for sunshine.

There were places I avoided too, though I didn't know why. I never climbed the gully that cut through the ridge near the rapids. I never strayed deep into the pine forest at the top of that ridge, where the dead needles lay deep on the ground like a reddish-brown carpet and the light was always grey and flat, no matter the weather. Walking alone in the forest, I often felt alien eyes on the nape of my neck, but when I turned, there was no one.

I found strange things: a tree covered in thousands of monarch butterflies, like so many orange and black eyes winking at me. One night, an owl dove out of her nest in the treeline as I crossed the back field, so close I felt her wings brush my hair, her talons nearly raking my scalp. And one autumn day, years ago, I had come upon an entire, perfect fawn skeleton, bleached white and curled in the brambles as though sleeping. But each time I brought my brothers to show them these miracles, they had vanished. Even though I retraced my steps to the exact place, there was no sign that the monarchs or the fawn skeleton or the owl nest had ever existed. It was no wonder my family considered me a liar.

I lay back again, my limbs heavy and warm. I listened to the chuckling stream at the edge of my awareness, picking out the places where it rushed over a rock or dropped into a small pool.

The murmuring voices crept up slowly. Louder and louder, but no clearer, as though I was listening to the sounds of a crowded party from the other side of a door. I heard traces of music, an instrument I couldn't name. A high-pitched thread of laughter broke my trance.

I opened my eyes and saw Jep sitting near the water's edge.

"What's so funny?"

Jep looked up. "I didn't laugh."

"I just heard you."

"Honest, Kit, I didn't."

I frowned towards the water. It bubbled on as it always had, the voices and music gone.

"What do you make of this?" My brother held out a fossilized shell, white ridges curving across the stone, with specks of clay in the cracks. He was always finding such treasures: arrowheads, beads, weathered pieces of broken glass, feathers, bones—the ones he hoarded in his orange crates.

I brushed some dried flakes of clay from the fossil and nodded my approval. When I handed it back to him, Jep's grin nearly split his face in two.

When our clothes had dried, we followed the path across the river and along to the yellow house. We found Rebekah reading in the garden under a parasol, like someone in a film.

Jep called out and clambered over the stile before I could stop him. Rebekah put aside the book to greet him. I leaned on the fence separating their garden from the river path as Jep showed her his fossil, then waved excitedly my way. Rebekah followed him down to the fence.

"No horse today?" she said.

"I'm letting him get fat in the summer field."

"We're out for a walk," Jep said. "Do you want to come?"

Rebekah met my eyes. "A walk would be lovely. Let me fetch my hat."

As we waited, I watched a honeybee dipping in and out of touch-me-not blossoms. Soon, she came down to the bottom of the garden, hat in place, as though we were about to promenade into town. I held out my arm to help her over the stile, but Jep grabbed her hand before she could reach for me and towed her down the path.

"How is Patroclus?" I heard him ask. "Has he caught any mice yet? One time Harriet caught eight mice in an afternoon!"

Rebekah met my eyes over his shoulder, and I could see laughter inside them. Then she inclined her head very seriously to respond to my brother.

"He is doing very well. Even my mother thinks so."

The three of us followed the path beside the river and up into the forest along the ridge. The pines were shady and cool in the afternoon sun, everything green and golden. The conversation turned from the adventures of Patroclus to a recent letter from Rebekah's grandparents.

"They got to see the King and Queen when the royal tour stopped in Montreal back in May. Apparently, there was a big parade, and my grand-mère saw the Queen's hat as they went by in the motorcade." Rebekah looked wistful. "Afterwards, they took a picnic up Mont Royal and ate it in the *parc* overlooking the city while a marching band played. I was so looking forward to it, but, well, I guess it doesn't matter now."

I wanted to take her hand, leap into her father's car, and drive us all the way to Mont Royal, just to bring back her smile.

"I know what will cheer you up," Jep said.

We both gave him a puzzled look.

"Come on."

He led us up the hill, skirting the deepest part of the forest, to the point where the trees suddenly fell away at the edge of the escarpment, and the whole valley unfolded before us like a table-cloth. In the distance, I could see Harrichford, the light glinting off the roof of the Catholic church. Green fields quilted with fences and hedgerows marched away into the distance.

Jep said, "Any Sunday afternoon you choose, you can have your own picnic, right here, with the best view in the entire world. All to yourself!"

He sat down on a rock and Rebekah sat next to him, tucking her skirt under her legs.

"It's absolutely perfect, Jep," she said.

"I know," my brother responded, and chucked a stray pebble off the cliff. I sat down on his other side. The limestone was warm, lichen crumbling beneath my hands. The wind blew fresh over the hill, and I swore I could smell Lake Huron in the breeze.

Jep flung another rock. "Why did you come here if you liked it so much in Montreal?"

"Jep, that's a rude question," I said, but I had been wondering something similar.

Rebekah traced a groove in the rock. "My father was in line for a promotion at the hospital," she said at last. "But just before Christmas, the board decided on someone else. Someone much younger, with less experience, but with a more . . . Canadian surname. My father thought we would be fine—he had his own practice, of course, not just his position at the hospital—but then many of his private patients stopped coming."

"Why?" Jep asked.

"Because he's German," I said, watching Rebekah's face in case I had it wrong. "Because of what's going on in Europe. People think Dr. Kromer must be just like them."

Rebekah laughed, a sharp, bitter sound. "As though all Germans are the same people, sharing one brain. As though the fact that my father has lived in Canada for twenty years doesn't mean anything—" She paused and took a deep breath to collect herself. "He looked for other positions, but it was the same everywhere. No one wanted a doctor named Kromer on their staff. It wasn't until he saw your mayor's advertisement in the newspaper that he had any hope." She sighed, and brushed bits of lichen from her hands. "So, we're here. For now. At least until things go back to normal."

Jep looked at her, eyes big. "I'm glad you're here and I hope you never leave."

She smiled. "In this moment, I'm glad I'm here too."

"And to celebrate we can have our first picnic right now," I said, reaching into my pocket and pulling out a bag of licorice. Jep tried to snatch it from my hand with a delighted squeal, but I held it high. After each of them had taken a piece or two, they fell into a conversation about their favourite movies. I leaned back on my elbows, savouring the licorice on my tongue.

I had spent hours up here on this cliff as a child, singing to the jays who hurry-scurried in the pines behind me, chipping flakes of lichen off the stone and letting them swirl away in the wind. It was strange to sit here now, watching the trailing smoke of half a dozen chimneys across the valley and a distant bank of clouds in the south promising rain late in the day, this time through Rebekah's eyes.

While Jep described his favourite bit of the most recent Roy Rogers movie, gesturing wildly with the licorice, Rebekah caught my eye over his shoulder and gave me a slow, private smile. I wanted to live in this moment forever, with her hair shining in the summer sunshine and the breeze flirting with the edge of her dress where it hung just over the edge of the cliff, and the whole world spread out below us.

REBEKAH

The clerk at the post office shook his head. "Nothing here for Kromer. Have you checked the telegraph office?"

I thanked him and stepped back out into the sunshine. I had written eight letters to Madeleine since we'd arrived in Harrichford and, so far, there had been no reply. Perhaps she'd gone on a holiday with her parents to the Eastern Townships. I was sure she would have written if she'd had the time.

My father was still at the chemist, so I sat on the bench outside the general store, nodding politely as people passed, surprised that I now recognized some of them. As I ran my fingertips nervously over the creases in my gloves, I remembered too clearly the slight tingle in my skin as Kit's fingers brushed my palm when she handed me a piece of licorice.

A shadow fell over my lap, and I looked up into Landon's smile.

"If I'd been born fifty years ago," he said, "I would have jumped on the first train west and made my fortune in the Yukon."

"Hardly a glamorous way to get rich," I said, catching a glimpse of myself in a shop window and pausing to adjust my hat.

I could picture him, in rolled pants and no shirt, wading barefoot through a river. We would live in a canvas tent and make fried fish and biscuits in a single skillet. At night, we would lie in our tent and count the stars. I could tell him the story of every constellation—

His hand cupped my elbow. "What are you thinking about?"

I blushed. "Nothing that concerns you." I drew my arm away, but not too quickly. "Didn't your maman teach you it is rude to intrude on people's thoughts?"

"My maman, bless her soul, did her best. It is the tragedy of her life to have such a wicked son."

"Wicked or stubborn?" We had reached the far end of the main street, where the houses abruptly gave way to rolling fields. If I didn't look behind me, it was as though Harrichford had ceased to exist.

"Which would you prefer?"

"Neither." I turned and began walking us back up the street. "If you are stubborn, then any attempt at change will make you worse, and if you are wicked, then only God can save you. In either case, nothing I say will make the slightest difference."

"You're right, I am both wicked and stubborn and many more terrible things besides." Landon stepped in front of me and I was forced to stop. "But I think you could change anything, or anyone, you set your mind to."

The wind blew his hair over his forehead, carrying with it the dust of the street and the smell of the farrier's shop farther down. He was looking at me earnestly, his eyes the copper colour of sunlight on honey.

Over his shoulder, I saw my father coming towards us. Landon must have seen my expression, since he pivoted away from me, already raising a hand in greeting.

"Dr. Kromer! What a pleasant surprise."

When my father reached us, he shook hands with Landon and asked after his family.

"They're well enough, sir. I was just explaining the work of haying to Rebekah."

I took the hint. "Landon mentioned that it is a long day's work. I had thought of bringing over some refreshments."

My father frowned. "I didn't know you were developing such an interest in country life, Rebekah."

Landon's voice was smooth as butter. "My mother was delighted with the cakes she brought us the other week. I'm sure she'd be grateful for more help in the kitchen tomorrow."

"I don't see why not," my father said. "As long as you promise, Rebekah, to be a help and not a hindrance to Mrs. McNair and to stay out of the sun as much as possible."

"Yes, Papa."

"I shall have her at your gate by dawn," he said to Landon, and walked around to climb into the driver's side of his car. "Come, Rebekah, we are expected at home."

I held out my hand to Landon. "Goodbye," I said.

"Until tomorrow, Miss Kromer." For a moment I was terrified that he would lean down to kiss my fingers, but instead, he shook my hand very properly and turned to walk up the street.

I climbed into the car and pretended to listen as my father expounded on the virtues of fresh air and good honest labour in the fields. My wrist buzzed where Landon had slipped his thumb beneath the cuff of my glove and pressed it against my pulse.

The next day dawned cool, with dew on every blade of grass, but by late morning it was scorching hot and dry. While Mrs. McNair drove the wagon, Kit and Jep took turns pitching forkfuls of hay into the back, where I worked to trample it down. The hay was itchy and dusty, getting under the collar of my dress and falling inside my stockings and shoes. Near the barn, I could see Landon pitching hay from the other wagon into the press, and Mr. McNair binding each finished bale with twine.

"Take them off!" Kit huffed, leaning on the pitchfork for a moment. "You'll break the hay with those shoes."

I nodded, and stripped off my shoes and stockings, tossing them on the wagon seat. The hay was sharp and splintery under my bare feet when I stepped lightly across it. As each new forkful showered down, it threw up a cloud of dust and pollen.

"You have to really squash it!" Jep yelled, heaving another forkful. "Knock the air out of it."

I jumped and stomped onto the sweet-smelling grass. My feet soon ached and sweat ran down my back. To distract myself, I pretended I was a maenad, crushing grapes underfoot in my madness. I was a bird, a wolf, a shaft of light. When I glanced down, Kit was looking up at me, smiling.

By midday, the sun was merciless and we stopped to rest. Mrs. McNair and I brought sandwiches and lemonade out to the shade of the trees in the hedgerow lining the south edge of the field. My arms trembled with the weight of the lemonade jug, and I was relieved when Landon came to take it from me, lifting it and drinking straight from the lip before passing it around. My mother would have been horrified, but I could imagine nothing more refreshing. The pile of sandwiches soon disappeared. After lunch, Mr. McNair fell asleep with his hat over his face in the long grass, and his wife stretched out next to him, fingers gently tracing his forearm.

Landon had thrown himself on the ground near my feet, his arms beneath his head. "So, what do you think of our country life, Miss Kromer? Does it match what you've read in books?"

"Don't tease," Kit said sharply. She was sitting a little apart from us, eating one of the jam tarts I had brought.

Landon plucked a grass stem. "Are we boring? Be honest."

I looked around at the grass and the blue sky, and everyone collapsed, tired, sweaty and at ease. "I could stay here forever."

Landon grinned. "Just wait until you've seen a dozen haying seasons come and go." He drew the grass stem up my bare calf, tickling me. "Then you'll wish yourself back in the city." The grass stem wriggled higher. I slapped it away.

"I'll keep you around to do all of my chores for me."

He rolled over onto his stomach. "Your wish is my command, lady. Say the word, and everything I have is yours."

"You're such an ass, Landon," Kit said, wiping her sticky fingers on her trousers.

"So, sheep and hay—that's your offer?" I said lightly.

Landon clutched his chest. "You wound me. Perhaps you prefer another? What sheep has my rival offered you? I will challenge him to a duel."

I did not look at Kit, smoothing my skirt down and tucking it under my legs. "No other offers," I said.

Kit stood up without speaking and walked off into the trees behind us.

"Where is she going?" I said, staring after her.

Landon shrugged. "Maybe the fair folk will do us a favour and finally take her back." He tipped back the lemonade jug, but it was empty. I had left the second one on the kitchen table, barely able to carry one.

"I'll get more—" I said, but Landon was already on his feet.

"Allow me. You should enjoy the shade."

He took the empty jug and jogged back towards the house.

"What did he mean about the fair folk taking her back?" I eyed the forest where Kit had disappeared.

"Just something Ma used to say." Jep bit into a tart, red jelly spilling down his hand. "Because of that day on the ice, and how she came back different."

"What happened?"

Jep glanced over at his parents. Both of them were now asleep, the dogs beside them. "It was a long time ago, in the winter," he said. "I was really little. Kit was ten and Landon had just turned twelve. We went out walking in the forest and on the way home we crossed the river at the wrong point—the ice was thin—and Kit went through. Landon got her out, somehow, and carried her back home. She was pretty much dead and Landon near scared out of his wits."

Jep offered me the last tart. When I shook my head, he smiled and took it for himself.

"She survived, obviously," Jep continued, words muffled by a mouthful of pastry. "But she was different. Had to learn all her numbers and letters over again, started hearing noises no one else could hear and seeing things that weren't there. She told me once that she heard voices in the river. She also started wearing Landon's clothes. Boy, was Ma mad about that. She also stole that horse of hers—"

"Stole?"

Jep blushed. "Well, not exactly," he said, and took a moment to suck crumbs from his fingers. "More like the McCutcheons had a half-broke pony nobody except the knacker wanted, and Kathleen cried until Pa let her bring it home. But there were other things—spoiled milk, a fire in the stovepipe. She was private and sulky, nothing like the sister we'd had before."

I tracked Landon's dark head across the field as he made his way back towards us.

"And because of that, you think she's some kind of *fée*?" My voice rose in disbelief.

"Shh," Jep put a hand on my arm, looking alarmed. "Don't ever name them. They don't like it."

"But you do think she's one of them?"

Jep lowered his voice. "She's a changeling. They took our sister under the water and sent back something else. At least, that's what Ma said."

Landon was now only a dozen yards away, the lemonade jug held over his head triumphantly. I took a deep breath. "Jep, most girls become a little clumsy and sulky around that age, even without a near-drowning. It's natural she'd want more privacy, more . . . She's not cursed, she was just growing up."

Jep looked at me, eyes serious. "There was no way she should have survived. The doctor couldn't explain it."

A chill rippled up my spine. The forest, though just as green and sun-drenched as a moment ago, loomed larger in my mind. A twig snapped behind me, and I whirled to see Kit stepping out of the trees, a little farther down from where she'd gone in.

She saw us looking. "What?"

I smiled. "You startled me. I thought you must be a coyote."

She gave me an odd look. "No coyotes around this time of day." Her gaze shifted to her brothers as Landon arrived with the lemonade. "We're losing daylight. Gotta get the rest of this hay into the loft."

KIT

My shoulders ached and, even with gloves, my hands were blistered from handling the pitchfork. But for once, I could wear Landon's shirt and trousers and my mother said nothing. I hauled and lifted and drove with no skirt to confine my legs or tight seams pulling under my arms.

My mother had prayed for the weather to hold, for the sky to stay unclouded, for the hay to dry sweet and true. I never heard my father pray out loud. He spoke all his prayers with his hands— nailing a fence rail as a prayer for protection, braiding leather reins as a call for strength and unity. I imagined him talking to the sun as we worked, asking it to linger a little longer and bless our harvest.

That night, after Dr. Kromer came to take Rebekah home, Landon, my father and I heaved the last load of bales up into the loft, where Jep and my mother wrestled them into place. My father braided a small doll out of a handful of hay, and my mother brought out the tiny loaf of bread she had baked, a thimbleful of blackberry jam spread in the centre. Under a sliver of moon, we walked out to the east corner of the field where my parents had woven a last uncut tuft of hay into a little house. They laid the doll and the bread inside and poured out a measure of spirits on the ground in front of it. My mother said the Lord's Prayer, while my father stared up at the night sky.

I shivered a little in the night air, so cool after the blistering heat of the day. I could feel them, all around us. God made every- thing, but the wee folk kept it running, as far as I understood. God kept the sun in the sky and made the hay grow and the pigs get fat, but it was the fair folk who had kept the field clear of stones, who kept the horses sound and the mildew from the hay. So we also owed thanks to them, according to my mother.

After my family headed back to the house for a late supper, I lingered in the field. Was the wind that lifted the arms of the doll so that it reached towards me a coincidence? That's what I told myself as I hurried back towards the orange glow of the kitchen window.

With the hay in, I wished for a week of rain as an excuse to rest, but the weather continued to be fair and dry. My mother was never one to put off for tomorrow what could be accomplished today, and she set me to painting the henhouse while Jep mucked out the pigsty and Landon went to check on the sheep. I was washing up at the pump before lunch when a commotion broke out.

"But you promised!" Jep yelled, his voice carrying through the kitchen window and out into the yard. I paused.

"I'm sorry, but that's the way it has to be." My father, his voice firm.

"It's not fair! You don't care about anything."

Heavy footsteps through the kitchen and then the slam of the door. As Jep ran past me, I saw that his cheeks were red with emotion. He disappeared into the barn, and I heard feet slapping the ladder as he climbed up to the hayloft. I shook my hands dry and slipped through the kitchen door.

My father sat in his usual chair, a ledger open on his lap. My mother was rinsing a colander full of raspberries, a pie crust sitting ready in the dish beside her. George the sheepdog slunk up to my knees and I petted him absently.

Landon chose that moment to return, leaving his boots at the front door and coming down the hall into the kitchen. "What's going on?"

My father didn't reply, still frowning over the paper, the pencil dwarfed in his hand. My mother sighed as she poured the berries into the pie. "Your father's decided to slaughter the black hog," she said. "It's past time."

My heart broke for Jep. He had raised that pig from a squirmy runt of a piglet he had to nurse by the fireside to a three-hundred-pound hog. He came when Jep called, letting him scratch his back with a willow switch, and we all knew that Jep had been sneaking him the best of the kitchen scraps for months. It was always going to end this way, but that didn't stop it hurting.

My father cleared his throat. "Between that hog, the six lambs, the rabbits and at least a couple of the chickens—that should see us through."

"Aw, poor Jeppy. He got real attached to that runt," Landon said.

"That runt is now a beast that will feed us for the winter or starve us when the stores run low and Jep keeps feeding him out of our larder. How did I raise such girls, to make so much fuss over a damn pig?" my father said with uncharacteristic vehemence, standing up and snatching his pipe from the table before marching past Landon and out onto the porch.

My brother stood aside to let him by, then went over to give my mother a kiss on the head.

"Those smell good," he said, leaning his chin on her head and reaching for the raspberries.

She slapped his hand. "Don't even think about it. So help me—"

"I know, I know," Landon said, putting his arms around her waist.

She sagged a little in his embrace, a smile creeping across her face. I couldn't remember the last time I had touched my mother, except for ducking a slap or a brisk rub to the cheek with a scratchy towel.

"Mrs. Kromer invited me for dinner next week," I heard Landon say.

"Did she now? You moving up in the world?"

A chuckle. "Anything's possible."

"I won't have you go looking a mess. You can leave your shirt out for ironing, and your trousers too."

"Thanks, Ma."

"I just hope Jep'll come out of his mood soon," she said. "We need to eat this winter."

"Leave it to me," Landon said, and he went out through the kitchen door, snagging a handful of raspberries as he went. I followed him out the door and across the yard.

"Aren't you taking Chelsea Fadden to the pictures next week?" I asked.

Landon stopped and turned to me. "What if I am?"

I swallowed. "This dinner—it's not the same as going on a picnic or taking her to the county fair."

Landon tipped the raspberries into his mouth. "So?" he said with his mouth full.

"Rebekah isn't like Anna or Chelsea or Sally. She's grown up differently. These things mean something to her parents. To her."

Landon swallowed and wiped his hands on his trousers. "I think Miss Kromer and I understand each other perfectly." His eyes narrowed on me. "What's it to you, anyway?"

"Nothing," I said quickly. "She's not the kind of girl you can string along, that's all."

"Sure." Landon stretched his arms over his head, looked around. "Where'd Jep get to? That boy wants a talking-to."

I nodded towards the back field. "He went that way."

"You'd think after all these years he would've hardened up a little."

"You'd think," I echoed.

Landon sighed and strode away towards the field, shoving both hands in his pockets. I waited until he was through the gate and out of sight before stealing into the barn and up the ladder.

I found Jep in the back corner of the loft, hunched into a miserable ball. It was hot and stuffy, with dust from the newly cut hay clouding the air. His face was tear-stained, shreds of hay stuck to it. I squeezed in beside him and put my arm around his shoulder.

"I knew it was going to happen," he whispered. "It's always the way."

I picked a piece of hay out of his hair, saying nothing.

Jep looked up at me, his eyes big in his round face. "Why can't I be like everyone else?"

"Maybe someone has to feel it," I said quietly, "so the rest of us don't have to."

He looked at his knees and I felt his shoulders tremble.

"You gave him a good life," I said. "Better than most pigs get. And because of him, we'll eat for another season. That's worth something, isn't it?"

"I guess it has to be." Jep sighed and leaned against me. I could feel sweat trickling down my back, but I didn't move away.

"Is it true what Rebekah said—that you raced her train into town?"

I nodded, and then I told him the story, with only a few exaggerations. By the time Ma came out into the yard yelling for us, Jep was smiling again, and the pig was, for the moment, forgotten.

REBEKAH

My mother had insisted on repaying the McNairs for their hospitality by inviting Landon to dinner exactly one week after the haying was done. Now the day had arrived and I was already sick of the whole affair. She had spent the better part of two days harrying Maria from one end of the house to the other—she'd polished the furniture and scrubbed the wood floors until I could see my reflection in them. I had wanted to tell Maman that it was only Landon McNair, that he would never notice a few fingerprints on the window glass or a chip in a plate. Judging by the mutinous curl of Maria's lip, she, too, thought it altogether too much fuss for a McNair.

My father drove off early on the day of the dinner, saying he had pressing business at the hospital, which I suspected was not all that urgent given it was a Saturday. I spent the better part of the morning hiding in my room, sewing the finishing touches on a new summer dress and reading poetry, while my mother and Maria chased each other around the ground floor.

In the afternoon, as I sat at the window reading, Kit rode up to the bottom of the garden and waved to me. I took my hat and bag and stole out the front door, then came around to her through the orchard, out of sight of the kitchen windows. Kit hopped off the horse and boosted me up on the saddle, then climbed up behind. We crossed the river, sluggish and shallow in the summer heat, and up to a field that arced like a bow towards the sky. Midsummer had baked the land into a golden quilt, and we slid off the horse and lay on the grass while Rat grazed nearby. It was warm in the sun, and warm, too, was Kit's half smirk when I said something clever. Three moles marched in a line just below her

earlobe, disappearing into the latest shirt she had stolen from
Landon. It was torn under the arm from pitching hay and had
another rip in the sleeve. I tugged at a loose thread dangling from
the tear.

"What do you do with your clothes? Don't you ever mend
them?"

Kit shrugged, lying back in the grass and chewing on a stem.
"It's from carrying you around on that damn horse. If I could only
get a moment's peace then maybe—"

I flung a handful of grass at her.

"And this is the thanks I get," she said, brushing it out of
her hair.

I reached into my bag. In my haste, I had gathered up my sewing box along with my handkerchief and book. "Let me make it up
to you then."

I took out the little box. It had belonged to my *arrière grand-
mère* and my mother would be distraught if she knew I had it out
here in the middle of a field. "Come on, take it off." Kit hesitated,
clutching a fold of the shirt. "Who's going to see you?" I gestured
to the empty field and the forest that skirted its edges.

Kit considered for another moment, then she drew the shirt
over her head, disappearing into a bundle of blue and white stripes.
I looked away. Below us, the river shimmered like a silver necklace
in the afternoon sun. A rustle and then the shirt was thrust into
my lap. I unsnapped the pearl-shell clasp of the box and drew out
a needle and thimble and some white thread.

Kit rolled over onto her stomach beside me, the hard angles
of her shoulder blades protruding from her back. I turned the
shirt inside out—it was still warm—and aligned the sides of
the tear under the arm. I threaded the needle and began with the

tiny, delicate stitches my grandmother had taught me. *"Comme de petites bouchées,"* she had said. Nip the cloth, just so. Kit watched me for the first minute and then became bored, reaching for my little bronze scissors. She began snipping bits of grass until I put out a hand to stop her.

"Ne fais pas ça," I said, eyes still on my work, my grandmother's voice in my ears. "It will wreck the blades."

She meekly returned them to me, and then pillowed her head on her arms.

"Tell me a story."

"I'm busy."

She looked up at me, squinting against the light. Her eyes were the deep warm brown of oak bark and earth after rain. "You can sew and talk at the same time. My mother does it all the time."

"All right, what story do you want?"

"Something good."

"There is a book in my bag." Kit rolled so she could reach across my lap. I kept my eyes firmly on the shirt in front of me and not on the length of pale flesh and the tiny berry of nipple that grazed my thigh. For a moment, her skin was sun-warmed and hot against my knees and then cool again, as she resettled on her stomach, the book lying open on the grass. My father would eat his beard if he saw a volume of poetry treated so.

"It's Tennyson."

A withering glare. "I know. We read 'The Charge of the Light Brigade' in school. I liked it, but then Landon chanted it every time we walked to school for a month until I punched him. So it's not my favourite anymore."

"That would ruin poetry for anyone."

I couldn't picture Landon as a child, only as a miniature version of himself as he was now. Kit claimed he'd had a nose too big for his face and knobby knees, but I'd put that down to sibling jealousy.

"He's always been a pig," Kit said absently, turning pages with grass-stained fingers. "What about this one?" Her hand stopped on an illustration I knew only too well, a poem I'd once recited endlessly to myself, acting it out in the privacy of my head.

"'The Lady of Shalott.'"

"Here." She held the book out to me, and I clung a little tighter to my needle.

"You read it," I said. As though I hadn't already memorized every word, as though she hadn't just reached through me and blindly touched my heart.

She read in a halting rhythm, fingers leaving faint stains on the pages as she turned them. Never had Tennyson been so butchered, but I didn't care. I was too distracted by her naked back and the shivers of her muscles as the wind traced them. I finished mending the first tear and began on the second, hardly noticing the needle now, all of my attention fixed on Kit.

A spike of pain as I pricked my thumb. I licked the blood away, my tongue warm against my skin. Kit's lips were still shaping unfamiliar sounds, stumbling over syllables.

I looked back down at the shirt, forced myself to breathe in time with the stitches. If one had the strength of mind to do so, time could be gathered and stitched and ordered.

The last tear was mended long before the poem was over. I looked away, towards the river, and imagined a wooden boat drifting in the current, my own face pale and beautiful. A Lancelot with Kit's face bending tenderly over the bow—

"Wait—she looks out the window and then she dies? That's stupid." Kit glared at the book.

"It's symbolic," I said, my mouth gone dry.

"Of what?"

"Of the forbidden, of the things we may want but cannot have or touch."

"Oh, like sin."

"Something like that. Here." I handed her the shirt, whole again. She took it from me, angling her shoulders away. I had the overwhelming urge to press my lips to the nape of her neck, right where the hair met flesh, and run my fingers down the straight planes of her back. Then the shirt was on, and she was staring back at me.

"We should go," Kit said quietly. "I'll be late for my chores."

I replaced everything in the sewing case and slipped it into my bag along with the book. Kit bounded to her feet and then extended a hand to help me up. She held on to my wrist for a moment before jogging off to catch the horse.

We rode back in silence through the waning afternoon. At the bottom of my garden, Kit stopped the horse beside the aspen trees, out of sight of the windows. I slid to the ground. Kit looked down at the shirt, smoothed it with her free hand. "You can't even tell it was ripped."

I smiled. "Thank my grand-mère."

Kit took a breath as though to say something, then let it out again in a quick sigh. "Well, goodbye then."

"I'll see you soon?" I didn't mean it to sound like a question.

Kit nodded. Then, quick as anything, she leaned down from the saddle and planted a kiss on my right cheekbone. She kicked Rat into a lope, and was off, raising one hand in farewell without looking back.

—

My mother nearly ran me over in the hallway.

"Rebekah! Not yet dressed? Hurry, *ma chérie*, he'll be here any moment."

The dinner. I had forgotten.

I flew up the stairs, astonished that she hadn't noticed my flushed face, my cheekbone burning like a brand. In my room, I pulled off my dusty clothes and reached for the dress my mother had picked out for me. The memory of Kit leaning across my knees, her nipple touching my thigh, flashed across my mind and my stomach swooped, as though I was falling from a great height.

Downstairs, I heard a knock at the door, followed by Maria's footsteps in the hall. I pulled my dress straight and buttoned the collar. Every happy moment I spent with Kit was borrowed against future heartbreak. To allow myself to imagine otherwise was beyond foolish.

I picked up my hairbrush and yanked it through my hair, wishing I had time to at least wash my face. I conjured up the memory of Landon tickling my leg with the grass stem, our chaste kiss in the wagon, his thumb pressed against my pulse. He was handsome, and clever, and he made me laugh. It was surely enough—more than most people had.

I heard his voice drifting up from the hallway as I smoothed my eyebrows and looked myself over in the mirror one final time. He wouldn't have come to dinner if he wasn't interested in me. I owed it to myself to see where this could lead.

A quarter of an hour later, we were all seated in the dining room. The table was laid with Maman's best china, fresh-cut flowers from the garden, and all eight candlesticks ablaze. Landon was sweating in his best clothes. He had already complimented the wallpaper, the crystal decanter, the flowers and the carpet. The conversation had run out of steam before the first course was finished.

My father cleared his throat. "How was the haying? I had hoped the weather would remain hot and dry for you."

"Yes, it did. Rebekah was a great help."

"And your mother, she is well?"

"Yes, sir."

"And your brother, Jeremy was it?"

"Jep," I said.

"Yes, Jep. How is he? Has his arm fully healed?"

"Good as new, sir. Nothing can keep Jep down for longer than a day or two."

"Good, good."

Silence washed through the room, lapped at my feet. I could hear the grandfather clock ticking in the next room. The Landon sitting across from me, so rigid and polite, was not the impertinent boy who had stolen a kiss. I saw our house through his eyes, the crisp folds of the curtains, the symmetrical lines of the books. A far cry from the rumpled mess of the McNair farm, with dogs underfoot and half-read newspapers, rising bread, and leather horse tack tossed over every surface. A dime store novel left dog-eared on the kitchen table, plants growing wild over the windowsills. Our house was sterile by comparison.

"Maria?" my mother called, two pink spots beginning to show on her cheeks. Her wineglass was empty, while mine and my father's were still half-full. Landon's, I noticed, was also empty. "We are ready for the soup now."

Maman had insisted on five courses, and had Maria bring them to the table one at a time as though a whole army of chefs had prepared them. Split pea and bacon soup, pork with apple-sauce, carrots in butter and brown sugar, a *tarte au gratin*, fluffy bread and goose liver paté, with *tarte aux pommes* for dessert. Landon ate with enthusiasm, pausing after every few bites to sip his wine. I picked at my food, sipped my wine and tried to follow a conversation that felt as though it were happening underwater.

"Where did you study, sir?" Landon asked.

My father dabbed his lips with a napkin. "First in Hamburg, at a small grammar school. I went to Berlin to begin my medical studies, but then the world war came, and of course I had to stop."

"You were a soldier?"

"An *Unterarzt*—a medic. The war took men apart and I tried my best to put them back together again. When it was over, I went back to Berlin to continue my studies, but nothing was the same. There was no money for research, no money for school."

"Even as a doctor?"

"I wasn't a true doctor yet. Just another young man with battle-field experience. After the war, people were angry with the govern-ment. We had fought and died and for what? So that our families could starve in the streets? But I was lucky. My mother's cousin was a nun who lived in Montreal, and she said I should come to Canada, that it was better here. So I studied hard and I wrote the exam, and they sent me a letter saying yes, I could go to medical school in Montreal. My parents and my uncles put together all their money, and there was just enough for a ticket on a ship from Hamburg and my first year's tuition."

I had heard this story at least a hundred times, each time coax-ing out a few more details. My father had arrived in Montreal on a frigid October night, stepping off the gangplank onto the quay in the Old Port. He looked around and took a deep breath. So this was Canada. It reeked of fish and diesel fumes and animal dung. If he was careful, he had just enough of his family's money left to live on for a year while he studied. There was no going back.

His cousin helped him find a flat on a small cobblestoned street northeast of McGill University. His roommate was a wiry Belgian studying chemistry one building over from the medical school. Busy with their studies, they rarely talked, but once in a while they would sit on the narrow balcony with the black iron railings overlooking the street and share a beer and talk about the life they'd left behind.

My father climbed the steep drive to St. Joseph's Hospital every morning before dawn, shoes sliding on the frozen cobblestones, the wind digging up and under the scarf his mother had knitted him before he left Hamburg.

The hospital corridors were narrow and crowded, officious nuns in their starched caps expertly elbowing medical students out of the way. My father spoke French, but everything here was in a guttural dialect muttered out of the sides of the mouth. He ended each day with a splitting headache, his mind reeling from one language to the next. He annotated his textbooks in German and English, some of it phonetically transcribed on the back of a notepad until he could find the time later, in his little railroad flat, to look up the word and cement it into the wall of knowledge he built, brick by brick, throughout those four long years.

"I will not lie to you, Mr. McNair, it was not easy. No one liked Germans in this country, so I did everything I could to become a French Canadian. I had promised my father that once I had my degree, I would go back home, but I became so immersed in the work of the hospital, with my colleagues and our research and my practice, I did not go back. And now ... well, it is good that we are here, instead of there."

"I am glad to know you do not share the views of the majority of your countrymen," Landon said.

An awkward silence followed. My father rarely discussed politics, but I knew he followed the news religiously. The situation in Germany hovered in our house like a distant thundercloud.

The silence was broken by Maria clearing away the dishes and returning with the *tarte aux pommes* and fresh cream, a childhood favourite of mine.

Our guest ate his first serving with relish and flattered my mother no end by requesting another slice. She cut him a full quarter of the *tarte* herself, heaping it with spoonfuls of cream.

"And you, Mrs. Kromer. How did you meet your husband? I imagine it was terribly romantic."

My mother laughed, setting down her wineglass. "Oh my dear, it was fate, wasn't it, Heinrich?"

"Now, Régine, I'm sure the boy really doesn't want to hear the details."

"It was very snowy that night." My mother's eyes were slightly glassy from the wine. "My parents and I had been invited to a Christmas party. I don't remember who was the host—"

"It was a Goodwin's party," my father said, a spoonful of cream paused halfway to his mouth.

At Landon's blank look, I added, "The department store. They held a big party every year and invited practically everyone in the city."

My mother was looking into the distance. "Of course, Mr. Goodwin. He was a friend of my father's. Such nice parties, with an orchestra and presents for the children and a big tree that touched the ceiling, covered in electric lights and silver paper chains."

"It sounds like a fairy tale," Landon said. He caught my gaze across the table, but I couldn't tell whether the glimmer in his eye was laughter.

"I was just seventeen and wearing a rose silk dress. I had the most charming pearl-drop earrings. I wonder what happened to them . . ."

"The party, Maman?" I said, trying to keep the edge out of my voice.

"Well, your father was there with his roommate, the Belgian. Heinrich was standing in the corner of the room, peering at everything from behind his spectacles. Everyone was dancing, but he wasn't." She beamed fondly at my father, who gave her a half smile in return.

"But he asked you to dance?" Landon asked.

"*Mon Dieu*, no. I asked him! In our day, it wasn't really done, but I didn't want to leave such a handsome boy by himself in the corner. So I took two glasses of rum punch from the table and I went right over to him, and I said . . . I said . . ." She collapsed into giggles.

My father picked up the thread. "She said, 'You look lost, jelly-bean. Care to dance?'"

"It sounds much better in French," my mother assured Landon.

"I was so nervous," my father said. "I was never a good dancer, and here was this pretty girl wanting me to lead her out onto the floor. It's a good thing you brought that punch."

Maman sighed. "We danced the whole night by the Christmas tree. My parents were scandalized, but I knew right away that he was the only man for me."

My father actually blushed. "You were the most beautiful girl I had ever seen."

"It *was* fate." My mother's voice cracked on the last word.

"A beautiful story," Landon said, politely ignoring the single tear that ran down my mother's cheek.

"Coffee?" I offered.

"Yes, please. I can't eat another bite."

I signalled to Maria, who clomped back through the kitchen door. Cherise would have had the coffee ready.

My mother was now weeping into her napkin.

"Shall we retire to the front room?" I asked.

"Of—of course," Landon said.

My father stood up from his chair and came around to my mother's end of the table. "I will join you in a moment," he said. "Madame Kromer is overtired."

I ushered Landon into the office and shut the door against my father's murmuring voice and my mother's hiccuping sobs.

"I'm sorry," I said. "My mother . . . she is sometimes like this. My *arrière grand-mère* was the same way."

"Sunny one moment, raining the next?"

Landon dropped onto the settee and threw one arm along the back of it.

"Something like that." I leaned against the desk. "I worry I will be the same."

"Never. You are far too cool and collected."

Kit's bare skin against my leg. A shiver ran through my stomach. "Not always."

Landon looked around. "Funny, the last time I was here, I didn't notice half of the things in this room. And you—I thought you were the doctor's secretary."

"Hardly."

"You were brilliant, though, so calm, reassuring."

"You liar. You kept asking for the real doctor."

"Only until I saw you with Jep. I think he was half in love with you before you'd finished asking his name."

"Don't be ridiculous." I sat down in the chair opposite him. "He is far too young to be in love with anyone."

"He's fourteen. That's old enough, isn't it?"

"I wouldn't know."

Maria chose that moment to back through the doorway with the coffee tray. I took it and sent her back to the kitchen with a nod. Landon was quiet as I poured and stirred, but when I handed him a cup, his fingers brushed my knuckle.

"Do you believe them?" Landon said. "Your parents, I mean. About fate and love at first sight."

I sipped my coffee. "I think such stories tend to snip out the complications and leave in only the parts that look best."

Landon shook his head. "So cynical. It's refreshing, really. Both of my siblings are daydreamers, and now here you are, like a breath of fresh air, ready to face the world exactly as it is."

I couldn't think of anything to say to that. After a moment, Landon got up and walked around the room, restless.

"What is it that you want, Rebekah?"

"Pardon?"

"I mean from your life—from all of this." His gesture took in the house, the town, the whole world.

"I—I don't know."

"Your father didn't cross an ocean and make something of himself so that you could spend your life as some society wife, decorated and hung up in a window for all to see."

His coffee cup and saucer clattered onto the desk, and he was kneeling at my feet, my hand clasped between his palms. "We are meant for more, you and me. So, tell me what you want?"

"I . . . I want to go to university."

"What's stopping you?"

I withdrew my hand. "Given everything that happened in Montreal, my father thinks that for now, I am better to stay at home and study. Perhaps someday I may persuade him to let me attend St. Hilda's College in Toronto, but not yet."

Landon got to his feet and walked to the window, pulling aside the closed curtain and staring into the darkness beyond. His fingers drummed on his trouser leg. "There is a world war coming—another one—and I'm going to join up. It's going to be my ticket out of here." He turned towards me. "Rebekah, you and I could—"

The door opened and my father stepped into the room. I glanced around to assure myself that Landon and I were an appropriate distance apart. Part of me felt as though he was still on his knees by my chair, his palms pressing my hand.

"Please accept my apologies, Mr. McNair," my father said. "My wife suffers from a nervous condition and sometimes requires medical attention. I hope you will not judge us too harshly."

Landon inclined his head. "Sir, your wife is a charming woman and gracious hostess. There is nothing to forgive."

My father allowed himself a small, relieved smile. He moved past me to the coffee tray and began pouring himself a cup. "I trust my daughter has been keeping you entertained?"

Landon's eyes glittered at me over my father's shoulder. "Oh yes, sir."

"I was thinking I could show you those books I mentioned earlier—"

I leapt to my feet, nearly sloshing my coffee onto the carpet. "Mr. McNair was just leaving, Papa."

"Oh?"

"Yes, he has a long day of . . ." I floundered.

"Roofing," Landon supplied. "My father thinks we're due for a storm in the next few days, and he wants our roof shingles replaced tomorrow."

"Right, well . . ."

"Thank you for a wonderful dinner. My compliments to your wife."

"I shall see you to the door."

"No, please, don't trouble yourself. Good night to you both." Landon shook hands with my father. His eyes hooked mine lightly as he disappeared into the hall. I heard the front door close behind him and his footsteps crunching down the drive until they were swallowed up by the hum of the cicadas.

My head was aching as though I had kept my teeth clenched for hours. My father sat down on the settee, raised his coffee cup to his lips, hesitated.

"*Un charmant jeune homme,*" he said at last.

"Yes, he is very charming," I murmured in English. I wanted to rest my head on my arms right there on the desk.

"So good, you know, with your mother. Very polite."

"He thought she was lovely."

"So understanding of—well." He took another sip.

I levered myself up from the chair and dropped a kiss on his forehead. "Good night, Papa."

"You're going to bed already?"

"It's quite late."

"Be very quiet going up. Your mother is sleeping."

"Don't worry, Papa."

As I started up the stairs, I heard him murmur, "Hmm, yes, very charming indeed."

AUGUST 1939

KIT

I STOOD IN THE RIVER, MY PANTS ROLLED TO THE KNEE. My hands were just under the surface, and the current tickled my wrists. A small shadow swam past my leg. I held my breath as it slowly moved between my palms, and then I lunged, quick as a cat. A tremendous splash and the fish danced away into deeper waters. I swore.

Rebekah laughed from her perch on a branch of the willow tree. She was leaning back against the trunk, a book in her lap, her hair loose, her feet and legs bare. Our shoes lay forgotten on the bank.

"I can't do it when you're watching me," I said.

She lifted an eyebrow. "I'm beginning to think you can't do it at all."

"I'm telling you it works. It just takes patience."

"And a fish to swim right into your hands."

I flapped an arm at her. "You're scaring them. Go do something else."

She stuck out her tongue, but she closed the book and climbed down from the tree onto the bank. A moment later, I heard a rustle and a splash as she waded to the other bank.

I shook my head and rolled my shoulders. I'd been fishing like this since I was a child, but never with an audience. I was beginning to worry that I'd be punished for my bragging.

It was a hot day. Every bit of moisture had been baked from the land, and the roads shimmered with false horizons. It was rare for Rebekah to turn up at the farm unannounced, but she'd appeared at the edge of the paddock just as Rat and I returned from an errand in town. I'd hurried to put the horse away and slip away while my mother was napping inside. The heat had driven us to this shady bend in the river, where one bank was cool and shaded by the willows that leaned over the water, and the other a series of flat rock shelves leading down to the river's edge, drenched in midafternoon sunlight.

Another shadow, bigger and slower this time. I let my eyes unfocus, my fingers move like plants in the current. I was another tree with my roots in the river. One heartbeat, another. The fish swam closer. I struck, seizing it with both hands and flipping it onto the bank. I crowed with triumph and looked around for Rebekah, but she had vanished around the bend.

I caught two more fish in quick succession, and cleaned them all with my knife, leaving the innards for the hawks. I wrapped the flesh in burdock leaves and placed it under a stone in the river to keep cool. Then I lay back on the rocks to dry my clothes.

The sun had tinted everything gold, the water flowing fast and clear a handspan from my feet. The shale was warm under my palms, the willows throwing blue-green shadows over the water.

Rebekah waded back towards me, her skirt bunched in her hands. Her hair fell down her back, tangled from her explorations along the river. She came up the flat stone steps and sat next to me, leaving a trail of damp footprints.

She leaned back on her hands, tilting her face up to the sky. I closed my eyes, the sun turning my eyelids a deep red.

"I wish it could be like this forever," she said.

"Like what? Hiding in the forest with no shoes?"

A damp foot kicked my ankle, gently. "I mean so peaceful," Rebekah said. "I'm always calm when I'm with you. Like this."

"My mother would say that's because I'm a daydreamer who doesn't know the meaning of hard work."

There was a shifting of cloth. I opened my eyes.

She had rolled onto her stomach and was propped on her elbows, looking at me intently. I swallowed. The sound of the river was loud between us. I could pick out the higher notes of the waterfall layered over the bubbling of the midstream.

"Your mother doesn't know you like I do," Rebekah said, and touched my forearm with her fingertip.

An ache spread from my chest down towards my stomach, stripping my breath. I was still, as still as I had been in the water, thinking myself a tree as the shadows moved between my legs. Then Rebekah leaned in and kissed me.

She tasted like sweet clover and sunlight. The scent of the river clung to her skin, and the ache in my chest shattered into a thousand bladed dandelion seeds, each lighter than a wish. The sunlight fell on us, around us, soaking into the rocks and the river and into us, alone and naked beneath our clothes.

She was the first to pull away. A tendril of hair had fallen across

her face, and I reached to brush it aside. She caught my wrist
with her hand. "If this isn't, you shouldn't—"

I leaned up to kiss each of her fingers where they held my arm.
Then I pressed my lips to her wrist, where a blue vein like a willow
branch forked under her skin.

"It is," I said. She pushed me back down onto the rock and
kissed me again, her hands twining around my shoulders and into
my hair.

The sky had turned from blue to pale yellow to pink when Rebekah
finally sat up and looked around.

"I have to go," she said, gathering her hair and twisting it
behind her head. I wanted to tug her back down into my arms,
but it would be dusk soon and the rest of the world would come
looking for us.

I retrieved the fish from the river as she shook out her skirt and
collected her shoes and stockings.

"Tell them you went fishing," I said as I handed the parcel
to her.

"We did go fishing," Rebekah said, and she gave me a smile
so full of happiness I nearly lost my footing. Then she turned
and went up the bank towards the path, the fish in one hand and
her shoes dangling from the other, stockings over her shoulder.
I spared a thought for the shy, overdressed girl I had met beside the
river back in spring.

As the sun dipped below the ridge and the air began to cool,
I walked home in a daze. Rat gave a nicker of welcome when I came
through the paddock. I patted his neck absently and went to do
the evening chores. Jep and Landon were already in the barn.

"Where've you been?" Landon asked, dropping hay into Daisy's stall. "Pa's been looking for you."

"Fishing," I said. I went to grab the milking pail, but it wasn't on the shelf.

"Jep's already doing it," Landon said, reproach in every line of his shoulders. "If you want to be useful, go bring in the horses."

"Sure," I said, and drifted to collect their halters. I was halfway out the door before Landon spoke again.

"How many?" he asked. I blinked back at him in confusion. "How many fish did you catch?"

I could still feel Rebekah's lips against my throat, her fingers in my hair.

"None," I said and turned to go.

"That's not like you," Landon said.

I shrugged. "Win some, lose some, I guess. I'll try again tomorrow."

A snort. "Like hell you will. Ma's on the warpath. If it was up to her, she'd chain you to the front porch like a dog—"

But I was already out the door and calling to the horses, still tasting sweet clover. I didn't bother to reply.

REBEKAH

After a week of bedrest and absolute silence, my mother had recovered. A few days after I'd first kissed Kit, Maman came fully dressed to the breakfast table and ate a soft-boiled egg with some toast, my father watching her anxiously from behind his newspaper.

After breakfast, she announced that she needed fresh air. She put on her oldest set of kid gloves and a big sun hat I remembered from picnics as a child. After badgering me into an old summer dress, she unearthed a set of rusty trowels from the garden shed behind the kitchen. Together we set about weeding and dead-heading the flower beds in the front yard. I knew nothing about gardening, but my mother would point at a plant and declare it *une mauvaise herbe*, and I would diligently dig it up and toss it on the burlap sacking she had dragged outside for this purpose.

The sky was overcast, but it was hot, wasps occasionally bothering us as we worked. Happiness fizzed like champagne bubbles in my chest, despite the unpleasant chore. Every time I closed my eyes, I was back on the riverbank, looking down at Kit, running my hand up an arm or tracing an earlobe with my tongue.

I pulled a particularly stubborn thistle from the earth. My mother dug her trowel into the dirt beside me.

"*C'est un gentil jeune homme*," she said, giving up on English since we were alone.

"Who is?"

"That McNair boy."

"Landon?"

"I know he isn't everything we'd hoped for. And his family, well. But he's smart, and he's ambitious and he clearly cares for you."

Irritation rippled through me, dissolving the champagne. "So, you think I should marry him."

"*Ma chérie*, this isn't like home. You may have to settle for something different than what you expected."

"But Papa said we'd only be here until everything blows over, and then we can return."

My mother said nothing, stabbing the earth.

"Maman?"

"This is a good place. Your father will do well here. So will you, if you apply yourself."

I snorted, tossing another thistle onto the burlap. "By marrying the first boy who comes calling? I thought you had your heart set on a lawyer or a medical student."

"He is a good boy, and he clearly likes you despite your father's . . . unfortunate background. Don't you like him, even a little bit?"

I bit my lip. The grass stem tickling my leg, the kiss in the wagon. His palms pressing mine, eyes lit with possibility.

"He makes me laugh, but . . . I don't know. I'm not sure it's enough."

Maman sat back on her heels and wiped her brow, streaking dirt across her skin. "I think it's time for some tea, don't you?"

While we washed up at the kitchen sink, Maria brought the little table from the upstairs parlour and two chairs from the dining room out into the garden. She laid the table with finger sandwiches, a plate of cookies and a crystal pitcher of cold tea, and Maman and I collapsed gratefully into the shade. It was a poor pantomime of our old life, but I was tired enough not to care. My mother ate two sandwiches and was on her third glass of tea before either of us had recovered enough to speak further.

"*Ma chérie*, your father and I are only thinking of your future."

"Maman—"

"No, listen. When I was your age, I was already engaged to your father and planning my wedding. You won't be young forever."

I dropped the remains of my sandwich on my plate, appetite lost.

"We aren't always going to be here, and I just want to be sure . . ." She swirled the cold tea in her glass, watching it intently.

Then in a quieter voice. "What if you turn out to be like me, if you develop the same . . . I don't know what I would do without your father's help. I can't bear the thought of you, alone, trying to manage." Her eyes threatened to brim over.

I took her hand. "I won't be alone. I promise. I'm just not ready yet."

"You do like him, don't you?"

"Of course."

"But not enough to marry him?"

"I . . ."

She withdrew her hand and wiped her eyes with her handkerchief. Across the garden, a cicada droned.

"Do you still write to Madeleine?"

I blinked. "Yes." Though not as much lately, I thought guiltily.

"Has she replied to your letters?"

"No, but she was going to stay with her cousins, so I don't expect she'll get them until the end of the summer."

My mother nodded, staring off into the distance.

"I had a friend like her. We were schoolgirls together, oh, many years ago now. Cassandra. We did everything together. Parties, dances, shopping. She was the daughter of my father's business partner. She came on our skiing holidays, even spent a whole summer with us when her parents went on a tour of the continent. We used to say that we would only marry twin brothers so that we could live together in a big house in the country."

I'd never heard this story before. "What happened?"

"We grew up. Her family moved to Boston and she married a stockbroker. I met your father a year later and married him."

Madeleine, her hand in mine as we glided around the ice rink.

Her ringlets brushing my face when she leaned in to kiss my cheek in greeting. I had never been so happy as the nights when she was curled up next to me in my single bed, her toes touching my ankles, her cheek on my shoulder.

Kit, her mouth under mine by the river. My hands on her shoulders, her arms around my waist. The chuckling water and the tall rushes hiding us from everything. I had walked home in a world soft with happiness.

"How can you stand it, being so far apart?"

My mother looked at me, her face serious. "I always knew it would end someday. We should have known better, but we carried on anyway. It was only after she moved away that I realized how close we had come to disaster."

My breath stopped. I had thought my desires were pinned tight against my ribs, buried from all eyes. My secret dreams of what it would be like to lean just a fraction closer and press my lips against Madeleine's. All the times I had dreamed of drinking in the scent of her skin.

My cheeks burned hot, and I stared at the grass under my feet.

Maman ran her finger along the rim of her glass. "My mother was not so understanding as I am. After she moved away, I was forbidden to write to Cassandra. When her letters arrived, your grand-mère burned them in the fireplace, right in front of me. Eventually, the letters stopped coming."

My throat felt tight as a piano string. "Is that why—?"

"No, *chérie*, you know there were other reasons to leave Montreal. But it was a good time for you to make a break too, before things got more complicated."

Tears threatened to spill down my cheeks. My mother opened her arms. "Come here, *ma chère*."

I fell on my knees and buried my head in her lap, crying all the tears I hadn't shed since we'd left our home. She stroked my hair.

"It's over now and there are other things in life, better things. Your father is a good man and I care for him very much. Without him, I would never have had you." She tipped up my chin to look into my face. "You are the best gift of my life." She brushed a strand of hair out of my face, unsticking it from my lips. "Promise me you won't write any more letters to Madeleine. It will only prolong the hurt."

I nodded. My mother handed me her handkerchief so I could wipe my eyes and blow my nose.

"Landon strikes me as a good man. You will at least think about it?"

"Yes, Maman." I got up off my knees and returned to my chair. She cleared her throat and offered me the plate of cookies. I took two and dunked one in my tea.

"I was thinking we should cut back those awful brambles near the fence. They look so untidy."

I nodded, the bite of cookie dissolving to ash in my mouth.

We worked for another hour or two, until my mother declared she'd had enough of gardening and would retire for a nap.

As we gathered up the tea things and started towards the kitchen, I asked, "Maman, where is Cassandra now? Is she still in Boston?"

My mother's step slowed. "She died in childbirth, nearly twenty years ago. A school friend of ours wrote to tell me. I suppose she is buried somewhere in Boston."

She carried on to the kitchen door, leaving me behind her with the tray of empty plates.

KIT

As punishment for missing evening chores, I spent every day for a week in the garden, weeding, gathering carrots and beets, and lugging water from the pump since the rain barrel was empty. It hadn't rained in almost a month and the garden was parched.

One afternoon, the sky overhead was striped with hazy clouds and the wind smelled of lake water. I would have bet good money a storm was blowing in, but it held off through the morning, the heat rising with each hour and the humidity sticking my shirt to my back.

I sloshed another two buckets of water around the roots of the beans and stomped back to the pump. I had occupied my thoughts all afternoon with daydreams of the Labour Day dance, when the whole town would turn out at the church hall in their best. Normally I had little interest in something so silly, but this year was different. This year Rebekah would be there.

As I came around the barn, I saw a strange shape in the back field. Too big for a human or a sheep. I walked closer. Had Jep left a pile of hay out in the open? Pa would kill him for wasting it.

The shape slowly resolved into Rat, collapsed on the ground. I dropped the buckets and began to run.

By the time I reached him, he was rolling and kicking on his back, twisting his long neck. His eyes rolled wildly, unseeing and glazed. Colic. Summer was the time for it.

I dropped to my knees as my horse writhed in agony, hooves striking in all directions. It was on my lips to shout for help, but town was a half-hour's ride away. Mrs. Crochett across the road had a telephone, but if I called the vet, what money did we have to pay him?

My horse flopped onto his side, breathing hard. I put my hands on either side of Rat's head, cupping his velvet temples, willing my breath to flow into him. His eyes rolled up at me, white crescents showing. He was in so much pain I couldn't watch. But here I was. I thought of the gun in the barn and the box of bullets on the shelf next to the kerosene lamp. I couldn't. I had to. Better me than anyone else.

I walked to the barn, willing my legs to move faster, to hurry to end his suffering. The gun was where it always was, hung over the door on two nails my father had punched into the frame when I was still too small to reach. Now, I grasped it easily. The bullets weren't on the shelf as I remembered. I had to search, rooting through the hoof picks, kerosene tins and rusted horseshoes. When I found them, I took two out of the box and clumsily loaded the shotgun, small flecks of hay and dust spinning in the sunlight that spilled through the door.

In the field, my horse lay still, flanks unmoving. I leaned the gun against the fence and walked over to him. I waited for his chest to move, for his lungs to fill. For him to climb to his feet and shake himself off like he did after a good dust bath. A fly landed on Rat's ear and for the first time, it didn't flick to shake off the insect.

I knelt and put my hand on his withers. They were still warm. The sunlight and the grass and my horse fractured into glittering prisms. My throat burned, my temples ached, and hot tears spilled down onto my shirtfront. I cried in a way I hadn't cried for other things, in a way I hadn't cried after I went through the ice or when my father switched me for cutting my hair. I sobbed, pushing my face against Rat's neck.

"Come back. Please come back," I choked out, but my horse remained silent and still, the warmth of his flesh evaporating into the empty grey sky.

It was a slow walk back to the barn. I unloaded the gun, replaced it above the door and put the bullets back in the box, avoiding the empty stall at the end of the stable. I dragged my feet up to the back door and into the kitchen. My mother stood at the stove, a simmering pot sending clouds of steam towards the ceiling.

I hovered for a long moment. Without turning around, my mother tapped the wooden spoon harder than necessary on the edge of the pot.

"Lord's sake, Kathleen. Either spit it out or get out of my kitchen. Having you trail around me like a *púca* is what gets me fretting."

"It's Rat, he's—" My throat spasmed, and I choked the word out in one great hiccup.

My mother paused, braced both hands on the counter. "How?"

"Colic," I said.

She sighed, a sound that seemed to contain all her sadness and frustration and hopelessness in one breath. "Perhaps it's best this way, *nighean*. He was getting on in years and another winter might've done him the same."

I nodded, not trusting myself to speak.

She came towards me, her face soft for once. "Go on with you. I can manage myself for a few hours."

I fled out the back door and nearly turned for the barn to saddle my horse before I remembered. I wheeled in the yard and took off for the forest. Thunder growled in the distance, and the western sky grew darker with incoming rain.

REBEKAH

Papa was waiting for me when Maman and I returned from a matinee at the movie theatre in Orangeville. It had been a disappointing film and the theatre had been close and stuffy. I longed to go upstairs and shed my stockings. Instead, I followed my father into the study, and he shut the door behind us.

"Please sit down," he said, and gestured to the settee. I sat. He took his usual place behind the desk and steepled his fingers.

"Papa?"

"I have some excellent news for you."

I said nothing, using the program from the movie theatre to fan myself.

"This afternoon, while you were out with your mother, someone came to see me."

"Oh?"

"Can you guess who it was?"

For a wild moment, I pictured Kit standing on the doorstep the way she had the day with the kitten. "I have no idea."

"It was Landon McNair."

"Oh."

"He came to ask my permission to take you to the Labour Day dance. I would have given my consent, but I am not one of those fathers who would agree to such a thing before consulting you. So."

I heard myself answer, "Yes, Papa."

"He told me about the plans the two of you had discussed—moving to Toronto once you're wed, and of him joining the naval academy."

I was too stunned to reply. That was not how I remembered our conversation.

"When I married your mother, I had nothing ahead of me but the promise of my career and the will to work. I see the same ambition and will in him."

"Yes, Papa."

He twisted his pen in its holder, looking into the middle distance. "I have done my best to shield you from the ugliness of the world, Rebekah, but I'm sure by now you are aware of how we are perceived. As though Germans were all one people, following that madman in spite of—" He paused and collected himself. "While I can understand the suspicion that falls on me, I will do anything to protect you from such bigotry."

"Papa—"

"If you marry, especially someone like Landon, it will make everything . . . easier."

I stared down at my hands. I read the papers too, often taking them out of the firebox in the kitchen and upstairs to my room. I knew far more about our situation than my father suspected. I hadn't failed to notice that fewer patients had come to see Papa in our last few months in Montreal, that party invitations seemed to get lost in the mail, that some neighbours crossed the street to avoid speaking to us.

My father leaned towards me. "I know how overwhelming this must be, especially for a girl your age. I told him I would speak with you. And if all is well after the dance, then he and I will talk more of this."

I stood up and walked around the desk, trying to control the trembling of my limbs, and bent to kiss the top of his head.

"Thank you, Papa. I will be happy to attend the dance with him."

He smiled up at me and patted my hand, dismissing me.

I slipped out of the study. Maria and my mother were in the dining room, heads together over a cookbook—they'd somehow achieved a détente. I snuck through the kitchen and out the back door, into the garden, breaking into a run closer to the fence. I clambered over the stile and kept running along the river path. The sky overhead was dark grey, the wind pulling at the tops of the trees and tossing the rushes in all directions. Soon the clouds cracked with thunder and lightning, and the sky broke open into sheets of rain. I was soaked to the skin in moments.

A figure was splashing across the ford, as wet as I was. Kit, with her hair plastered to her skull. I met her at the bank, and we embraced. The crash of the rain all around us made speaking impossible. When she pulled back, I saw that streaks of tears were mingled with rain on her face. I kissed her without thinking, and she clung to me as though I was a spar in the wreck of the storm.

There was a white flash of lightning close overhead. As thunder cracked, Kit took my arm and we ran through the deluge, deep into the forest, along a path I had never travelled. The trees were larger here, but even their canopy couldn't keep off the fat drops that found their way inside my collar. We scrambled up the ridge, Kit tugging me by the hand, right, then left, until there was no path ahead of us and we were running through a pine forest, the ground carpeted with rust-coloured needles, the tree trunks around us black and slick with rain.

Ahead, I saw a clearing, and at its middle a cottage. We stumbled our way to it and then inside. Kit shut the door behind us.

The place was bare of furniture, with a simple dirt floor and no windows. There was a stone hearth along one wall and a pile of ancient firewood in the corner. The rain hammered on the wooden roof above us.

"Who lives here?" I asked.

Kit was already stacking logs in the hearth and peeling kindling with her pocketknife. "Dunno. Whoever it is hasn't been here in a long time."

There was the scratch of a match and the smell of sulphur, and a moment later, orange firelight flared against the wall. I sank down next to Kit in front of the fire and leaned my head on her shoulder.

"Rat's dead," she said in a flat voice. Everything I had intended to say about Landon and my father evaporated on my tongue.

"Oh, Kit, I'm sorry. I'm so sorry." I wrapped my arms around her. She tensed for a moment, and then sagged against me.

"If I had known this was his last summer, I would have—" She drew a great shuddering sigh.

"I know," I said.

Thunder rolled in the silence between us and the rain fell steadily on the roof over our heads. I leaned in and kissed her.

KIT

Her face was wet, her lips cold at first. Her dress was soaked and painted on her shoulders. She put her hands on my cheeks, the heat of her mouth a stark contrast to her icy fingers. I ran my hands up her arms and down her back, a storm inside me. She fisted my shirt in her fingers, pushed me back until I lay flat on the dirt floor.

The firelight threw a gold wash over the ceiling, and everything became blurry except Rebekah. I could count the beads of water clinging to her eyelashes. She climbed on top of me.

I shivered despite the fire. "Rebekah—"

"Hush," she said, leaning down to kiss my neck, her fingers already undoing my shirt buttons, hands sliding down my chest. When she had my shirt crumpled in a damp heap beside us, she reached behind her neck, unhooked her dress and pulled it over her head.

She had a look in her eyes I'd never seen before, a wild look, like she was a fey creature fashioned out of holly vines and blackthorn branches. I couldn't tell whether she was going to kiss me again or bite out my throat.

Slowly, gently, I ran my palms down her ribs, let my thumbs rest on the curves of her hips. She half closed her eyes. I did it again. She put her hands over mine and guided them down her thighs, across her garter, along her stockings.

Thunder cracked above us and she jumped, shock rippling through her skin. I drew my palms up her back and she leaned down, letting her full weight sink on top of me, her shoulders on mine, her hips pinning my thighs. She was shivering. I kissed her and her hair came tumbling down like wet silk, curtaining us both in a humid tent of breath and skin and raindrops. I wrapped my fingers in it, trying to breathe warmth back into both of us.

She licked a droplet off my cheekbone, ran her hands down my chest and further, unhooked my belt.

"It's all right to cry," she said.

"I'm not." But perhaps I was, because my skin was unravelling, my whole self unspooling against her fingers as she unbuttoned my pants, reached inside. I froze.

"I—"

She guided my hand under the edge of her slip. "I want this. Do you want this?"

With my whole self spun out between her fingers, a cobweb strung between fence posts, I couldn't speak. Instead, I pulled her face close to mine.

"Yes," I whispered against her lips.

REBEKAH

Afterwards, we lay tangled in front of the dying embers of the fire. The thunder had rolled on, taking the worst of the storm with it. The rain still drummed on the roof.

Kit stroked my hair, our body heat a comforting blanket against the damp. Everything felt far away: Landon, the situation in Europe, my father's worries. The whole world outside of our little circle of skin and breath and damp clothes was a blurry memory.

"Run away with me." Kit's voice was barely a whisper.

I settled my head more comfortably against her bare shoulder. "Shall we grow wings and fly to the moon?"

Kit's hand paused against my scalp, then resumed its motion. "We'll jump the freight train one night and be on the other side of Lake Superior by dawn. No one would be able to follow us."

I closed my eyes. "What would we eat? Where would we sleep?"

"We'll walk towards the setting sun, until we find the perfect place. I'll build us a willow cabin by the lakeshore. We'll live off fish and berries and dewdrops. I'll whistle down a flock of birds and make you a coat of feathers."

I laughed. "If we have to rely on your fishing skills, we'll starve."

"I mean it. We don't need anyone else, Rebekah." Kit rolled onto her side, pressed her nose against my cheek. "It could be just you and me, forever."

I opened my mouth to say something about Landon, but I couldn't bring myself to ruin this moment, this one perfect moment. Instead, I traced my finger down Kit's forehead, across the bridge of her nose, her lips. The dying firelight set her hair aglow in the darkness. I leaned in and kissed her, a promise and an apology together.

KIT

The lights of the church hall flickered like fireflies, drawing everyone in town towards the music and laughter. It was a calm night, deep with the hum of crickets. The breeze rustling the aspens along the road carried a hint of autumn in its teeth. I could hear voices before I saw groups of people drifting towards the dance hall. I was wearing Landon's third-best shirt (stolen that morning while he was out doing chores) and my cleanest trousers. I had polished my boots until they shone.

Blanketed in darkness and the sound of crickets, I wanted to stay here, the future still unwrapped and shining before me, to savour this moment like a lemon drop. But my treacherous feet continued to move forward, and soon, I was at the door of the church hall.

It was hot inside, and humid with bodies and drink and laughter. The long hall was crowded near to bursting. The wall in front of the kitchen pass-through was lined with tables groaning under bowls of punch and bottles of beer, cakes and cookies and every type of dessert the women of Harrichford County could bake. I spotted my mother's famous raspberry pie among them, already more than half gone. The dance floor was jammed with couples, the band in the corner doing their level best to keep them happy. I could see Jep among the musicians, sawing on his fiddle alongside a drummer, a man playing an accordion and another on an upright bass. I recognized the jaunty reel they were playing—one of Jep's standards.

Everyone was in their nicest clothes, their best hair and their poorest manners. I spied my father in the kitchen doorway, beer in hand, laughing with some townspeople, the mayor among them. Pa's face was red, from the heat or the alcohol, and he looked relaxed, happy even, in a way I hadn't seen in weeks.

I walked over to the pass-through and glanced into the kitchen, where I spotted my mother with the church ladies. With the tables set and the dance in full motion, they could swig sherry and gossip freely.

"Well, you never can tell," Mrs. Crochett said, refilling my mother's glass. "For all we know, they could be among us right now."

I took a shortbread cookie from a plate. It seemed the impending war in Europe was all anyone could talk about.

"I don't know, Susan," my mother said. "Even here? Who would be interested in Harrichford of all places?"

I deliberately turned my shoulder to the kitchen, looking out over the dance floor.

"My sister in Toronto says there's German spies all over the country. Operating in secret, spreading chaos." That was Amelia Gorseman, the mayor's wife.

"It could be anyone. Just think." Mrs. Crochett again.

I heard the chink of a glass hitting the wooden table. "Well, not just anyone," said Mrs. Gorseman. "Some are more likely than others, when you think about it."

I turned slightly to see the group of them staring in the same direction. Dr. and Mrs. Kromer were standing at the edge of the dance floor, Rebekah's mother wearing a fancy silk dress and a coat too warm for this weather. Dr. Kromer stood like a fence post, forcing others to go around him. They both looked miserable.

"You can never be too careful," Mrs. Crotchett whispered, loud enough that I could hear her. I pivoted away from the kitchen and towards the Kromers, muttering apologies when I bumped an elbow or a shoulder as I passed. I ignored the stares the way I always did. You would have thought these people would be used to me wearing trousers by now.

I sidestepped a couple leaning on each other and laughing and beyond them glimpsed Rebekah, a relaxed smile on her face I had only seen levelled at me or, occasionally, at her cat. The dancers pivoted and traded sides, and I lost her blue dress in the crowd. I orbited the hall, moving past the band and towards the kitchen again.

I found Landon, or at least the back of his head. He was dancing with eyes only for his partner. I wondered who he had asked this time: Chelsea, from the drugstore. Anna, Mr. Nelson's daughter. Susan Dale, the dairy maid, had been making eyes at him in the post office a week ago. I'd teased him, wanting to know whom to lay odds on, but he'd only smiled to himself and told me I'd have to wait and see. Given his expression now, I couldn't imagine he had decided upon Susan.

Then the dancers turned, traded partners, spun and traded again and I saw her blue dress before I saw her face. Rebekah was caught in the circle of Landon's arms, her skirt flaring out around both of them as they spun in a tight circle. Her dark hair stark against his white shirt, his hand holding hers. A hateful part of my mind noted what a beautiful pair they made. They turned and turned and her smiling face caught mine. I didn't stay to see whether her eyes registered dismay or shock or apology before I turned on my heel and cut through the crowd, ducking and shoving until I was back outside.

The night felt cool by comparison, and I shivered as I walked away. Through the pool cast by the overhead light above the doorway, past a group of schoolboys huddled around a beer they'd lifted from the tables, past a couple kissing in the permissive shadow under a tree.

Twenty more yards brought me to the old stable behind the hall. The door swung open easily, and I stepped inside, shutting myself in. The walls did nothing to block out the music but it was blessedly dark in here. I sagged against the wooden parade bleachers, stored here when they weren't needed.

Fingernails tapped against the door. I opened it a crack and she slid inside, a tumble of blue silk dress and perfume.

"Did you really think you were going to get away that easily?" Rebekah whispered, pushing the door closed and pulling me towards her all in one movement.

She kissed me, her nails digging into the nape of my neck. I kissed her back like I was drowning. Landon's smirk was in the back of my head and I thrust him away, pulling Rebekah closer to me, my arm around her waist, my palm on her cheek. She sighed into my mouth. Back in the hall, the accordion launched into a rendition of "Beer Barrel Polka," greeted with shouts and cheers and the sound of dozens of feet stomping wooden floorboards.

She had her fingers in my hair and I had my mouth halfway up her thigh when boots crunched on the gravel outside the stable. I pulled away, stopping her gasp with a firm grip on her waist.

"Rebekah?"

I'd have known Landon's voice anywhere. Her eyes were wide and bright in the darkness, gazing down at me. I shook my head silently.

"Rebekah?"

I ran my tongue up the inside of her thigh, nuzzled the soft flesh at its peak.

She leaned back against the wall, every muscle trembling. I licked higher. Her other hand fell out of the darkness and grasped my hair, hard enough to hurt. The boots crunched closer, until they were on the other side of the wall from us. I imagined him looking around, tugging his left earlobe the way he always did when searching for something he couldn't believe he'd lost.

I turned my cheek and bit Rebekah's thigh, hard enough to leave a mark, enough to make her drop my hair and clap both hands over her mouth to stifle a groan.

The boots twisted in the gravel, pivoting one way and the other. A muffled curse. Then they retreated, swallowed up in the whirl of noise and laughter of the dance hall.

We remained still. I could feel her pulse under my cheek, the growing warmth at the place where I bit her. After a long moment, I untangled myself from her skirt and slid back up the wall until we were face to face once more. She was flushed, stray tendrils of hair loosened and falling across her forehead. I tucked them behind her ears.

"You are an idiot," she said, breathless, mouthing more than speaking the words. I buried my face in her neck.

"Run away with me," I said.

"Kit—"

I pulled back and cupped her face between my hands. What little light seeped in through the cracks in the wall turned the lines of her face into a woodcut.

"Tomorrow night."

She softened under my hands, looking down and away. "There are things you don't—"

"I don't care." I kissed her. After a moment, she pulled away.

"I have to get back."

"I'll be waiting for you."

She kissed me once more, and then the stable door creaked and she was gone.

I counted a hundred heartbeats in the darkness, then another hundred more just to be careful. I slipped out and away through town. The sounds of the party followed me like a scent on the wind, and I felt more than heard the music long after I had turned off Main Street onto the old pony track that would take me on a winding route across country and eventually back to the farm.

A three-quarter moon lit my path and the coyotes were yipping in the pine forest on the ridge. For once, I had nowhere to be, no one expecting me, no chores to do. For this one night, I was free.

I flopped down in the field and looked up at the sky, picking out the summer crown and the two dippers. I imagined a sunrise over a field of water. The stars wheeled slowly overhead, cold and remote as ever.

I had a sugar tin filled with what little money I'd saved. It wouldn't get us far, but it would tide us over until I found work. We could ride the train to Toronto or all the way to Halifax, somewhere no one knew us. Out to the prairies to a homestead farm, or on to the mountains and north to the rivers of the Yukon. I would do anything—shine shoes, sell papers. Surely someone would hire me with my hair cut short and my imitation of Landon's cocky swagger. I'd send a postcard to my parents once we were settled, let them know I was all right. Jep—I felt a little stab of pain when I thought of my little brother. I would take him with us if I could. Maybe send for him in a year or two.

REBEKAH

I took a moment to smooth my dress and adjust my stockings. The air was chill against the sweat on my bare arms. I leaned against the wall of the church hall, wishing suddenly for a cigarette so I would have an excuse to stand out here alone for a few more minutes. So I could slow my heartbeat before I had to face the music again.

Landon had arrived at our doorstep at exactly seven o'clock, in a clean shirt and polished shoes. My mother had made a fuss over letting us walk together to the church hall. My father had finally persuaded her to travel ahead with him in the car, to arrive in style.

When we got there, I drank the glass of punch Landon brought me, and then another. He turned out to be a surprisingly good dancer, whirling me around the floor with careful steps. If I ignored the off-key band and the country people who bumped shoulders with us, it was almost like being back home. This felt easy, reassuring. Stepping backward each time Landon stepped forward, his shoulder firm under my hand, the way people glanced at us approvingly from the sidelines. For once, I didn't have to fight to keep myself nailed tight like a canvas stretched in a frame. I knew this dance, these gestures. It could be so easy. If I wanted it, it could always be like this.

The feeling vanished the moment I saw Kit. Her stricken face, eyes wide with shock and betrayal and a hundred other painful things I didn't want to name. The dance swung around again, and I craned over Landon's shoulder, but Kit was gone. I stuttered some excuse about being overheated and slipped out of his arms and out the nearest door. Luckily, I had heard the stable door creak.

The music in the hall wound down, to applause and shouts of disappointment. The dance was ending. I firmly shoved all thoughts of Kit aside, squeezed my trembling hands into fists and went to find my parents.

They were in a corner, looking as uncomfortable as when we'd arrived. All around, people were collecting their coats and hats, calling good night to each other. A group of hungry boys lurked around the dessert table, hoping for extras, as the women collected the dishes and began to clean up.

"There you are!" Landon was at my elbow, holding a cup of water. "Where did you go?"

"I felt a little faint," I said, channelling my best Olivia de Havilland. I took the glass from him and sipped. "I needed some air."

He frowned. "I looked around outside, but I didn't see you."

Damn. "I went into the ladies' room afterwards to freshen up." I smiled up at him, willing my heart to stop beating so fast, my hands not to shake. My thigh still burned where Kit had sunk her teeth into it.

"Do you want to sit down? Here, let's—"

"No, I'm all right now." I turned from him to my parents. "Maman, are you quite well?"

She was looking pale and overwhelmed, my father floating at her elbow, their coats over his arm. I took my mother's coat from him and wrapped it around her shoulders. She felt as small as a child under my hands.

"We should get you home," I said, rubbing her shoulders.

"That would be best," my father said. "The car—she can lie down in the back seat."

Landon took my arm. "I'll see Rebekah home safe, sir. Please go on ahead."

"No," I said, undoing Landon's grip. "Thank you, but I need to take my mother home. Someone should be with her in the car."

I didn't pause to see what expression registered on his face, just put my arm around Maman's shoulders and began ushering her away. Landon faded into the crowd somewhere behind us.

As we passed the kitchen, I caught sight of Caroline McNair shaking out a tablecloth. I ducked my head and steered Maman towards the far door, my father trailing in our wake. Voices echoed more loudly as the hall emptied, amplified by drink and the late hour. The musicians, about to pack away their instruments, stood near the stage, gulping the dregs of their beer.

Outside, the partygoers were dispersing into the night, small groups of two and three weaving off towards their beds. My mother sighed and leaned into me as the three of us crossed the road beside the church and began walking to the car, which my father had parked beside the graveyard. I felt as though I was underwater, all sounds muffled by the slosh of water in my ears. My feet ached from dancing and my mouth felt hot and swollen, as though Kit's teeth still grazed my lip. There would be time later, after my parents were asleep, when I could sink into bed and let my thoughts spill onto the pillow.

There was a shout in the darkness, then raucous laughter and the sound of boots against gravel. I peered ahead, but the noise could have come from any direction.

"*Ils ont les dents du fond qui baignent,*" my father murmured, disapproval soaking each word. Drunken idiots. Still, he moved a little closer to us.

"Not far now, Maman," I said, but it was as much to comfort myself as her. The willow trees lining the graveyard sighed in an invisible breeze. It would have been a pleasant night for a walk home, the perfect setting to steal a few kisses in the shadows on the way. I couldn't decide if I was glad that I had left both Landon and Kit behind.

Another surge of voices, followed by the smash of breaking glass. Drunken laughter, louder now. Maman hung tighter to my father as we rounded the edge of the graveyard. There was his car, nearly invisible in the dark except for the faint metallic reflection that caught any trace of light and flicked it back. There were shapes surrounding it—men, I realized, too slowly.

My father stopped us short, but not before I saw the terrible words scratched into the side of the car, glinting silver where the black paint had been ripped away. The passenger window was smashed in.

A flicker, like an orange firefly in the dark—more laughter—a lighter, for a cigarette? No, too bright, and moving towards the open window.

"*Wir werden langsam zurückkehren,*" my father said quietly. We will go back slowly. He must have been extremely shaken to lapse into German. The figures turned at the sound of his voice.

"Look what I found, boys," a voice slurred.

The group of young men started towards us. I started to edge backwards, towards the church, but my feet slowed as thumbs flicked cigarette lighters in a chorus of clicks and their faces became ghoulish in the orange flames. They were faces I recognized. Young men who had held the door for me at the general store, who had passed me in the street pushing a wheelbarrow. The one at the edge of the group could have been the boy who took our bags at the train station, all those months ago.

My father stepped forward. "We don't want any trouble. I wish to take my family home."

"No trouble? Shoulda thought of that before you move to Harrichford, Kraut. We don't need your kind around here."

"I am not what you think of me, I assure you." My father's English was strained, and the strange, formal sentence seemed to hit the group with an invisible force. They thought he was mocking them.

"Speak real English, traitor. Bet you can't wait to see us all crushed under Hitler's boot."

"Bet he's feeding them information."

"Poisoning the wells."

"Spying like the dirty Hun he is."

My father took another hesitant step forward. "Gentlemen, I assure you—"

There was the smell of liquor, not on their breath, but fresh and sharp. They'd poured alcohol on the seats of the car and those lighters were still flickering in the dark. The men moved towards us, a couple of them feinting and lunging, laughing when my mother shrieked in terror. My father stood there, his tall frame hunched. I saw him clearly in that moment, no longer a man of intellect, former army medic and powerhouse of authority, but an aging veteran from a war two decades in the past, who hadn't so much as thrown a punch since I was born. Suddenly, all I could feel was anger at him for being so frail and short-sighted and, above all, for being helpless to protect me.

"Hey!" A voice boomed behind us. I nearly jumped out of my skin. "What's going on here?"

"Nothing to do with you, McNair."

Landon strode into the circle of men, putting himself between them and us. He seemed taller and more menacing, nothing like the young gentleman who had been twirling me around the dance floor. His tie was loose, his sleeves already rolled up.

"Jamie Hutcheons, does your mother know you're out this late?"

"Watch it, McNair. This is none of your business."

"Tom Sevlich, I'd recognize your fat mouth anywhere. And is that little Mickey Isaacs I see back there?"

"I mean it. Just go home. Leave us to do what needs doing."

"As if I'd leave anything to you, Hutcheons. Go home, all of you, before you do something stupid."

A mutinous muttering, one voice rising above the others, "Kraut-lover."

"What did you say?" Landon's voice had an edge to it I'd never heard.

"You heard me."

"Get on home. I won't tell you again."

"Or what?"

Landon darted forward, his fists raised. The whole group of boys flinched, and Landon laughed mirthlessly.

One by one they slunk away, turning back every so often to shoot us murderous glances. Landon went after them, shooing them away down the street. I relaxed my grip on my mother's arm.

When he came back to us, he asked, "Are you all all right? Did they hurt you?" He glanced over the three of us, though his eyes stayed longest on me.

"We're fine," I said, when my parents didn't respond. My mother was trembling against me and my father was staring off into the distance as though he wasn't here.

"Stay put," Landon said, and he went to check the car. I didn't want to look again at the words carved into Papa's beautiful black car, the one he was so proud of, but they kept drawing my eye like a magnet.

Landon was back in a moment. "The front seat is a mess of glass, but you should be all right in the back. Get in, and I'll drive you home."

I expected my father to put up at least a token resistance, but instead he followed us meekly, waiting as Landon and I handed Maman into the car and then climbing in after me.

I was so grateful when the car roared to life at Landon's touch, even though the seats reeked of alcohol. My mother lay down in my lap, crying quietly now. I didn't let go of her hand the whole drive home. The shock of the encounter had driven the soft warmth of the punch straight out of my blood, and I was now painfully sober and alert.

The car rattled out of town and into a deeper darkness. I flinched every time we passed a group of people on the road. Landon's hands were tense on the wheel, and I suddenly wondered when he'd learned to drive.

When we pulled into the lane in front of the yellow house, my father seemed to shake off his daze. Gravely, he guided my mother out of the car and half-carried her up to the house, waving off Landon's offer of help. The front door squeaked open and then shut. Landon and I were left alone beside the car.

He was staring at me as though I was a glass orchid or perhaps an unexploded grenade. I wasn't sure which was more accurate.

"Thank you," I said, my voice hoarse from swallowing my fear.

"It was nothing—"

"No," I insisted. "I don't know what we would have done if you hadn't shown up when you did. I was so rude to you in the hall, and we'd been having such a good time until—"

A wave of dizziness took my feet out from under me and I sagged against the car, my chest tight. Landon caught my elbow and led me to the front steps, where we sat together on the bottom stair. Impressions shuffled through my mind too fast for me to keep up—the taste of rum punch, Kit's lips on my neck, the flicker of lighters and hideous laughter, Landon's hand on the small of my back, my father staring motionless out of the car window.

Hot tears dripped down my nose. Landon hesitated, then put his arm around me and I leaned into him. His chest was warm and solid, his arm a comforting weight against my back. His shirt smelled faintly of sweat and alcohol—from the car, I realized—and a little of sunshine and harsh soap. I pictured him scrubbing up before the dance and let out a hysterical giggle.

"Here," Landon said. He pulled a flask from his pocket and offered it to me. I took one swallow and then another, and soon my hands had stopped trembling and I no longer felt like crying and laughing at the same time. I sat up a little straighter and he removed his arm. I handed him back the flask and he took his own, longer, swallow from it.

"I was afraid something like this would happen," he said, his voice low in the dark.

"What do you mean?"

"The way people have been acting, with everyone so jumpy and on edge about the war. It was only a matter of time before Hutcheons and the others . . . I only wish I'd thought to head it off before it happened."

I was ashamed to admit that the thought of something like this hadn't even crossed my mind. I'd been too busy with Kit and Landon, caught up in my own drama. The countries in the headlines of Papa's newspapers had seemed a long way away.

Landon looked at his feet, fiddling with the cap on his flask. "If there is a war, I'm joining up."

I stayed quiet, watching his thumb and forefinger twist the cap to and fro.

"I want you to know, though, that I meant what I said before. When it's all over, you and I could—I mean, if we have an understanding, then . . ."

All traces of the smooth-tongued charmer I'd met earlier in the summer were gone. The bravado he'd summoned to drive off the drunken townsfolk had also vanished. Instead, I saw a young man who was out of his depth and knew it, yet was still determined to play the best hand he could.

I touched his knee. "I understand."

He placed his hand over mine and we sat there for a long moment, listening to the susurrus of wind through the branches of the apple trees. I wasn't cold, but a shiver ran through me all the same.

Finally, Landon stirred, tucking the flask back in his pocket.

"I should go. My parents will be wondering where I got to. I'll come by tomorrow and see how you are."

"Do you want to take the car? I'm sure Papa would be fine with that."

"No, thank you. I know a shortcut along the river."

He leaned in and gave me a kiss, as delicate as the one he'd stolen in the cart all those months ago. Then he got up from the step. I watched him round the orchard and head off towards the river path. All summer, I had assumed that only Kit knew that path, but obviously Landon knew it just as well. I wondered what it said that he had always arrived by the road, walking straight up the drive to the front door, and what it said about me that I had assumed he knew no other way.

KIT

When I got home, the barn was a silhouette against the sky, haloed by the lantern my mother had left burning on the front porch. I had been gone longer than I realized.

When I entered the barn from the far side, I heard a tuneless humming and the clank of the water pump. Landon was in the yard filling a bucket. His sleeves were rolled up, and his boots shone wet in the light where water had spilled.

Another summer, years and years ago. A younger Landon, in the shimmery heat of mid-summer, dust from the yard rising all around us. I came home after climbing trees in my church clothes and he'd saved me a beating, washing the dirt and sap off my dress and hands before my mother noticed, his skinny arms working the yard pump with all his might.

Tonight, he was levering it one-handed, adult muscles tensing under his shirtsleeves. I could slip away, disappear into the hayloft. I could walk back across the river to the Kromers' house and steal through Rebekah's bedroom window. I could leave and never come back.

Landon turned, the bucket in one hand, the red spark of a cigarette dangling from his lips, and started towards the barn. I knew the moment he noticed me, because he stopped and plucked the cigarette free, exhaling a cloud of smoke into the air.

"Kathleen. Didn't see you at the hall."

I stepped out from the shadow of the door. "I didn't feel like dancing."

He took another long drag, his eyes taking in his shirt and my pants, now damp from lying in the field.

"Out visiting?" The cloud of smoke wafted over my chest.

My heart beat faster. "No, just walking. Looking for coyotes."

He smirked. "What were you going to do, kick 'em to death?"

The gun. "Left it in the barn."

He dropped the butt, crushed it with the toe of his boot.

"Going to be some changes around here," he said without looking up. "When the war comes, I'm going to enlist. Afterwards I'll be able to start over somewhere else, really make something of myself. Something our family can be proud of." He looked up at me. "But I'm guessing she already told you that."

I felt the blood drain from my face. He knew. He'd known all along.

Landon sighed. "You surprised? I've been courting her for months. Did you think she'd be content to play soldiers with you in the woods forever?"

Cold lemonade and hay scattered from the wagon. Sunlight on the river and the taste of sweet clover. The night of the thunderstorm, her hair tangled in my fingers. Nausea rose in my throat, and I had to take small breaths to keep my vision clear.

My brother was still talking. "Just let her go, Kathleen, and we can forget all of this. I promise I won't tell anyone. Just—"

I punched him so hard I broke my third knuckle. He stumbled backwards, dropping the bucket. I charged, shoving him into the water trough, and pulled back to punch him again, but this time he was ready for me, catching my arm with one hand, yanking it sideways. We both tumbled onto the ground, where he broke my nose with one blow. Blinded, I kneed him in the stomach and he rolled off me. There was blood in my eyes and the yard was slippery with water. A commotion on the porch, voices shouting, my parents and Jep running towards us.

I clambered to my feet. Landon did the same. I lunged again, but he caught me and tossed me into the trough without much effort. I didn't feel the metal edge slice my arm as I climbed out and staggered across the yard towards him. My father grabbed the back of my shirt.

"What the hell is going on?" he demanded.

My mother and Jep were standing a few feet away, horrified faces half-lit by the lights from inside the house. Landon and I looked at each other. He had a black eye starting.

"Ask him," I said, tugging myself out of my father's grip.

"Kathleen heard that I'm gonna marry the doctor's girl. She's—"

"That's enough," my father growled. "Everyone in the house. Now." I turned towards the porch.

"Not you," my father said, grabbing my shoulder.

My mother and my brothers disappeared inside, while my father fetched the lantern from the porch. I gingerly touched my nose, my fingers coming away sticky with blood. My father pumped clean water into the bucket. He pulled out a handkerchief from his pocket and soaked it. As I held the lantern, he cleaned my face, the water in the bucket slowly turning pink. He examined my hand and, with a shrug, said that my knuckle would heal on its own.

"Now hold still," he said. I opened my mouth to say that I was, but he grabbed my chin in one hand and with one white-hot painful jerk, realigned my nose. I was ashamed to feel tears pouring down my cheeks. He handed me the handkerchief and I wiped the snot and blood and salt water from my face as he emptied the bucket onto the dirt and hung it on the pump handle.

Silence, except for the low murmurs of the sheep, and the far-off bark of a coyote. My father looked at me. "Oh, Kit. What am I going to do with you?"

"I'm sorry," I said.

"What were you fighting about?"

"He thought I'd taken something of his."

"And had you?"

Very quietly, I said, "Nothing that belonged to him."

Pa sighed, brushed his hands dry on his trousers. "Come inside. It's too late to mend anything tonight. We'll sort it out in the morning."

He started towards the house, the gold light from the window catching his silhouette and throwing an exaggerated shadow over the ground. I could see the blurred shapes of my mother and my brothers through the glass. The faint sound of dishes being stacked in a cupboard. A tall shadow turned and looked out at me, before disappearing farther inside.

"Kit?" My father was near the door, looking back at me.
I followed.

REBEKAH

I lay on my bed, staring up at the ceiling, willing the shadows to resolve
into some useful portent that would help me decide. Kit wanted me
to cut all ties and plunge overboard into adventure. Landon wanted
me to anchor myself here and be his port in the coming storm.

But Harrichford, a town I had tolerated then slowly grown to
like, was no longer the safe haven my father had believed it to be.
I grew cold when I thought of how much worse the night could
have been if Landon hadn't come walking along the road.

I sat up and gathered Patroclus into my arms against his sleepy
protests and nuzzled the soft fur of his head. My parents had come
here, seeking less prejudice, yes, but also in the hope of protecting
me from my worst impulses. They had done everything they could
to protect me. Now, it was my turn to protect them.

I went to the little writing desk under the window and pulled
out fresh paper. The words came almost too easily, fuelled by every
romance novel I'd devoured, every film Madeleine and I had seen
together. I sealed the envelope and addressed it in my best looped
script, set it carefully on the desk.

I pulled out a second sheet of paper and picked up my pen.
But these words would not come. I sat and stared at the blank
page for a long time, picking up and discarding every phrase that
came to mind. There simply weren't enough words, or the right
words, to explain what I needed to say. There was no way to say
what I wanted, how I felt, without creating more trouble.

Out in the garden, the river caught tiny flecks of moonlight. I closed my eyes, allowing myself to imagine a different future. I imagined I packed my suitcase and stole down the back stairs and out along the river to meet Kit. I saw us running for the train, laughing as we swung aboard the boxcar. Riding until the sun rose to greet us across the shining expanse of Lake Superior. A coat of feathers, a breakfast of morning dew.

I pictured the way her hair fell against her cheek, the jut of a collarbone under the loose edge of a shirt, the taste of her skin. I remembered every stolen grin, every slight smirk that was only for me. I gathered them all, one by one, and bound them tightly together, dropped them deep into myself alongside every other thing that belonged to the old Rebekah, the one who was weak and selfish and headstrong. I buried every moment with Kit beside my most wild and precious memories.

I crumpled the blank page and tossed it aside. Then I wiped my eyes, put on my dressing gown and went across the landing to my parents' room. My soft knock silenced their murmuring.

My father opened the door, looking older than I had ever seen him.

"*Chérie*, come in. None of us can sleep after tonight."

I sat next to my mother on the bed. She was still in her party dress, her expression as fragile as tissue paper. I took a deep breath to quiet the waves inside me and let the tears that had been hovering behind my eyes brim to the surface. I had to make this performance the best of my life so far.

"Papa." I let my voice waver on the second syllable. "I want to go home."

—

Later, I would remember that dawn as a series of stereoscope slides: endless in dimension, but static and unmoving. My mother packing her winter coat into a trunk. The kitchen, pristine in the grey light. The back garden heavy with the nodding heads of gold-enrod and asters. Patroclus curled inside his travelling basket. The train station, empty save for us and the ticket master, with geo-metrical shadows thrown across the floor by the window frames. The 5 a.m. passenger train pulling in, steam billowing against the peach dawn sky. My father's beard scratching my forehead as he gave me a goodbye kiss. My mother's perfume as she settled next to me, then leaned to look out the window.

My father, so small and alone on the platform, receding into the distance, sliding soundlessly away and out of reach.

KIT

I lay awake long after my family had gone to bed, plagued by both the pain in my nose and a restless energy. My brother wanted to marry Rebekah. Rebekah hadn't said anything about it to me. Which meant, in all likelihood, that Landon was lying. If he was, then I would beg Rebekah to escape with me, just as we'd planned. If he was telling the truth, I would leave this place for good.

Before dawn, I gave up on trying to sleep. I pulled my ruck-sack out from under the bed and began filling it with clothing, my scarf and hat, matches and a couple of candle stubs, my other pocketknife. My life savings—twenty-eight dollars and sixty-four cents—I wrapped in a sock and hid in the bottom. The soaked and bloodied clothes from last night were ruined, so I pulled on a pair of work trousers and the blue striped shirt Rebekah had mended on a sunny afternoon that felt like years ago now.

I tiptoed down the stairs. Gordie raised his head from beside the stove, but then subsided when he saw it was me. I went to the cupboard and pulled out some stale biscuits and cured bacon. It wasn't much but it would last us for at least a day or two. I shooed Gordie back to the kitchen and stole out the back door, easing the hinges shut. In the barn, I lit a hooded lantern and found my father's shears, oiled and waiting in their leather case. It didn't take long to crop my hair close to my scalp, dark strands falling in the straw around me. I kicked them under the door into Pete's stall and replaced the shears. When I checked my reflection in the water bucket, the lack of hair had changed the angle of my jaw and my eyes seemed more gold in the orange light. It would have to do. I put out the lantern and left the barn.

A cool wind traced my ears and tickled my scalp as I crossed the back fields. The eastern sky was just beginning to lighten. I vaulted over the fence and was soon swallowed up in darkness of the forest.

I reached the river and crossed the ford, careful to step from stone to stone to keep my boots dry. It was a short way along the path to the bottom of the Kromers' garden. The yellow house was unlit, the windows blank.

I took a handful of green acorns from below the oak at the edge of the orchard, and threw them, one after the other, at Rebekah's window. Silence, except for the tap, tap of the acorns bouncing off the glass and onto the roof. I emptied my palm and still nothing.

I stole around the edge of the house, keeping below the windows, crouched below the edge of the porch. Dr. Kromer's car was parked close to the steps, but I paid it little attention, craning to see through the front windows if anyone was awake.

A crunch of gravel as footsteps approached from the road. I ducked below the edge of the porch. The steps grew closer, then boots thumped on the porch boards. I raised myself just enough to see.

It was Landon, looking as underslept as me. He had changed his clothes, but his boots were still stained with mud from our fight. He knocked once, twice, and then a third time. I ducked, leaning my back against the bricks, heart pounding out of my chest.

The door opened at last.

"Mr. McNair." The even, soft-spoken tones of Dr. Kromer.

"Dr. Kromer. I apologize for calling so early, but I promised Miss Kromer I would look in on you today, after—"

"That is very kind of you. We are fine. I must thank you again for your assistance last night."

"Is there anything more I can do? Bring you some groceries from town or fetch your mail if you prefer not to . . . ?"

"That is kind, but not necessary. I will be leaving Harrichford before the week is over."

"Leaving? But—"

"Yes. Madame and my daughter have gone ahead, on the early train. I will be following them as soon as I have settled my affairs here and can arrange for our belongings to be shipped."

"But, sir, you haven't—"

The roaring in my ears was so loud I lost the rest of Landon's words. Gone. She was gone. Without a word of goodbye or an explanation. My skin prickled all over like a horse bothered by flies.

Dr. Kromer's voice penetrated my shock. "You may have had an understanding, yes, but this has nothing to do with you or your character. My daughter asked me to give you this." A rustling. I craned my neck and caught a glimpse of Dr. Kromer handing Landon a white envelope. "She was so very sorry to go—such tears!—but I hope you will understand that, for now, Montreal is the safest place for her."

I dropped my head to my knees. She was well and truly lost to me now. Last night—the memory of the stable pierced me like a hot blade. Had she known, even then, that she was leaving? Landon's words drifted across my mind. Playing soldiers. That's all I was to her.

I didn't wait to hear more of their conversation, but crept around the side of the house and then ran down the garden, vaulted the fence and leapt across the ford, the stones sliding away under my feet. The trees reached for the sky around me like a fleet of ships' masts in the early light. Rebekah's face in the darkness. Her hands knotted in my hair. The river, with the sun slicing down like a blade on my neck, her lips on mine. I slowed to a jog, cutting through the narrowest end of the forest. Her smile, at the dance. Landon's expression after I punched him—so shocked, as though I had no right to anything.

I reach the other end of the valley, and the ground begins to climb. The hill grows so steep I am forced to all fours, heaving myself up between rocks, the trees clinging to their sides with gnarled root fingers.

At the top of the hill, I pause to look down. The next valley spreads below me. The lights of Harrichford are behind me, back the way I'd come. A train whistles in the distance.

I start running downhill, towards the tracks that curve west, away from the village. I wish I could reverse time and erase our first meeting, erase all the moments that clatter together like shards of broken glass in my chest.

A dark shape in the distance. The freight train that thunders past from Orangeville every dawn. I put on another burst of speed. The wind flits across the edges of the grass in answer. The train doesn't stop at our station, but it has to slow to take the bridge over the river. I pull alongside the tracks, the crashing wheels squealing as the brakes engage, the beast slowing and shuddering as it begins to shunt over the bridge. I focus on a red boxcar, coming up behind me. Reach towards the hulking metal and lose my nerve, stumble back. I scramble upright. Only a few cars left. I focus on the second last one. Imagine myself riding my horse, jumping fences with ease, gliding up and over any obstacle. The train whistles again, the engine already across the bridge. It begins to pick up speed. I sprint, leap and catch the ladder with both fists, landing with a jarring slam against the metal siding. In a moment I am inside the sliding door, the last boxcar hurtling over the bridge, swept away in a river of metal and smoke, towards a field of shining water.

I hear and don't hear the faint laughter that follows me, see and do not see the blue-green lights that dance behind in my footprints.

SEPTEMBER 1941

IT WAS A BRIGHT AUTUMN MORNING, THE SKY YELLOW
and pink with dawn, the leaves covering the road the red and
orange of early fall. It had rained overnight, but the clouds were
gone now, and the rooftops shone in the early light, moisture
clinging to the windowpanes of the old truck that rattled along
the road from the north.

A sixteen-year-old boy stood alone on the station platform.
Sault Ste. Marie was a small town, and no one else was waiting for
the 7 a.m. westbound train. The standard issue duffle was heavy
on his shoulder and he dropped it near his feet. He'd tried on his
uniform last night and everything had fit. When he'd walked into
the kitchen, his mother had pressed her hand to her mouth and
pushed past him into the bedroom and shut the door. His little
sister had begged to try on the hat and giggled when it slipped
down over her ears. His great-uncle had nodded, face expression-
less, and slipped a pack of cigarettes into the boy's hand. He had
tried smoking one a moment ago, but he'd coughed and retched
on the taste. He'd stubbed it out and returned it to the packet,
determined to try again later, when he wasn't so nerved up.

The papers folded carefully in his breast pocket crinkled every time he shifted his weight from one foot to the other. He'd considered wearing his uniform for the journey, but the thought of turning up at Portage la Prairie with a gravy stain on the pants was enough to keep it stowed in his duffle. The morning had turned out to be colder than he'd expected, however, and so he'd slipped on the jacket. He wasn't really in the air force, not yet, and so it was probably all right to wear just one piece of the uniform for now. There was no one around to see him, anyway. The boy scrubbed his sweaty palms against his trousers, swallowing past the lump in his throat.

Maybe something would happen and the train would be delayed, and he wouldn't be able to get to basic until tomorrow night. That wouldn't be so bad. If it was because of the train, the air force would understand. Then he could spend one more night at home in his own bed, with Trigger curled around his knees, and he could pet his dog's soft ears until he fell asleep. One more night. Tomorrow he'd be ready to go.

He heard the truck before he saw it. A dirty brown thing, with mud splashed on its fenders and a cracked windscreen. It rumbled up and stopped across from the station, belching smoke from the tailpipe. There was a pause before the passenger door opened and a young man stepped out lightly onto the street, a small rucksack over his shoulder. He leaned back into the cab to shake hands with the driver, and then the passenger door clunked shut and the truck carried on, a cloud of dark fumes fading in the air behind it.

The young man wore a heavy flannel jacket and a wool cap pulled down over his ears. His trousers were dusty and mended at the knees. He crossed the road and walked around the far side of the station building, neatly avoiding the ticketing desk inside, and hopped the fence to the platform. The boy watched as the young man scanned for a guard, and then strolled casually towards him. The boy kept his eyes on the tracks, pretending to be looking for the train. He didn't want any trouble, and he didn't want to get mixed up in whatever this stranger was about to do. Train hopping was a serious offence, according to his great-uncle.

The young man seemed to be only a few years older than the boy, but definitely old enough that if he walked through town without a uniform, he'd draw comment. The boy straightened his spine. He wasn't yellow. He'd lined up with all the other boys—or rather, men—outside the recruitment office and talked his way in. It didn't matter that his mother and sister had cried when his letter came, or that he hadn't heard from his father in months. He was doing the right thing.

The young man stopped a few feet away from the boy. He pulled a cigarette out of his breast pocket and stuck it in the corner of his mouth with a practised, easy gesture. He rummaged through his other pockets, coming up empty-handed.

"Hey, you got a light? I musta dropped mine in the damn truck."

Wordlessly, the boy took the lighter from his pocket and tossed it to the stranger, who caught it one-handed, quick as anything. He heard the click, and then a slow sigh.

"Thanks." The stranger held the lighter out to him.

The boy shuffled closer and took it back. "You're welcome," he said, because his mother had raised him to be polite.

The stranger looked up at the sky and blew smoke out his nostrils. "Damn foreman wouldn't let me smoke all the way down here."

The boy looked down the tracks again. If only the train would hurry up and arrive.

"You headed to basic?" The stranger nodded towards his jacket, and for a sickening moment, the boy had the crazed thought that he was an air force inspector, come to keep an eye on new recruits, and he would be in trouble for wearing his jacket without the rest of the uniform. The thought of getting demerits before he'd even started brought panicky tears to his eyes. It was hard to take a full breath.

"Hey hey, kid, it's all right." The stranger was next to him, a hand on his shoulder. "Just breathe."

The boy took a ragged breath in, mortified to feel tears starting to leak out of the corners of his eyes. He squeezed his fist so his nails bit into his palm, and the pain brought the world back into shaky focus. The man was looking down at him, brown eyes full of concern.

"You got your papers?" the stranger asked.

The boy nodded.

"Mind if I see them?"

The boy dug into his breast pocket and handed them over. He sniffed and drew the back of his hand across his nose. Thank God his great-uncle wasn't around to see him like this.

The stranger dropped his cigarette to the platform and stubbed it out with his boot. "Well, now, isn't this the funniest thing."

The boy swiped a hand across his eyes and looked up at him. The man was examining his papers, a thin smile playing at the corners of his mouth.

"What's funny?"

"Well, it seems like you got my papers by accident."

"What?" The boy reached to tug the letter back, but the stranger moved it away.

"I've been up north, working. Expected to pick up my letter in town after the conversation I had in the recruitment tent a few weeks back, but someone told me it had already been claimed. Figured if I came here, I'd find the culprit and I was right."

"But . . . that's my name on it. C. McNeil."

"Oh, the army does this all the time. That idiot at the recruitment office typed up my name wrong. It should say McNair."

"I don't—"

"Got the birth year right, though. 1921, huh? I've been told I look young for my age too." The man gave the boy a penetrating look, and the boy felt the ground give under his feet.

The stranger stared at the letter a moment longer and then seemed to come to a decision. "Listen, kid, give me your duffle and your jacket, and just go on home."

The sick feeling in the boy's stomach ebbed a little. "But I have all my stuff, and my mom, she thinks—"

A train whistled in the distance.

The stranger looked quickly around the platform and dug into his trouser pocket for a ten-dollar bill. "I'll pay you for your kit, and your ticket. Least I can do."

The boy hesitated. The train whistled again, a little closer this time.

"Kid, go home. Your mom needs you more than the air force does."

That look on her face last night. The boy would have done anything to take it away.

He snatched the bill from the stranger's hand and shoved the duffle towards him with his foot. The boy stripped off his jacket as the man pulled off his coat and they traded. The flannel was warm and worn soft by a hundred washings. When the boy looked up, the stranger had put on the uniform jacket and taken off the wool hat, revealing short brown hair that fell just past his ears.

"Why are you doing this?" the boy asked.

"You remind me of somebody," the stranger said, tugging his wool hat over the boy's head.

As the train pulled into the station, the man tucked the papers and ticket into the breast pocket of his jacket. He picked up the duffle, then paused and turned back.

"Hey, kid, what does the C stand for?" he shouted, over the noise of the breaks and the train hissing to a stop.

"Christopher!" the boy shouted.

The stranger laughed, shaking his head as though he couldn't quite believe it. "Perfect!" he said, and then he climbed aboard the train, and the conductor pulled the ladder up and the passenger car was moving away from the platform, picking up speed.

Christopher McNeil watched the train until it was out of sight, and then he tucked his hands into the pockets of his new flannel coat and headed home.

PART TWO

DECEMBER 1942

KIT

THE WORST PART OF NIGHT OPS WAS THE LACK OF WINDOWS. The knowledge that hell could arrive at any moment, from above or below and I wouldn't see it coming. A searchlight could pin us and bring a Messerschmitt like a diving hawk, or a curtain of flak could rise up from the ground like a deadly fountain—there was no way for me to know.

Ranbir Singh sat opposite me in the cabin, carefully adjusting the dials on the wireless relay.

My headphones crackled. "Searchlights coming up, Skip." Gerald Wilkins, our upper gunman.

"I see them." Our pilot, Pete Belmont, always sounded slightly bored, no matter what was happening. "McNair?"

I glanced at the map. "If we go a bit left, we can get around them and back in line, Skip."

"Going left."

I kept my eyes on the map, numb to the bumps and shudders of turbulence as *Friday's Girl* hurtled through the night sky over Germany. The map rendered the world below in orderly inked lines—here a town, there a curve of coastline. They were updated daily, fuelled by reconnaissance ops and telegraphs from the front lines, as the Nazis did their best to place flak lines and searchlights. At twenty thousand feet in the air, in the pitch dark, we were only as good as the latest information.

I marked our position on the map and noted the time on my watch.

"Three minutes to target, Skipper," I said.

"Okay, Navigator," Pete's voice was nasal coming through the intercom. "Bomb aimer, do you see it yet?"

"I see it, Skipper. They're lit up down there like a fireworks show."

"Steady goes."

Another bump and weave. I stretched my shoulders beneath my flight suit and spared a thought for Laurie Hartwick, lying facedown in the bomb aimer's glass fishbowl.

A crackle on the radio, and Ranbir took quick, furious notes.

"Pathfinders at point three two northeast. Beginning descent approach," he repeated to me. I sketched the positioning triangles, numbers scrolling through my mind as the aircraft tilted and dove. I found our position, ticked it with the pencil.

"Two minutes, Skip."

"Doors opening," Laurie said. The crunch and crank of the bomb doors below us. I tried not to think what would happen if flak hit our belly now.

A new voice, higher pitched. "Skipper, I've got one to our port and coming in."

"Keep an eye, Thompson. Nearly there." Our newest rear gunner, crammed in the back turret, strapped into his heating suit and no doubt getting shocked by the wiring in his gear every few minutes. I'd joked with Simon that he'd grow used to it after a few flights, maybe even enjoy it. Simon had said—but, of course, it was James Thompson back there now, not Simon. Simon had had to bail out three months ago, over the lines. There'd been no news since, but we didn't expect any. I didn't know what to hope for him.

I glanced again at my watch and made another mark. "One minute, Skip." Ten miles and we would be over our target, a munitions factory in the Ruhr valley. The bombs rattled in their casings just below my feet.

"Flares ahead, one o'clock," Wilkins said.

I frowned at the map. They should have been dead ahead. "You sure?"

"I can see them, McNair."

Ranbir looked at me, tension in his face.

"Starting approach," said Pete. "Bomb aimer, you have control."

"Yes, Skip, adjusting course oh three one . . ."

"Hartwick, can you see those flares?"

"Yes, McNair. Looks like everyone's dead on. Thirty seconds, Skipper."

I'd learned to track aircraft by the sound of their engines, easily picking out the higher buzz of the Luftwaffe fighters from the slower, monotonous hum of our fellow bombers, the Halifaxes a few tones flatter than the Lancasters. Our Hurricanes had a slight hitch in the propeller drone.

The whole kite shuddered with the blowback of a Messerschmitt winging overhead, too close for comfort. There was an answering whine as one of our Hurricane escorts took off after it.

The anemometer indicated 210 mph, and the map said we should be nearly on top of the target. But *directly* ahead, not three points to starboard. I redid my calculations. Either the map was wrong or I was. It didn't make sense, unless—

"Hartwick, hold!" I said.

"What's wrong, McNair?"

"The pathfinders are off, Skip."

"No." This was from Edouard Vanier, our flight engineer in his seat next to the pilot. "The whole squadron marked it."

A whistle and a whoosh from close by. "*Jenny's Joy*'s away," said Wilkins. Our bomber squadron was dropping on the lit target, dozens of bombs falling away into the abyss.

Another whistle. "*Trident* too," said Thompson.

"Ten seconds to target," Laurie said from below.

"It's a decoy!" I gasped, "Hold, hold! We're off—we're all off."

The distant boom of the first explosions below. "Right on the flares," the engineer said.

"McNair, are you sure about this?" Pete said.

"Yes, Skip."

"Then where the hell are we going?" Vanier's voice was tight, panicked.

"Language, Vanier," in Pete's icy, calm tone.

I shut my eyes, pictured the night sky over Harrichford. "Skip, can you see Orion's Belt?"

"I can see it. On our port."

"Steer for it. Count twenty and we'll be over it."

"This is insane—" Wilkins started.

"Bomb aimer, prepare for new target in fifteen seconds. Gunners, eyes up."

Silence. The engine shuddered as Pete steered us north. The drone of nearby bombers was overlaid by the higher whine of the fighter escort.

"They've found us," Thompson said, and there was the crack-crack of the rear gun and the kite rocked side to side.

"All yours, Hartwick!" said Pete.

"Five seconds," the bombardier said. "Four, three . . ."

Laurie fought to keep the aircraft steady as the cages released and the bombs went tumbling down into the dark. Silence as everyone held their breath, waiting for him to take the photograph proving we'd completed our op.

"Photo done. Skip, you have control."

"You better have been right about that, McNair," Vanier said.

"Hold tight, lads," said Pete.

Friday's Girl went into a dive, curving sharply down and to the left, Thompson and Wilkins's guns cracking in disjointed harmony. We jerked up and to the right, the familiar corkscrew manoeuvre that was our Lancaster's only defence against an enemy fighter.

"McNair, get us out of here," said Pete.

"One eight five," I said, jerking in my seat and clutching my pencil with one hand. The aircraft yawed violently to the left, sending Ranbir's tea thermos tumbling to the floor.

"I told you to keep that strapped down," I said.

"Thought Thompson might want some," the wireless operator quipped.

A buzz as a Messerschmitt skimmed past our tail in pursuit. I stared at the map, breathing in and out as evenly as I could. There was nothing to do but keep time and mark the distances.

Another staccato crack from the upper gun and then the crescendo slide of an engine failing and falling.

"Got 'im!" came Wilkins's satisfied shout.

"Two more, on our starboard," in Vanier's smooth French accent.

"I see him," said Thompson. Another crack-crack of gunfire. A buzz as two Luftwaffe fighters soared underneath our squadron. The shriek of an engine pushed to the limit and stalled. I held my breath—the boom that followed echoed through the clouds and thrummed the metal wall next to my ear. No one spoke.

"*Scout's Honour*," Pete said soberly. A fighter had risen up out of the dark, silent as death, and opened fire straight into the belly of the bomber. It was everyone's worst nightmare. No one bothered to ask about bail-outs. When fourteen thousand pounds' worth of explosives went off at once, there was no hope of escape.

"Bomb aimer, get those doors shut. McNair, how far to the coast?"

"Thirty minutes, Skip. Flak line in ten."

Our escort dropped back to chase the Luftwaffe towards Dresden, and we continued on, climbing high into the night and levelling out. The intercom was silent, all of us sobered by the reminder that death rode alongside, clinging to our wingtips and breathing down our shirt collars. Ranbir retrieved his thermos and poured himself a cup, downing several gulps. I pretended not to notice his hand shake.

It had been hard to imagine it being like this, back in training. In Portage la Prairie, and later at air observation school in Rivers, flying had felt like an exhilarating adventure. A challenge to test my knowledge and reflexes, but still a war game. The actual conflict had felt far away across the ocean. Now, I could only shake my head. None of us could have pictured what we were in for.

Thirty minutes later, we staggered out of the flak line and over the Channel.

"Engineer, report?"

"Not bad. Lost the far starboard engine, but we should have enough fuel to get us back."

"See that we do," Pete said.

"Uh, Skipper?"

"Yes, Thompson?"

"Our near port engine is leaking something."

"Can you see what it is?"

"I think it's oil."

"Vanier?"

A pause while the engineer checked the fuel gauges.

"Skipper, it's fuel. Rebalancing."

"Right. McNair, can you get us home any faster than this?"

"Not unless Wilkins gets out and pushes."

The port engine spluttered and died, leaving only two coughing us forward.

"We have fuel for another thirty miles." Vanier's voice was tight.

I made some quick measurements. "It's thirty-seven to Lincolnshire base."

"We can make it," Pete said firmly. "If not, you can bail out over the coast."

"I don't really like swimming, in case anyone's forgotten," Laurie said.

"Well, if Hartwick's going to be such a big girl's blouse about a little water—"

"We'll glide the last few," Pete said firmly. "Everyone quiet, and eyes on the waypoints."

I counted the miles against my watch, imagining the fuel gauges falling lower with every second. The remaining engines began to falter at mile twenty-four. We ran out of fuel at mile twenty-nine.

"Steady. I'll bring her down slow," was all Pete said.

Over the sound of the metal sheets screaming and the remaining engine grinding, our bomb aimer shouted, "We could do with some of that famous luck of yours, McNair."

"I might have used it all up beating you at cards last week," I said through gritted teeth.

The last engine cut out and we were gliding, tilting side to side, the darkness yawing and heaving with us inside it. I could hear Vanier swearing in the cockpit.

"Prepare to bail out," came Pete's order. I rolled and stuffed the map into my jacket, grabbed the compass. Ranbir and I heaved the doors open, cold air rushing and swirling around the interior. My chute was a heavy weight on my back. Outside the door, the world rushed by at a dizzying speed, turning and twisting in a way that roiled my stomach. We were coming down too hard, too fast. There was no chance of bailing out now.

"What do you figure?" I shouted to Ranbir over the noise of the wind. "Broken legs or burnt to a crisp?"

He gave me a look of such pure terror I regretted my words. I knotted my hand through the webbing and pulled him close to me, putting his head under my arm. "Don't let go!"

We hit the runway hard and bounced, wheels screaming at the impact. Then down again and skidding sideways in a hail of gravel and dirt and engine exhaust. The walls shook so violently I expected them to shake loose. The whole world became a tumult of smoke and dust and burnt rubber and screeching metal, spun out of control. I held Ranbir's head tight to my chest and closed my eyes against the grit and the blinding rush of wind.

Silence. I opened my eyes, and saw the door open beside us, revealing only the ground. The aircraft had come to rest on its side.

Thompson was already out of the bomber when Ranbir and I crawled from under the wing. Pete and Vanier appeared a moment later, stripping off their chutes. Laurie and Wilkins were nearby doing the same. Vanier paused long enough to reassure himself we were all alive and then went off to trade notes with the ground crew.

"Skipper, you're supposed to fly the aircraft, not plow fields with it," I said, thumping Pete on the back.

He punched me in the arm, face relaxing into a grin. "Next time we'll trade places. You fly the bird and I'll read a map upside down and backwards."

The ground crew, or erks, as we called them, jogged out to the aircraft, and a bustle of activity sprung up around us as they shouted and prepared to move our bruised and smoking bomber off the runway. We started towards the waiting transport trucks. All around was the deafening roar and whine of the rest of the squadron landing. Trucks wheeled in among the aircraft, stretcher bearers jogging out to the Hurricanes as they glided out of the sky and onto the grass.

Once we were seated under the canvas awning in the back of the truck, Wilkins took a generous gulp from the flask he'd taken from his pocket and then handed it around. "Some of the boys have put together a little shindig for us tomorrow night. Panto, drinkies, a few girls coming up from the village."

"What for?"

"What do you mean, what for? It's Christmas Eve."

I had forgotten. I had forgotten that beyond the relentless schedule of night ops and briefings and terror-fuelled flights, it was Christmas.

Wilkins and Thompson fell into conversation. I could see the skipper and Vanier through the opening in the canvas, their heads together over paperwork, debating the finer details of the mission log before handing it over to the erks. I sighed, knowing it would be at least another hour of debrief back at the base before I could enjoy breakfast.

Ranbir sat next to me, unusually silent.

"Looking forward to the panto?" I asked him. "I wonder which one they'll pick this year."

He rubbed at the tip of his ear just under his turban. "How did you know?" he asked quietly. "About the target. That the pathfinders were off. It doesn't make sense."

I shrugged. "Intuition, I guess." How else to explain the feeling I had sometimes, looking at the charts. That sense in my gut of magnets clicking when we were on course, an unsettling void when we weren't. Ranbir gave me a measured look, and then drew breath like he was about to ask another question when Laurie jumped into the truck and plunked himself down between us. He smelled like machine oil and sweat and a flight suit gone too long unwashed.

"Nothing like coming home to a day of leave and a Christmas party. Up for a rematch, McNair? Or did you use up all your luck climbing out of that wreck?"

I laughed and put an arm around his shoulders. "Hardly. I'm going to have a drink, you're going to have a bath, and then I'm going to fleece you at cards all over again."

"Not likely," Laurie said, and then Pete and Vanier climbed aboard, and Wilkins winked and hollered at the WRAF driver and we were trundling across the airfield to base, back on the ground and alive, against all odds.

REBEKAH

It was cold in the communications room, despite our little coal stove and my woollen socks. All winter, the icy winds off the Atlantic Ocean had crept through the barracks windows and into the underground tunnels and under every closed door. I had almost forgotten what it felt like to be warm. That day in the hayfield with the McNairs, with the sunshine baked into my skin, seemed like a childhood memory, hazy around the edges.

The headset pinched the way it always did, and my fingers had cramped hours ago. I stared at the desktop, found the swirl in the grain that looked like an owl and the darker mark that reminded me of an old man's face. A steady rhythm of beeps and clicks streamed through my ears: Morse code. The long desk shook as women on either side of me wrote staccato shorthand, pausing only to adjust dials on the receivers in front of them. After months of this work, I could record messages perfectly while my mind drifted. More than once I'd looked down and been shocked to realize I'd written to the end of a slip and couldn't recall any of it.

Devil's Battery was built on the farthest eastern point of Halifax Harbour, across the bay from the city proper. As far as everyone else knew, it was just another coastal defence installation, designed to protect both the city and the hundreds of ships that came into the harbour every week. But navy intelligence had commissioned this underground room and recruited all the women in it for another vital purpose: to eavesdrop on enemy ships and U-boats, record their messages and pass them up the chain to the code breakers.

There were other "huff-duff" stations, as we called them, up and down the eastern coast. I didn't know their names or precisely where they were, though I had once overheard the Kettle—which was what my roommate, Elaine, had nicknamed Commander Davis because she was as steady and indestructible as a copper-bottomed kettle—instruct a telegraphist to send a dictated code to Bermuda. Beyond that, I could only imagine.

A blip, like a streak of lightning, came through the earphones. I turned the dial to home in on it. I'd been tracking this German U-boat for most of the day, only to lose her a few hours ago. Another blip, and another. I locked the signal, and a satisfying stream of noise came into my ears. I wrote quickly, translating effortlessly. As I reached the end of what I could gather, Petty Officer Mathers drew up to my desk. Her hand hovered near the edge of the page as I made the last few marks, and then she snatched it and hurried off to the plotting room. I sagged a little in my chair and rubbed my eyes.

We had returned to Montreal from Harrichford and were trying to pick up the threads of our old lives when the war broke out. The government forced my father to register as an enemy alien, and while he was allowed to practise medicine, he had few patients. With no one willing to rent to a family with a German name, he sold most of our belongings and we'd moved in with my mother's parents. When my uncle Leo enlisted, Tante Yvonne moved in too, along with her teenage daughter, Sabine. Six months later, my cousin Hélène arrived with three kids under five. Her husband had enlisted, and she could no longer afford to pay their rent in Outremont.

My grandparents' house, which had always felt large, became crowded and noisy. After my father was called up to the military ward at the hospital, he worked day and night and we rarely saw him. My mother withdrew into a quiet despair and spent much of

her time upstairs in bed. Tante Yvonne and Hélène often went to
sit with her. I could smell the cigarette smoke curling under the
bedroom door and hear the chink of coffee cups as they listened to
the radio. Sabine soon found a job as a grocery clerk, which left my
grand-mère and me to look after Hélène's children.

I barely survived that year of dirty diapers, endless laundry, tan-
trums, and a crowded kitchen humid with cooking smells. I had
no time to read and barely a moment to myself, except when I was
sent out to do the shopping. Few of my old friends were around,
and the ones who were had either married or had joined up or were
working in the naval yards. When I saw the recruitment poster for
the Women's Royal Canadian Naval Service in the store window, it
had been a lifesaver. A few weeks later, I had enlisted in the Wrens.

The bell rang, signalling the end of my watch. The next group of
girls entered the room, saluted Petty Officer Mathers, and lined up
behind our chairs. I rose to my feet, feeling my legs protest, managed a crisp salute and filed out of the door with the others. After
working our eight-hour shift, we walked through the drafty tunnels to the hidden exit, too tired to talk. The men bunked at Elkins
Barracks, but the women had our own smaller living quarters in
the lower levels of the administrative building.

Back in my room, I took off my jacket and laid it carefully on
the end of the bedspread, then sat on my bed and rolled my shoulders. Elaine came in a moment later and collapsed onto her bunk
with a loud sigh, spreading her arms wide.

"I thought that shift would never end."

My roommate had a pleasant, round face and black hair she
faithfully pin-curled every night, even though it nearly always fell
out of its shape before noon the next day.

After the chaos of my grandparents' house, followed by the crowded sleeping quarters in Galt during training, I would have taken a screaming parakeet as a roommate if it meant sharing with only one other living thing. Elaine had proven to be decent company and, if not tidy, at least she was obedient to naval discipline.

"Thank God we're going ashore for two days," she said.

I rolled my eyes. The naval culture that insisted on speaking as though we were living on a ship despite everyone being on land had lost its novelty precisely five seconds after I'd been introduced to the idea.

"No one is 'going ashore.' We're just walking out the gate," I said, pulling off my shoes and wiggling my toes.

Elaine made a face. "You're no fun, Becca. Don't you ever wish we were on a real boat?"

"Not even slightly." I lay back on my bed, pulled out my battered copy of *Kitty Foyle* with a sigh. I was looking forward to two quiet days of sleep, reading, and perhaps bundling up to walk along the shore.

"A group of us are bumming a ride from the boys into Halifax," Elaine said, holding her leg in the air and scrutinizing the curve of her calf. "Janey has an uncle who has an apartment in town. He's away, and he's left her the key, so we can all kip there for two nights and be back aboard by Thursday."

"That sounds lovely," I said, turning a page.

"Come along. It's been ages since you went anywhere."

"No, thank you."

A shadow fell over my page. I looked up. Elaine had her hands on her hips and was wearing the same expression as the day she'd turned up carrying a pair of scissors and a box of pins and declared that she couldn't bear to look at the sad state of my hair any longer. I did like my hair shorter, and curled, but I'd die before admitting it.

"Becca, it's Christmas. I won't leave you here to sulk in your bunk while the rest of us drink punch."

I groaned, putting the book over my face. She pulled it aside. "You're coming, end of discussion. Get out of that uniform and I'll have Dot in the laundry press it for you before we leave."

It was impossible to resist Elaine under full sail. Her enthusiasm swept up everyone in its path, until it was easier to simply accept that she was going to make your life better. I dragged myself off the bed, shed my uniform and went to the lavs to scrub my face.

An hour later, the two of us, along with Elaine's friends Sara, Janey and Dot, trudged through the snow to the main gate. I swore the wind at Devil's Battery got a running start from Greenland. Our uniform coats were warm enough, but my fingers ached with the cold, even with my hands jammed in my pockets.

There was a slight delay as we each handed our leave passes over for inspection, and then we were on our way down the road, snow-flakes swirling in our wake. Elaine and her friends kept up a steady stream of chatter about the boys from the *Stadaconda*, and Christmas letters from home, and the dance hall we were headed for.

Half a mile down the road, a car appeared on its way from Elkins. Dot took off her hat and waved at it frantically. The car crunched to a halt in the snow and Elaine leaned through the passenger window, her red lips lifted in a contagious smile.

"Now where might you boys be off to?" she asked. The three soldiers in the car grinned right back at her.

"The city, where else?"

As if on cue, Janey rubbed her arms and shivered. "Elaine, it's so cold. Let's just go back."

Protests from inside the car. "Where are you headed? We can give you a lift."

"Oh, we couldn't possibly ask," Dot said. Elaine cooed, "We don't want to be any trouble." In a moment we were all squished into the car, Dot and Elaine up front on the gear box, and Janey, Sara and I in the back seat with the third boy.

"Becca, you're sitting on my coat!" Sara hissed.

I sighed and squeezed even closer to the door.

The soldier—he'd introduced himself as Ben—patted his lap. "You can sit here, darling. Plenty of room." Sara made a disgusted noise and edged my way, but within a few minutes, she was giggling and flirting like the rest of them.

With all of us piled inside, the car grew warm. A flask was passed around and I took a sip, the liquor burning my throat. I looked out the window at the evergreens nearly swallowed up in soft drifts.

My last letter from home had arrived in November, addressed in my mother's loopy cursive. She wrote that she'd been galvanized into action by a Croix-Rouge poster and was furiously knitting socks. Most of them were of dubious quality (the pair she had sent me were of two different sizes), but I was pleased that she was keeping herself occupied. I wrote back, telling her about Elaine's antics and the East Coast weather and every other insignificant thing I could think of. It had been drummed into me from the moment I arrived at Devil's Battery that no one could know the true nature of what we did here. Everything I heard over the radio—U-boat positions, coded chatter between the admiralty, troop movements—had to remain secret. So I told my parents that I was a file clerk for the Royal Navy, making my job sound very boring and monotonous, and hoped my mother wouldn't press me into more lies.

At last, the car rattled into Africville. The clapboard houses were anonymous humps under the snow, showing only tiny winks of light at the edges of the blackout paper as we drove past. The harbour was slate-blue water that looked colder than ice, the outlines of dozens of ships crammed together along the wharf. When we reached the border between Africville and downtown, Elaine tugged the driver's sleeve.

"Here is fine," she said, gathering her coat around her. The soldiers were reluctant to let us go, citing the weather, the neighbourhood, the better drinks they were going to find downtown. It was only when Janey promised that we'd meet them later, near the waterfront, that they pulled over to the sidewalk and let us out. The others waved until the car disappeared around a corner, and then we began walking in the opposite direction. Everyone touched their hair, blotted lipstick, smoothed their uniforms, all the while comparing the relative merits of our recent chauffeurs.

"Becca, come here," Elaine said, stopping me so she could twirl a few of my curls back into place.

Janey reached into her pocket. "You hang on to this since you're always the responsible one. It's at the corner of Oxford and Norwood, just south of the Citadel. Third floor." She handed me a silver house key with a wink. I slipped it into the inner pocket of my uniform.

"Come on!" cried Dot from farther up the block. "It's freezing—let's get inside."

The Bluebird Club was a two-storey clapboard building, its neon sign dark and lifeless. But the sound of trumpets and drums flooded out through the windows, and a handful of young men in uniform stood out on the sidewalk, smoking and laughing.

We had to wait at the door to get in, each of us blowing on our fingers and stamping our feet to keep warm. I missed my bunk and my book already.

As we waited, a car skidded to a halt near the stage entrance. A young woman climbed hastily out of the back seat, wildly under-dressed for the weather in a beaded gown and a short coat, and caught the hem of her dress in the door as she closed it. She made an incoherent noise of distress, opening the door just as the car drove off again. There was a tearing noise as a long strip of fabric ripped free. The woman stared at her dress, on the edge of tears, then picked up the piece and hurried towards the stage entrance.

Elaine and the others were nearly at the door.

"I'll be back in a moment," I called, and slid away from them.

"Becca, where are you going?" Sara called after me.

"I dropped my glove on the street. You go inside, I'll be right behind you."

Any reply was swallowed up as the group of them were pulled into the light and music that briefly spilled out before the door closed.

I darted down the side of the building. The woman was open-ing the stage door when I caught up with her.

"I saw what happened to your dress," I said. "Can I help?"

She looked me over, assessing my uniform and demeanour in one shrewd glance. "You got a size four frock good enough to sing in hidden under there?"

"No such luck."

"Well then, thank you, but I'll just have to tell 'em I can't per-form tonight."

I asked, "Do you have a sewing kit? Even a few pins?"

"I'd make it worse if I tried to mend it. Anyway, I'm supposed to be on in five. There's no point."

"We'll see about that."

Four and a half minutes later, I bit off the tail of the thread. A quick whipstitch had done nothing more than piece the dress back together, but it would do for now.

"You'll need to get that mended properly," I said, standing up from where I had crouched in front of her, "but it will hold for tonight."

The woman spun one way, then the other, the peach silk swishing. From the stage, no one would be able to tell it had been torn. On the other side of the curtain, I heard wild applause and a man's voice over a microphone, introducing the next act.

"You're a lifesaver. Thank you," the woman said, leaning forward to kiss me on the cheek. "I'm Hatti Dano."

"Rebekah . . . Beauxdons," I said, and we clasped hands briefly. I'd hesitated a little on my last name: my father had thought it wise I enlist under my mother's name, given how people were about Germans.

"Well, Miss Beauxdons, you ever need anything, you come see me. I don't forget my debts."

She threw me a dazzling smile and walked out onto the stage, her arms spread wide to welcome the cheers and whistles that greeted her. I returned the sewing kit to a harried stagehand and went down onto the dance hall floor.

It was crowded and noisy, couples twirling and jiving as Hatti launched into "Somebody Else Is Taking My Place." I squeezed and slithered my way through the uniforms in the crowd: navy blue, army grey, and here and there an air force cap. The women were a blend of drab Canadian Women's Army and Wrens mixed with local girls in their best dresses.

I found Dot and Janey at a table near the far wall, drinks in hand, with three army boys hanging on their every word. Elaine and Sara were already dancing, Elaine giving me a cheerful wave as she blew past. I sat down in the only empty chair and tried to fall into the rhythm of their conversation. The third boy glanced in my direction, and then turned back to Dot, who was describing how she and Janey had snuck a boat out in the summer and nearly capsized off Purcell Landing. This story, which I'd heard at least six times before, grew more embellished with each retelling.

I considered catching the soldier's attention and coaxing a drink out of him, but I simply didn't feel like all that smiling and nodding. I excused myself from the table and made my own way towards the bar.

I downed my first in three quick swallows as Hatti finished her first song. She launched into the next with scarcely a pause for breath, looking lovely up there. If nothing else, I could console myself with the thought that I had made at least one person's night better than my own. I ordered a second drink and carried it back towards our table.

An elbow with a lieutenant's chevrons slammed painfully into my ribs. The drink sloshed over my wrist, and I was ready to snap at the navy boy who'd hit me. He turned.

"Excuse—Rebekah? Rebekah Kromer?"

And there, looking down at me in shock, as couples swirled all around us, was Landon McNair.

"You cut your hair," Landon said, leaning in so that I could hear him.

"So did you," I said, grinning. He'd bought me a drink to replace the one he'd spilled, and we made our way back to the table where Dot and Janey were still sitting with their dates. Elaine had joined them. I introduced Landon as a friend from home, and they shook hands very politely. When Landon offered to buy the next round and disappeared back to the bar, Elaine raised a suggestive eyebrow at me.

"It's not like that," I said. "We were neighbours for a little while."

Elaine's eyebrow arched higher. I avoided her eyes by polishing off my drink.

"It was a long time ago, and anyway, we were very young."

Landon chose that moment to return to the table and caught the tail end.

"What, Rebekah, you're already telling them my faults?" To Sara and Elaine he added, "It's a long list."

Elaine laughed and helped herself to one of the glasses Landon set down. "Becca never mentioned she had such a handsome neighbour." She winked at me.

Landon threw me a look. "She didn't?"

I took one of the glasses and drained it in one quick, burning swallow. "Let's dance."

The floor was crowded, but Landon steered us away from tables and chairs and other couples. It felt both strange and good to have his arms around me, to look up into his brown eyes. All at once we were back at the Labour Day dance, all those years ago, spinning on the floor. I stumbled, struck by the sudden memory of Kit's mouth against my thigh in the dark stable, Landon's boots crunching the gravel outside. Glass shards on the seat of the car. Snarling laughter.

"Are you all right?" Landon asked.

The lights burned brighter, and the music warped and spun, seeming to enter my ears at two different angles. "I just need some air," I said.

"Let's get you outside." He held my elbow as we threaded our way to the front door. The cold hit me like a wall, sending gooseflesh down my neck. The world stabilized a little. I took a deep breath, and another.

"Better?" Landon's coat collar brushed his cheekbones, and the wind soon turned his nose red. I shivered, pulling my coat closer around me. "We can't stay out here too long," he said.

But where was there to go? I couldn't return to Devil's Battery with a man in tow, no more than he could walk me down to the docks and onto his ship. What I really wanted was to go home to Harrichford, to the little bedroom under the gable with my own bed and Patroclus wrapped around my ankles and the comforting sounds of my parents talking in the parlour. To Kit leaning over the fence. Tears pricked my eyes and I reached into my pocket for my handkerchief. Janey's key was cold against my fingers.

"Can we walk for a bit?" I said.

He nodded and we set out towards the Citadel. We walked in silence for a few minutes as my head cleared.

"What's it like, out on the ocean?" I asked at last.

He shrugged, seeming to come out of deep thought. "Well, it's big and wet and sometimes blue." I pushed his shoulder with my own. A familiar slanting grin lifted one corner of his mouth. "Oh, I don't know. It's boring, mostly. Nothing to stare at but waves for days on end. The water isn't usually blue, though. It's sometimes black and sometimes green, purple or grey like rock."

He took my hand, his palm warm. I steered us towards the flat, Janey's directions from earlier in the evening watery in my mind.

"And it's bloody cold. The kind of wind that crawls up one trouser leg and down the other, freezing everything in between. And the rain—I'd never seen a rainstorm that lasted seven days, but out on the sea I've been in ice storms that lasted more than a week, waves high enough to flood the whole ship."

"Weren't you scared?"

His grip tightened on my hand. "No, not of the water. The real danger is those damn U-boats. We spend all our time hunting for them."

"Have you found any?"

He responded with what I suspect was a highly embellished account of a chase up the coast through a terrible storm only to have the sub escape without a trace. His story carried us past the Citadel and onto a quiet street.

"That sounds as exciting as it is dangerous."

"You can't even imagine, Rebekah. The tension when everyone is on high alert? Every shadow in the water could be a Nazi sub lurking to sink us."

I thought of the coded messages I caught and passed along every shift, the bustling tension of the plotting room, the elusive traces of U-boats through my headset, the knowledge that missing even a single blip could spell disaster for our ships out at sea.

"You're right, I can't imagine it," I said.

"Well, I'm sure filing, or whatever, has its own thrills," he replied, after a moment.

I smiled to myself. "You have no idea."

We arrived outside a nondescript three-storey building. I checked the street signs, then pulled out Janey's key.

Landon looked around, realizing I'd had a destination in mind all along. "Where are we?"

"A friend's house. Let's go inside for a minute to warm up."

We climbed up two sets of squeaky stairs, to the third floor. I unlocked the door and eased it open. The apartment had the stale feel of rooms left clean but abandoned. There was a worn carpet on the floor of the main room, a tiny kitchenette and a bedroom but no bed. Five girls would be hard-pressed to sleep comfortably here tonight.

I sank to the floor with a sigh and leaned up against the wall. Landon copied me.

"Are you all right?"

"My feet hurt a little."

Landon leaned over and unbuckled my shoe, drawing my foot onto his knee. I sighed as he pressed into my arch with both thumbs. I shouldn't have allowed him to do this, but it had been so long since someone had touched me with tender intention, I couldn't resist. The last time was when my mother hugged me goodbye at the train station.

Landon's fingers dug into my sole, easing months of stiffness from sitting at the desk and hurrying across from the barracks to the station at all hours. Maybe I groaned, because he paused.

"Why did you stop?" I asked.

"To make sure you're okay."

"I'm perfectly okay," I said, and placed my other foot in his lap.

He obediently unbuckled my second shoe. "As you wish, oh princess of the nine worlds, empress of all filing clerks—ow," he said, as I playfully hit him.

The flat was cold, but I was growing warmer by the moment. I took off my coat and dropped it to the side. Landon resumed massaging my feet, my skin buzzing under the pressure of his fingers. He had grown into his features, the years filling out his jaw and sharpening his cheekbones. The cocky young man I remembered was all but replaced by this self-assured lieutenant.

I put my hand against the side of his face, smooth to look at but rough with stubble under my palm. "I'd like to see you with a beard. You would look handsome," I said.

"I'm not opposed, but the navy might have something to say about that."

"After all of this is over, then. Promise me."

He chuckled. "I promise."

I tugged at his collar, until he unbuttoned his coat and shrugged it off.

"And what would the navy say about you luring an innocent young woman to an abandoned flat and then stealing her shoes?" I said. We were so close I could count each of his eyelashes.

He leaned even closer, and I caught the smell of the aftershave on his neck. "I would say you're the one who lured me. You're not as innocent as you pretend to be, Miss Kromer."

"It's Miss Beauxdons now," I whispered.

I wanted to bury my nose in the hollow of his neck, feel the weight of his arms around me. Landon seemed more alive, more vivid to me than anyone else in the world. I wanted to snatch this moment from the air and capture it like a flower immortalized in amber.

"I missed you," he said, and there was a slight catch in his voice. "I never stopped thinking about you, from the moment you left. I hoped—"

I kissed him, the freezing air of the flat rushing between us like a chaperone, and then his arm came around my waist and pulled me to him, and his cap was in my fist, and we were tumbling down together, the carpet soft beneath us.

—

Afterwards, I lay on top of him, my skirt still bunched around my waist, my head on his shoulder. He had one hand behind his head as the other idly stroked my thigh.

"Marry me," Landon whispered in my ear.

I pushed myself up to look into his face. "Really?"

He nodded. "And when this is all over, I promise we'll go anywhere you want. Just marry me, so I know I'll have someone to come home to."

I laid my head back on his chest. "In Paris, on the steps of Notre-Dame."

"Done."

"With a thousand white doves, and me in a dress with a train that flows all the way down the stairs."

"A cake with seven tiers and a musket salute."

"We'll honeymoon in the West Indies."

He laughed, a deep rumble that I felt through my chest. "Where the nights are much warmer than this, I promise." He kissed my temple.

"The Taj Mahal, the Tower of London—"

He pressed his nose against my cheek. "Whatever you like. I'll go anywhere, as long as it's with you."

For a moment, I heard a different voice in my ear, felt a different hand stroking my skin while dying firelight played on the rafters overhead. Another whispered promise I had answered and broken with silence.

The memory burst like a soap bubble, and all at once, I was painfully aware of this grey and dingy room, the carpet rough under my bare knees. The pressure of tears rose somewhere deep behind my eyes. Landon's hand on my thigh grew heavy, and the cloying smell of his aftershave hung around us. A shiver ran up my legs and into my chest.

I turned and kissed the edge of his mouth. "God, it's cold," I said, clambering to my feet. I set about straightening my clothes.

Landon knelt long enough to fasten his trousers and then stood. He shook out my coat and helped me into it before putting on his own. In the hallway, I relocked the apartment door and then reached to tug his hat into place. He leaned down to kiss me, but I ducked out of his reach. Landon chased me down the stairs, his buoyant laugh the same as I remembered.

I let him catch me in the foyer. I closed my eyes, crushed my memories tight in my palm and tilted my face up for his kiss, trying to recapture the giddy thrill from earlier. I still felt empty and had to work to imagine myself the kind of girl I knew Landon wanted me to be, the role I was supposed to play here.

I looped my arm through his, leaning against his shoulder. I pointed us towards the street that would lead us back to the Bluebird Club.

"Come on, Lieutenant McNair. It's your last night in town and you owe me another dance."

KIT

"And that, boys, is how it's done," I said, dropping my cards face up. A royal flush beamed up at me as a chorus of groans ran around the table. "Pay up, Hartwick," I said.

Laurie rolled his eyes, shoving his small pile of cigarettes, coins and pound notes towards me.

"I swear to God, McNair, you cheat. And I'm going to prove it someday."

"I look forward to it," I said, stuffing the money and cigarettes into my breast pocket. Laurie's eyes caught and held mine for a fraction longer than necessary. I looked away at last, my own eyes landing on Wilkins. "Maybe while you're at it, you can find out where our gunner keeps putting all that good drink." Laughter all around. Wilkins raised his glass in a mock toast to me.

"Or who took Thompson's virginity," Pete said drily. Another round of laughter. The newest gunner blushed and stared into his beer. The skipper shook his head and gathered up the cards, beginning to shuffle again.

Around us, the mess hall was crowded and sweaty with dozens of bodies dancing, drinking, gaming and shouting over the music provided by the ad hoc band in the corner. It was only twenty-three hundred, but the brass had called off all missions for Christmas Eve, so we were all free to get stinking drunk.

The panto had been a hoot—C Squadron's version of "Little Red Riding Hood." Their bomb aimer got done up in a cape and wig to look like the girl, and a chubby engineer in an oversized robe and glasses was the grandmother. The squadron leader had dressed like the Kaiser, adding a pair of furry ears and mitts to make him the wolf. Everyone cheered when all the gunners dressed as woodcutters came in and chopped him down, rescuing the "women," and laughed even harder when Granny's nightgown went over his head to reveal enormous bloomers. After the finale—a misty-eyed rendition of "While Shepherds Watched Their Flocks by Night"—the senior officers retreated to their own mess, and the party moved into high gear.

The girls here were from the nearby village, the ones who worked in the shops and ran the telegraph office and the bakery and hung around the gates of the airbase on their days off. I knew a few of them—Annette, Mary-Anne and her cousin Gwen—but tonight they were a more alluring version of themselves, wearing their Sunday best, red lips and painted-on stockings in place of nylons. They had the same aim as everyone else: to get drunk as quickly as possible.

The band had attempted to play some proper Christmas carols, but had been shouted down, and now they were wheezing their way through a version of "Jingle Jangle Jingle" while couples spun around the floor.

The whisky had burned a long column of fire down my centre, dissipating the cold, metallic fear of last night. I had a pocket full of cigarettes and enough cash that I could afford to lose a few games in the coming week. I could even buy a postcard and mail it home, tell my parents happy Christmas. For a moment, the truth choked me. I couldn't write home to my parents, just as I couldn't write to my brothers. Landon had likely signed up right away and was somewhere in this mess. But Jep? I couldn't imagine him in combat. Surely, he wasn't old enough.

And even if I wrote to them, what would I say? How could I even begin to explain where I'd been and what I was doing? How to explain Christopher McNair and his life to them? I might not survive the war, and if I did—

Mary-Anne tumbled into my lap, giggling uproariously, as Ranbir collapsed into the chair next to me, panting.

"That's it, I'm down for the count," he said. "Find someone else to be your whirling dervish."

"But you promised me three dances. I put on my best shoes and everything." She extended her foot into his lap, her hemline slipping another six inches up her thigh.

"I'll dance with you, darling," I said.

Mary-Anne wriggled around to face me. I caught the gin on her breath. "You would?"

I looked at Ranbir over her shoulder. He threw up his hands in surrender. "She's all yours, McNair. Maybe you'll have better stamina than me."

"That's a certainty," drawled Vanier, and laughter rippled around the table.

I drained the last of my whisky as Mary-Anne pulled me to my feet. "Take my place, Singh. And someone should tell Skipper the ace of clubs has this nice little dent in the top corner."

I heard Pete cursing as Mary-Anne dragged me out into the crush. She was a good dancer, light on her feet, twisting and jiving. I spun her out and pulled her back in, getting frantic with the music and the rush of alcohol to my head. Everything was fuzzy and blurred, so that I didn't notice the absences—Jacob and Mark and the rest of the *Scout's Honour* crew. Mary-Anne's hand was warm and slightly sweaty in mine, her skirt swishing against my arm when I caught her around the waist, her body leaning into me and then spinning out again. We were whirling, faster and faster, the engine whining into a screech, Ranbir's shoulder squeezed beneath my arm, the world tumbling, the smell of burning oil and rubber, that bubbly panic in my throat—

A pair of arms caught us both as I stumbled.

"Easy, easy." Laurie steadied me as I lurched sideways, nearly colliding with another couple. Mary-Anne continued spinning, straight into the arms of someone else. She glanced back, concerned, but Laurie waved her off.

"Carry on, doll. My friend here needs some air." He put an arm around my shoulders and guided me out of the mess hall and into the night.

The whisky was sour in my mouth, burning when I inhaled, but the night air felt good. We walked away from the circle of the overhead light, then Laurie pulled us back against a nearby wall. A sentry went past, shivering in his overcoat. Laurie and I exchanged a glance and I had to bite back a laugh. I was drunk, I realized distantly, completely drunk for the first time in I didn't remember how long.

Laurie leaned next to me, pulled a cigarette pack out of his shirt pocket and offered me one. I took it and bent to the match he struck. We stood there for a while, my skin steaming slightly in the chill. I noted how quiet and calm it was, appreciating that there was no one trying to kill me at this precise moment. The distant sounds of the party trickled out of the mess hall, hitting a tantalizingly familiar note. Something about the circle of yellow light that spilled out from the building behind us and being here in the dark, with Laurie's shoulder touching mine. I shook the feeling away and took a drag of my cigarette. We fell to discussing the panto.

"I have no idea where they got a nightgown to fit Jameson," I said, flicking ash into the dirt. "I think Skipper might've gotten some ideas."

Laurie snorted. "Well, if you like that sort of thing—"

"I don't."

He took another drag of his cigarette, then said, "But you know who would have looked good up on that stage?"

I pretended I didn't know where this was headed. Laurie crushed his cigarette butt underfoot, then picked it up and tucked it into his breast pocket. The man could inhale an entire smoke in one breath, the result of long practice.

"Why didn't you get up there in that little red number? With no beard and those legs of yours, you'd have been ten times more convincing than Jameson."

I scraped a nail against the wall behind me. "I don't do that sort of thing. Besides, it's funnier with the beard."

"Oh, c'mon, we'd find you a wig and some pearls—"

"No."

"Fine, be a stick-in-the-mud."

I said nothing, watching my cigarette burn down to the filter a hair's breadth at a time.

"By the way"—Laurie turned to face me, planting one shoulder against the wall—"you cheated me out of a week's winnings. You owe me."

"Or what?" I couldn't help myself from provoking that spark in his eye.

"Or I tell everyone you count cards. It's not like you'd ever win in an honest game."

"I would too."

"Prove it."

In the distance, the door to the mess hall opened and light and the sound of "Fools Rush In" spilled out, along with several figures who stumbled unsteadily in our direction.

"Your bunk, ten minutes," I said. "I'll bring the cards—"

"No, it'll be dice, and I'll bring them, you lousy cheat. Don't be late." He looked like he was going to say something more, but then he turned and disappeared around the end of the building. I counted to one hundred and twenty, then strolled back towards the mess hall, intending to take the long route to the barracks.

I was walking along the hall's far side when footsteps crunching on gravel caught my attention. I stopped, glanced around. Hearing voices, I stepped into the shadow of a doorway.

My eyes were enough adjusted to the dark to see two figures standing close together—as close as Laurie and I had been—but not touching. One of them had a bicycle. They were talking earnestly. Furtively. As I watched, the man with the bicycle took something the other man handed to him and pocketed it. I held my breath. We'd been warned about spies, of course. The Germans were treacherous, as Station Commander Worthing never tired of reminding us.

The last murmured words between them were still too soft for me to catch. Then the man with the bicycle turned it around and stepped lightly on board, coasting silently downhill and away from the mess. Soon, he was lost in the dark. The other man remained where he was for a moment, looking down at the object in his hand. Then he straightened. I shrank back against the doorway as he glanced around, and then he walked off in the direction of the party, whistling a half-hearted tune.

When I entered the barracks, Laurie was already in his bunk with his feet up, reading, his jacket undone at the collar. I shut the door carefully behind me. We were alone.

"You're late."

"I got lost."

Laurie smiled, a tired, honest smile so different from the rakish grin he wore everywhere else.

"Let's get this over with then." He gestured to a waiting set of dice and a flask on a nearby table.

We played in earnest silence, passing the flask back and forth. Laurie won the first game easily, but I took the next three.

After my third win, Laurie slammed his hand onto the table, then pointed at me.

"No way someone can win that many in a row. How are you doing it?"

I leaned back in my chair, out of range of his finger, and spread my hands. "I swear, Laurie, I don't even know how to cheat at craps."

"Prove it." He pushed the dice towards me and propped his book up on the edge of the table opposite me. "Eight no-pass. Roll has to hit the book."

I gathered the dice into my palm, as Laurie took another long drink from the flask. "Eight pass," I said quietly, squeezed my hand around the dice and threw them. They rattled across the tabletop, hit the book with a satisfying sound and tumbled to a standstill. Two and six. Laurie threw the book to the floor and lunged towards me as I grabbed the dice and leapt out of my chair. He caught me a few steps later and shoved me back against the wall.

"You cheating bastard," he growled. He had me pinned by both shoulders, his face inches from mine.

Laurie had size on me, but he hadn't spent eighteen years tickling trout and wrestling Landon. As though I was accepting defeat, I let my shoulders go slack, and his grip instinctively loosened. Fast as a snake, I ducked under his arm and twisted. I pinned him against the wall, my hands tight on the balance points just above his elbows, my hip pressed between his legs. His eyes were glassy as he absorbed what had just happened. I leaned in until our noses almost touched.

"I don't cheat," I said.

"I'll tell everyone you keep loaded dice in your pocket and an ace up your sleeve," Laurie said. Whisky fumes clouded my face.

"You wouldn't dare."

"Wouldn't I? You better be nice to me, make me forget all about this little incident."

I bit my lip. Cards and games were like navigating. I didn't cheat; I simply picked the numbers that felt right, that aligned like buttons snapping into place in my head. I did count cards, but I would die before admitting it. My mother had taught me how when I was ten and recovering from drowning, as a way to help me relearn my numbers. Landon had been furious when I started beating him.

Laurie was still looking at me, a little unsteady, his eyes narrowed. I leaned slightly towards him, but his hand was firm on my shoulder, pressing me down.

The dice slipped from my hand, bouncing on the floor like hailstones. His trousers were already half unbuttoned, hidden by the coat. I knelt and undid the rest of them, pressed my forehead against the top of his thigh. His skin was warm and slightly goose-pimpled in the cool air. Laurie closed his eyes, leaned back against the wall.

"That Gwen is a firecracker," he said quietly. "But maybe too sensible for my purposes."

I chuckled, muffling the sound by pressing my nose into his leg. His hand tightened on the back of my head. "You owe me, McNair."

He groaned when I took him in my mouth.

"When this is all over, I'm gonna ask her to marry me. And we're going to find a little place on the lakeside, downriver from my parents."

I moved my tongue, sucked in my cheeks. His thighs quivered under my palms.

"And I'll be the envy of the town, for bringing home the prettiest English girl the world's ever seen."

I fisted my hands in his trouser legs, the coat falling on either side of my face, a heavy wool curtain that reduced the world to darkness and breath and skin.

"You'll see, Christopher. We'll win and everything will be good again."

I took him deep into my throat, still feeling the burn of whisky on the back of my tongue.

"I'll go home and then"—he gasped, loud in the emptiness of the room—"everything will be okay. You'll see."

I pressed my forehead into the cleft of his thighs and closed my eyes. Through the open window, the faint music resolved into "Silent Night," a chorus of drunken voices chasing each verse. It was Christmas Eve, and all was well, all was bright.

FEBRUARY 1943

REBEKAH

AFTER ANOTHER RETCH, I COULD FINALLY CATCH MY breath, the sides of the toilet bowl cold against my hands. I contemplated staying hidden in here for a few minutes longer, but I'd already been gone longer from the communications room than I'd intended, and soon Mathers would send someone looking for me. This was the third time this week I'd been sick. I wanted to blame the tinned beef in the mess, but no one else was ill.

I stood at the sink, washed my hands and rinsed out my mouth. The Becca in the mirror looked sallow from so many months spent in the windowless rooms of Devil's Battery. I'd taken walks on my shore leave days, bundled up against the fierce Atlantic wind, but the weak winter sunlight had done little to brighten my complexion. And while I'd been sick and barely able to eat for weeks, my uniform still felt snug. I shoved that thought away.

Back in the communications room, I slipped into my chair next to Elaine and pulled on my headset. She gave me a glance, but nothing more, her attention riveted on the clamour that streamed through our ears from across the Atlantic.

I held out against the nausea until the watch change bell rang, and then managed to salute the Kettle as she came in to supervise the shift change, to tidy my station and make way for the next girl, and to walk sedately out of the room. As soon as I was around the corner in the corridor, I bolted for the bathroom. There was nothing left to purge, but still I retched and retched. When the last spasm passed, I splashed cold water on my face and then waited until I could hear no one moving in the corridor before I left.

My room was empty and I sank down on the bed gratefully as the world spun. I was shaking with hunger, but the thought of food made me feel ill all over again. I lay back on the pillow and closed my eyes. I would have given anything to be home right now, lying in my own bed. To have my mother come in with a cool cloth for my forehead and to gently stroke my hair, the way she had when I was little.

All those times I had feigned a headache to avoid a social engagement, all the times I had resented her fussing attentions and driven her out of my room—I would have taken them back in a heartbeat if it meant she was here now, singing me *"Parlez-moi d'amour"* until I fell asleep.

The door to the room opened and Elaine backed carefully in.

"I brought you this from the mess." A cup of tea and a piece of bread with butter. My stomach heaved at the smell, but I forced myself to sit up and hold the cup in my lap. Elaine set the bread on the end table and sat down on my bed.

"Still not feeling well?" she said, reaching the back of her hand to my forehead.

"I'm sure it will pass," I said. "Probably just about to have the painters in."

The sympathy in Elaine's eyes flickered into something else.

"What?" I said. "You know how I get."

"I do," Elaine said. I took a sip of tea, grimaced at the taste and forced myself to take another swallow.

"Only . . ." Elaine hesitated. "Normally that only lasts a week. You've been sick on and off for a month."

"Have I?" I wrinkled my brow. "I'm sure it hasn't been that long—"

"Becca, I'm not an idiot," Elaine hissed.

I stared at her.

She arched her eyebrows. "I've three older sisters back in Fredericton, all married. You think I haven't noticed?"

At once, all the fight went out of me and I sank, boneless, against my pillow. As exhausting as it was hiding the truth from others, it had been even more tiring trying to hide it from myself.

"Whose is it?" my roommate asked, typically blunt.

I took a deep breath. "You remember Landon, from that night at the Bluebird Club back at Christmas?"

"Who?"

"The boy from Harrichford. I told you about him, the one who I—"

"Oh right, him." Elaine said the last word as though it was something sour, or perhaps I just imagined it.

"Yes . . . Well, that night we went for a walk and it was cold and we stepped into Janey's uncle's flat to warm up before coming back to the club and, well . . ."

She raised her eyebrows at me, passing judgment and absolving me in the same expression.

"He shipped out the next day and I haven't had a letter since."

"Was he . . . was it serious? Or do you think he's found someone else?"

Outside in the corridor, there was the noise of dozens of footsteps. Dinner had ended and women were returning to their rooms.

I missed you. I never stopped thinking about you. Marry me.

"He seemed pretty serious," I said quietly.

Elaine leaned closer to me. "You have to tell him."

"But what if he—maybe he won't . . ." Tears gathered in the corners of my eyes.

Elaine took my hand and squeezed it. "Write to him. If he's the kind of man you think he is, he'll come through for you."

"You really think so?"

"You shouldn't have to do this alone, Becca."

I smiled, a wavering, watery sort of smile. "Fine," I said. "I'll write to him."

Elaine patted my leg and got to her feet. "I'll tell the others you're under the weather because the painters are in," she said, winking. She took my half-empty cup and left me.

I lay on my bed, staring at the ceiling. Landon would know what to do. He would find a way to come back, just for a week or two, and we would get everything sorted.

KIT

"McNair!"

"Yes, sir?"

"What am I looking at?" Station Commander Worthing's jowls shook with indignation. He had shaved earlier in the day, but I could already detect stubble.

"That would be a pig, sir."

"A pig?"

"Yes, sir. And it appears to be wearing Jerry colours." I didn't think Worthing could turn a deeper shade of eggplant, but he proved me wrong.

"In the officers' mess hall." He bit each of the words off as though they offended him, which on reflection, I supposed they did.

"Correct, sir," I said, adding a dash of puzzlement to my expression. "Is there something wrong, sir?"

Behind the officer, the rest of the *Friday's Girl* crew could hardly keep themselves together. Laurie had to brace his shoulder against Thompson's to keep the gunner upright. Vanier was chewing his moustache hard in an attempt to hide his grin, while Wilkins clutched Ranbir's arm with white knuckles, covering his laughter with a coughing fit. Our skipper, standing to one side, seemed torn between laughter and the purple indignation of the CO.

The pig, standing on the table in the officers' mess, continued eating the remains of their tea. It had taken half the day for us to catch the bugger and paint him up. The Führer's moustache on his nose had been Thompson's *pièce de résistance*.

"An absolute disgrace," Worthing bellowed.

"I quite agree, sir," I said. "I'll just get it out of here, shall I?"

"You insolent pup. You think I don't know that you put this animal here in the first place?"

"I can't really take all the credit, sir." I caught Thompson's eye over the CO's shoulder. "It was the pig's idea to eat the scones."

"Shut up before you regret it, McNair. I expect better from a flying officer of your experience. Consider yourself on thin ice."

Worthing eyed the rest of the crew. "You are all a disgrace to the uniform and the British Empire. This is precisely why we should never have let a single Commonwealth hooligan into the RAF.

Do you think we won the Battle of Britain by tolerating farm animals in the barracks?"

I put on my blankest expression. "Oh, I think 'farm animals' is a little harsh, sir. They can't help being Scottish."

Worthing's cheeks purpled to new depths. "Clean this up, all of you! And get that goddamn animal out of my sight. I expect this mess hall to be gleaming before this evening's briefing, which gives you exactly one hour to get it done or I'll have you horsewhipped as an example to every man on this base."

He stormed out. In the ringing silence that followed his exit, we all held our breath. The pig licked the plate clean, then clambered down off the table and trotted out the door.

By the time I had caught the pig, washed him off and returned him to the nearby farm, the others had nearly finished cleaning the mess hall.

"You took your time," Wilkins said. His Sheffield accent bent every vowel in several directions. I shrugged and accepted the rag that Vanier handed to me and began wiping the chairs.

"It would have been funnier if it were a goat," said Thompson. He was on his knees scrubbing the last of the jam from the floor.

"But we didn't have a goat, did we?" said Wilkins. "So we made do."

"I have to agree," Ranbir said, shaking a mop out the window. "A goat would have caused even more havoc."

I rolled my eyes. Trust our Australian and Indian air force representatives to stick together.

"It was highly amusing, if ill advised," Pete said, stacking plates on the table. "McNair, did you forget that we are here to co-operate with the Royal Air Force, not plot the best way to make Commander Worthing's head explode?"

"No one tell the Krauts," Laurie quipped. "If their spies smuggle enough pigs in to eat all the officers' scones, the entire British Army will crumble."

"Enough," Pete said firmly. "Finish up and get on with whatever else it is you do with your downtime. Don't even think about being late for the general briefing. Oh, and be sure to thank McNair for your next two weeks of punishment detail."

A chorus of "Yes, Skipper" followed him out of the room, his dignity undermined by the stack of dirty plates wobbling in his arms.

Thompson shrugged and looked around at the rest of us. "So, what'll it be next? I saw a place down the way with this great big turkey—"

"*Non, non,*" Vanier said. The engineer's accent reminded me of Rebekah's, though his was broader and flatter. I pushed the thought of Rebekah away as quickly as I was able. "We should rest on our victory," Vanier continued. "That way we can plan something truly *magnifique* for later. *Par exemple*, have you considered what we could do with a cow?"

He was met with laughter and claps on the back.

"McNair?" Pete had his head around the door, his expression stern.

"Coming, Skip," I said.

Flight briefings at Lincolnshire base were held in a windowless interior room. I nodded politely to the RAF police on duty outside the door as I went inside. All the pilots and navigators for tonight's op were seated at rows of wooden tables facing the front of the room. There was a huge curtain across the wall, and in front of it stood Station Commander Worthing and the wing commanders, along with other senior officers and our designated spook.

I dropped into a seat next to the skipper. He said nothing, merely pushing the stack of charts, a compass and pencil in my direction. There was a time when Pete had been in on every stunt we pulled.

Back in Rivers, he was the first to suggest tobogganing on sheets of scrap metal down the hill behind the barracks and building a voluptuous snowman in the likeness of Rita Hayworth outside our instructor's hut. Being promoted to squadron leader and captaining more than two dozen missions with our *Friday's Girl* crew had taken its toll, and he had become more serious, focused on keeping us all alive during ops and home for breakfast. I couldn't blame him.

Worthing cleared his throat, the cue for us to fall silent and pay attention. As the police began to shut the door, a figure slipped through, darting to a seat in a row just ahead of me. I craned my neck. It was Isaak Keyserling, a Czech navigator who had arrived in Lincolnshire a few months earlier on a sprog crew fresh out of training. When most of that crew had bought the farm in a dambusting op, the remaining men had been split and reassigned to fill gaps in other squadrons. Navigator Keyserling had just been transferred to a place on the *Siren*, but like all survivors of ill-fated missions, superstition followed him like a shadow. As he settled in the chair next to his skipper, I noticed his hair and uniform were damp.

Once the door was locked and well-guarded, Wing Commander Sandish, a skinny RAF airman with his hair lacquered into place, called out the roll to ensure everyone was present. Then Worthing stepped up to the podium and nodded. Sandish pulled a thick cord and the curtain parted to reveal a map of Europe the length and height of the wall, and a chorus of groans went around the room, mine among them. On the map were strips of blue tape showing our flight path and the target for tonight's op. The Ruhr valley—ironically called Happy Valley—was the most fiercely defended stretch of Germany, with thousands of searchlights, anti-aircraft guns and radar sweepers waiting to catch us. As if that weren't enough, it was also guarded by a swarm of night fighters as thick as flies over a dead sheep, ready to hunt us across the continent.

Worthing silenced us with a stern look and began delivering target objectives and timing details. I grabbed my pencil to mark everything we would need on the charts. Pete did the same, underlining and filling in information as necessary. A stream of numbers, coordinates, landmarks, heights and speeds sped through my ears and onto the chart. As the intelligence officer added his thoughts, I crosshatched the location of known flak lines, and circled searchlight locations.

An hour later, we were released to last supper and our personal preparations. Prank forgotten, we went quietly to dinner and then to the crew room to suit up and gather our chutes and life jackets.

I had earned the nickname "Lucky McNair" on my very first op with *Friday's Girl*. We took flak through the windshield and still managed to hit our target over Belgium before limping home, crew miraculously intact save for a nasty gash on Vanier's hand. I couldn't take any credit for it, truly, since it had been Wilkins's aim and Pete's steady hand that got us out, not my lucky guess that a spiral dive and sharp turn to the right would send our Luftwaffe pursuer spinning down into the ocean, the wings stripped clean off him. Still, the name stuck and with it came rituals. I'd learned to graciously accept the kisses on the head and slaps from my crewmates.

Nearby, I saw a man struggling with his flight suit, his hands shaking too much to close the snaps. I gently took the lapels and zipped them closed over his chest. Isaak looked up at me, his blue eyes scared.

"With all the zippers, you'd think it would be warmer," I said, lifting his life jacket and holding it out for him. Isaak slid his arms through and tightened it around his waist.

"Sometimes it is too warm," he said, not meeting my eyes.

I put a hand on his shoulder. "Joffrey's a good skipper and he knows that Halifax inside and out. You're in good hands."

Isaak wouldn't meet my eyes, but he let my hand linger for a moment before he shook it off. I watched him hurry through the crew room to catch up to the rest of the *Siren*'s crew.

When all of us were kitted out, we strolled out to wait for the trucks on the lawn outside the barracks. Laurie lit a cigarette, smoking his last of the day while we were still far from the aircraft and the fuel lines.

"I still can't believe they let that Kraut in. You couldn't pay me enough to fly with him," he muttered, sending a dark look towards Isaak's hunched figure.

Vanier followed Laurie's gaze. "I heard he was a defector who volunteered to fly against the Luftwaffe. Better to have him in one of our planes than one of theirs."

Laurie scowled. "That's a pretty story. I'm surprised you believe it, Vanier."

"If he is a spook," Ranbir said, tugging his life jacket straight, "he's a terrible one. He openly admits where he came from, and with that Czech accent? I would give the Jerrys a little more credit."

The trucks rumbled up to the lawn and men began climbing on board. Laurie dropped his cigarette and ground his heel into it.

"Even so, you stay away from him, McNair. He's bad luck."

We clambered into the nearest truck, which carried us out towards the airfield, and onwards, into the jaws of hell.

APRIL 1943

REBEKAH

MY APPETITE HAD RETURNED AT LAST. I'D INHALED MY toast and eggs at breakfast and was eyeing the leftover slice on Elaine's plate when the mail trolley came around, and an envelope nearly fell onto my crumb-covered plate. My heart began beating faster as I picked it up and scanned it for an address. There was an army postmark in the corner.

Elaine noticed. "Is that—?"

"I don't know."

I slit the envelope open with my butter knife and unfolded the contents. It was written on army letterhead. Elaine leaned on my shoulder, reading alongside me.

Dear Rebekah,

Hello from basic. I've been here a few weeks already, but you would hardly recognize me. I had a postcard from Landon last month saying he'd bumped into you in Halifax at Christmas. I'm going to be passing through there next week. If you've the time, I thought I

could treat you to lunch for the chance to see a friendly face before
I head out. Write back and let me know where and when.
Jep McNair

I dropped the letter on my plate. Elaine picked it up and skimmed it, a little frown between her brows.

"Who is Jep?"

I sighed, flicked a fingernail against my empty teacup. "Someone I knew in Harrichford." I couldn't bring myself to explain any more about the McNairs.

"So nothing from Landon yet?"

I shook my head. I'd let out my uniform skirt twice already, and yet it once again cut painfully into my stomach. My mother had owned a corset that could be tight-laced to conceal any curve, but there was no way I could write home and ask her to send it without explaining the reason why.

I had written Landon four letters and had a fifth half-finished in my trunk. The last I'd sent had begged him to write back and reassure me that he would help. I'd hated the pleading tone but couldn't help myself. In the unfinished fifth letter, I told him in plain language what was happening and what I needed. Perhaps he hadn't understood my hints. Perhaps a mail ship had been destroyed—it happened all the time. There were a thousand reasonable explanations for his silence.

Elaine glanced around and then ducked her head close to mine. "Have you thought about what you're going to do? I mean, you can't hide it forever."

I bit my lip. Did Elaine think I would suddenly have a different answer from the last time she'd asked that question a week ago?

"I'll think of something," I said, as I shoved back my chair and marched off to the wireless room, trying to ignore that the floor beneath my feet was a cracking, shifting sheet of ice, threatening to shatter under me at any moment.

The café was just off Main Street, squeezed between a laundry and a pawn shop. I arrived first, but I decided to wait outside under the awning. My uniform was a comfortable shield against most questions, but I shuddered to think what my mother would say about me sitting alone in a city café.

It was my only day ashore this week and I was glad to be away from Devil's Battery. I was so sick of knocking elbows at dinner, of spending my days surrounded by people, of having to keep my face composed and pleasant at all hours of the day and night. I was tired to my bones, as though my very soul was sick of itself. There was nothing for it, however, but to keep on going. There was a war on, after all.

When I'd replied to Jep, suggesting today's date and the café where I now stood, I had felt cheerful about seeing a familiar face. But when this morning arrived and brought with it an overcast day and a mild headache, I had wanted to stay in bed and doze and reread the letters my mother had written to me. It was the thought of Jep arriving here only to be puzzled by my absence that had pushed me into the day.

"Miss Kromer?"

I turned. He had the same rounded features, emphasized by the cap on his head, but the puppy fat had been replaced with muscle. His cheeks were red, as though he'd been running.

"Jep!" I didn't have to force my smile. We shook hands, slightly clumsily, and then he opened the door and ushered me inside.

Jep found us a table at the far end of the café. He pulled out my chair, but not quite far enough, so I had to wriggle in. He sat opposite me, squeezing his cap in his hands, as I took off my gloves and scarf.

"So," I said, smiling.

"So." He smiled back at me. I had expected him to look older in his uniform, but even with the muscles, he looked like a boy dressed up in his father's clothes. His close haircut looked so raw against his scalp, I wanted to reach out and smooth it.

"How is your family?" I asked.

"They're well. My father joined the Home Guard, just as a volunteer, but they've been doing drills on the main street and going around doing blackout inspections. He takes a shift guarding the train station once a week."

I smiled, imagining Dermot in his felt hat, armband on his shoulder, marching up and down in front of the empty station, his expression gruff.

"Ma's added an extra garden and she's been knitting for the Red Cross, and they've put up blackout papering. She wanted to join up as a nurse after she saw one of those films."

"I pity anyone who had to face your mother on the battlefield, nurse or no," I said.

Jep shrugged. "I talked her out of it. Told her she had to stay home so she could give us the whole hero's welcome when we get back."

Silence fell across the table. The question of Kit burned on my tongue like a peppercorn.

"Oh, and Landon joined up with the navy too, but I guess you know that already." Jep gave an awkward chuckle.

"Any idea where he is now?"

Jep shrugged. "Somewhere in the North Atlantic, I imagine. But loose lips and all that."

"Of course," I said.

A waitress arrived to take our order.

"But look at you, all kitted out in navy gear yourself," Jep said, when she had disappeared. "Do they make you wear those silly hats like the boys?"

I told him about our drills, semaphore flags and learning Morse code. The inane tradition of referring to everything as though we were at sea, even though Devil's Battery was a series of clapboard buildings and underground bunkers. Our sandwiches arrived as I was explaining it all.

Jep was delighted with the slang. "Could you pass me the salt? It's on your starboard," he said and giggled. All at once, we were back in Harrichford, sharing licorice on a clifftop. An ache bloomed inside me. That memory belonged to another girl, much younger and more innocent than me. I could hardly reconcile that it had been me in that cottage kissing Kit in the firelight, or that Landon had sat stiffly at my dinner table and complimented my mother's glassware. It felt as though I'd read it in a book and had forgotten half the plot.

Jep made all the usual complaints about basic training in Brampton. His impression of their drill sergeant made me snort so hard we drew the attention of other diners. We were quieter after that.

He insisted on paying for lunch. After he escorted me back outside, Jep said, "You have the whole day off, then?"

"Yes, but I have some errands I should—"

"Lead the way!" He offered me his arm, and I couldn't think of a reason to say no.

It began to rain as we walked through town. Jep waited outside while I turned my spare shoes in for mending. Then he followed me to a bookshop, where I browsed self-consciously for a few minutes, and left without buying anything. Soon, we were back out on the street again, the sky dripping relentlessly.

"You really don't have to stay with me," I said. His face fell. "I mean, you're welcome to, of course, but I wouldn't want to keep you from the rest of your afternoon. I will be quite all right on my own."

"Alone in the big city? What kind of man do you take me for?" Jep said, chest puffing up with affront. I stifled a smile. Halifax was barely even a town compared to Montreal, and Jep was only eighteen.

"Shall we see a film?" I suggested.

When we arrived at the theatre, however, the next showing wasn't until the evening. Jep suggested getting food, but we had just eaten, so he went to the concession and brought back two lukewarm teas, and we stood under the awning in front of the theatre and chatted, the rain dripping down the awning's fringes and a cold breeze lifting the edge of my skirt.

Having exhausted all possible topics of conversation, we lapsed into silence. I was beginning to feel chilled and miserable, wishing I hadn't agreed to lunch, wishing a hundred small, irrational things, when Jep said abruptly, "She never came home."

I didn't need to ask who he was talking about. "They had a fight—Landon and Kit—and then she just disappeared. We looked everywhere, for weeks. She never came back."

He paused. "Late one night, I even went out alone and stood in the forest and whistled for them. I thought if anyone would know where she'd gone, it would be . . . But I heard nothing." He looked at me from under his cap, his eyes wide.

"I don't know where Kit is," I said.

Jep looked at the ground.

"I'm sorry." I reached for his sleeve, squeezed the arm beneath it. "I truly am."

Jep gave a strange half-smile. "She liked you best. I figured if anyone knew what had happened to her, it would be you."

I shook my head. "For all the hours we spent together, she was a mystery to me." My words fell onto the sidewalk and washed away with the rainwater down a nearby culvert.

Jep sniffed, took off his cap and swiped a hand over his shorn head before replacing it. "I guess I should be getting back."

We walked down to the harbour in silence, each alone with our own thoughts.

At the checkpoint, I hugged him goodbye. His uniform was damp against my cheek, and he held me delicately, as if I was a fledgling bird he was terrified to crush. In that moment, a hundred things I hadn't said or thought to ask came flooding into my mouth, and I swallowed them, seeing his face trembling on the edge of control.

"I'll see you soon," I said, and squeezed his arm. He nodded and then pulled himself to attention.

"Permission to disembark?"

"Permission granted, soldier," I said, and he saluted me smartly. The last I saw of him, he was walking down the dock, shoulders hunched against the rain.

KIT

I sat back against the wall, grateful that my sheepskin coat insulated me from the worst of the damp. The dirt floor was cold underneath me, but at least it was dry. The sound of rain trickling

off the gutters reminded me of the river back home. I was beginning to doze off when Laurie ducked through the doorway and
back under the shelter of the roof, buttoning his trousers.

"Now I know why the Brits are in such a damn mood all the
time," he said, running a hand through his wet hair. "It comes
from pissing in the rain your whole life."

"What's your excuse?"

Laurie flicked water at me.

I leaned my head against the wall, ignoring the slightly spongy
wood. A bombed-out gardener's shed on the outskirts of a nearby
estate wouldn't have been my first choice for a liaison, but in
Lincolnshire in mid-April, we couldn't afford to be picky.

Laurie sat down opposite me, leaning against an old potting
table, his long legs straight out in front of him. He pulled a cheese
sandwich out of his coat pocket and handed me half. The bread was
squished and the cheese a little rubbery, but I wolfed it down just
the same. I wanted to go sit next to him, lean against his shoulder
and rest my forehead on his neck, but it wasn't a good idea. Laurie
and I had established a strict, unspoken set of rules. No lingering
touches, except in the heat of the moment when he would let me
hold his thighs or his hips, as he ran his hand through my hair; no
talking during; no loitering around afterwards for fear of being
caught; and certainly no kissing. We picked our moments. Early
morning, after debrief and breakfast, when everyone else had collapsed into an exhausted sleep. The hour after mission briefing,
when we wouldn't be missed and others would assume we were
napping or bathing or throwing up—any of the usual pre-flight rituals. This moment was rare, sitting in silence sharing a sandwich.
Normally he would have been out the door and halfway back to
base by now.

I said as much to him.

Laurie rolled his eyes. "Don't feel special. I just don't fancy a long walk in the rain. I'll go when it clears up."

He dug into his coat pocket and produced a slightly squashed bar of chocolate, tossed it over to me.

"What is this, a tip?"

"It's from my mum."

"Then she meant it for you." I tried to hand it back.

He shook his head. "They keep us so crammed with chocolate here I can't stand the stuff anymore."

"Suit yourself." I tucked into the candy with enthusiasm. After so many years staring yearningly at the glass jars of candy in the general store at home, I could never get enough sweets.

"Doesn't your mother send you anything?"

"My mother doesn't know I'm here. We don't exactly get along."

"No?"

"No."

We sat a moment longer in silence, Laurie staring at the rain as it fell through the holes in the roof.

"I have three sisters, all at home in Edmonton," he said at last. "One's married, one's in the CWAC, and the youngest is at home with my parents. She's the one who writes mostly."

He reached into his jacket and handed me a rumpled postcard. The picture was a cat on a cottage porch. I turned it over.

Dear Laurie, Happy New Year from all of us! It wasn't the same without you. Mum's been making Christmas cake with carrots and no rum. Isabel says hi and hopes you're coming home soon. All our love, Winnie.

"She sounds sweet," I said, as Laurie snatched the postcard back and stowed it safely in his jacket once more.

"She's just sixteen and the nicest girl you'd ever meet. I wouldn't let her within ten miles of you."

I grinned. "Want to keep me all to yourself, do you?"

Laurie kicked me viciously in the shin. I drew my knees to my chest, out of range.

"What about you?" Laurie said. "You have a girl waiting back home?"

"No, nothing like that."

"Really? No one you think about when you cross the flak, or just before you fall asleep?"

Dark hair spilling like a curtain beside my cheek. The sun red on my eyelids and the taste of clover. I shook my head.

He gave me a pitying look. "That's sad. Everyone should have someone like my Gwen."

I wasn't in the mood to hear another soliloquy about Gwen. "I'm going out now," I said.

"Unlikely."

I waved my pass and then replaced it in my pocket. "I got per-mission. Twenty-four hours of freedom and I'm not going to waste them all on you." I hauled myself to my feet.

"Maybe do us both a favour and find yourself a bit of skirt."

"Why? You worried I'm getting too attached?" Laurie's jaw tightened, and I immediately regretted the words. "Don't worry. I'll hitch my star to the first girl who's better looking than you."

"Good luck with that."

I stepped over his legs to reach the door. "Wait a few before you head out."

"I know, I know," he said, and sighed, reaching into his breast pocket for a cigarette.

I looked around before heading out onto the path that threaded the edge of the estate. It was still raining, and there was no one about, but it paid to be cautious.

REBEKAH

The wireless room was silent, as always, save for the scratching of pencils against paper and the occasional shifting of feet. I hung my jacket over the back of my chair and sat in my usual place, settled the headset on my ears and tuned the dial to my assigned channel. It had been quiet for days on the Atlantic, which left my mind plenty of time to worry about what exactly I was going to do.

Panicked in the middle of the night two weeks ago, I had written to my mother, telling her that Landon and I were engaged, but that he'd shipped out again before we could get married. That I now had found myself in a family way and wanted to please come stay with them to wait for Landon to return. I'd had no reply yet and couldn't help but wonder why.

I hadn't mentioned this to Elaine. I didn't want her to think of me as a child who needed her parents to solve her problems. Or, worse, as a child whose parents wouldn't help her.

A blip in the wireless noise, a German coded signal that flashed by too fast for me to untangle. Then another, and another. I scribbled quickly, all my attention now locked on the faint beeps and taps that indicated a U-boat lurking somewhere in the depths of the Atlantic, reaching out to its fellows.

The other girls were taking notes furiously too, the duty officer marching down the rows and snatching dictations as fast as they were completed. I let the signals flow down my arm onto the page, not sparing a moment to try and decode them for myself. We were the net. It was our job to catch the messages. It was for someone else far away, in Bermuda or England or Florida, to dissect their meaning.

Still, it wasn't hard to piece together what was happening. A fleet of U-boats, circling, hunting something. The frantic Morse blips of the Royal Navy ran through my mind like water, too late, too slow. The U-boats chattered to each other brazenly now, not caring who might be listening, certain of their targets. I wrote at a feverish pace, passing off one, two, five slips to the officer, hardly noticing as she slid each one from my desk.

The convoy's signals flickered frantically and then went silent. Around the room, girls were tight-lipped and pale. Next to me, Janey wrote with tears tracking down her cheeks. She had a brother in the merchant marine.

I snatched another piece of paper. I had never felt so small and so anonymous in this vast machine, knowing that somewhere over the ocean, guns were firing and men were dying, ships exploding into flame, people killed outright and drowning, and through it all the U-boats knifing like sharks to pick their prey.

Everyone, including me, gave a sigh of relief when the shift bell rang. I breathed in so deeply I came close to popping a button. The group of us filed quietly back towards the dorms, with none of the usual chatter or giggles. As I passed Elaine in the hallway, on her way to work the night shift, she pulled me aside.

"This arrived for you this afternoon." A letter.

"Thanks." I stuffed it in my pocket.

She started down the hallway, then turned back. "A group of us were thinking of having a picnic down by the water on our shore day later this week. You should come."

"Yeah, all right," I said. I could do with some sunshine and fresh air. It would maybe take my mind off things.

Elaine beamed, and then hurried to join the tail end of the night watch.

In my room, I sank down on the bed to tug off my shoes. I dug my thumbs into my soles, massaging until the circulation returned to my feet. I pulled the letter out of my pocket and lay back on the bed to read it.

I felt a lump rise in my throat at the sight of my mother's familiar handwriting.

Ma chère fille,
We received your letter of April fourth. We have all been fine
here. I have been keeping very busy with the Croix-Rouge. Just
last week we held a benefit for the troops at the Ritz-Carlton,
and everyone was so splendid about it. I wore my peacock green
gown—you remember the one with the beaded collar? When I saw
Ambassador Moffat's wife, she told me how impressed she was
with you joining up and doing your part—

I skimmed through a page and a half of details about the event, names of important guests and what food they had served and who had said what to my mother and how much money had been raised. A tight bubble rose in my chest. How could she be so focused on dresses and fine food and social politics when there was a war on?

I found what I was looking for in the final paragraphs.

I have considered your situation, and you must understand
what a terrible position you have put us all in. Your grand-père
has been in poor health over the past year, and we have all had to

have a care for his weak heart. Since you left, your grand-mère has had to give up attending daily mass in order to help Hélène care for the grandchildren. Your father is still working long hours at the military hospital, and I, of course, have been very busy with my volunteering.

I had a quiet word with your grand-mère about the circumstances you have found yourself in re: engaged to Landon, and I'm afraid she made it clear that unless you are properly married, she cannot allow you back under her roof. We are very lucky that my parents have supported us throughout this difficult time, and I fear what would happen if anything were to change. I know you will understand.

I've included a little something to help you with your dilemma (don't tell your papa!) and I have absolute confidence that you will sort it all out for the best. I look forward to seeing you at home again, when the war effort can spare you, and we can all continue on as before.

Beaucoup d'amour pour toi,

Maman

Tucked inside the envelope was a hundred and fifty dollars. I stared down at the money, unable to stop the tears that spilled over my cheeks. Even in my worst imaginings, it had never occurred to me that I wouldn't be allowed to come home. My mother's message was very clear: if I used her money to take care of this "dilemma" on my own, then I could return to my grandparents' house and everything would be fine. But this was the extent of what she was willing to do.

A sob rose in my throat. How many long hours had I spent at my mother's bedside, tending to her every need? When she couldn't leave her room, it had fallen to me to instruct the servants, play host to our guests, and keep my father company. I had been her closest confidante my entire life . . . No amount of money could make me forgive this betrayal.

More than ever, now, I had to reach Landon, make it clear how dire the situation was. Surely, once he knew that I couldn't go home, he would find a way to help me.

I got up and went to my trunk. I stuffed my mother's letter and the envelope of cash down at the bottom and opened the book of Whitman's poetry where I had hidden my latest unfinished letter to Landon. It wasn't there. I pawed through my trunk, checked all my pockets, my other books. Nothing.

I stood, looking around the room with new eyes. The book on my bedside table had slipped down between the table and the wall. The covers on my bed were as neat and tight as they always were, but my pillow—the pillowcase was the wrong side up, showing the slight stain I always put face down. I ran my finger along the mattress edge, where it met the bedframe. It was off by two inches, overlapping the wood. Someone had searched my room. If they had found that letter—

There was a knock at the door. I straightened, as guilty as if I'd been caught doing something wrong. More knocking, rapid and officious.

I opened the door. Petty Officer Mathers stood just outside. She took in my creased uniform and lack of shoes.

"Miss Beauxdons?"

I saluted automatically. "Yes, ma'am?"

"Commander Davis would like to see you, immediately."

"Yes, ma'am. If I could have one moment . . ." I glanced at my feet.

Mathers nodded, remaining in the doorway as I sat on the bed to put on my shoes. After I'd tidied my hair and put on my hat, I followed Mathers out of my room, down the corridor and up two flights of stairs to the top floor of the building. I had never been up here before. Each small office emitted the clack and whir of typewriters and telegraphers. I caught glimpses of tables spread with maps and papers, a few rooms with large naval charts pinned to their walls. Mathers didn't slow, and I was forced to walk quickly as she led me to the very end of the building. She stopped abruptly outside a door on the left and knocked twice.

"Enter!" came the brisk and unmistakable voice of our commanding officer.

Mathers opened the door and stepped inside. "Miss Beauxdons, ma'am."

The Kettle didn't look up from the papers she was reading, glasses perched on her nose.

"Very good, Mathers. Wait outside, please."

Petty Officer Mathers saluted and threw me a single, disdainful look before she stepped out and shut the door behind her.

I stood in the middle of the office, taking in the large window, the desk scattered with papers and pencils, the walls blank save for a map of the Atlantic seaboard. Cryptic little coloured labels had been pinned up and down the coast.

"So," the Kettle said, setting aside her paperwork. My attention snapped to her as she leaned back in her chair and folded her hands. "Miss Beauxdons, isn't it?"

"Yes, ma'am."

There were two chairs in front of the desk, but she did not invite me to sit.

"It has come to our attention that you enlisted in my division under a false name."

My knees went weak. "Ma'am?"

She picked up a folder from the desk, flipped it open and read aloud. "Miss Rebekah Marie Beauxdons, born 1922 in Montreal, Canada. Is that correct?"

"Yes, ma'am. Only—"

"Only?" The Kettle arched an eyebrow.

"Beauxdons is my mother's maiden name."

"I see."

"My father's surname is—"

"Kromer. Heinrich Kromer, born 1899 in Hamburg, arrived in Canada May 1920." She put the folder down on the desk. "Did you really think that, given you work for the intelligence arm of the Royal Navy, we wouldn't find out who your father is?"

I looked at my feet. "I'm sorry, ma'am. My father advised me to enlist under my mother's name, in the hope that—so that I would be spared any consequences."

The Kettle shook her head. "Your father has been a registered enemy alien for the past four years and, in that time, he has shown himself to be nothing other than an unremarkable physician with no ties to his homeland. The only thing he has done wrong was to encourage you to enlist under a false name." I opened my mouth to protest, but Davis waved her hand. "An understandable action, in the circumstances."

"Thank you, ma'am." There was a long pause, and I found myself leaning back towards the door. "If that is all, ma'am . . ."

"It's not." The Kettle sighed and withdrew a smaller sheet of paper from the folder. I bit back a gasp. My unsent letter to Landon, the one that had been in my trunk.

"Do you recognize this?" Commander Davis asked, turning the page towards me.

I nodded, tension building in my chest.

"Do you have anything you wish to tell me?"

"No, ma'am."

"Nothing at all?"

I shook my head, clenching my jaw to keep it from trembling. The Kettle sighed again, picked up the letter, and began to read aloud.

"I can't believe it of you—that you would promise me such sweet things and then no word for months. You must know the terrible situation you have put me in."

"Please, stop," I whispered, unable to meet her eyes.

"You admit it, then?"

I squeezed my eyes shut and nodded, not trusting my voice.

Davis sighed and I heard the chair creak as she resettled her weight. I forced my eyes open. She was staring at the desk, sparing me the full force of her gaze. "You stupid, stupid girl," she said at last. "As though I can stand to lose even one of you right now, let alone one of my best. Has he taken care of you, at least? You've heard back from him?"

"Ma'am?"

She put a finger to each temple and closed her eyes. "Please tell me your fiancé is overjoyed by this news and is paying for your train ticket home to your loving family until your convalescence is over."

Tears stung the edges of my eyes. I locked my fingers tighter together behind my back. "Ma'am."

The Kettle took off her glasses and pinched the bridge of her nose. Then she looked up at me. "Miss Beauxdons, given your conduct, you give me no choice but to discharge you, effective immediately.

Given the secrecy of what we do here, you will be discharged quietly to avoid drawing undue attention, but let me be clear that the lack of a public drumming out is a reflection on our work, and not a lenient view of your situation."

She drew in a breath and continued in a slightly quieter voice. "You will return your uniform and all ranking identifiers to Petty Officer Mathers, collect your personal effects, and vacate the premises by eighteen hundred tonight. You will not speak to the other girls. You are not to enter the mess hall or have any further contact with members of your unit. Failure to comply will result in disorderly conduct charges and further action. Do I make myself clear?"

I saluted, fingers trembling. "Yes, ma'am."

"I need not remind you that strictest secrecy is to be upheld. On pain of charges of treason. When anyone asks you what you did at Devil's Battery, you will tell them—?"

"I was a file clerk, ma'am. I had little to do with the actual war. It was mostly copying troop lists and collating."

"See that you remember that." The Kettle's eyes softened just a little. "Good luck, Beauxdons. I am truly sorry it ended this way."

"No more than I am, ma'am," I whispered.

"Close the door on your way out."

I did.

KIT

I was about to step out of the woods that surrounded the estate when I saw someone coming up the road towards me. I shrank back among the branches, holding my breath. As he drew closer, I recognized Isaak, his coat collar turned up against the damp. He passed close by my hiding place, heading towards the village.

I counted fifty heartbeats, and then stepped quietly out of the trees and followed him, keeping to the edge of the road, trusting the greenery to hide me.

I trailed him into the village and watched him enter the local pub. I stood under the eaves of a nearby building and smoked a cigarette while I waited. Finally, hunger and curiosity drew me inside.

The pub was only partly full. The smell of beer and meat pies wafted into my nose as I entered, shaking water off my coat and hat. I ordered a pint at the bar and took myself to a table in the corner, not too far from the fire. It was pleasant to sit and drink without someone's elbows in my ribs, without the constant jockeying and joking that buoyed up all conversation in the mess.

Isaak was in a far corner, his back to me. Sitting across the table from him was an older man, stocky and bearded, wearing civilian clothes—the man on the bicycle I had seen the night of the Christmas party, I was sure of it. As they talked, his gaze darted around every few minutes to see who might be observing them.

I drank my beer and pretended to read the newspaper while keeping watch from the corner of my eye. I couldn't hear what they were saying, but I could read the emotions on the man's face. Distress, anger. He gestured with his hands, growing more agitated, until Isaak motioned for him to contain himself. They were no longer drinking, too absorbed in their argument.

At last, the bearded man stood up and stalked out of the pub, snatching his jacket from the hook near the door. Isaak sank his head in his hands and sat like a statue for a few moments. I was about to steal out quietly when he got to his feet and hurried out the door.

I counted to twenty and then followed him. The rain had let up and left a misty haze in its wake. I lit another smoke and strolled along the street, trying to look like an airman out on a day pass and without a care in the world. I caught sight of them together up ahead. I stamped out my cigarette and walked faster.

At the next crossroads, they stopped, and the man turned to Isaak. I ducked behind a hedge and peered around it. The man said something I couldn't hear at this distance. They stood there together for another long, silent moment, as if arrested by the desire to say more. Then the bearded man walked away down the lane to the right. Isaak watched him go, and then continued up the road, hands in his pockets. I skirted the hedge, trying to time my steps to Isaak's, as we made the long climb back towards the base.

I tried to decide what to do. If I went straight to Commander Worthing, he would no doubt ask how long I had been suspicious of Isaak and I would have to confess that I had said nothing since December.

Isaak slowed and looked around quickly enough to make me shrink into the hedgerow. Then he stepped off the road and through a gate. I crept after him.

He was on the lee side of a stone wall. I didn't think, I simply acted. I drew my pistol and leapt through the gate and onto him, sending us both tumbling into the mud and the wet grass. Isaak's yelp of surprise was loud, as was our combined breathing as he struggled to push me off him. His hands locked around my throat. I wrestled my arm free and pointed the pistol at his head.

"Shut it," I hissed. Isaak's death grip on my neck loosened, just a little.

"McNair? What the fuck are you doing?"

"I could ask you the same thing. Who was that man?"

"What man?"

"The man in the pub. The man you were talking to."

"He's no one."

I adjusted my grip on the pistol. "I saw you with him the night of the Christmas party. He had a bicycle."

Isaak sagged a little underneath me. "He's a friend. No one important."

"You're late to briefings, you sneak off base alone—"

"It's not what you think!"

"The Station Commander will be the best judge of that. I'm arresting you on suspicion of treason and—"

"No, no. I'm not a traitor." There was a hitch in his voice.

"I know what I saw."

"No, you really don't."

It took me a moment to realize that he was laughing, not sobbing in fear.

"Shut up," I growled. "If you think they're going to go easy on you for selling secrets to the Germans, then you're—"

"You idiot. If I was a spook, do you really think I'd meet my contact in the village pub on a Wednesday afternoon?"

"Maybe you're a really stupid spook."

Isaak groaned, trying to ease the pressure of my weight on his ribs. "I have more reason to hate the Nazis than you—than anyone. Let me up."

I stood, letting Isaak sit up but keeping my pistol trained on him.

"Look, I will tell you, but you have to swear to me that you'll keep it quiet."

"I can't promise—"

"It's nothing that compromises the war effort or helps the enemy. It has nothing to do with the war whatsoever."

I frowned. "Then why all the sneaking around?"

Isaak picked grass off his boot. "You wouldn't understand."

"But you're going to tell me or I'm going to drag you back to base and into Worthing's office."

Isaak's face crumpled. "I'm not a spy, McNair. Please, I would do anything to kill them, to pay them back for what they did, for what they're doing." He looked up at me, his expression now anguished. "They killed my father. They burned my home. They took my friends." His voice hitched. "They tried to take me, but I ran, I left them behind . . ."

I slackened my grip on the gun, letting it rest on my knee. "Why?"

Isaak sighed. "I don't know how you say it in English. That man I spoke to, he is not just my friend; he is more like a brother, like a . . ."

All the pieces fell into place. The night of the Christmas party. Isaak's uniform rumpled and damp during briefings. The intensity of their conversation in the pub.

I lowered the gun. Isaak gathered his feet under him as though he was about to bolt as he waited for my response. I holstered the pistol and brushed the mud from my knees.

"I understand. I understand perfectly. That night of the party, he was giving you a Christmas present."

Isaak blushed a deep scarlet that made his pale eyebrows stand out even more. "Yes." He tilted his right hand to show me a metal ring, soldered at the edges, on his third finger.

"Then why were you arguing just now?"

"You were spying on us?"

"Can you blame me?"

He sighed. "There is something I want to do, but Matthew doesn't approve. He is worried for me, always."

"He must care for you very much."

Isaak nodded. "I am very lucky."

I held out a hand and tugged the man to his feet. "Come on, I'm starving. Let's go see if there's anything worth eating in that pub."

"There isn't," Isaak grumbled, falling in step with me as we turned our feet towards the village. "A whole bloody empire and the British still don't know what good food is."

"Well, then we'll drink until we don't care whether it's good or not."

Isaak laughed. "Cheers to that."

REBEKAH

Petty Officer Mathers escorted me back to my room and stood guard outside the door as I took off my uniform and badges and dressed in civilian clothes, now uncomfortably tight around the midriff. After I was ready, I sat for a long moment on the bed, staring at nothing. Maybe if I stayed here on this bed, time would stop and I wouldn't have to move forward.

Landon and I had come to an understanding that night, hadn't we? Perhaps I could have insisted we find a chaplain first thing the next morning, but before my head had fully cleared, Landon was onboard his ship and miles out of harbour, part of a convoy headed to Europe. He wouldn't have had any way of reaching me now. Not for the first time, I considered a more terrible reason as to why he hadn't replied.

From her post outside the door, Mathers coughed pointedly. I pulled my suitcase out from under my bed and began mechanically packing my books, my grand-mère's sewing kit, and my mother's letter with the cash. Everything else I tipped into my trunk, hardly caring if anything broke or got creased. I would have no chance to say goodbye to Elaine, though she would likely be able to work out for herself what had happened. For a moment I wondered who would take my place as her roommate. Which girl would sit at my desk in the communications room and place the headset over her ears. I wondered if she would find the owl in the wood grain, as I had.

Then Mathers knocked on the door, and I picked up my suitcase.

She walked with me out to the entrance of Devil's Battery, where a car waited for me. As the driver loaded my trunk into the rear seat, I turned to her, unsure whether to say goodbye, but she was already marching away. I got into the passenger seat and tucked my battered leather suitcase between my knees. The driver climbed in, and we drove through the gates, which closed promptly behind us. The Royal Navy was well and truly done with me.

It was a beautiful evening. The golden light on the bay seemed to mock me. The harbour was crowded with ships, and I could just see the guide ropes that held the submarine nets as they were raised up for the evening.

"So where's a girl like you going so late in the day?" the driver asked. He was a sergeant, judging by the chevrons on his arm. He had a nice smile.

It was on the tip of my tongue to say "nowhere," but I didn't want his pity. "To visit my aunt in town. She's sick and needs a hand with the kids."

"That's a shame," he said, tucking a cigarette between his lips and lighting it with one hand. "I was hoping you were a bird on leave and you could join some of us downtown. I know a nice place for dancing."

"Sorry, but my aunt is expecting me."

My driver chatted on amiably, saving me the trouble of sharing any more about myself by explaining that he was recently promoted, off on leave for a week and planning to meet an old school friend in the city. I murmured politely at the appropriate intervals, but it was only by keeping myself as still as possible that I avoided breaking into hyperventilating sobs.

At last, we rounded the curve of the bay and the city grew ahead of us. I could see the edge of the Citadel silhouetted against the ocean. I squeezed my memory, trying to remember the best way to Janey's uncle's apartment. Not that I had a key.

"A right turn up here, if you don't mind," I said, interrupting the sergeant's story about a fishing trip with his school chums.

He nodded and resumed talking. As the turnoff approached, he didn't slow the car, but continued straight. I turned to look at the street as it passed and then back at him.

"That was it, back—never mind. You can take the next turn up the hill."

He responded by pressing the gas pedal a little harder. "Are you sure you don't want to come out with us?"

The next street slid past, and the next.

"No, thank you. Here's fine. Let me off on the next block."

"My friend's a funny guy, always lots of laughs. And the place is nice—I think you'd like it."

"I really can't," I said, one hand gripping my suitcase handle. "I'm sorry. I can't let my aunt down."

"Really?" He flashed a grin at me, but it somehow felt less nice than before. "A girl like you, in civvies, leaving the base with all your kit to visit an aunt? It's a good story, darling, but you can't fool me."

"Let me out," I said firmly, my other hand on the door handle.

"Oh, come on, have a few drinks with us, some dancing. Your 'aunt' can wait." He slid his hand across the gearbox and onto my leg, pushing up under my skirt. I slapped him.

That startled him, and he took his foot off the gas long enough for the car to slow. I pulled hard at the door handle and the door flew open and I tumbled out into the road, scraping my knee badly as I landed. The car braked as I scrambled to my feet, surprised to find the suitcase still clutched in my left hand. I started running. The car circled in the road and drew up alongside me.

"Aw, come on, darling, don't be that way," the sergeant said out his window, the car crawling at the same rate as my footsteps. I didn't reply, concentrating on walking as fast as I could.

He followed me for another block, alternately wheedling and chastising me, until his patience ran out. "Stone cold bitch. You tease! Go to hell!" He slammed the car into a U-turn and disappeared back towards the harbour, taking my trunk with him.

I kept on for another few blocks until I was so out of breath I had to sit on my suitcase. I realized my knee was trickling blood and I wiped it away with my handkerchief. I had lost my hat somewhere. My face was sweaty and my hair stuck to my forehead.

I didn't recognize this part of the city. All thought of finding Janey's uncle's apartment vanished as I surveyed the blank, anonymous houses on either side of the street. My only option was to walk towards the harbour until I found a landmark I recognized and make my way to the train station from there.

It was a long, uncomfortable walk in the dark. My suitcase seemed to grow heavier with every step, no matter how often I switched hands. I sweated under my coat, but the night air chilled me when I took it off. Every block, I came closer to collapsing onto the sidewalk in defeat.

I heard the music before I turned the corner and saw the crowd of people standing outside a two-storey building. Shafts of light went off like a photographer's flash as the door opened at regular intervals. I paused on the other side of the road and stared at the familiar facade of the Bluebird Club. The handful of people who caught sight of me glanced immediately away, as though I was too painful to look at.

I stood for a long moment, watching couples walk arm-in-arm into the warmly lit doorway, as snatches of brass and drums spilled out into the night. I thought of the Becca who had walked out those doors with Landon, leaning on his arm like the couples I saw now, and I wished more than anything to reach back in time and strangle her.

Then I hefted my suitcase and crossed the road to the stage door. I knocked twice.

The man who opened it was the same one I had seen that December night; tall and broad-shouldered, almost blocking the doorway with his bulk. He scowled down at me, raised his eyebrows in a silent question.

"Hatti Dano, please."

He shook his head, but as he started to shut the door, I threw myself against it with a ferocity that alarmed both of us.

"Please, she knows me. My name is Becca. Tell her it's about the peach silk."

He contemplated me for a long moment, then said, "Wait here." He shut the door.

I stood on the gravel, staring at my scuffed shoes, feeling my shoulders ache and my stomach growl. The silent, frenetic battle I'd witnessed in the wireless room earlier today seemed to belong to another life, like a fever dream. Any moment I was going to be shaken awake by my mother and find myself safe in my own bed.

At last, the door opened again. "This way." The man gestured for me to follow him, and I did. He led me down a narrow corridor, then stopped outside a door with a handwritten sign that read "Miss Dano" and knocked.

"Enter!" She sang it. He opened the door.

The dressing room was little more than a broom closet made over with a mirror and a folding screen. Hatti was sitting at her vanity, putting a layer of mascara on her lashes, her hair not yet unwrapped from its satin scarf. A feather fan and boa were on the floor next to her stool. Her eyes met mine in the mirror as I hovered on the threshold, and then they widened in surprise.

Hatti set down her brush. "Thank you, Blink. I can take it from here."

At the man's gesture, I squeezed into the room, next to an overflowing rack of costumes and a sewing mannequin pinned with fabric swatches. The door shut behind me. I felt very drab in this brightly lit space of feathers and sequins.

"Sorry, it's a bit tight," Hatti said, turning to face me. "When I talked Albert into giving me my own dressing room, this isn't exactly what I had in mind." She was dazzling, with her full lips rimmed in red and kohl around her eyes. She folded her hands in her lap, clearly waiting for me to begin.

I swallowed. "I don't know if you remember me," I stuttered, "but I fixed your dress—"

"Yes, I remember."

"You said that if I ever needed anything, anything at all . . ."

The room swam in my vision and that was when I gave in and collapsed to the floor.

JULY 1943

KIT

WE TOOK TO MEETING AT THE VILLAGE PUB WHENEVER Isaak and I could get some hours of leave. On this particular afternoon, Matthew had joined us, and we ordered pints and sat outside under an awning. Last night's op had been a close call, with a Luftwaffe fighter gliding up underneath us and firing into the belly of *Friday's Girl,* only missing by inches. I was still shaking off the nerves, and it was pleasant to sit in the garden and put my feet up on an empty chair.

I kept quiet, observing them, as Isaak reminisced about his childhood in Prague and Matthew talked about growing up in a mining town in Northumberland. He was too old to enlist, though he had tried several times at the beginning of the war. Instead, he worked as a mechanic in the village, fixing up vehicles and farm equipment. The soldered metal ring on Isaak's finger had come from his shop.

It wasn't obvious, certainly not in their words or in their gestures. They were as careful as Laurie and I were. If one knew where to look, however, it was clear. Both of Matthew's feet were oriented towards Isaak under the table, and Isaak's shoulders were turned to face him, subtly excluding me.

Matthew's laughter shook me out of my thoughts, back to the garden and the warm glass of beer in my hand.

"And I ran home with my trousers in my hands, and thanked God my family weren't farmers," he concluded. Isaak giggled, looking over at me. I grinned with a levity I didn't feel and took another gulp of beer.

"What about you?" Isaak said to me. "You grew up on a farm, no? Are Canadian sheep just as bad?"

I let them persuade me into talking about my family's farm, and every hare-brained stunt I'd ever pulled. It felt easier to tell these stories now, as though I was recounting the antics of a favourite cousin and not my younger self. Encouraged by Isaak's incredulous expressions, I exaggerated Landon's various courtships of every girl in the county, and Jep's habit of leaving gates open behind him, with disastrous results. Watching Matthew laugh loudly enough to draw looks from passersby, I wished my little brother could be here. Jep would like this pub, with its cheerful striped awning and the twittering of sparrows in the hedge near us. He and Isaak would be good friends.

Then, just as quickly, I was horrified at the thought of Jep in a flight suit, watching his cheerful face disappear behind the glass of a Hurricane. As I got up from the table, insisting I would stand the next round, a prickle of gooseflesh ran down my arms. All the way to the bar, I fought a sense of creeping dread, as though my careless wish might draw my brother here, and into further danger.

The shadows had grown long by the time we finished our third round. I looked at my watch and realized it was time to head back to base.

Matthew walked with us as far as the edge of the village. Isaak and I carried on, and when we reached the place where the road crossed a small stream, he stopped on the bridge, looking down into the ravine of green moss and wildflowers. I leaned next to him.

"Do you ever think, Christopher, that maybe we aren't doing the right thing?" he said.

I swallowed. "I try not to think, as best I can." It wasn't talked about at the base, but everyone knew. Victory, at any cost, was the goal of Bomber Command.

"I don't expect you to understand what it was like. To you—Germans, Czechs—we are all one people, but the Führer . . . before he brought destruction to Britain, he destroyed us first."

I nodded. Everything I knew had been filtered through newspaper columns, radio broadcasts, speeches from politicians. It had seemed like such a cut-and-dried conflict. Germany was out to conquer the world and the Allies had to stop it, but of course the truth was more complicated.

Isaak took a shaky breath. "They were going to make me enlist. They had ways, terrible ways, to make sure you obeyed. But after my father was killed and my friends were taken away—all men like me, who had done nothing except gather in the wrong bars—I had nothing left to lose. So I escaped to France and then came here. I wanted to fight, I wanted to kill them—for my father, my friends, my little sister."

He turned bleak eyes towards me. "Do you know who works in those factories we fly over every night? Women, children, prisoners of war. People rounded up and forced to work, like slaves."

I felt cold. I had seen what remained of London, after the Blitz, on my way up to Lincolnshire.

"I'm sorry," I said quietly. "But we have to break the supply chains. It's the only way."

I wasn't sure if I believed it anymore, but what else was there to do? The dark belly of a bomber, thousands of feet in the air, was not a place of moral nuance. When our guns fired on a Schwalbe intent on dropping us from the sky, we either killed or were killed. The last eighteen months had made that very clear to me.

"Sometimes I think you are right," Isaak said, "but I cannot do it anymore. My friends, my family, people just like me—they are the ones below us at night. They are the ones in the centre of the flare targets, and I cannot . . . I cannot—"

"You want to get out," I said bluntly.

"I am not a coward," Isaak said, his voice harsh. "But I can't do this."

Everything that had been drilled into me about cowardice and dodging one's duty hammered at my skull, telling me to go straight back to base and report Isaak's planned desertion to Worthing.

Instead, I moved closer to him and placed a hand on his arm. "How?"

"I'll pick a night next week when the weather's bad and we're stood down. I need you to cover for me, to buy me some time to get away. I'll meet Matthew on the road and then we can head north to—"

I held up a hand. "Don't tell me the rest."

Isaak gave a shaky laugh. "Right, of course."

I watched the current below us pull a stray flower blossom down the stream. "Don't risk meeting him on the road. I know a good place." I led him away towards the estate to show him the abandoned gardener's shed.

REBEKAH

I nestled the final bead into place, securing it with three lock stitches. I snipped the tail of the thread, shook out Hatti's dress and laid it over the sofa arm. Whoever had made the costume had barely tacked the beads into place along the hem. I defied even one to drop off now.

I heaved myself to my feet and replaced the dress on its hanger. Hatti had flown out of the dressing room fifteen minutes earlier in a cloud of feathers and perfume, leaving me to tidy the makeup brushes and discarded clothes. I stretched, feeling the bones in my spine pop, and went out into the corridor.

I followed the sound of cymbals and trumpets into the wings. Blink was there, standing guard at the stage door, and he gave me a nod as I passed. My usual stool was perched at stage left, hidden from the audience by a thick red curtain, but it gave me a clear view. The best seat in the house, Hatti liked to joke when she came tumbling into the wings just long enough for me to hustle her out of one dress and into another, the band playing an interval with little snare drum snaps of anticipation.

She was halfway through "Shoo-Shoo Baby" and the dance hall was starting to heat up. I'd seen her routine many times by now, but she always seemed to add something new. A different fan twirl, a new line of banter with the crowd, a new trill at the end of a note. It made sense, given that most of the patrons came here often and she couldn't afford to bore them. A nudge at my elbow and Blink pressed a cold drink into my hand. I smiled my thanks and settled in to watch the rest of the song.

The old me would have been scandalized by Hatti's bare thighs, by her dance moves, by the suggestive remarks of the band backstage.

The new me found it wonderful and strange. In this world, my condition barely warranted a second glance. Here, I was simply Becca, Hatti's *costumière* and friend, with all the implied nuance. There were no family names here, no reputations to preserve. I was free.

Hatti and I lived on opposite sides of the clock. She stayed up until two or three in the morning at the dance hall, then came home and slept until noon before going back in for rehearsals, or out for drinks with friends. I, on the other hand, had been moulded into an early riser, first by the military and now by the demands of my bladder and the fact that sleeping had become more uncomfortable by the week.

Her apartment was on the second floor of a tall, narrow building in the north end of Africville. To reach it, I had to climb a set of steep stairs with a carpet runner that had once been red and gold but was now a muddy brown. It had just one bedroom, a small kitchenette with a stove, and a bathroom with an ancient clawfoot tub. A small balcony off the sitting room overlooked the street, with a slip of the harbour waters visible through the rooftops to the east. Hatti took the bedroom, as was her right, and I slept on the ancient sofa in the living room. The landlady lived on the third floor with her eleven-year-old son, and the ground-floor apartment was tenanted by a family of seven, whose arguments and crashing dishes often kept me awake.

That first morning after I was kicked off the base, I woke to sunlight streaming through the narrow balcony door, and Hatti's faint snores from the bedroom. I scrubbed the kitchen and made breakfast for us both from what little was in the cupboards. Then I sat, at a loss, in the tiny living room.

Hatti's costume from the night before lay crumpled in a heap. Several of its feathers were bedraggled and the back seam was torn.

I took the dress and my sewing kit into the better light on the balcony. By the time Hatti stumbled out of bed, I had rendered the
torn seam invisible and straightened and reattached the feathers.
When I came back inside, I found Hatti at the kitchen table in a
nylon robe, feet on the opposite chair, eating a jam-slathered biscuit
and reading a magazine. She took one look at me, at the mended
dress in my arms, at the clean kitchen and nodded. "You can stay."

I was Hatti's *costumière*, but I also took in mending and laundry from our neighbours to earn some cash. Hatti refused to
accept anything for rent, insisting that I was a guest, but I used
my ration coupons to bring home food for the week and bought
soap and toothpaste. Every day I swept and tidied the small apartment, aired out the bedding, emptied the ashtrays and washed
the dishes. Gradually Hatti's bachelor living quarters had grown
clean and bright, smelling more of soap and fresh salt air than
stale cigarettes.

I soon outgrew the clothes I'd arrived in and scoured rag bins
and charity shops for others. When she wasn't wearing her performance attire, Hatti lived exclusively in morning robes, tailored
pants, blouses and a seemingly inexhaustible collection of silk
scarves and hats.

Some nights, I managed to stay up until Hatti came home,
fired up from a night of performing, and we talked and drank and
smoked until dawn. She taught me all the words to "Hitler Has
Only Got One Ball" and jokes so filthy my mother would have
blushed. Some nights, too, after a few drinks, she would pull me
into the bedroom and we'd mess around, all sweaty breasts and
gin-soaked lips, and she'd fall asleep in my arms, as boneless as
a starfish. I'd lie awake, staring out the open window at the little
patch of sky I could see between the buildings, feeling the breeze

drift over my naked skin. If I sometimes thought of a different pair of eyes reflecting firelight while Hatti's mouth moved over me, what did it matter? I was certain she did the same.

When Hatti's landlady, Mrs. Tsu, found out that I was a woman of education, she agreed to lower Hatti's rent by a dollar if I would teach her son English in the evenings. Wei was a bright boy, though not much interested in lessons. I had only a few books with me and so, when we had exhausted *Kitty Foyle* and *Leaves of Grass* and Mrs. Tsu's battered copy of the Bible, I scavenged the local shops and came up with some hard-boiled novels a young boy might enjoy. I spent my evenings on the front steps of Mrs. Tsu's building, listening to Wei read in a faltering voice about the detective's clever attempts to catch the criminal, and the woman with long legs who came to seduce him.

A few weeks after arriving at Hatti's, I had replied to my mother's letter with a brief note to say that I had left the navy and was staying with a girlfriend. That I was doing well, and there was no need to worry. She could read into that whatever she liked. I didn't mention the money she had sent and mailed the letter with no return address. I had intended to write another letter, filling her in on my life and letting her know where she could write to me, but as time passed, I always found an excuse to put it off.

While I was certain Hatti could have helped me find the right kind of doctor, by the time I had found my bearings and settled into this new life, I was already more than halfway along. Somewhere between stumbling into Hatti's dressing room that night and now, I had stopped thinking of my condition as a problem to be solved and started considering it an unexpected adventure. I kept the cash my mother had sent me in an envelope in my suitcase, adding the few dollars each week I earned from sewing and mending. It wasn't much of a nest egg, but it was mine.

For the first time in my life, my time was my own. No military bells, no interruptions from my mother, sweeping through the house in one of her moods, nor instructions from my father with his rigid sense of decorum. I ate when I was hungry and worked while the light was good and laughed with Hatti into the night. In the late sunlight of summer evenings, I would sit on the balcony looking out towards the harbour and count the ships on the silver water, cigarette smoke curling from between my fingers, feeling an exquisite kind of happiness I was hard-pressed to name.

KIT

The following week was overcast, with a heat that covered the ground and refused to lift. On the day that the *Siren* and her crew were stood down, I rose early and spent the morning doing small, unpleasant tasks so I wouldn't be tempted to seek out Isaak: mending a shirt, darning socks, polishing my boots and getting my hair cut. I was tense, failing to laugh at a particularly rude joke Vanier told over lunch in the mess. Later, Laurie followed me to the barracks to demand I tell him what was wrong.

"Nothing, I'm just hot." I threw myself down on my bunk and pulled out the army edition of *Kitty Foyle* I had read over seven times by now, flipping to a random page. "I'm not in the mood for cards, Hartwick." He lingered by my bed until I glared up at him. "Isn't there anyone else you can lose to?"

"Fuck you too, McNair," he muttered and stalked out. I stared at the page without reading a word, telling myself it wasn't my fault that my bad mood was catching.

The *Siren* may have had the night off, but *Friday's Girl* did not. The briefing room was hot and cramped, and the place heated more with every man who entered. Worthing was already sweating in his uniform, big rivulets running down the sides of his neck, and Sandish's moustache drooped.

At last, the doors opened again and the remainder of the crews joined us. I sat between Pete and Vanier, as far from Laurie as I could get, while the room slowly filled with gunners, bomb aimers, engineers and wireless operators. The faces in this room shifted from night to night, men suddenly disappearing and being replaced just as quickly. I was ashamed to realize I could no longer name the crew of *Scout's Honour* or picture their faces. They had washed away in the tide of blood and smoke that billowed over the Channel.

There was a knock at the door, and another wing commander entered, followed by Isaak. I sat up, immediately tense. As Isaak found a seat on the other side of the room, the WC jogged quickly to the front and whispered in Worthing's ear, handing him a folder. Worthing scowled before waving the man away. He flipped open the folder and scowled at it as well, then slapped the folder shut.

"Flying Officer Keyserling."

Isaak looked up.

"It seems we need one more gunner. Since you have the most ops in a turret before you became a navigator, you'll be joining the boys going up in one of the Stirlings on the decoy mission."

Sandish consulted a clipboard. "*Washington* is available, sir."

I was on my feet before I knew what I was doing. "Sir, that plane isn't fit to fly."

"McNair, sit down," Pete whispered, but I ignored him.

"Sir, it should have been decommissioned weeks ago, with the engine trouble it had on its last flight." My voice seemed to be coming from very far away.

"Thank you for your input, McNair." Worthing stared me down like an outraged bull. "But Bomber Command is confident in their choice."

"They are flying targets! Do you know how many Stirlings we've lost since—"

A sharp yank on my elbow brought me back into my seat. "Shut up or you'll get us thrown out of here," the skipper hissed in my ear. The men around me whispered to each other, the disciplined silence disturbed by my outburst.

Sandish took a deep breath, mustering even more gravitas than usual. "*Washington* is fit to fly. She was personally inspected by Sergeant Hedley and his men."

"I'm surprised the chief erk took his head out of his ass long enough to have a look," Laurie drawled from farther down the row. Pete whipped around to glare in his direction.

"Pilot Officer Belmont, do you need a moment to restore discipline to your crew?" Sandish snapped.

"No, sir," Pete said. "The heat, sir—it's making everyone forget themselves."

I glanced over at Isaak. He was pale, resolutely staring at a spot somewhere beyond the chalkboard.

Worthing stepped forward, leaving Sandish to puff and splutter. "You all have your assignments," he said. "Dismissed."

I stood and started towards Isaak, but Pete grabbed my bicep and forcibly steered me out of the room and into a side corridor.

"What were you thinking?" he said in a furious whisper. "Contradicting a ranking officer?"

"I was only saying what everyone else was thinking, Skipper."

"And was everyone else thinking about the best way to spook the *Washington*'s crew? The best way to shake the men before a flight?"

"I didn't—"

"You know as well as I do that morale is hanging by a thread around here. Your insightful comments in there did no one any favours."

"But the chief erk is a drunk and that kite is—"

"You could have come to me, to Sandish, to anyone with that concern, instead of running your mouth off in there."

He was right, dammit, but I was scanning the rapidly departing airmen for Isaak.

"McNair, are you listening to me?"

"Yes, Skip. I'm sorry. Next time, I will voice my concerns to you in private."

Pete opened his mouth to reply but caught sight of something over my shoulder. "Hartwick!" he thundered and strode past me, muttering, "We'll finish this later."

Free, I darted through the crowds now heading towards the mess hall. Isaak wasn't there or in the barracks or the privies. Outside again, I heard an uptick in noise and commotion from the hangars. Isaak wouldn't have run for it. He wouldn't be as stupid as to—

I took off at a quick jog. The heat was still oppressive, the clouds heavy with unfallen rain. The lawn beside the kitchens was empty. I turned, looked down the hill towards the fence. A figure was striding determinedly towards it. Isaak.

I sprinted for him, not caring who saw me. I grabbed the back of his jacket before he could haul himself up the chain-link. He gave a yelp of surprise and we tumbled onto the grass. He rolled and came up on his knees, raising his fists, and then he saw it was me.

"I wasn't supposed to go up tonight," he said. "I won't. I can't leave Matthew waiting, in the dark—"

Tears were pooling in his eyes. I glanced around to make sure no one was watching us. "Listen to me," I said. "We'll get you out of this. You can say you're sick, you have the runs, you're feverish . . ."

Isaak shook his head miserably. "They'll know I'm faking. I had a medical just yesterday. They'll label me LMF."

Lack of moral fibre. We'd had only one such case on this base and, after they'd shipped him off to somewhere in Wales, his name was never mentioned again.

Isaak looked up at me. "I'm not a coward, I'm not. But I can't do this."

"I know, I know," I said, rubbing his shoulders the way I would calm a spooked horse. He sat there, shuddering with barely contained sobs as I looked out past the fence at the green fields, the distant forest and the piling of clouds on the horizon. The breeze smelled of damp earth and ozone. It would rain before the night was out.

I said, "I have an idea."

"Bomb going now," Laurie said. I braced myself as *Friday's Girl* rose suddenly in the air, free of the weight of the bomb casings. There was a distant boom far beneath us.

"Incendiaries now," said Thompson. "Nice and bright."

"New course, McNair," Pete said.

"Round to port, Skip. Three four oh." My mouth moved and my pencil never left the chart, but my mind was far outside this metal box. *Friday's Girl* droned, all four engines straining against the wind and time, the sound of Hurricanes chasing the Luftwaffe above and below us. My thoughts were with the *Washington*, where Isaak was locked in the rear turret, alone and freezing despite the electric suit. And in the tumbled-down garden shed back in Lincolnshire, where Matthew was waiting for him.

We banked sharply, turning towards the Channel and home, Pete steering for the coordinates I'd spit into the headset. I checked and rechecked my calculations, my watch reflecting the single light over the nav desk. I could just see Ranbir's face opposite me, thrown into grotesque relief.

My plan was pure insanity. Isaak would do his duty as usual while the bombing run went ahead, and then, on the return, go silent as they went through the flak lines. He would already have his chute on and the chances of any of his crew taking the risk of going to the rear turret to check on him were low. If they did, he would simply lie limp and hold his breath. Rear gunners were exposed and easy targets: he wouldn't be the first or the last one to silently die while his crewmates celebrated a successful return. Then, when they were across the Channel and just over the shore, he would bail out. Silently, quietly. The drop would be short, so he'd have to time his chute opening carefully, but with a little luck, he'd land in a field ten miles from the base, ditch the chute and uniform, and then make his way to the estate and Matthew.

It was stupid and crazy, but once I'd suggested it, Isaak's tears disappeared. I'd emphasized the risk—the short drop, the dangers of being seen by anti-aircraft and mistaken for an enemy pilot. It would be safer to wait until another night. Matthew would understand.

"I can't wait any longer," Isaak had said, and then he'd leaned in and kissed my cheek with such tenderness. "It'll be all right, you'll see."

After his footsteps had faded away, I sat in the early twilight, looking out at the clouds that roiled ever closer across the field.

A boom and then another. The plane jagged side to side, rattling equipment. I couldn't see what was happening outside, and the sounds were too distorted to arrange into any clear picture. Not for the first time, I wished I were in Laurie's place, lying in the belly of the plane within a clear glass dome, looking down over the landscape. More dangerous, yes, but at least I'd be able to see what was happening.

"Flak coming up from our starboard side," Wilkins called.

"I can feel it," said Thompson.

"I can see it," Laurie chimed in.

I glanced at the map. There was no flak line marked. It must be a new installation. I reached for the pencil. "Skip, how far would you say—"

A sudden whoosh and then a burning smash as shrapnel came through the windshield. Metal screeched on metal and I heard Vanier's yelp and the scream of a fighter grazing the roof of our plane. I was on the floor, looking up at the nav desk. A burst of machine gun fire from our upper and rear turrets.

"Report!" came Pete's sharp order through the headset.

"Jerry on our starboard, Skip," said Wilkins, his words punctuated by more gunfire.

Thompson's voice now. "I see him." The side of my head felt hot and numb, my ears ringing and my headset dangling half off my neck.

I tried to speak but my tongue was thick in my mouth. Everything seemed very far away and very close at the same time. I was a giant stretched out on the floor and their voices were tiny buzzing flies in my ears.

Ranbir crouched next to me. "McNair? McNair, can you hear me?"

The floor was sticky. I touched my left ear, and my hand came away black in the dim light of the cabin. My helmet was torn, one earmuff hanging limp. More gunfire, the plane lurching left to right in the dark. I rolled with it, too stunned to resist.

"Vanier, I need you back here." Ranbir's voice was tight, his hands shaking as he grabbed my shoulder.

"A little busy at the moment," Vanier replied.

The plane plunged, then veered left, wove up and down. Ranbir clutched my jacket, holding me in place. *Friday's Girl* groaned and protested, her weight working against the quick manoeuvres. Another splutter of gunfire from the turrets.

"Do you see him?" Pete asked.

"I got him dead to rights," came Thompson's crackled reply. Another staccato of machine gun fire, and under my ribs I felt the whole plane shudder in response.

"Got him! Right in the mouth!" Thompson cried. My right ear filled with gleeful shouts.

"You got him?" Pete asked.

"He's gone, down and burning."

"I see him now," said the skipper. "Singh, what's going on back there?"

"McNair's been hit."

Another set of hands grabbed my head. I winced as a flashlight beam pointed directly down into my face. Vanier rolled me onto my right side and held me in place by the shoulder.

"How is he?"

"Hard to say, Skipper." Vanier looked at Ranbir. "Hand me that med kit."

Pete's voice cracked. "Singh, I need you to pick up the nav. Vanier will see to him."

"Another one to port," came Wilkins's voice as Ranbir moved to the nav desk.

More staccato gunfire and then a sudden drop in altitude that sent my stomach lurching and something skittering across the floor of the plane. More shots and then a whine that increased in pitch until it was a scream. I wanted to block my ears, but Vanier held my arms at my sides.

An explosion, so close it buffeted the plane sideways. Laurie whooped over the headset.

"Got 'em!"

"Nice shot, Thompson!"

"Vanier, I need you back up front." Pete's voice was eerily calm against a backdrop of explosions and engine noise.

"One moment, Skip." He pressed a wad of bandage against my ear, and I stifled a moan. It burned, and the pressure spiked through my head and into the backs of my eyes. "McNair, can you hear me?" I took two deep breaths. Opened my eyes. Vanier's stupid moustache was inches from my face.

"I'm flattered but normally I insist a man buy me dinner first," I croaked. There was laughter over the intercom and the engineer sighed with relief.

"Bad news, Skip, he's still alive." Vanier squeezed my shoulder before springing up and returning to the cockpit.

"Takes more than that to put down Lucky McNair," Laurie drawled from below me. I smiled and immediately regretted it.

"All right, hush up everyone. McNair, break time is over." The pilot's voice seemed even drier than before, if that was possible.

I sat up, mentally checking all my limbs. I was intact, except for the wet trickle behind my left ear.

"On my way, Skip," I said. I let Ranbir help me back into the nav seat and wrap a bandage tight enough to hurt around my forehead. I picked up the pencil and looked at my watch. "Anyone have eyes on a tower spire?"

I felt rather than heard six sighs of relief over the mics.

"No, too much cloud," said Pete.

"I see it, Skip," Laurie said. "Portside and down, just past our tail."

"Okay." I drew three quick lines, the numbers aligning and shifting in my head.

"Skipper, turn port, oh seven one. Prepare for the next flak line in twenty minutes."

The bandage was soaked through and leaking by the time we descended to the runway. Ranbir had handed me an extra roll of the stuff to press against my head, but I had still dripped blood on the nav desk and my flight suit and the charts. As the aircraft came to a standstill and the engines died, we were quickly surrounded by ground crew. I stepped out of the doors, avoiding the pool of blood—I deliberately refused to think of it as mine—on the floor. Vanier leapt out of the cockpit and began shouting orders at the erks. The skipper met me near *Friday's* nose, his icy composure cracking a little at the sight of me.

I held up my hands. "I'm all right. It looks worse than it is."

An arm wrapped around my shoulders from behind and hugged me tight.

"You had us worried there for a moment, McNair." Laurie's smile was in place, but his eyes betrayed real concern. "Lord knows we need someone to keep this flying circus on course."

"Are you telling me McNair was navigating those last few miles?" Wilkins said, shaking free of his life vest. "By all the wrong turns, I assumed it was Singh."

"Nice shooting, Wilkins," I said. "I can only assume the Kraut hung in the air wearing red panties to make it easier for you."

As our crew made its way towards the trucks, I looked around at the kites already landed. I hadn't spotted the *Washington* before our truck was bumping its way back to the base.

"To medical, McNair. We'll handle the debrief." Pete's tone left no room for argument, and I let Ranbir lead me to the medical bay, where the soaked bandage was removed and my head doused in alcohol, and a few stray pieces of flak were picked out of my scalp. I was lucky, the nurse told me. Head wounds always bleed, she said, as she sutured my skin together, and mine would heal, likely without much of a scar. I thought, suddenly, of my brother, lying in the dirt of the sheep field.

She rebandaged me and gave me a shot of penicillin and a slip that excused me from duty for two days. I was hardly listening, my attention focused on the sound of aircraft landing out in the field. I told Ranbir I was going to go lie down in the barracks, but instead I walked back to the airfield.

Most of the bombers were back, along with the majority of the Hurricanes.

I pulled the nearest erk aside. "Has the *Washington* come back yet?"

He grunted a negative and shook off my grip, giving my bandaged head a look.

I walked all around the field, my head throbbing. The bandage grew warm with fresh blood, but I couldn't rest. I searched the hangars, one by one, until the chief erk caught me and threw me out, threatening to call the nurses.

Unable to let go, I sat down against the outside wall of a hangar, out of everyone's way, and waited.

The light in the east grew steadily. It had rained here while we were gone, and the ground was damp. The sky was less overcast, the pink-red dawn blushing the underbelly of mauve clouds. A trio of Hurricanes came in, without their bomber. The three pilots conferred quietly with the ground crew and then piled into a waiting truck alongside the crew of a Halifax that had landed a few minutes earlier. After the trucks went off, it was quiet except for the sounds of the mechanics hauling the planes into the hangars and beginning their repairs.

A light wind ruffled my hair where it wasn't trapped beneath the bandages. My mouth was dry and my eyes burned with lack of sleep. The whole world seemed brighter and sharper, every sound magnified against the silence of the dawn.

And that is how I heard it. The low, far-off drone of an engine in trouble. I stood up, scanning the sky. I spotted a bomber flying low and unsteadily, a single Spitfire flying escort off its port. As it drew closer, I could see smoke billowing from under the left wing. At least one engine down, maybe two. It stumbled in the air, falling two dozen feet before righting itself. By now the sound was unmistakable, and the ground crew had reappeared on the tarmac, looking up just as I was, watching the Stirling limp towards the base. The chief erk came out, took one look and swore, sending his underlings for the firehoses, the medics, and stretchers.

I strained to see her markings as she careened onto the runway, one wing scraping the ground and then rocking up again. There was the squeal of brakes and a huge billow of smoke and the smell of charred rubber and burning oil, and then the firehoses were around her and the runway was a flurry of activity and shouting. I stayed where I was.

The smoke cleared around the nose enough to reveal a crown over crossed swords. *Duchess.* Men were swarming the wreckage now, pulling off loose sheets of metal, stretcher-bearers sprinting towards the aircraft. Shouted orders. The hiss of water on hot metal. Medics crawling into the carcass.

Black body bags were beginning to emerge. The pilot was lifted out of the cockpit and put on a stretcher, his face and torso bloodied. Medics began running him towards the infirmary. I rushed forward to intercept them.

"Is there anyone else?"

The pilot looked up at me, the side of his face burned. Several hands reached to pull me away but I shook them off, jogging to keep up with the stretcher.

"The *Washington*, was she behind you?"

He exhaled a shaky breath. "Took a dead hit," he wheezed. "Poor bastards didn't have a chance."

I grabbed the edge of the stretcher, halting its movement. "Did you see anyone bail out?"

He gave me a pitying look through his remaining eye. "They're in pieces over France, boy."

I let go, and the medics pushed on, rushing him into a nearby truck and roaring off to the medical bay. People swarmed past me. The *Duchess* groaned and creaked as the erks stripped away the burnt engines and hauled her into the hangar.

Overhead, the sky grew brighter, throwing a red wash over the bricks and the gravel, the windows reflecting back the same shade. I waited where I was as the field emptied and the morning rose higher, but no other aircraft came.

I stood in the open field for one last moment and breathed in a wind that smelled like sea salt and crushed grass and engine oil. Then I turned and walked down the lane to the gate, flashed my leave pass at the guard without speaking. The road was deserted. I turned my feet downhill and began the long walk to the gardener's shed.

REBEKAH

"FINE, IF THAT'S HOW YOU FEEL!"

"It is!"

The door slammed shut behind her, and Hatti pounded down the stairs.

It was an autumn heat wave, the sun slamming down on the asphalt streets like a hammer. The plants wilted in the heat, the concrete breathed dust so fine it seemed to hang in the air. The gulls were silent and the waves moved sluggishly against the harbour wall. The whole city held its breath for rain and the fall's cool embrace.

It had started as a silly argument over a shirt she'd left on the couch and spiralled out of my control before I could stop it. Hatti was hungover and cranky; I was sleepless and irritable. I regretted my words, but not enough to chase after her. The apartment was stifling even with the shades drawn. I'd propped open the door to the balcony in the hope of enticing the smallest breeze inside. I paced around, fanning myself with a folded newspaper, feeling the sweat drip down my lower back and pool between my breasts. I was heavy, the baby in my pelvis pulling me off-kilter and weighing down my bones. A single fly buzzed around the ceiling, bumping senselessly off the plaster.

I was an interloper, a guest who had overstayed her welcome in Hatti's otherwise single and unburdened life. The baby might come any time now. I wished for it. To be free of the waiting and the weight and this never-ending "in-between" that held me in thrall. Every hot day pooled and glistened and flooded into the next, until it felt like I had lived these months a dozen times over, doomed to a purgatory of sweat and tinned beans and peeling tile and starched cotton. I had work that needed doing, but I couldn't stomach the idea of drawing a bundle of cloth into my lap and trying to wield a needle with my sweaty fingers. There was always tomorrow.

I shut the balcony door and locked up the apartment, then went down the stairs, pausing to catch my breath at the bottom.

Most anyone who had the means had left the city, while those who didn't huddled in the shade of storefront awnings and under the trees on the cooler lawns on the north side of town. The shore, when I reached it, was a strip of dusty, dirty sand in front of some old pilings supporting a dock. I stripped off my shoes and waded into the water. It was cool and I felt my temper ease.

Last night, when the heat had finally broken enough for me to fall into a light sleep, I had dreamed again. These dreams had been happening since I got pregnant, at first only confusing snatches of colour and conversations, scenes that felt like memories but not my own. In one I stood on the deck of a ship, the whole ocean turned luminescent green and yellow beneath me. In another I flew through clouds and smoke, the heat of a fire singeing my belly. The faster I flew, the higher the flames reached until they seemed to touch my skin and I awoke gasping and sweating in the dark.

Last night's dream was of the day we'd spent haying in the summer heat. I trailed behind, trying to catch up to the wagon as Kit and Jep pitched hay. The wagon was floating on water and the horses were made of mechanical gears, chugging forward. Across the field, I could see a great wave of grass headed for the wagon and I cried out a warning, but Kit and Jep carried on, oblivious. The grass was tangled around my legs and I couldn't run to them, and all the time the wave was coming and the metal horses walked on.

I'd woken alone on the couch, fierce sun already pouring in through the balcony door. My head pounded, and the air felt heavy and thick in my lungs, my whole body swollen and aching with a pressure I couldn't release.

The dream had brought with it a hundred moments I hadn't let myself think about in years. I thought of them now, as I walked along the beach. The smell of the air as Kit and I came back from the river after our first kiss, the bubbling, giddy feeling in my chest. The old stable behind the church hall, Kit's hot breath on my thigh and the sharp edge of the shelf in my back. Dozens of smiles, snatches of conversation. The field and the graze of a nipple against my knee. And finally, the night in the cottage, with the rain drumming on the roof. How Kit had pushed the hair back from my face and kissed me as though I was the cure for drowning.

I didn't notice the tears until they dripped onto my belly. I had waddled my way to the edge of a pier and could go no farther. There was nothing to do but scrub my face on my sleeve and begin the long, slow walk back to the apartment.

KIT

The crew room was more crowded than usual that evening. Everywhere I turned, someone bumped my shoulder or belched in my face. Half an American fighter squadron had come down on our airstrip in an emergency landing a few days earlier, and the airmen had made themselves right at home while our erks fixed their Thunderbolts. With space in the barracks already limited, the presence of another half-dozen men caused tempers to flare. They had smoked, drunk and cheated their way through card games in the mess hall, and always pushed ahead in line to get to the food first. I wasn't sorry that tonight they were finally heading back to their home field in Yorkshire.

As the rest of us put on our gear in the usual subdued manner before night ops, the Americans were loud and boisterous, glad to be leaving rather than setting out across the Channel. Their voices carried clearly through the shuffling and zips and quiet cursing that always accompanied a gearing up.

"I don't know why they let 'em in in the first place. Last thing a fellow wants is some pansy leering at him."

"Or copping a feel in a bunk."

The Yank flyers laughed loudly, earning a few smirks and glares in response. My heart started thudding in my ears. Next to me, Ranbir folded his uniform carefully and placed it in his locker, and Wilkins and Vanier exchanged glances.

The thud of a boot hitting the floor. "If it were up to me, I'd line 'em all up and shoot 'em."

A few of our boys were openly paying attention now, including Isaak's former crewmates assigned to the *Siren*. Laurie caught my eye and shook his head almost imperceptibly.

The *Siren*'s engineer now chimed in. He'd played the grand-mother at the panto, back at Christmas. "I knew one, a blond fel-low, pasty-faced and as soft as melted butter." This was followed by an explosion of questions, indignation and disbelief.

Mutters flew around the crew room. "Disgusting." "Shouldn't have been drafted in the first place." "A disgrace to the uniform."

I balled my hands into fists, nails biting into my palms.

"Where is he, Patterson? I say we go get him and drum him out of the air force."

"Bought the farm a month or so back."

One of the American pilots grinned. "Least the Krauts are good for something. If they hadn't got him, I would have."

A chorus of braying approval.

I was across the room and standing over their bench before I knew what I was doing. "Care to repeat that, you dog-faced Yank?"

It took them a moment to register my presence, but once they did, they focused on me like a pack of coyotes. The dark-haired, clean-shaven one with a pilot's double wings on his breast stood up and wiped his upper lip with the back of his hand, slowly, insolently. He looked around at his friends.

"Look, boys, I found his girlfriend."

I feinted at him and suddenly the whole crew were on their feet, every muscle tense and bristling. A muscle twitched under the American pilot's eye.

"Gentlemen, we're here to do a job, as I'm sure you are." Pete's calm tone grated on my nerves.

"Sure, sure." The pilot spread his hands wide in a gesture of helplessness. "But your bitch of a lapdog here needs to apologize."

"McNair?" There was a clear warning in Pete's voice. I felt the ghost of Isaak's hand on my shoulder, his tears, the press of his lips against my cheekbone in the twilight. Cold anger flared in my stomach.

"I'll apologize," I said quietly, "as soon as this yellow bastard apologizes for disgracing the name of men braver and better than him."

An intake of breath all around. The pilot looked me in the eye, and then carefully and deliberately spat on the floor at my feet. "I don't apologize to faggots," he said. "And I'm glad that nasty little pansy's dead. If I ever meet the Jerry who did it, I'll shake his hand and thank him for a job well—"

My fist sent him staggering into the bench. I was dimly aware of shouts and other brawls breaking out around us. The pilot snarled and launched himself at me. I ducked, only to receive a blow to the shoulder from one of his mates. I squared myself up to hit the pilot again and then Pete and Vanier and Wilkins were between us, arms out, trying to shout over the noise. Vanier grabbed my arm and began dragging me towards the door.

Pete had placed himself in front of the pilot and was using his most reasonable voice as Vanier hauled me outside and shut the door behind us. He dragged me across the lawn.

"Vanier, I'm sorry, I just—"

"Take a walk, Christopher," he said gruffly, giving me a rough push. "Cool your head."

"I—"

He dug into his pocket and flipped me a cigarette. "Just go. We'll deal with this."

The wind on the field was sharp and clean, tugging at my flight suit and jacket. My shoulder ached where I'd been struck. As the cold air cleared my head, I began to burn with shame and regret.

I'd been an idiot. I shouldn't have lost my temper. Isaak was dead, after all. It didn't matter to him what some idiot Yank yammered on about.

I trudged around the field while the other airmen began to gather on the far side of the building. Pete was going to kill me. No doubt I'd be confined to barracks. In fact, I'd be lucky to keep my rank. I could already picture Sandish's moustache quivering with fury. Then I realized I didn't care—it wasn't as if they could afford to throw any of us away.

I turned up the lane, unwilling to return to the others just yet. The wind died, leaving a silence in its wake that pulled at my skin. I could see a forest on the other side of the fence, the same one that ran along the edge of the estate where Laurie and I had found the gardener's shed. The trees were older, tall and well spaced, with a carpet of leaves underfoot. It reminded me of the forests of my childhood, of autumn days spent walking in the woods alongside the river. There was something achingly familiar about the way the sunlight strained through the canopy overhead, the bird calls and the smell of the air. As though someone had been in a room ahead of me and left just before I entered, trailing a whiff of perfume. My pulse was loud in my ears, and the birdsong died away. My feet slowed and then stopped.

The wind came at me down the lane, racing up the road as though it was chasing me, gathering speed and dust and bits of twigs and leaves and flowers, swirling and twisting. I threw my arm across my face, squeezed my eyes shut and was showered with road dust and grit, leaves and flower petals and ash dropping at my feet. Then the wind was gone, spent. I dusted off my palms, spat into the grass at the verge. A dust devil, nothing more. I'd chased them across fields as a child, hoping to catch them. Rebekah would have laughed at my superstitious fear, telling me it was no more than a ripple in the—

Rebekah. Warm lips pressed against mine, the heat of shale rock against my back. Dark brown eyes, straight brows furrowed with mock reproof. A grey kitten. A door shut in my face. A thunderstorm and rain-damp skin under my tongue. Fiddle music, the smell of hay in the sunshine, my finger tracing the lines of her palm. Every memory came bursting through me like a firework. My anger flickered and died.

A horn honked. I looked over my shoulder to see the trucks pulling up to the crowd of waiting airmen. The forest beckoned and I considered what it would cost me to scale that fence, to disappear into it like I had as a child, avoiding my mother's chores.

I jogged towards the trucks, leaving the trees behind me.

REBEKAH

I staggered into the apartment, dripping sweat. It was as empty and stuffy as when I had left. I ran myself a tepid bath and made myself a drink while I waited for the tub to fill. The water cooled my skin and I lay in it for a long time, staring at the ceiling, my thoughts drifting. I would need to find a new book for Wei soon. He was nearly through the last one I'd purchased. The smell of machine oil drifted through the apartment. Perhaps someone was running a car on the street below, wasting fuel.

Finally, I heaved myself out of the bath and let the water drain. I wrapped myself in one of Hatti's old robes and padded into the kitchen. It was too hot to cook, but I was hungry. A quick poke through the cupboards revealed a tin of fruit and some jelly powder. I mixed them together with some ice cubes and poured the concoction into a mould to set in the fridge. Hatti liked fruit jellies, and I owed her an apology.

The apartment seemed a little cooler now. I sat on the couch and picked up a shift I'd been meaning to mend. When I bent down to get my sewing kit, a stab of pain lanced through my abdomen, so sharp it took my breath away.

KIT

"There you are!" Thompson said, waving me over. He handed me my life belt. "You left it on the floor of the crew room."

"Thanks, I was just—" I glanced around, but the Americans were already aboard one of the trucks.

"Skipper's been looking all over for you." Thompson jerked his head towards a waiting vehicle.

I started towards it, and a wave of pain ripped through my abdomen. I stumbled.

"Where'd you go?" Thompson said. "We've been waiting for ages."

"I went for a walk, to clear my head—"

"Right. It was at sixes and sevens for a moment there, but Skip and Wilkins got the Yanks to back off, especially once the lads from the *Duchess* got into it. 'Spect there'll be some blowback from on high, but not until tomorrow."

"Probably." I bit back a gasp as another lightning strike of pain went through my gut. I saw Pete waiting near the truck, looking sterner than ever.

"Get in, Thompson," he said when we got closer. "I'd like a quick word with McNair." Thompson flashed me a sympathetic smile and climbed aboard.

"Sir—"

"I don't know where you've been for the past half-hour and I suspect I won't like the answer, even if you decide to tell me the truth for once."

I looked at my feet. "I'm sorry, sir. About earlier."

"It was a stupid and selfish thing to do."

I looked up at him in shock.

Pete drew me farther away from the trucks. "Those men are our allies!" he hissed. "They risk their skins every night to see that our boys make it back home in one piece. I cannot have you start-ing petty fights and I will not tolerate that kind of behaviour from any member of this crew. Do I make myself clear?"

I stared at my boots. "Yessir."

"I've already informed Sandish. You are to report to his office at eleven hundred tomorrow. The Americans are calling for your head. They're telling anyone who will listen that you punched a higher-ranking officer."

I opened my mouth, but Pete kept going.

"If you want my advice, don't run your mouth off to Sandish and you might get away with a stern warning and punishment detail. And for God's sake, don't tell him what the argument was about."

I pressed my lips together and nodded. Pete cleared his throat and looked around, stepping closer to me. "For what it's worth, I'm sorry about your friend. In other circumstances, I would have gladly stood up for his memory."

I swallowed, feeling the slight burn of tears at the back of my throat. Pete clapped me on the shoulder, once, twice, and then steered me towards the truck.

—

When I opened my eyes, I was on the carpet, on my hands and knees, and the pain had subsided. I staggered to my feet and went to put on my nightgown. Then I collected the shift and the sewing kit and sat back down on the sofa.

Just as I had the thread through the eye of the needle, another wave passed through me, and I nearly pricked my thumb. Now I knew what this was, but I didn't want to believe it. The baby was early, by at least two weeks. I forced myself to breathe calmly and sew, nipping tiny bites in the cloth, one at a time, thinking of my grand-mère. I coughed, the taste of road dust in my mouth. There was a buzz I couldn't shake from my ears.

The next wave came after thirty stitches.

The truck engine roared, and Laurie turned to me. "Where on earth have you been? I thought the skipper was going to have some kind of fit."

"I went for a walk," I said.

Laurie eyed me, clearly wanting to ask questions, but seemed to think better of it. "Get through tonight and then we'll all have a few days off. I've been looking forward to some more sleep, myself."

I nodded, staring down at my palms.

I closed my eyes, bit my cheek to avoid crying out. I wondered what my father had told women in childbirth. I'd never attended one. I had always assumed my mother would be there to guide me through it when it was my time. I pushed that thought away before

I dissolved in panic. I lay back on the sofa and forced myself to breathe evenly. Think of something nice, something calm.

What if Hatti didn't come home tonight?

I pushed that thought away too and rifled through my memory for something that would slow my heartbeat. The day on the cliff, when the sky was fresh and blue. The fields and roads laid out before me like a miniature model. The taste of licorice on my tongue.

"McNair?"

I shook myself back to the present. We were the only two left in the truck, the other men having shuffled out and onto the field.

"Laurie, something's wrong."

"What are you talking about?" His eyes flicked to the still-healing scar over my ear.

"I don't know—I just have a bad feeling, about tonight."

He looked around, then said in a quieter voice, "You're just nerved up, that's all."

"No, it's more than that."

"Chip-chop, lads," the driver said over her shoulder. "I've got another bunch to bring from C Squadron."

Laurie and I clambered out and the truck rumbled away. All around us, aircraft were fuelling up, testing their engines, mechanics crawling over them like ants.

Laurie put an arm around my shoulders. "Listen, Christopher, have a nip of this." He passed me his flask. I took it, and when he continued to stare at me, unscrewed it and took a swallow. The brandy burned all the way down. I felt overheated, as though we stood in the blazing sun, but a moment later the air was cool and brisk, the same as it had been all evening. I tried to return the flask but the bomb aimer pushed it back. "You hang on to it, just in case."

I slipped it into an inner pocket of my flight suit. Laurie was trying so hard, I couldn't bring myself to pull him down into madness alongside me.

The next contraction drew me out of my memory and pulled a gasp of pain from my lips. Hatti still wasn't home. I started to panic, and the next lightning crack of pain sent me off the sofa and onto the carpet. Mrs. Tsu. She could call the midwife. She was only a flight of stairs away. I had to make it up those stairs.

But I couldn't go in my nightgown. I stood up, looking around for Hatti's robe, but another contraction sent me stumbling to the door without it. I hauled the door open and headed towards the staircase. A burning rose in my throat and I thought I might be sick. I sat down on the bottom step and held my knees until it passed.

Every step was like climbing a mountain. I clung to the banister, staring up at the next floor, so far above me. I had to get to her. I hauled myself up another step, clinging to the banister with all my strength.

The airfield was ordered chaos, men running in every direction, engines gunning as each crew mustered for takeoff. As I approached *Friday's Girl*, I saw the American pilots standing in a tight circle near their kites. They glanced in my direction and then turned away, talking among themselves.

Wilkins and Thompson ruffled my hair—"For good luck," Wilkins laughed—before climbing into the turrets. Vanier was running last-minute checks with the erks. Ranbir climbed aboard just ahead of me. Laurie shook my hand, squeezing my palm, his eyes searching my face.

"We're still on for cards later, yeah?"

I nodded. He gave me a grin and climbed into the bomb aimer's coffin below the belly of the aircraft, his face distended through the fish-bubble glass.

Near the top of the stairs, the pain returned. I lost my handhold on the rail and the staircase yawned behind me as I felt my balance tilt. I threw myself forward onto the landing. My knees burned where they'd hit the stair lip and I skinned my hand. The carpet was cool under my cheek. Mrs. Tsu's door loomed above me. I tried to get up but my legs wouldn't obey me.

The door opened a crack and Wei peered down at me.

"Wei," I croaked, "get your mother. Tell her—tell her—"

Another contraction tore my pelvis in two and I doubled over on the floor. "Please," I gasped. When I looked up, the door was closed.

"McNair?" Ranbir was holding out his hand to haul me on board. I grabbed it. Vanier leapt nimbly in, and Ranbir shut the door. As the crew ran through a pre-flight check, I sat at the nav desk and stared at the charts. The lines swayed and blurred together. I blinked. The marks in my neat pencil script seemed like an unfamiliar code. Whatever was happening to me, whatever else would happen when we got back, I would deal with it then. For now, I needed to focus.

I slipped on my headset, listening to the familiar banter. A few minutes later, Pete's voice cut through for final checks.

"Nav, go," I said and picked up my pencil.

Voices above my head.

"What's going on?" Is it the Kettle? She's found me. They're going to drag me back to Devil's Battery. I try to tell her I can't put on my headset; I am having a baby.

Footsteps past my ear, quick and light. A hand on my cheek. An unfamiliar voice says, "She's coming. Your friend. Wei's gone to get her. It's going to take two of us to move you."

I crack open my eyes. A wrinkled face looks down at me. Mrs. Tsu. The edges of her chin and mouth are soft. There are rings on her fingers, cool against my skin. "No good you having a baby on the staircase. Ruin my good carpets."

"Hatti?" I manage to croak.

"Wei will get her. He runs fast. Faster than me." She gives a wheezing, crackling laugh. "Rest now. When your friend comes, we take you downstairs."

"But I don't want to—" Another shudder of pain moves through me, sending sparkling lights behind my eyes. I hiss through my teeth. Mrs. Tsu's hand is tight in mine, her fingers stroking my arm.

"Would you look at those searchlights," Wilkins says.

Laurie now. "Like Christmas down there."

"How many, you reckon?" Pete says.

"At least a thousand."

"McNair, any way around this?"

I stare at the map. "No, Skip. It's all over the coastline. Though there might be a small break in it just to port."

Friday's Girl weaves through the air. We've taken flak damage over Hanover, but all four engines are still up and we've dropped on target as planned. We're making good time back towards the Channel, and have already ducked through two flak lines and evaded a group of night fighters.

"Three minutes to the coast, Skip," I say.

"Keep a weather eye, Wilkins. See any breaks?"

Silence. Then, "Just off to your ten, Skip. There's a break in the line."

Pete sucks in a breath. "It'll be like threading a needle. McNair, you mark that?"

There are sparkling lights in my vision, and even when I blink they cloud my eyes. "Sorry, Skip, again?"

"Off our ten, what's there?"

I look over the charts. "A river."

"Good as anything. Hartwick, you reckon we can fly low and get under those beams?"

"Better than staying up here, Skip."

"Right, Thompson, keep your eyes peeled. We're headed for that gap. Hold tight, lads."

My stomach swoops as the plane begins to dive.

Pounding footsteps on the stairs, strong enough to shake the carpet under my cheek.

"What's going on—oh, Becca. Becca!" Someone is shaking my shoulder. My stomach swoops as though I'm falling and then I open my eyes.

"Hatti?"

She puts her face close to mine and feels my forehead. "Clammy and cold. We have to get her downstairs. Where's the midwife?"

"No," I manage to gasp as another contraction sends me writhing on the carpet.

"Help me get her downstairs."

"No, no, I want to stay here. It's too early. The baby can't come yet."

"Honey, this baby's coming whether you want it now or not."

Hands scoop under my shoulders and my calves, and then I am weightless, born down and down. I'm falling. Someone is puffing and swearing in Cantonese.

"Mind the banister. Nearly there, Becca, hang on."

"One to starboard beam."

"Two on our tail."

"You see them, Thompson?"

The competing rat-tat of machine gun fire, and then a Luftwaffe fighter strafes the side of our plane, the bullets striking the other side of the metal sheeting, inches from my head. *Friday's Girl* rocks, tumbling to the left.

"I can't see him!" Thompson's voice, higher, a little panicked.

"Above you!" Laurie yells. "Coming round to port."

The plane wobbles in the air and loses another dozen feet of height.

"McNair, how wide did you say this river is?"

"I didn't, Skip."

"Let's hope that luck of yours holds."

Another cracking rhythm.

"Got one!" yells Thompson.

"Keep your hat on, kid. There's two more of them," Wilkins says.

A soft cushion under my back. Someone is tucking a towel under my hips, lifting the hem of my nightgown.

"I'm going for the ambulance."

"What about the midwife? My son will be back any moment."

"No, she needs an ambulance."

Hatti is next to me, kissing the top of my head. "Hang in there, doll. I'll be back soon."

"Hatti!" I try to call after her, but my voice breaks. Another wave of pain leaves me gasping and sweating. By the time my vision clears, the door has already swung shut.

Mrs. Tsu tucks a blanket over my lap. I don't want it, I'm too hot already.

"You do need the ambulance. The baby is turned, won't come out without help."

I stare at the thin blue line we are following on the chart, eyes darting reflexively to the anemometer.

"A little faster, Skip."

"I'm pushing as hard as I can."

"Careful, those lights are following us."

"I'm weaving, Hartwick. McNair, how much farther?"

"Two minutes to the coast."

"Skipper! They've got us coned!"

My heart skips a beat. If two searchlights lock us in the sky, it's only too easy for a fighter or the flak guns to pick us off.

"Not yet they don't!"

Friday's Girl yaws to starboard and then plummets so fast I feel my breath disappear. Flak ricochets off our side like burning hailstones.

"We're out of it."

"Wilkins, on your starboard, just above us."

"Pull up, Skipper." Vanier now, voice tight.

"Not yet. We'll get under them."

"Skip—"

"Watch that temp gauge, Vanier."

Rat-tat-tat. Rat-tat-tat. A boom as an aircraft hits the ground and explodes below us.

Rat-tat. Rat-tat. Fingernails drumming on the wooden table next to my head. It is summer. I am lying in tall grass, the sun warm

on my limbs. The taste of jam tart on my lips. The smell of hot
green grass. The pain starts beneath my hip bones and knifes
across my belly.

Friday's Girl screams, all her rivets straining as we pull to port and
then up. The buzz of a fighter overhead, then behind us. I cling to
the nav desk as the aircraft jars side to side, moving up by inches.

"Looks like we've shaken them," Pete says.

"They're turning back now," Laurie says. "Thompson, can you
see them?"

Silence.

"Thompson, can you see anything?"

"Thompson?"

Then, "Singh, check the rear turret."

"Yes, Skipper."

A hand strokes my forehead. "Shh, just breathe, *ma chérie*. Just
breathe."

"Maman?" I moan, opening my eyes. I am on the couch, my
hands pressed flat against the blanket. Sweat has dampened
my nightshirt, making me shiver. I feel my body shifting, changing,
growing longer and heavier, my fingers merging into one great
paddle that bats ineffectively at the edge of the sofa. It's hard to
breathe. Dimly, some part of my mind knows this is a fever, that
Hatti has been gone too long, that I am in danger.

"He's gone, Skip. That last fighter must have . . ."

Silence on the intercom. We are out over the Channel now,
shrouded in darkness, leaving the chaos of the flak line behind.

"Singh, can you take the rear turret?"

"No, we'll need wireless over the coast. Wilkins, you'll have to be our eyes."

"Yes, Skipper."

"Dover coastline in three minutes, Skip," I say. I am clammy under my suit.

I can smell smoke and fuel. The apartment is dark now, the lights have gone out. The world slides sideways and underneath me. I shake my head, pain lancing down and through me, faster now, won't let me catch my breath. How am I supposed to give birth in this chaos? I open my mouth to tell them to turn off that engine—

A tremendous crash, exploding through the side of the plane in a wall of heat and shredded metal. I am thrown to the opposite wall, my shoulder slamming against the struts.

"They're here!" Wilkins yells. Gunfire, a shrieking engine that whirs faster and then dies.

"Must have followed us from the coast to get the jump on us."

The wind is screaming past the hole in the side of the plane. Two more fighters streak past, rolling up and overhead.

"We've lost both port engines, Skip."

I see Ranbir crumpled in the rear of the cabin. I edge my way past the hole in the skin, clinging to the webbing.

"McNair, we need the nearest landing strip."

I reach Ranbir, roll him over. I'm scrambling for the med kit, there is blood on his face, on his shoulder, his eyes are glassed.

"I can't see them!" Wilkins screams from the upper turret. "Hartwick, where are they?"

"McNair, report! I need that landing strip."

I gather Ranbir in my arms, pull off his helmet, hold my palm to his mouth. He rolls limply into my lap.

"We're losing fuel in the near starboard engine, sir."

There are hands, holding me up, voices, the flicker of a face in my vision—

"Quickly now, the ambulance is waiting!"

"She's lost too much blood. It's happening here or not at all."

"McNair!"

"Yes, Skip, coming." I let Ranbir roll to the floor and claw my way back to the nav desk. The charts are scattered, trembling in the wind. I pin one down and struggle to read it. "Skip, you need to turn starboard in—"

Another explosion, closer and from below. The floor erupts, nearly tearing the world in two.

A hand pressing mine. "Becca, can you hear me?" I know that voice. My eyelids flutter. There is a faint light now, figures larger than life against an orange glow.

I look down. The belly of the plane is in flames. I am clinging to the webbing, my feet dangling over the edge of nothing. From below, I hear a shout. Laurie. The fire is climbing.

"Prepare to bail." Pete's voice. "McNair, get to the wireless, tell them where we are."

I look over. The wireless is shot to pieces, half of the wires dangling loose. A strangled yell from below my feet. My lungs crackle and pop, my chest aches when I take a breath. I'm drowning, I realize. My hand slipping to the floor.

I drop to my knees and reach down. "Grab on!" I yell. I clasp the hand that is reaching towards me. I pull with all my strength.

"You have to push. We're doing everything we can, but you have to help us."

I pull Laurie into my arms. Haul my chute over my shoulders, buckle the belt. The flames are higher now. I can feel the heat on my face.

"All hands, bail—"

A crash of glass from up front. I pull Laurie with me to the floor as a hail of shards whip past us from the cockpit.

"Skipper? Pete!" The plane tilts down near vertical, the wings howling as air rushes through the holes ripped in her skin.

The ragged sound of my breath in my throat. There is a great weight on my abdomen, like someone pushing down. I cough and splutter. Laurie is hot and limp against my shoulder. I can hear the engines dying, smoke blowing through the cockpit too fast to choke on. "Nearly there, love." I lock my arms around him and we roll out of the plane into a cold nothing, the screaming of the wounded engines fading, the plane growing smaller above us. I am falling through the air, plummeting at a breath-ripping speed towards the earth, weighed down and heavy. My fingers are numb, the rip cord whipping. I yank. A sudden brake, muscles screaming, the baby slipping down towards the dark water. A white canopy fluttering like a dying sail, the plane is a comet in the sky. I inhale and choke, not air but water. Bubbles rushing past my cheeks, rising up to the surface. I follow. I'm tangled in the lines, pulled back under black water, salt stinging my neck, white ghost drifting in the waves. The voices again, louder. I cannot let the lights lead me astray. A black silhouette blotting out the sky, then an explosion of flame and heat. Ash, snowflakes whirling, cold cruel water swallowing me. A light in the dark below. Whispering voices. I am falling as softly as in snow. Someone in the distance calling my name. The cold wind numbing me into nothing. A blue-green body skimming mine, don't fall asleep, follow the lights follow the lights, we're almost home.

In the distance, a thin, breathless wail.

NOVEMBER 1943

REBEKAH

THE TRAIN ROCKED FROM SIDE TO SIDE, WEAK WINTER sunlight flashing in stripes through the windows onto our little corner of the third-class car. The same seat we had been sitting in for two days. Adelaide had cried from Trois-Rivières to Toronto without drawing breath and was now, miraculously, asleep in my arms. My legs were cramped, my dress stained with spit-up and spilled milk and all the other small disasters that had befallen this infant and her mother across half the country. We were alone, and I could stretch my calves across to the facing seat and place my bags on the floor within easy reach.

If only my mother were here next to me, offering to hold the baby while I slept—that thought was laughable to the point of tears. I seemed constantly on the verge of either hysterical laughter or endless sobs. I couldn't map my own mind from one moment to the next. There was only the great catastrophe of the present. A wet diaper, a hungry mouth, the tiny, contented sighs of her sleeping. Adelaide didn't care whether I could name the trees we passed, or how much money was hidden in the inner lining of my suitcase, only that I provided the most basic needs and that she survived. Beyond that I was nothing, and I embraced it wholeheartedly.

I had written to my mother the week after Adelaide's birth to say that, though the labour had been difficult, the baby and I were doing well. Delusional with fatigue, I had suggested that we come to Montreal to visit my parents at Christmas so they could meet their granddaughter. Some naive part of me believed that if my family could only meet the tiny miracle that was Adelaide, they would fall in love with her as I had, and all would be forgiven. My grand-mère would change her mind, and the short visit would inevitably extend into a permanent home for both of us.

Instead, my mother had taken a month to write back, her letter complaining about the noise that Hélène's children made throughout the house and how it was simply too crowded and too chaotic for anyone to bear. That there wasn't going to be much of a Christmas anyway, since my father worked around the clock, and they had hardly enough beds to go around as it was, never mind any space for guests. Not a single word inquiring after her granddaughter.

I burned the letter in the kitchen stove while Adelaide drooled down my back. As the paper charred, I considered my options.

A pregnant *costumière* who cooked and kept house had fit seamlessly into Hatti's life, but a squalling infant filling the apartment with dirty diapers less so. While Hatti hadn't said anything, she had found more and more reasons to be out of the house, sometimes for whole nights at a time. It was no one's fault, but it was clear that my life with her had run its course. I had no illusions about how difficult it would be if I struck out alone, a single woman with an illegitimate child and no income. Adelaide deserved a chance at happiness, deserved a real family.

It had taken me a whole day to write the letter, in between feeding and changing and playing with my daughter. I'd filled Hatti's sitting room with crumpled balls of wasted paper. She had even offered to write it for me, but this was something I had to do myself. My penance, as if Caroline McNair would know if these contrite words, begging her forgiveness and her help, weren't in my own hand. The three weeks waiting for a reply had been agony, as sleepless and delusional as the first month of Adelaide's life. Caroline's message, when it came, was ambiguous.

I wish to meet my granddaughter. Bring her at your convenience.

No promise of sanctuary or hint of what might await me.

A few days later, I had cleaned the apartment one last time, stocked the kitchen cupboards with jelly packets and tinned fruit, and crammed Adelaide's necessities into a second-hand ruck-sack and my few belongings into my old suitcase. Mrs. Tsu hugged me tightly on the staircase, wishing me good luck, and Wei shyly gave me a Bible verse he had painstakingly copied onto a piece of cardboard.

Hatti came with us to the train station, kissing both me and Adelaide goodbye, pressing some money into my hands and making me promise to write to her. I cried the first thirty miles out of Halifax, and then fell asleep, Adelaide bundled to my chest.

Outside the window, the countryside flashed by in a flickering of bare trees and muddy fields, ragged fingers of snow clutching the hills and gullies. I barely remembered this scenery from four and a half years ago, though I could picture that earlier Rebekah, sitting in first class, her hair neatly curled, gloves and hat perfectly in place.

So determined to make the best of things. Nothing like the puffy-eyed woman who stared back at me in the window's reflection. Adelaide shifted in her sleep, mouth opening and closing like a fish.

"Excuse me." An older woman in a smart travelling coat stood in the aisle beside us. "May I?"

My feet were still resting brazenly on the opposite seat. I pulled them back and rearranged our belongings, and she settled across from us. All traces of my irritation vanished as she caught sight of my child's sleeping face.

"What a precious angel. Has he given you much trouble on the journey?

It was dark by the time we arrived in Harrichford. The conductor helped me down to the platform, handed me my bags, folded up the train steps and, without a backwards glance, leapt aboard. The train rattled off into the night.

The station was empty. It began to rain, a winter sleet with the edge of snow in it. I wanted to slide down the brick wall and sob hysterically. I wanted my father to appear out of the darkness and whisk us away in his car. Instead, I waited on the bench for a half-hour, while Adelaide slept fitfully, her fist tugging on the blanket, mouth screwed up in anger in her dreams. At last I faced the truth. No one was coming to meet us. I waited until the rain let up a little, and then I resettled my daughter in her blanket, picked up my suitcase and rucksack, and started walking.

Harrichford had changed since I'd last seen it. There were new shops along the main street, and the town extended a little farther than I recalled, so it took longer to reach the open countryside. Several cars passed us, their headlights bouncing crazily in the dark, but no one stopped. When I turned off onto the side road, the ground became more uneven, and in places I walked ankle-deep in mud. It wasn't long before my coat was soaked through and my shoes damp with slush. Miraculously, Adelaide slept soundly in my arms, her dead weight numbing my elbow.

We were both wet to the bone by the time I crossed the bridge and finally saw the light of the McNairs' kitchen window in the dark. I didn't know how my feet carried me down the drive to the door. No dogs barked the alarm. I stumbled up the front porch and knocked, resting my forehead on the door frame, feeling hot and cold at the same time. Adelaide stirred in my arms, beginning to fuss.

The door opened, and Dermot McNair stood there, looking a little more grey and worn than the last time I saw him. He stared at me for a moment and then his face broke into a smile.

"Why, Miss Kromer! We weren't expecting you until next week."

I'm not sure what I said in response. The warmth coming out of the house was dizzying, the light sending spots through my vision.

"I was going to bring the cart up and collect you—"

"Dermot! Whoever it is, bring them inside and shut the door."

I would have recognized Caroline's sharp voice anywhere. "We aren't in the business of heating the whole neighbour—"

Dermot opened the door wider as she came up behind him. She froze, the reprimand dropping from her lips. She stared at me, and I saw myself as she must have seen me in that moment, soaked and shivering, in a third-hand coat and muddy boots.

"Hello, Mrs. McNair," I said. "I'm sorry to arrive so late."

"Come inside." She nudged Dermot out of the way with her hip and ushered me through the door.

I followed her into the kitchen, and she drew back the chair closest to the stove for me. I sat, stunned by the sudden change to warmth and light, still clutching Adelaide to my chest.

"Take her things, Dermot. She can have the second bedroom,"
I heard Caroline say, and then the bag was tugged from my hand
and I heard slow, steady footsteps going up the stairs. Caroline set
a mug of something hot down on the tabletop in front of me. The
smell of it made me dizzy with hunger. When had I last eaten?

"There now, you drink that. Give me the wee bairn. You're half-
frozen and dead on your feet." Gentle but insistent hands drew
Adelaide from my arms. A flicker of panic ran through me, but
Caroline had her safely on her shoulder, where my daughter grizzled
a little. "There, there, you've come quite a ways. What's her name?"

"Adelaide."

"Such a pretty name. All's better now, darling, all's better."

I looked up, but Caroline was talking to the baby, not to me.
I wrapped my fingers around the mug and let the heat sink into
my bones. I hadn't realized how chilled they were until they began
to thaw.

Caroline put Adelaide on her hip and went to the stove. I
thought vaguely that I should be tending to my daughter, but
holding the cup and bringing it to my lips took all my effort. It was
bitter—chicory—but it was warm and satisfying.

Before I had finished half the mug, Caroline had put a bowl
of hot oatmeal studded with chunks of apple, and two slices of
bread drizzled with honey, in front of me. As I ate, she sat at the
other end of the table holding my daughter, now wrapped in a
dry blanket, stroking her fine hair and looking into her sleeping
face. Dermot sat beside her, chewing thoughtfully on an unlit pipe
stem and gazing at his wife and granddaughter. I spooned the oatmeal into my mouth, too exhausted to make conversation or worry
about table manners. The kitchen was silent, save for the sound of
a clock ticking in the front room.

I finished my bowlful and sat back with a heavy sigh. Warmth had returned to my limbs, and with it my exhaustion doubled. At some unspoken signal, Dermot stood up, tucked his pipe in his pocket and went upstairs. Caroline handed me back the baby and refilled my mug. Then she sat down again, in the same place as before. Adelaide wriggled in my arms, waved her tiny fists and then settled again. I would need to feed her soon, but the thought of climbing the stairs to the bedroom made me want to weep.

Caroline waited until we could no longer hear Dermot moving around on the upper floor. Then she smoothed the tabletop with her fingers, the wood worn soft from her doing exactly the same thing hundreds of times.

"That boy always did have the devil's streak in him."

I couldn't think of anything to say in response. After a long silence, Caroline stirred at the far end of the table. "You go on upstairs and rest. I'll get done with these dishes."

I started to protest but she waved me off, and I was too tired to argue, so I climbed the steep, narrow staircase to the tiny room. As I nursed her, Adelaide fell asleep. I envied her, looking down at the perfect curve of her eyelids and the slight quiver to her upper lip as she breathed. I wanted to wake her, raise her head to my cheek and cling to the tiny, warm body that was both me and not-me—and the only certainty in my life at this moment.

Instead, I lay her down gently on the bed, undressed as quietly as I could, crawled onto the cold mattress next to her and stared at the outline of the trees through the window until sleep mercifully claimed me.

When I woke, everything was bright and washed in early winter daylight. Miracle of miracles, my daughter had slept through. All the shadows and curves of the previous night had been replaced with sunlight that revealed the worn edges of the banister and the cracks in the whitewash as I descended the stairs, Adelaide fed and content in my arms.

Caroline had started breakfast, and Dermot sat at the table in the chair I had taken last night, a steaming mug of chicory coffee untouched before him.

"Put the bairn down over there." Caroline nodded towards a small cradle, close to the stove. I walked over, then hesitated. Caroline must have seen my reluctance. "She'll be fine. Old Gordie'll keep a close eye."

I glanced down to see a dog I recognized, with more white around his muzzle now and rheumy eyes that met mine patiently. I could think of worse child-minders. I placed Adelaide in the cradle and the dog lay down next to it, clearly planning to stay until further notice.

Caroline directed me to the dish cupboard and I laid the table while she piled up griddle cakes and bacon. The meal was a silent affair. Dermot carefully cut and transferred each bite of his breakfast to his mouth, chewing slowly as though it pained him as Caroline stared into the middle distance, lost in thought. I had little appetite but forced myself to eat every bite. Adelaide remained quiet too, perhaps tired from our journey, perhaps as stunned as I was by the sudden change in our circumstances.

At last, Dermot put his cutlery to the side, plate empty. He got to his feet, bracing one hand on the table, and put his hat on his head.

"It is nice to see you again, Miss Kromer," he said, looking my way for the first time.

I blinked. "You as well, sir." He nodded, pausing to touch the top of his wife's head before heading out the kitchen door into the yard.

Caroline was still lost in thought. I collected the dishes and washed and dried them, fumbling through cupboards to find where they belonged. I cleaned the counter boards and the table and swept the kitchen, while she sat on, her coffee long cold. When Adelaide began to wail, I retreated to the bedroom to nurse her. She fussed and spat, finally falling into a light sleep. I left her on the bed, hemmed in by rolled blankets, and returned to the kitchen.

As I entered, Caroline said, "Sit down." Not unkindly.

I sank into the nearest chair, at the far corner of the table.

"You had every intention to marry?" she asked.

I swallowed the lump in my throat. "Yes."

"Was there a ring?"

I shook my head. "A promise of one, after . . ."

"You've had no word?"

"No, but—"

"My Dermot, he's got a cousin in St. John's who said a few ships went down a month ago, but the navy's keeping it quiet. I haven't had a letter from Landon in nearly a year. I'm starting to think . . . Well, never you mind."

There was a long silence.

"You know that my youngest, Jep, he . . . We got a telegram, a few months ago."

My heart skipped a beat. The round-faced boy in my father's study, clutching a broken arm. Jep licking spilled jam from his hand, playing the fiddle the night of the dance. A hunched figure walking away in the rain.

"I'm so sorry," I said, feeling as though something had punctured my lungs.

Caroline nodded, accepting my sympathy.

I tightened my grip on the tabletop. "I don't suppose . . . Did you ever—did Kit—?"

"Kathleen?" Caroline glanced at me in surprise, then shook her head. "It's been, what, four years now? The Lord only knows where that girl is."

I looked down at my fingers, their tips pressed white against the wood grain.

"You ever see him?"

It took a moment for me to understand she was asking about Jep. "Yes, ma'am, once. We had lunch together, the day before he shipped out."

"Where?"

"In Halifax."

"What did you talk about?"

"His time in training, the usual complaints and pranks. To be honest, we spent more of our time talking about home, about our favourite memories."

"How did he seem?" There was the barest catch in her voice.

I took a deep breath. "He was good. Happy, making friends. He was looking forward to shipping out."

She smiled. "That's my Jep all right. I'm glad he saw a friendly face from home, before, before . . ."

"Me too," I said quickly, to forestall the shining bead in the corner of her left eye.

Caroline got up from the table and rinsed her mug in the sink. I stayed still, balanced on a tightrope high above this farmhouse. Certain that if I flinched, my daughter and I would plummet to our doom. I didn't know who I could pray to anymore, what I believed in. Perhaps I believed only in the wire itself, even as it cut my feet. *Please, please.* The wind moved in invisible, soundless circles around my ankles. *Please.*

A thin wail from upstairs. I got to my feet, but Caroline waved me down and went up herself. She returned with Adelaide in her arms. Every muscle sparked with the impulse to take her, but I restrained myself. She carried my daughter back to her chair at the table, bouncing her gently against one hip and sat. I held my breath.

"My first granddaughter," Caroline said, stroking Adelaide's head. "You know, she is the spitting image of Kathleen at her age. All eyes and barely any hair."

I pocketed that piece of knowledge for later, for when my heart wasn't racing. She was gazing at Adelaide with a grandmother's love, tracing her cheeks, taking her tiny fists and waving them gently up and down.

"You met Jep in Halifax, and he proposed that afternoon. It was a quiet, hurried ceremony." I opened my mouth to protest but she continued. "One of many performed that week, I imagine, before the troop ships went out. You celebrated with a meal and a night at the hotel. A perfectly respectable wedding night. And then he shipped out the next day. You wrote him, I assume, when you knew?"

I nodded, numb to the core.

"It's a shame how many letters go missing every week. Impossible to predict which boats will arrive and which will disappear under the Atlantic." She was still looking at Adelaide, counting her knuckles. My daughter stared back, equally entranced. "It's monstrous to imagine how many words of grief and love and life-changing news are lost forever that way, and never reach their intended home. You must have been devastated when he never replied."

"Yes, ma'am." A flood of tears, the cold tiles at Devil's Battery. Bile and the smell of typewriter oil.

"I'll never forget that man walking down the laneway with the telegram," Caroline said. "Smart dressed, he was. Almost too fancy, for delivering such news. It seems they didn't have a chance to update Jep's file with his new married status. At the moment, his pension is willed to me. We must change that, as soon as possible."

The numbness was giving way to burning sparks, like a limb shaken back to life.

"But, that's not—"

Caroline looked up, her gaze pinning me to my chair. "This is my granddaughter, yes?"

"Yes. Yes, she is."

"Then we need say no more about it."

"But the records—"

"You leave all that and Father Bradley to me. My grandchild is home where she belongs. That's all that matters."

"Thank you," I whispered, ashamed to feel tears burning the back of my throat. "Thank you, thank you."

Adelaide began to twist and squall, maybe feeling my distress, but more likely, simply wet and restless on account of it.

I stood to reach for her but Caroline was already on her feet.

"I'll take care of the bairn. You can't be doing chores in that getup. There's some old dresses of mine and Kathleen's in a trunk in the attic. Take what you need and we can hem them later. The pigpen needs a good digging out, and I fancy this little one won't mind rocking in the sunshine while we work."

I fled upstairs before she could see me start to cry. In the cold, dim light of the attic, I pawed through the trunk and came across a red-and-black-checked dress Kit once threatened to drown in the swamp. I held it to my face to stifle my sobs, and the smell of dust and old sunlight and a past I could never reclaim came pouring down my throat.

PART THREE

MARCH 1947

"OF ALL THE STUBBORN, PIG-HEADED ANIMALS—JENNY,
stand still!"

I slapped the cow's rump as she sidled away from the stool
again, nearly kicking over the bucket. She turned and gave me a
sidelong look as I shuffled the stool closer and took up milking
again. Caroline made this look easy, but I still found it a boring,
thankless chore that needed repeating twice a day. Jenny was picky
and moody, and no matter how many times Dermot had suggested
it, I couldn't bring myself to sing to a cow.

At last, her milk came down and I soon had a half-pail to bring
inside. I turned the cow out into the muddy paddock and checked
that the pigs we'd kept over the winter were happily eating yesterday's slops. I knew Caroline was hoping for two litters of piglets this year, and the sow was already looking bulkier. The smell
of pig manure had bothered me early on, but I barely noticed it
now, just as I barely noticed the mud that coated my boots or the
rough fabric of the coat I wore against the chill. I walked across

the yard carrying the milk pail. It was early March, and the wind still had teeth, snow lying in ragged patches on the ground.

"Adelaide?"

There was a rustle and a clucking from the henhouse, and my daughter emerged, carrying a little basket as though it was made of spun glass.

"Mumma, Susan *avait trois oeufs* this morning," she said, beaming up at me as we walked towards the house.

"*C'est bien, ma chérie,*" I replied, smiling back.

I had been skeptical when Caroline had insisted that Adelaide be given a chore of her own, thinking no three-year-old should be trusted with animals or eggs, but I had been forced to admit I had worried without cause. Adelaide adored the chickens and took pride in feeding them and collecting their eggs every morning. Caroline was less pleased that she had named each of them after the characters in *Swallows and Amazons*, but I was frankly impressed my daughter could tell the hens apart.

Inside, we shucked off our boots, and after I set down my pail, I took the eggs and sent Adelaide to wash up. Caroline was at the stove stirring the oatmeal, Dermot in his usual seat at the kitchen table, only the top of his head visible over his newspaper. I strained the milk and added a slosh to the pot, along with a handful of walnuts and dried apples. Adelaide, freshly clean, bounced across the kitchen and climbed into Dermot's lap. He rested his beard on her head, turning a page of the paper. Caroline had already heated a frying pan, and I cracked the eggs into it.

"Adelaide, the bowls," Caroline said without turning around from the stove. My daughter sighed and slipped from Dermot's lap to retrieve the bowls from the lower cupboard. One by one, she put them on the table, and then clambered into her own chair. Caroline dished out the food and the kitchen filled with the sounds of scraping spoons.

"I think the sow is pregnant again," I said.

Caroline nodded. "I hope so."

"I'll check on her," Dermot said, sipping his coffee. "Was thinking of refitting Pete's old stall for her when her time comes. Should be warm enough in there."

Caroline nodded. "No sense letting it stand empty."

"Wild leeks should be out," Dermot said, "maybe even some fiddleheads."

"Too early for those," Caroline said. "Another month at least."

Dermot shrugged, a gesture that meant he disagreed but didn't want the argument. "Sally told me she saw some on the east side of the ridge."

"When did you see Sally?" Caroline reached to steady Adelaide's hand before she tipped a bite of egg into her lap.

"Yesterday, at the post office. I went to see if there'd been any word from Landon. It's been so long since the war ended."

I wiped Adelaide's mouth with a napkin and helped her scoop the last of the oatmeal onto her spoon.

"We'd have heard," Caroline said in a tight voice. She got up to collect our plates and ferry them to the sink.

"Go and get that big basket from the attic," I said to Adelaide. "*Le grand panier.*" She darted up the stairs, leaving the rest of her egg uneaten. Caroline tsked over the waste of food as I scraped the egg into the slop bowl, but I couldn't fault my daughter for inheriting my dislike of eggs.

Dermot stood and placed his newspaper in the firebox. He took his hat from the peg by the door and went out into the yard,

Gordie at his heels. I watched the two of them amble across the yard to the barn.

"I might go help him," I said.

Caroline glanced out the window after him and shook her head. "It's good to see him up and about. I'll check on him every hour or so. Can't get himself into too much mischief out there anyway."

We both knew that was untrue, the memory of Dermot's illness sitting in the silence between us. He'd caught influenza the winter before this one and been bedridden for over a month, coughing blood before the end of it. Caroline had stayed up nearly every night by his bedside, watching him fight to breathe. He'd never fully recovered, and the smallest chore left him huffing and wheezing. Without discussing it, she and I had split the work of the farm between us, leaving Dermot small tasks that would occupy him for days at a time but didn't demand hard labour. She had sold their flock of sheep and cancelled the lease on the summer pasture. She'd also sold the back fields to a neighbour, and with them went the responsibility to maintain the fences. We didn't need the land anyway. With only one cow, one horse, a few pigs and a flock of chickens, the costs of running the farm had gone down significantly. I'd thought her ruthless, to strip away their livelihood so quickly, but I could see now that she had taken the steps that had saved us. Between our vegetable garden and livestock, the trout in the river, foraging the forest, and Jep's war pension that arrived each month, we'd fared better than many families over the past few years.

Adelaide came back down the stairs, carrying a basket nearly as big as she was. Caroline handed us a couple of biscuits wrapped in newspaper.

"If there are any wild leeks, they'll be up under the maples on the other side of the river. Take only the leaves, mind, and only a few from each patch."

The wind was fresh as Adelaide and I walked along the back fence. I carried the basket, and Adelaide scampered at my heels, darting from one delight to the next. A lingering patch of snow in a tree shadow holding one perfect rabbit print. A blackbird singing from the tip of a leaning fence post. It was cold in the shadows, but a faint sun warmed the eastern side of the hill as we went down into the forest.

"Why didn't we bring Daisy?" Adelaide asked, as we joined the wider path along the river, its banks hidden by dead rushes. "She could carry the picnic."

"We don't need a great big horse to carry one basket," I said.

I kept a keen eye for fiddleheads along the riverbank, but as Caroline had predicted, it was too early. We came to the bend where the river ran slower and deeper, the place Kit had caught fish for me years ago. The willow tree I'd climbed that day had blown down last year, forming a natural bridge across the water. I rarely came down here, since I'd found if I lingered, the ghosts of my past came rustling around my feet.

Adelaide crouched on the bank, poking at the water with a small stick. She turned and looked up at me. "You can hear them too, right, Mumma?"

"Hear what, *ma chérie?*"

"The people in the water. Do they tell you secrets too?"

A shiver ran up my spine.

"*Allons-y.* Grand-mère said we might find leeks up the ridge."

I held out my hand and she took it, abandoning the stick on the bank. Our boots squelched as we walked across the broad willow trunk and took the path leading up the long back slope of the ridge.

The sun strengthened as we climbed. Shafts of light came down through the branches, lighting up small patches of brown and green on the forest floor. Adelaide darted ahead of me, weaving between the trees. She found the first patch of newly sprouted leeks, and we carefully cut a few leaves with my pocketknife and put them in the basket alongside the biscuits. I found another patch a few minutes later.

The day grew warm enough that Adelaide shed her coat. I carried it along with the basket as she roamed ahead, chattering to me in an English-French pidgin language all her own. She glanced back every few steps to make sure I followed. The maple trees gave way to tall pines, and the forest floor grew flat and featureless beneath our feet. Small dregs of snow clung to the shadowed sides of the trees.

Near noon, we came across a small clearing in the middle of the pines. I'd noticed it from a long way off, lit up by the sunlight beaming down through the opening in the canopy. Though the spring grass hadn't yet taken hold anywhere else, the clearing was a tangle of bright green. Adelaide galloped towards it, with me at her heels.

The chilled shade of the forest gave way to summer warmth against my arms. At the centre of the clearing, there was already a profusion of wildflowers—buttercups and Queen Anne's lace and black-eyed Susans, a tangle of wild cucumber vine threading them together like beads on a string. It was beautiful, a burst of colour in this otherwise drab spring forest. Adelaide gave a giggle of delight and stumbled after a yellow and black butterfly that skirted the flowers.

Among the greenery was a group of weathered fieldstones, each as big as a pumpkin. They were seated firmly in the earth, and beneath the spring plants I could see a web of old, dead grasses nested around them. These stones, whatever they were, had been here a long time.

In the centre, where the wildflowers grew most densely, the ground sank down a little, as though it had been hollowed out and then filled in again. Adelaide circled the stones, chasing the butterfly that zipped just beyond her reach. I looked around. This place felt familiar, somehow, but I couldn't quite place it. Like a whiff of smoke on the breeze, caught and then lost again in a moment.

I frowned. It was far too early for butterflies. Too early for these wildflowers. The stones formed the outline of a square, with a gap on one side, about three paces across. To one side of the hollow, there was a pile of smaller stones, and mixed with the stones was something black and powdery. Charcoal.

I whirled around, looking at the clearing with new eyes. The size was right, the pile of stones and charcoal where the fireplace had been, and the gap in the stones lined up with the doorway I remembered. But it wasn't possible. This couldn't be the same cottage where Kit and I took refuge that night? The foundations looked as though they had crumbled decades ago. But there was the fireplace, and there the collapsed earth where the floorboards had been, and there the doorway, opening like a mouth, through which the butterfly was leading Adelaide—straight into the centre of the ancient cottage walls.

I dropped the basket and ran forward, propelled by breathless fear. I caught my daughter's arm and pulled her back before she could step inside the stones. The butterfly vanished, as quickly as it had appeared. The light overhead faded, as the sun passed behind a cloud and I shivered a little in the chill that followed. There was no birdsong, only the hissing of wind through the pines all around us.

"*Allons-y, chérie.*" I lifted my daughter into my arms and ran away from the clearing, abandoning the basket and the leeks, looking back only once to reassure myself that nothing had followed us.

APRIL 1947

KIT

I HAD WALKED FOR SEVERAL MILES BEFORE SOMEONE stopped for me. A mail truck pulled over onto the shoulder, and a grizzled head leaned out the driver's window.

"Where you headed, son?"

"Next county over."

"Get in."

I swung aboard and the truck engine guttered and caught, rumbling back into life. We travelled a few minutes in silence before he spoke again.

"So, where'd you serve?"

After that terrible night over the Channel, I'd been given a week's survivor's leave. I'd gone to London and tried to lose myself in the city, in the bottom of a glass drunk anywhere that would have me. It didn't help. I saw Pete's face above every double-winged pilot's badge, heard Laurie's low chuckle just behind my left ear. After I'd dragged myself back to the Lincolnshire base, the rest of the squadron avoided me. I couldn't blame them.

When Sandish called me into his office, I assumed it was to deliver my delayed punishment for the fight with the Americans. Instead, something like compassion crossed his thin, pinched face as he told me I was being promoted to flight lieutenant and reassigned to a base in Norfolk. I stood outside of his office for a long moment after he dismissed me, clutching my transfer papers, stunned.

For the rest of the war, I flew with the Pathfinders, an elite squadron tasked with guiding the main force across the Channel and marking their targets with flares ahead of a bombing raid. The gold eagle on my chest and the increase in wages was a bitter consolation. I would have given it all up to feel Laurie's arm around my shoulder or to coax one more shy smile out of Ranbir. But I carried on, surviving.

After VE Day, everyone wanted to get home as fast as possible, but there weren't enough ships to carry them. I couldn't imagine sitting around doing nothing while waiting for a ride home, so I stayed in the air force. I didn't think they would turn down a decorated officer volunteering for duty. And I was right.

For the first few months, our squadron flew dozens of missions to Germany and back, transporting liberated POWs home to England. Then, when the Pathfinders were finally stood down, I talked my way into a few Red Cross supply flights. After that, I stayed to demobilize the training bases and distribute the materiel and personnel worth keeping among the Commonwealth forces. The barracks were emptier, the mess halls quiet, corridors that had been teeming with men for years now echoing and empty. When my name at last came up for a ticket back to Canada, it was the autumn of 1946 and I had run out of reasons not to go home. And so, quite suddenly, I found myself in Toronto on a rainy afternoon, with a couple of medals in my pocket and no clothes worth wearing except my uniform.

I walked into Simpsons and up to the second floor. No one bothered me as I browsed the men's section and, for the first time in my life, picked out new clothes for myself that weren't stolen from my brother or borrowed from a friend. I found trousers and shirts, a winter jacket, a woollen hat and some gloves. A pair of sturdy boots. I looked for a blue shirt to replace the one Rebekah had mended for me years ago, but I couldn't find one that was the right colour.

The salesgirl gave me a warm smile as she wrapped my purchases, then asked me how long I'd been back and if I had any plans for the evening. A couple of years ago, I would have invited her out for a drink. But instead I thanked her, used the store washroom to change into my new clothes, and got out of there.

I walked through the city without really seeing anything, sidling past other pedestrians and dodging streetcars until my stomach growled. My feet had brought me to the doorway of a Chinese restaurant, and from inside came the tantalizing smell of fried dumplings and thick noodles. I took a seat near the window and stuffed myself with hot, rich food, washing it down with cheap beer. It tasted better than anything I'd eaten in years.

I could have enrolled in university, given that Veterans Affairs was handing out money to anyone who wanted to attend. But I hadn't the faintest idea what I would study. The air force had asked me to stay on and train sprogs, but I'd had enough of flying and paperwork to last me a lifetime. The money was there if I wanted to buy land, or a business, or even furniture, but I couldn't think of anything I wanted to do.

That night, I found a room in a boarding house just up the block, full of returning vets like me. The next day I walked down to the docks and found a job loading cargo on and off the barges that travelled the length of Lake Ontario. It didn't pay much, but it covered my rent and kept me in cigarettes and cheap liquor. I barely touched the money I'd made during the war, and when my gratuity came through, I deposited it at the bank and didn't think about it after that.

My shifts at the docks were long and punishing, but I welcomed the muscle aches and the bone-deep exhaustion that kept my mind firmly in the present. Only after a day of work could I drop into a blank, dreamless sleep. On my days off, restless and driven by a ceaseless energy, I took to walking the city, along the lakeshore, up towards York, the miles disappearing under my feet.

I still wasn't used to how little attention I drew in the world. It had been easy in my uniform—everyone saw the chevrons and the badges and the rest followed. But it seemed miraculous to me that I could order a drink, sit alone in a restaurant, walk down any street and no one gave me a second glance. That winter passed in a fog of hard labour, cheap, filling meals in the Chinese restaurant, and cold nights sleeping in my dingy rented room with the cracked window.

At least once a week, I thought about writing to my parents and went so far as to buy a postcard. But I couldn't think what to say. After so many years, where would I even begin? As for Rebekah—who knew where she was or if she even remembered me. But I thought about her, late at night in my lumpy bed, in a way I hadn't dared let myself throughout the war. As though, by not thinking about her in those days, I could protect her from everything I'd lived through.

It was a dream, in the end, that set my course. I'd spent my day off roaming the lakeshore, the ice broken up and melted, and the wind whipping the water into whitecaps. I became chilled to my core, despite taking nips from the flask in my coat pocket.

Back in my room, I'd fallen asleep with my clothes on. In my dream, I stood on the ridge overlooking Harrichford, the sky lit up with a thousand searchlights. In the distance, I could see birds as big as aircraft gliding down towards the village. I had called the birds here, but I couldn't remember why. My parents were somewhere in the valley below and I had to warn them. I stepped to the edge of the cliff and leapt. It was like remembering a skill I'd had as a child and forgotten until now, the way I found purchase in the air and twisted, until I was gliding towards the valley, faster and faster. The birds were diving now too, and the screech of incendiaries was in my ears, fading into the sound of spring frogs singing beside the river. Then I was on the bridge in Lincolnshire, looking down at the stream, the same one I'd stood on with Isaak. I turned to him, but it was Jep next to me. My brother looked as he had at fourteen. He cradled a piglet in his arms, his eyes wide as he stared up at me.

"Can we go now?" he asked, a rush of wings all around us, the birds descending.

I woke in the dark to a warm, steady wind blowing through my cracked window, the thin curtain flapping above my head. As midnight rain rolled across the lake and into the city, I felt winter withdraw its claws at last, and knew I couldn't put it off any longer.

The next morning, I packed my things and left my key with the landlady, having paid up until the end of the week. Then I walked downtown and caught the midmorning train to Orangeville.

The truck came over a small rise and I saw Harrichford's church spire in the distance.

"You can let me off here," I said, cutting off the driver in the middle of his story—something about the Home Guard parading with a cannon around the town square.

"You sure, son?" He looked around at the rolling fields on every side. "We're miles from anywhere."

"It's all right, I know the way from here," I said.

The truck engine faded into the distance as I started across the nearest field, my rucksack over my shoulder. The wind blew fresh from the east, tearing away the lingering clouds. Only a few miles and I would be home.

REBEKAH

The morning dawned wet, but the sky soon grew clear and the air sweet. I tied my hair back out of my eyes with a handkerchief and put on trousers suitable for gardening, then went out in the vegetable garden to dig over the bean patch while Adelaide helped Caroline hang freshly washed sheets on the line and air out the quilts. Dermot had taken Daisy into town and wasn't expected back until dinner. The earth was heavy and dark on my shovel, and the day warm. Everywhere there was the sound of water trickling and birds chirping in the still-bare branches.

Gordie, who had been asleep on the porch, raised his head and gave a sharp whoof of alarm. There was someone coming down the drive. I paused, leaning on my shovel, and watched them. It wasn't a neighbour—by now I knew them all from a distance.

The sheepdog heaved himself to his feet and ran down the steps, barking madly, racing towards the stranger. The dog circled, barking, then the person crouched down and offered a hand, and Gordie backed away, growling.

I glanced around the side of the house to where Adelaide and Caroline were working. Then I walked up the drive, still gripping the shovel.

Gordie took a few steps forward and sniffed the stranger's hand. His tail began to wag. He sniffed again and danced backwards. Then he leapt on the stranger and the two of them went down in a tumble of paws and limbs and tail.

I hurried forward, ready to call Gordie off, but as I drew closer, I heard laughter amid the dog's excited yips. The stranger was rolling around in the dirt with the dog, wrestling and hugging him all at once.

In response to my sharp whistle, Gordie came to me, but he quivered with excitement at my heel. The stranger picked themselves off the ground, brushing dirt from their clothes and turned towards me.

"Talk about a welcome—"

In front of me stood a figure in muddy boots and a jacket too heavy for the warm day. A head of brown hair growing out of its cropped military cut. Dirt on their face from wrestling with the dog. I took it all in slowly, scarcely trusting myself to breathe. Thick, straight brows over brown eyes, with a few crow's feet at the edges. All traces of adolescent softness gone. Shoulders wider and more boldly cut. It was as though a skilled sculptor had taken a chisel to every feature and fashioned them into a sharper, purer version. The one I'd always seen, underneath.

My shovel hit the dirt with a thud.

KIT

She had cut her hair and pulled it back under a kerchief. She was wearing—were those Jep's pants? Her knees and hands were stained with dirt, and her skin was freckled and chapped where the sun touched it. She bore almost no resemblance to the girl I'd met eight years ago. She had gained muscle, her wrists thicker, her face filled out and with more colour. But the eyes were the same.

I took two steps towards her. The shovel lay in the dirt. I wanted to reach out and pull her into my arms, bury my face in her hair.

"Rebekah, I—"

A small figure darted around the side of the house and raced towards us.

"Mumma, Mumma! *Regardes ça!*" A child was coming towards us, hands cupped carefully. She didn't even glance at me, all her focus on whatever she held.

Rebekah leaned down to see. "Oh, a toad. So tiny! Can you go put him back in the garden now?"

"Grand-mère said I could keep him."

Rebekah looked sidelong at me. "He belongs in the garden, *ma chérie.*"

The child followed Rebekah's gaze and immediately hid behind her mother.

"Go on, now. There's a good girl."

The child lingered, assessing me with big eyes. "Do you want to see my toad?"

"I'd love to." I knelt and the child opened her hands to allow me to peek at the creature. It was no bigger than my thumbnail.

"He is lovely," I said. "But your mother is right. He will be happier in the garden."

"You can put him where I was digging," Rebekah said. The child closed her hands and wandered away, looking over her shoulder at me as she went.

I stood up. "So."

"So," Rebekah echoed, staring at me as though I might disappear any moment.

My eyes followed the child as she rounded the edge of the house and disappeared. "I didn't expect to find you here."

Rebekah picked up the shovel. "Can't say I expected to be here. Her name is Adelaide."

"She's charming."

"Yes, she is."

The east wind stirred the grass alongside the drive. The house looked older, the roof not as straight as it once was, the shutters dropping flakes of paint. Everything seemed faded, like a photograph left exposed too long.

"How long have you—?"

"About three years."

She now stood with her feet planted, leaning on the shovel. No gloves, no hat. I recognized the kerchief on her head as an old one of my father's.

"My parents?"

"Dermot's in town. Caroline's hanging the laundry. She's—"

I picked up my bag and walked up to the house, across the porch and through the front door. It didn't squeak the way I remembered.

My mother was standing at the kitchen table, holding an armful of quilt, her back to me. At the sound of the door, she spoke over her shoulder. "Rebekah, Adelaide said something about a stranger on our . . ." She turned and caught sight of me, her words dying in the air. The quilt fell limp to the table.

"Hello," I said, from the doorway.

She inhaled sharply, once, twice, and then opened her arms. I stepped forward and hugged her, feeling her shoulder blades shake under my hands. I was a head taller than her now, looking down at her red hair streaked with grey. She smelled just the way I remembered.

She stepped away from me long enough to wallop me on the arm. "Where in the name of all saints have you been, you wicked, wicked child?" she cried, and then pulled me in for another hug. "We thought you were dead too," she sobbed into my shoulder. Another few blows to my back. "You ungrateful, selfish creature. How could you do this to your father and me?"

I hugged her tightly and apologized over and over.

At last, I got her to sit down at the table. I pulled some tea from my pack and heated the kettle on the stove. She sat, clutching the edge of the table with one hand, staring at me much the same way Rebekah had—as though I was a ghost who might vanish at any moment. I placed the mug in front of her, but she only looked at it until I sat down beside her and let her hold my hand as she drank it.

"Your father will be home soon. Perhaps I should go and meet him on the road, to prepare him. You know the Kromer girl is here now, with her daughter?"

"Yes, we, uh, met on my way in."

"Oh good, yes, Rebekah's been such a help with everything here, everything. A good hand in the garden. A decent horsewoman, would you believe it? And Adelaide, such a bright little thing, full of mischief, just like . . ." She paused to sip her tea. "Your father will be so happy to see you. He was so worried, you know, when you . . . when you . . ." Another flood of tears threatened to fall.

I covered her hand with mine. She wiped her eyes and took a gulp of tea. I looked around the kitchen, noting the cracked plaster, the soot-stained ceiling over the stove, the furniture from my childhood. My eyes settled on the mantel, where my father's pipe sat in its usual place.

"Where's Jep?" I said. "The army shipped home earlier than anyone, lucky ba— devils. I would've thought he'd be here by . . ."

That's when I noticed the piece of paper next to the pipe. A black-bordered telegram, leaning beside a photograph of my brother.

REBEKAH

Caroline came out of the house, red-eyed, and went out along the road to meet her husband. A short time later, Dermot came down the driveway at a canter and leapt from the saddle like a man a third his age. He charged up the porch to grasp Kit in a fierce embrace. Caroline followed a short while later on foot.

I slipped away to the barn with Adelaide to look at the piglets and give the McNairs some privacy. Caroline and Dermot had believed all their children to be lost forever. To be reunited? Well, that was the stuff of fairy tales. I listened to Adelaide tell me the name of each piglet as I scratched the sow behind the ears, thinking of my own parents, now lost to me.

A few months after arriving at the farm, I had written to my mother again, telling her that I was living with Mr. and Mrs. McNair, that Adelaide was healthy and growing well, and that I hoped they would meet their granddaughter someday. I had received her reply six weeks later, in an envelope with a coffee-ring stain on the front. She wrote that she was grateful to our former neighbours for their charity and that, if I ever decided to visit Montreal, to please telegram in advance, as she and Father were very busy. I had taken savage pleasure in tearing the letter into small pieces and letting the wind drag them from my fingers and across the hayfields. We'd had no communication since.

Dermot and Caroline had been the kindest, most generous and occasionally indulgent grandparents my daughter could have asked for. To let myself wish that my parents had made a different choice felt ungrateful in the face of everything the McNairs had done for us.

On the morning after Kit's return, I went out to the barn in a poor temper to search for the milk pail, and found them already at the milking stool, leaning against Jenny's flank and singing quietly. I stopped at the door, caught between surprise and embarrassment. I could only see their legs and two hands pulling with practised ease. The singing paused, the only indication that Kit had heard me.

"Maeve used to like it when I sang. Pa always says you get more milk that way."

"I tried singing but it made her angry."

"Maybe you didn't pick the right tune."

I hovered in the doorway listening to the milk splash, suddenly aware that I was wearing one of Dermot's old coats, two sizes too big for me, and that my hair was a rat's nest.

Kit finished and brought the milking stool and the pail to the door. I stepped back to let them pass, and Kit slid by without touching me.

In the yard, Kit turned back. "I've finished feeding and watering. Eggs are already inside. Better hurry if you want breakfast." They went off to the house humming the same tune as I balled my hands into fists. I had been out here in all weather doing chores for the past three and a half years, and yet Kit was treating me like I was still some lily-handed doctor's daughter. When I came in the kitchen door a few minutes later, everyone was seated, and Kit was ladling maple syrup onto Adelaide's plate.

"Rebekah, there you are," said Caroline. "Hurry and get washed. I doubt the pancakes will last long with these three at the table."

I stormed up to my room, washed my face, and yanked a comb through my hair, wishing absurdly for Elaine's nimble fingers and curling rags. I'd never taken anything the McNairs had given me for granted, and I'd done my share of the work to keep this place running while Kit had been off elsewhere, doing God knows what. To see how easily Caroline and Dermot forgave them, how smoothly Kit picked up the threads of their old life here, when I'd struggled to prove myself every day for years—the comb caught on a particularly tight knot and I winced. It wasn't fair. So many times, now, my life had been overturned in an instant. More than anything, I realized, I was afraid that Kit's return signalled the end of my time here.

My anger had ebbed by the time I returned to the kitchen. As I took my seat, Dermot was engrossed in his newspaper, Caroline was wiping syrup from the table where Adelaide had dripped it, clearly too busy staring at Kit to mind her fork. I didn't dare look at Kit, unsure of what I'd see in their expression and also unsure how I would feel about whatever I saw.

In the days that followed, I found reasons to be anywhere Kit wasn't—out in the vegetable garden, or riding Daisy to town and back, or upstairs teaching Adelaide her letters. Kit, by contrast, threw themselves into the upkeep of the farm with a discipline and energy I'd never witnessed from them. As spring marched on, the porch gained a new coat of paint, the paddock fences were mended, weeds pulled, and a new flower bed dug for Caroline. Kit helped Dermot refurbish Pete's old stall into a larger pen for the piglets and replaced the damaged shingles on the barn roof.

Chores that had gone undone for years as Caroline and Dermot and I struggled to make ends meet were finished in a matter of days. Caroline sang to herself in the kitchen, and Dermot walked with a renewed spring in his step. Unless I dragged her away, Adelaide followed Kit around the farm, chattering and constantly underfoot.

I returned from town one afternoon with a bag of sugar and found Kit and Caroline in a fit of giggles on the porch, darning socks. Kit caught sight of me and sobered immediately.

"What's so funny?" I asked, setting the bag on the steps and sitting down to rest my feet for a moment.

"Never you mind," Caroline said, shaking her head. "I sent Adelaide inside ten minutes ago for my glasses and she hasn't come back." She leaned towards Kit. "Remind you of anyone else at that age?"

I expected Kit to bristle, but instead they shrugged and said with a smile, "Jep was worse." I shook my head as I went inside.

Tasks that I remembered Kit despising—laundry, dishes, anything that could be termed women's work—were no longer a point of contention. They were as cheerful setting tables and hanging laundry as they were with any outdoor chore. Their cooking hadn't improved, however, and I wasn't proud to admit that I took a small measure of comfort from that.

KIT

Despite my mother's pleading, I refused to take one of the beds in the attic. I couldn't very well turn Rebekah and Adelaide out of my childhood bedroom, but neither could I bring myself to sleep in my brothers' old room. I had gone up there only once since coming back, to fetch an extra blanket. The attic seemed smaller, the ceiling nearly as low as a Lancaster's cabin, the windows tiny and airless, and then there was Jep's abandoned bed, with his collections of rocks and tin soldiers and the odd scraps of wood Landon and I had whittled into toys for him over the years. I fled back out into the spring sunshine.

I took to spending my nights in the hayloft. It had been empty of hay for years, so I made myself a cot out of old crates and layers of horse blankets and slept with the loft doors flung wide open to the stars. I could sit dangling my legs over the edge of the loft and smoke in peace, with fresh air blowing over my face and lulling me into enough calm to close my eyes for at least a few hours each night.

That first morning home, I awoke to the sound of a chickadee calling, liquid notes bouncing off the sky. The air was damp, and for a moment, I was in the gardener's shed in Lincolnshire. I was in an underwater grotto. I was back in the cottage with Rebekah, breathing in the humid smell of damp earth and our mingled breath. I reached out from under the blankets, feeling for smooth skin or slender fingers—and opened my eyes to the hayloft, dawn sunlight slanting across the ceiling.

I had stumbled down the ladder and out to the water pump. Looking around, I could only see the decay and neglect that had gathered in every corner of the farm: the chipped paint, the broken boards, the rickety chicken coop, the overgrown apple trees. It had been an easy choice to do all the things my parents hadn't been able to take on themselves while I was away. That it gave me an excuse to avoid Rebekah was another benefit. She had been prickly and distant ever since I'd come home, quick to leave any room I entered, using Adelaide as an excuse to be anywhere I wasn't.

I could see how hard the past few years had been on her and on my parents. Painting a few boards and replacing roof shingles seemed the very least I could do to make up for being gone for so long and leaving them to fend for themselves during hard times.

Rebekah had laid a fierce claim on Daisy, our old cart horse, and so when I went anywhere, I walked. The fields and the forest were the same, with the trees newly budded and the smell of mud and growing things in the air. The trails I walked were overgrown, and somehow the distances were shorter. The climb to the ridge I'd remembered as so long disappeared under my boots. The clifftop where we had once eaten licorice no longer overlooked an endless vista, but a small and unremarkable countryside. The river was simply a slender waterway running through Harrichford County, no more than a stream, really. The pathways I could have walked backwards and blindfolded as a child had changed enough that I no longer knew precisely where I was at all times.

At the farm, Adelaide followed me like a duckling. For the first few days, she was quiet, observing me as though I was a stray cat she hoped to tame. I ignored her. It didn't take long, however, before she was chattering at me in a half-French slang I barely understood. I listened and apparently nodded at the right moments, and from then on, she was a shadow that clung to me no matter the angle of the sun.

My parents had aged more than I had expected. My father, especially, had more grey than black in his hair, and was worn out by even the simplest chores. After he went to bed the first night, my mother told me of his illness and miraculous recovery. I was heartsick that I hadn't been there to help, and said as much, expecting my mother to scold me for running away. Instead, she took my hand and patted it.

"You're home now," she said.

I swallowed. "When I left, I didn't know—" I faltered. She and my father had known only Kathleen, just as Laurie and Isaak and the others had known only Christopher. As for who was sitting at the table with her now, I couldn't even begin to explain it to myself, let alone to her.

My mother looked at Jep's photo on the mantelpiece for a long moment. "What's done is gone and can't be called back. I'm just glad you came home." She squeezed my hand, and I knew that was the last we would ever say about it.

Rebekah continued to leave any room I entered and watched my conversations with Adelaide with fierce attention. I stayed out of her way as much as possible, but I knew we could only go on avoiding each other for so long.

JUNE 1947

REBEKAH

MY DAUGHTER WASN'T ANYWHERE IN THE HOUSE.

"Adelaide!" I called from the porch. Gordie flattened his ears at my shrill tone. I stomped down the steps, half of me worried she'd wandered off into the forest alone, and the other half irritated at her recent discovery of disobedience. I went through the yard and round to the side of the barn, where I found her hammering shingles into place on the roof of the new chicken coop, crouched between Kit's arms, chubby fingers clutching the hammer under Kit's steady grip.

"One more!" Kit said, and together they swung the hammer and tapped a nail home.

Adelaide beamed with happiness when she caught sight of me. "Mumma, we're making a new home for chickens. I'm building it myself!"

I exchanged an unintended glance with Kit, whose legs created a safe barrier between Adelaide and the five-foot drop to the ground, and we almost smiled at each other.

"Adelaide, get down from there. You'll fall and break your neck."

"I won't!"

Kit took the hammer and laid it aside, then gathered up Adelaide. "Your ma said to come down, so we're going down."

I didn't take a full breath until they were both back on the ground. Adelaide came to hug my skirt and show me the nail still clutched in her fist. I pried it out of her fingers, and sent her inside to Caroline with a gentle push to the back of her head.

Kit had been gathering up the tools into a bucket, but stopped to watch Adelaide go.

"I wasn't aware we needed a new coop," I said, trying for a neutral tone, but hearing the ice slip through anyway. "The old one held up fine."

Kit shrugged, ran one hand down a corner post. "Even before I left, it was shot through with dry rot. I meant to fix it that summer, but well . . ." The words hung unspoken between us.

"I wanted to go with you," I said.

Kit looked around quickly. "Not here." They walked around the barn to the vegetable garden. I followed.

In the garden, Kit picked up a hoe and began hilling potatoes. I watched them, arms folded. The hoe bit and turned in silence for a few moments. Then Kit said, "Landon made it sound so final, I couldn't—"

"You didn't think to ask me? I could have told you he had it wrong."

Kit's smile was small and sad. "By the time I arrived, you were gone. I had no idea how to reach you."

I swallowed. "Something happened, that night of the dance. We had to leave, quickly." A lighter flame in the darkness. The reflections of shattered glass across the road. "It wasn't about you or Landon at all."

"I thought you'd make your choice." The hoe paused. "Seeing Adelaide, well . . ."

I began attacking the weeds growing up among the tomato plants. We worked in silence for a few minutes.

"Where did you go?" I asked finally.

Kit shrugged and kicked a clod of earth off the hoe. "I hopped a freight train, headed west. Where did you go?"

"To Montreal, then to Halifax with the navy."

"I made it to Lake Superior. Saw the sun rise over the water, just as we'd planned. It wasn't as impressive as the Atlantic turned out to be, but at the time, it seemed the most beautiful thing I'd ever seen."

"What did you do? Up there, I meant."

"I worked in a logging camp."

"But how—?"

"It's true," Kit said. "Believe what you want."

They leaned forward to pull on a particularly stubborn weed that refused to budge. I wrapped my hand around the base of it. Another heave and it came free, showering bits of earth over both of us.

Kit spat into the dirt and tossed the weed aside. There was mud on their cheekbone. Standing this close, their face was both familiar and strange. The eyes, though, the eyes were the same.

I picked up the hoe and began weeding the bean plants, as Kit checked the cabbages for slugs. We managed half the row in silence, and then I thought of the uniform I'd seen them wash and hang to dry the week they arrived.

"So how did you get from a logging camp to the air force?"

The explanation carried us through tending the rest of the garden and into the afternoon. Kit had unearthed a bucket of ancient paint and a couple of brushes from the barn, and Adelaide joined us in painting the new chicken coop.

"And then the CO says to me, 'I expect my men to behave better than animals,' and I said, 'Sir, they can't help it, they're Scottish!'"

I laughed. Our brushes swished across the boards, Adelaide getting more paint on the grass than anything else.

"What happened to the pig?" she asked.

"Oh, I eventually caught him, washed him off and took him back home. I left the moustache on, though, as a little reminder of his adventure."

"I'm surprised they didn't kick you out," I said lightly, dipping my brush.

"Worse—they handed me some medals and promoted me instead," Kit said.

I laughed. Kit kept their eyes fixed on the chicken coop, but I caught the faint blush that crept into their cheeks.

"Did you ever crash?" Adelaide asked, all innocence.

"*Chérie*, those are not funny stories," I said. "Maybe Kit would rather not—"

"Yes. Several times," Kit said, crouching down to my daughter's height and continuing to paint. "There was one time we were flying back and our plane got hit, so I had to jump out with my parachute, over the Channel."

"Did you die?" Adelaide asked, wide-eyed.

"No," said Kit. "I was rescued."

"By who?"

I was half listening, expecting to hear another wild story about the bravery of the merchant marine or the local coast guard.

"Selkies," Kit said, very seriously.

"You mean, like the ones in grand-mère's stories?"

"Exactly like them."

I could not contain my snort. "You expect me to believe you were rescued by mythical seal people?"

Kit gave a one-shouldered shrug. "I know what I saw. One moment I was in the water, tangled in my chute and drowning. The next moment, I woke up safe and alive."

Adelaide's brush had paused. "Where did they take you?"

"To an underwater cave, all blue and green and sparkling with mussel shells set into the walls. I slept on a bed of kelp, and they bathed my injuries with sea water and tied them up tightly with seaweed. Took off their seal skins and wrapped me in them, so I was all toasty warm in their fur. I slept like a babe."

Adelaide was listening so hard her brush was now dripping white paint onto her shoes. I put it gently back in the tin. "What did you eat?"

"They brought me oysters and giant clams and fish. I built myself a little fire in the cave and cooked up the most delicious chowder you'd ever taste."

"I thought selkies didn't like fire," I said, climbing up the ladder to paint the roof trim.

Kit looked up at me. "They don't, but they knew I was injured and they were very brave. They stayed and fed me soup for three days and three nights. By the time the soup was all gone, I was better."

"What did they look like?" Adelaide asked. She had plunked herself down on the grass, painting entirely abandoned.

Kit thought for a moment. "Well, when they were seals, they were beautiful, dark colours—brown and black and deep grey, with big eyes and whiskers like a dog. And when they took off their skin, they were like people, but different. They had long fingers and webbed toes, dark hair and dark eyes. I remember their fingers were always cold."

"Were they naked?"

I caught Kit's eye for a fraction of a second. Over Adelaide's head, Kit said, "I don't remember, but I suppose they must have been."

I cleared my throat. "None of this explains how you got back to England."

Kit grinned and resumed painting. "Well, on the morning of the fourth day, I woke up and the selkies were gone. I went out of the cave and onto the beach, and there were hundreds of gulls, circling and screeching and nesting on the cliffs. So I sat down and whistled a tune and they all came flying to me, swirling around my head, hundreds and hundreds of them. When I stopped whistling, the birds flew away and I was sitting in a pile of feathers. I stitched all of them into a coat, and then I flew up the cliff and across the countryside, back to the base. I strolled inside the officers' mess just in time for tea, and boy, were they surprised to see me! I was so hungry from all that flying, I sat right down and ate all their lunch, every last bit." They emphasized the last word by tapping Adelaide's nose with the end of the paintbrush. My daughter shrieked with laughter.

I rolled my eyes. "You expect me to believe that out of everyone in that whole channel, the selkies picked you? Why?"

The magic of the story evaporated in an instant. Kit dipped the paintbrush and added a few strokes to the boards. "I don't know," they said softly. Their gaze became distant, lost in a private grief. I could have bitten off my tongue, I felt so clumsy and cruel.

"I know why," said Adelaide. She was now threading dandelions together in a crown. "Because they knew you were like them."

"What?" Kit and I said at the same time, glancing at each other.

"Grand-mère told me. You're part selkie. So they recognized you," Adelaide continued.

"I suppose so," Kit said quietly.

"That makes me part selkie too, right, Mumma?"

I swallowed. "Yes, darling, I guess it does."

"But I've never seen the ocean."

"You did once, love. A long time ago, when you were very small. I dipped your toes in the sea." I'd never wanted my daughter to be afraid of water, so the day before we got on the train, I'd put her smallest toe in the icy Atlantic.

Adelaide shrugged. "I'd rather be a faerie. Less wet and you get to live in the forest and talk to the birds." She got up and put the flower crown on Kit's head, then bounced away into the house, painting and selkies forgotten.

As I climbed back down the ladder and helped Kit wash our paintbrushes at the pump, I said, "You shouldn't fill her head with such nonsense."

"You didn't mind my nonsense once upon a time," Kit replied, peeling a bit of paint from a fingernail.

I opened my mouth but couldn't think of any reply. So I turned on my heel and followed my daughter into the house.

KIT

That night, my parents went to sleep early, exhausted by a day of outdoor work. Adelaide insisted that I be the one to put her to bed. I sat on the edge of the quilt and told her the story of the selkies and the birds one more time. When I emerged from the bedroom,

I saw a flicker of movement at the top of the stairs, but by the time I returned to the kitchen, Rebekah was pulling the kettle off the stove.

The night was mild, so we drank our tea on the front porch. I noted the wasps' nests clustered under the eaves, the opaque cobwebs in the corners. The brick wall was cool and sweating a fine, chalky ash that fell on us as we sat under the porch light.

"Looks like rain tomorrow," I said, gazing up at the clouds blotting out the stars.

"Good thing you finished fixing the barn roof," she said, sipping her tea. My hand still ached, and my neck was sunburnt from the week I had spent up there, ripping up shingles and throwing them down into the woodpile, hammering in the new ones my father had planed.

"I was thinking of taking Adelaide to the movies next week," Rebekah said. "You could come, if you like."

"I would."

"Well, that's lucky, because Adelaide insists she won't go unless you come." Her smile was slanted in the lamplight. For the first time since coming home, I saw the ghost of the girl I'd met all those years ago, wading across the river with her skirt above her knees.

"She's a great kid," I said. "You should be proud of her."

"She is, isn't she?"

Somewhere in the distance, an owl tested its voice, vowels trembling up and down a scale. Rebekah stood up and shook out her skirt. Brick dust and pine needles fell to the boards. She tossed the dregs of her tea over the railing.

As we went down the hall, blinking, into the bright kitchen, Rebekah stopped in the doorway.

"There's something you should know about Adelaide," she said, staring down at her empty mug. "Your mother wouldn't want me to say it, but you should know that—"

"If this is about you and Jep, Ma already told me."

Rebekah looked up from her hands. "What if I told you, it wasn't . . . that she's actually—"

"She's your daughter," I said quietly. "That's all that matters. I don't care about any of the rest." I gently pried the mug from her grip and went to the sink.

Rebekah stayed in the doorway for a long moment, and then I felt her join me, the warm pressure of her arm against mine. I wanted to touch her wrist, trace the veins that ran from elbow to palm. I wanted to taste her knuckles with my tongue.

Instead, we washed the dishes, standing side by side without speaking. And then she went up to bed and I walked out to the hayloft alone.

The day of our outing dawned wet and raining. My head ached, above my left ear, the way it often did now on rainy days. Adelaide was fretful, refusing to eat her porridge and dawdling when Rebekah told her to go change into her town clothes. It was enough to put Rebekah into a sour temper as well, and it was on the tip of my tongue to suggest we go another day.

Adelaide stomped up the stairs to the bedroom as Rebekah clattered the breakfast dishes into the sink.

"I don't know what's gotten into her," she said.

My mother looked up from putting on her boots near the door. "It's like I warned you, that devil's streak in her, from . . ." She caught herself and shook her head. "Well, you know what I mean.

I'm going to rescue the strawberries before the birds get them. Your father got it into his head to walk over to the Gorsemans', so if you meet him on the way to town, tell him to hurry home if he wants a hot lunch."

She went out, the kitchen door swinging shut behind her.

Rebekah and I shared a look. "You know, Landon used to kick every stair on the way up, when he didn't get his way," I said.

Rebekah snorted. "Very comforting, Kit. Thank you."

I chuckled as Adelaide stomped back down the stairs, dressed but with her hair in shambles. Rebekah sighed and went to coax it into a braid.

The rain had let up a little by the time we were ready to leave. It was a long way to Orangeville and I hoped we'd be able to hitch a ride at least partway. Adelaide's mood lightened as we went, and it wasn't long until she was marching ahead of us, singing a wartime tune I'd regretted teaching her almost immediately.

Rebekah hung back to walk with me, her arm brushing mine every few steps. At that moment, I didn't care if we ever made it to the movies. I would have been content walking along the wet road, the air heavy with the smell of lilacs from a nearby hedgerow, Adelaide running ahead of us and Rebekah at my shoulder.

No one else was out in this weather, not even in cars. The rain and the damp wind on my face reminded me of the Lincolnshire base, of afternoons in the gardener's shed with Laurie. I thought of his sisters in Edmonton. I should write to them again, to make sure they were getting on all right.

Just then I noticed something slumped at the side of the road ahead. I touched Rebekah's wrist, and we began to jog towards it, overtaking Adelaide. As we came closer, my heart lurched into my mouth. I rushed forward and fell to my knees beside my father, where he lay crumpled in the ditch.

I shook his shoulder, but he didn't respond, eyes wide and staring into the distance. I placed my palm in front of his mouth and could just feel the faint warmth of his breath on my skin. Rebekah crouched beside me as I took off my coat and covered him with it.

"Is he alive?"

"Barely. We need a doctor."

"First we need to get him out of the damp."

Rebekah called to Adelaide, "*Chérie*, run home and tell Grandma to hitch up Daisy to the cart and come to the crossroads."

"I don't want to. It's so far."

"Do as you're told!" Rebekah snapped, with an edge in her voice I'd never heard before. Adelaide was startled into tears, but she turned and ran back the way we had come.

Rebekah said, "Kit, you need to fetch the doctor."

"I'm not leaving him," I heard myself say.

"All right, I'll go." Rebekah pulled off her coat and folded it into a pillow, slid it gently under my father's head. "Your mother will be here soon. I'll bring the doctor from town."

I nodded. She hesitated a moment and her fingers brushed the top of my head. Then she took off running down the road towards Harrichford.

The rain turned to a drizzle, a fine mist that might have come straight off the English Channel. The sound of Rebekah's footsteps on the road faded, until all I could hear was the whisper of wind in the trees overhead and the gentle pat-pat of rain on the dirt road. My father gave a great shudder and a spasm ran through him, tightening all his muscles in sequence. I gripped his hand and brushed the hair from his forehead, feeling helpless.

"Pa," I said, and his hand tightened on my own for a fraction of a second. Whether it meant he could hear me or it was a trick of the seizure, I had no idea. "You would have loved flying. It was like being a bird, seeing the whole world spread out like a painting."

As I sat beside him in the rain, I told him about flight training in Manitoba, and how the fields fell away to tiny blocks of colour below us. Of coming home from our night missions.

"You can't even imagine the stars, Papa. They were so clear and bright above the clouds. It was cold, but when the moon was out, everything was silver and ice. Vanier used to say that they looked like a handful of snow crystals thrown across polished black ice. I thought you would like that. You would have liked him."

I kept talking, about anything I could think of, every memory, every beautiful thing I'd ever seen, plucking them out of the tapestry of the war and stringing them into a necklace of shining lights.

At last, I heard the jingle of a harness and the sound of hooves on the road, coming up at a quick trot. My mother drew Daisy to a halt, Adelaide beside her, looking miserable.

My mother jumped down and hurried to us. "Let's get him home, quickly now."

Together we lifted my father as carefully as we could and laid him in the pile of quilts in the back of the cart. I sat with him as she drove us home, the cart jagging side to side. We staggered up the steps with him and laid him down on the living room floor. I hauled Landon's old cot from the attic and set it up next to the fireplace, and by the time the doctor's car came down the drive, we had stripped off his wet clothes and rewrapped him in warm blankets.

The doctor was a young, round-faced man with a thick neck and rosy cheeks. Once he and Rebekah had joined my mother at Pa's bedside, I went out into the rain to unhitch Daisy and put away the cart, knowing that my father would be furious at the thought of me leaving an animal out in the wet a moment longer than necessary. I spent some time in the barn brushing her before I led her to her stall.

Soon Adelaide came to find me, tears dripping down her cheeks. "Is Grandpa going to be okay?"

I crouched next to her. "The doctor is here to help him. You did a good thing, running home so fast and bringing the cart back."

She sniffed, wiped her nose on her sleeve. "Can I see him?"

"Not until the doctor leaves. But there is a special tea I want to make for him. I have everything I need except ten perfect butter-cups and a four-leaf clover."

Adelaide brightened. "There's lots of buttercups in the field. I'll get them." She darted out of the barn, tears forgotten. I stood up and walked back towards the house.

REBEKAH

Dermot lingered for three days, incoherent and slurring, unable to move and trembling like a leaf. Dr. Healy came to look in on him every day, sometimes twice, but each visit ended with a quiet whisper to Caroline and a shake of the head. The doctor couldn't say if he would recover, or if he did, how much of his former self would remain. When Dermot showed no improvement by the end of the second day, Caroline summoned Father Bradley to perform the last rites.

Every moment that Kit wasn't at Dermot's side, they were doing chores or urging Caroline to rest and eat something. At night, Kit slept in a chair next to their father's bed while Caroline went upstairs, exhausted. Adelaide was fretful and underfoot, too young to understand what was happening, but old enough to know that it was bad. Kit sent her off on invented errands—for strands of spider silk, or the smallest pea shoot in the garden, or seven perfectly round pebbles. Kit gathered all these treasures into tiny sachets they sewed from quilt patches, and Adelaide reverently placed them under Dermot's pillow.

On the third night, Dermot slipped into a false sleep, his eyes closing and his breath becoming shallow and faster. Caroline refused to leave his side, sitting by the bed and holding his hand long into the night. Only when Kit was nodding from exhaustion was I able to coax them upstairs and into the bed next to Adelaide. I sat vigil with Caroline, brewing endless pots of tea, and stitching a rag doll for my daughter to keep my hands busy.

At three o'clock in the morning, Dermot opened his eyes and looked at his wife, his mouth trembling with the effort to smile.

I slipped out to the porch and sat on the steps smoking a cigarette until the short summer night was over and a red dawn glowed on the horizon.

The following Sunday was bright and clear, as cruelly beautiful a summer afternoon as anyone could imagine for a funeral. We walked to the church in town, following the hearse. Adelaide was in her soberest dress, her hair pulled back and tamed with a black ribbon. I had put on my grey jacket and skirt and tugged gloves over the calluses on my hands. Kit looked alien and withdrawn in their uniform, the jacket pulled tight to the neck, cap slightly askew. Caroline was a pale waif of the woman I had come to know. The tears on her cheeks fell and dried, leaving salt streaks that glittered every time she lifted her head to look up at the hearse.

The church was as full as I had seen it these past few months, every citizen of Harrichford come to pay their respects. Kit escorted Caroline down the centre aisle to a place in the front pew. I intended to take a seat farther back with Adelaide, but Caroline reached for us, and so I sat in the front row next to Kit, Adelaide between us. She was too young to really understand what was happening, though I had tried to explain while tying her hair back earlier that morning.

"Grandpa was sick, but now he's gone somewhere else. Somewhere nice."

"Somewhere with medicine?"

"Something like that."

She turned around in the chair, her expression as serious as any adult's. "Is he with Daddy?"

"With—?"

"That's what Grandma said. That he is in heaven with my daddy, that they will be having tea together all the time and that there are lots of flowers there."

I sighed. "Yes, *chérie*, that's where he is."

"Good." She rearranged herself in her chair and took up playing with the hem of her dress, the matter as resolved as a near four-year-old could manage.

After the burial, there was a reception with food and drinks in the church hall. Kit pocketed a handful of cookies and whisked Adelaide out the door. I watched Caroline carefully and drew her away from the gathering when she became tired, saying our thanks to everyone.

The last of the afternoon passed slowly, the house feeling empty without Dermot at the table with his newspaper, the smell of his pipe smoke filling the air. Kit and I dismantled the cot in the living room and returned it to the attic. I expected Caroline to retire early, but instead she attacked the housework like a madwoman, scrubbing the kitchen floor and the table, washing the sheets and blankets and cleaning the cupboards with feverish intensity.

We ate sandwiches for dinner, and afterwards we sat on in the kitchen with the door open to catch the evening breeze. Adelaide played with her new doll, while I stared at nothing.

"Will you tell the story?" Kit asked.

Caroline looked up slowly, as though returning from a great distance.

"Please?"

She took a breath, and began the story of Corin and Siobhan, one I'd heard Dermot tell at least a dozen times since Adelaide and I had come to live here. Caroline stayed true to his version, until she came to the part after Corin brought the seal-woman back.

"Siobhan became a sullen, quiet woman who rarely spoke and sat for hours staring out at the sea like one who is dead and has gone on living." Caroline fell silent, and I saw her shoulders shake. Adelaide came to lean against my knee, and I lifted her up into my lap.

"What happened next?" I asked, to bring Caroline back to us.

She drew a breath and continued. "Siobhan stayed with him another three years, until one day, she was gone." She shook her head. "I never liked Dermot's ending. The way his mother told the tale, Siobhan dove into the sea and it welcomed her with open arms. She dove down and down until her lungs were pure fire and the light above glimmered smaller and smaller."

Adelaide's eyes were wide. "And then she died?"

Caroline snorted. "Of course not. She drew in a deep breath of water, and her legs fused and became a tail, her arms shortened into flippers. Dark, wet fur grew over her body and her body curved into a slippery shadow made for gliding through the ocean."

"But she didn't have her skin! Corin burned it."

"It was only a smelly old sealskin. She never needed it to change back because she always knew who she was. In here." Caroline leaned forward to tap Adelaide gently in the centre of her chest.

I wanted to protest that she couldn't change the rules in the middle of the story. Then I looked over at Kit, who was gazing at the stove, a thousand miles away. The lamplight played on the bare skin of their throat, where their shirt collar had fallen open.

I leaned down to pick up Adelaide's doll from the floor. "Come on, darling, time for bed."

"But I'm not tired," she protested, even as her eyelids drooped.

I carried her upstairs, stripped off her dress and answered a dozen or more questions about selkies before she fell asleep, one arm clutching the doll. I'd just got up and was straightening my skirt, when I heard Caroline go into her bedroom and close the door.

Downstairs, the kitchen was empty. I finished the dishes and then sat on the porch and read, in the slanting evening light, trying to keep myself from thinking too much.

After the sun went down, I headed to the barn. I hesitated at the bottom of the ladder to the hayloft, then climbed resolutely.

Kit was sitting on an empty crate near the open door of the loft, looking out over the fields. It was dim in the loft, and I could see the red tip of a cigarette between their fingers.

I sat down next to them. "Hey, fly boy, you got a light?"

A ghost of a smile trickled over Kit's face, and they obediently handed me a cigarette and then leaned over to flick the lighter for me. We sat and smoked in silence, gazing out through the door.

"Someday, I'm going to find out what you did during the war, to learn such terrible language," they said.

I smiled. "I was a file clerk."

"Of course."

Kit smoked like a soldier, sucking in the tobacco as though it might be snatched from them at any moment. When the cigarette was finished, they stubbed it out and put the butt in their jacket pocket. The familiarity of it made me smile.

Outside, the light continued to fade, until we were in a world of greys and blues and shadows. Kit drew a flask from their pocket and took a long swallow before offering it to me. I took a sip, the sharp liquor making my eyes water. As I handed it back, the last of the twilight caught the metal, illuminating an engraving just below my thumb. LH.

Kit took another long swallow.

"I left without saying goodbye," they said quietly. "Pa was so kind to me that night, and I just disappeared on him. On Ma. Eight years." They looked sickened and haunted. "I didn't mean to do it, it just sort of happened, and by the time I realized what I'd done, I couldn't get back."

"You were angry," I said.

Kit nodded. "But with Landon. And you. My father fixed my nose after the fight."

"What fight?"

As we sat in the deepening night, Kit told me everything. The fight with Landon, then running away. Training in Portage la Prairie. About Matthew and Isaak. About Laurie. Parts that seemed more like half-remembered dreams. I struggled to understand, until I remembered the voices in the river and the stone foundation in the pine forest.

"Did you love him?"

Kit gave me an unreadable look. "Laurie? I don't know, maybe. He saved my life, in more ways than I can count. And then, when it was my turn, I . . . I failed him. I failed all of them."

I touched their knee. "That wasn't your fault."

Kit looked down at my hand. "What about Landon?"

"What about him?"

"Would you have married him?"

I looked away. "I don't know. I thought I wanted to. You were gone and he was there." Kit nodded, looking out over the dark fields. "I'm sorry, this must be hard to hear."

"No." A hand covered mine in the dark. "I guess the question should be whether you regret not marrying him."

"Sometimes, because your mother wouldn't have had to invent the whole lie about Jep. But I can't regret the past. It brought me Adelaide."

Kit smiled. "I didn't think I could become even half as attached to a creature other than you, and then you bring this tiny French-speaking dervish into my life and—"

I leaned forward and kissed them. Kit's arms folded around my waist and I climbed into their lap and we overbalanced and fell off the crate, onto the floor. Kit was somehow different, yet smelled the same, tasted the same. Every place they touched me lit up, like I was being painted back into existence. The parts of me that had only belonged to Adelaide for so long, sticky toddler fingers on my arms and my legs, my face so sunburnt and chapped. Kit touched me like I was something beautiful and rare. Not someone's daughter or mother, not a fake wife or a fake widow or a prize, but a wild creature who'd consented to being tamed for only this moment.

They had scars I didn't remember, muscles and creases that were not there before. A neat line of hair missing from their scalp just above one ear. I had invoked the memory of the cottage so many times—the rain, the cold air, the sound of breathing in my ear and the angle of a collarbone—that to be here now, again, was surreal. As though I was kissing Kit and my memory of Kit and their younger self and this familiar stranger all at once.

Afterwards, we lay curled together in front of the open doors, looking out over the moonlit landscape. As Kit traced me from my shoulder down to my waist with light, feathery strokes, I explained how I lost my place in the WRCNS, the letter from my mother, my time staying with Hatti, the train ride back to Harrichford.

Kit pressed a kiss into the nape of my neck. "I would have come back sooner, if I'd known."

I squeezed their fingers. "No one can fly that far, idiot."

"I would have. I would have whistled up a wind and flown in my coat of feathers."

"I know."

Their breathing fell into a slow rhythm, warm against the back of my neck, and the arm over my waist grew slack and heavy. I lay awake in the dark, listening to the crickets outside the loft door. All around us, I felt the rush of phantom wings.

AUGUST 1947

KIT

A FEW DAYS AFTER THE FUNERAL, MY MOTHER HAD announced that she couldn't bear to sleep in the master bedroom alone, and that she would move into the smaller room with Adelaide. When Rebekah and I protested, she gave us her steely glare and said that she would welcome the company of her grandchild and that Rebekah deserved some privacy. So my mother carried her things into Adelaide's room and Rebekah moved into the larger bedroom. I kept my cot out in the hayloft for appearances, but in truth I spent every night with her. If my mother knew, she said nothing. For the first time in my life, I was content with our mutual silence.

The rest of that summer blazed with a warmth that was both bittersweet and wonderful. I missed my father every day. The smallest detail of his presence would bring tears to my eyes: a half-mended piece of tack, the slowly dwindling stack of folded newspapers in the firebox, the scent of pipe smoke that dissipated a little more each day and yet remained caught in the lapels of his old jacket and hidden in corners of rooms. His pipe now sat on the mantelpiece next to Jep's photograph. I helped Rebekah pack away his clothes in the attic, interspersed with cedar shavings.

Our lives fell into a gentle routine. Every month, two cheques arrived, one addressed to Jep's wife and the other to Christopher McNair. If my mother saw that name and wondered, she never said anything to me. With that income, plus the produce of the farm, we managed. The four of us watched the fireworks in town on Dominion Day, went on picnics, swam in the river, and one weekend hitchhiked into Orangeville to see *Donald's Dilemma*. My mother doted even more on Adelaide, spending long hours teaching her to bake or reading her stories, which left Rebekah and me time to wander the forest as we once had, though we never went far or for long. During the day I worked outside, and in the evening, I carved wooden animals for Adelaide while my mother told stories. At night, I still sometimes dreamed I was back inside the Lanc, spiralling down towards the Channel, Laurie's face melting away as he screamed, but when I woke sweating and shaking, Rebekah was there to wind her arms around me. If I buried my face in her hair and reminded myself that I was home, I found I could sleep again.

By early August, the garden had grown to spectacular heights and the pigs were fat. One Sunday afternoon, after the sticky walk home from church, no one had the energy for anything except drinking glasses of lemonade and dozing. My mother went upstairs to nap and Rebekah sat at the kitchen table, pinning and then cutting a pattern for a new dress. I sat beside her scrubbing an old piece of harness in a bucket for the sake of feeling cold water on my hands. Only Adelaide seemed unaffected, crouched on the floorboards near the open front door, having a whispered conversation with her doll.

When I heard a motor car in the drive, I thought it was Mrs. Gorseman coming to check in on my mother. I didn't bother to get up, since she always found her own way in. Gordie gave a soft wuffle, the sort of bark he used for familiar people, and there were footsteps on the front porch.

I looked up to see a figure in the open front doorway, silhouetted against the golden sunlight. Tall, bulky, with a cap on his head and heavy boots.

I froze, my hands in the wash basin, soap bubbles breaking silently on the surface. The dress pattern on the table fluttered and then stilled under Rebekah's hand. Only Adelaide remained absorbed in her conversation with her doll, not even looking up.

The figure took another step into the house. His face was bearded and fleshier than I remembered, with deep lines etched on the brow under the cap. A jacket despite the heat of the day. A large rucksack on his shoulder, causing his whole torso to lean to the right.

The pack dropped with a thud onto the floor, startling Adelaide, who clutched her doll and gazed up at him. He tugged the cap from his head, one hand ruffling his short hair with a gesture so familiar it took my breath away.

"Hello, little bird," he said as he knelt.

Rebekah grabbed the edge of the table, her knuckles white. Adelaide stared, transfixed, at the newcomer. I had the overwhelming urge to scoop her up in my arms, away from him, as though he were a rattlesnake she had stumbled upon in the woods.

"Is there anyone else at home?" he asked her. I placed my hand over Rebekah's.

Adelaide looked over her shoulder and his gaze followed, squinting a little in the dim indoor light. He handed her his

cap and stood. I knew the moment his eyes adjusted, because he
stopped dead.

"Kathleen?"

I couldn't think of anything to say, too thrown by his presence.
I moved my hand, but not before his eyes had flicked down and
noticed. His mouth hardened a little.

"Well, this isn't exactly the hero's welcome I expected. No 'Hello,
brother dear. Thank God, you're alive—we've all been worried sick.'"

"Hello, Landon," I said. "Welcome home."

REBEKAH

I sent Adelaide upstairs to wake Caroline and busied myself with
making dinner. My hands trembled as I filled a pot with water and
began chopping vegetables. Landon sat down in Dermot's chair
with a sigh. Kit put away my dressmaking supplies and hung the
clean tack beside the stove, and then hovered at the opposite end
of the table, as if unwilling to sit down but equally unwilling to
leave the room. I wanted more than anything to feel the reassurance of Kit's arms around me, but we kept a scrupulous distance
between us.

When Caroline came downstairs, bleary-eyed, Landon jumped
to his feet to embrace her. Though I couldn't remember him being
that tall in Halifax, he towered over his mother. Adelaide came
and hugged my legs. I handed her a piece of carrot to forestall any
questions.

Landon wiped his mother's tears with his sleeve. "I ran into
Mr. Gorseman in town. He told me about Pa," he said. "I'm so sorry.
I should've been here. That damn steamship—" Caroline took his
arm and led him out onto the porch.

Adelaide helped Kit set the table.

"Who is that?"

"My older brother," Kit said, catching a fork before it could hit the floor.

"Is he your brother too?" Adelaide asked me.

"No, sweetheart," I said, beginning to peel potatoes. "Grand-mère is his mother, just like she's Kit's mother."

"And your mother."

"Sort of," I said.

"Where was he?"

Kit swept her up and swung her around the kitchen. "He was off fighting in the war."

Adelaide squealed with delight. "Like you?"

"Yes, but I was in the air and he was on a ship."

"Did we know he was coming?"

"No," I said, catching my knuckle with the peeler and wincing. "Go fetch *trois grosses tomates* from the garden, please. Don't squish them."

Kit set Adelaide down, and she spread her arms like a plane and whooshed out the back door. We were alone in the kitchen. They took the peeler from my hand, lifted my finger and kissed away the blood.

"Does Landon know?"

I shrugged. "I have no idea. He never replied to my letters."

Caroline and Landon chose that moment to return from the porch and we sprang apart. He helped Caroline into her chair as though she were a woman twice her age. Kit finished peeling the potatoes while I fried the fish we'd caught yesterday.

Dinner was a strange affair. Landon talked for most of the meal, describing his adventures in the navy—daring rescues, near-misses with U-boats and the liberation of Antwerp.

"The people lined the harbour, end to end, when we sailed in," he said, putting another piece of fish into his mouth. "They'd been starving for months under the Kraut's boot, and we arrived with food and supplies, like Father Christmas come early!"

Caroline and Adelaide were rapt. Kit ate quietly, saying nothing to disagree, while all I could do was push the fish around my plate with my fork. The man sitting across from me was no longer the boy who'd teased me with a grass stem in the hayfield or the young lieutenant I'd danced with, and more, in Halifax, but a seasoned navy vet, with a sailor's rough manners and colourful language. He reminded me of the men I'd seen on shore leave in Halifax, the ones who roamed the city in schools like fish, or perhaps sharks.

"Who would like dessert?" I said, standing up and beginning to collect plates. Landon broke off in mid-story, looking at me in surprise, but then quickly back at Caroline. I stacked the dishes in the sink and brought the jelly to the table.

"Raspberry, my favourite! How did you know?" Landon said.

I smiled at him blandly. "It's my daughter's favourite too."

After that, only Adelaide ate dessert with enthusiasm.

After dinner, Landon chivvied us into a card game. I let Adelaide have a second helping of dessert, as she watched Kit win a pack of cigarettes from Landon. At the end of the game, Caroline announced it was time for bed and carried Adelaide upstairs, over her protests. Kit slipped out the door to finish the evening chores as I went to the sink to wash the supper dishes.

Landon came to stand at my elbow, eating the last of the jelly straight from the bowl.

"This was delicious. Have you always been such a good cook?"

"Yes," I said, and handed him a drying cloth. We worked in silence for a few moments.

Landon cleared his throat. "So, there was a guy I knew, in the navy, a real card sharp—"

The plate I was holding crashed back into the sink. "Why didn't you reply to my letters?"

"Letters?" Landon's face was blank.

"I sent you several letters. You never replied."

Landon slowly dried a milk jug. "I only got one letter, nearly six months after . . ."

"Six months," I repeated. I'd been living with Hatti for weeks at that point.

"The mail system was terrible. Besides, we only got letters when we put in at port."

"Why didn't you write back after you knew?"

Landon put the jug on the counter. "It's not like I could've done anything."

"You should have written!"

"I knew you were a smart girl and would figure it out." He took my hand. "If there had been any way, I would have come back to you and made it right. I'm sorry you had to go through that alone."

I opened my mouth to say that I hadn't been alone, not really, and he brushed his thumb along my jaw. "You were always so strong, and capable, no matter what anyone said."

How many nights had I lain awake in Halifax, wishing to hear those exact words? Landon dropped his hand slowly. I felt dizzy.

"Besides," he continued lightly, "how could I be sure it was even mine?"

I stared at him, so shocked I didn't know how to react. Finally, I hissed, "How dare you?"

He raised the towel in surrender. "Think how it looked to me. You seemed to know what you were up to that night—"

"She's yours. But I've never told her and I'm never going to. Adelaide thinks Jep was her father." Landon opened his mouth to protest, but I pressed on. "And that is the way it has to be. I have the marriage document to prove it."

"I assume that was my mother's doing."

"None of that matters," I snapped. "But if you tell Adelaide anything different . . ."

"Sure, sure," Landon said. "Your secret's safe with me."

"You can finish the dishes," I said, and I went upstairs and sat on my bed with the door closed and my head in my hands. Our bubble of happiness seemed to have burst.

The next morning, I slept late. With Adelaide now sharing a room with Caroline, I was no longer kicked awake before dawn by restless little feet. I groaned, pressing both palms to my eyes, but the thought of Landon possibly alone in the kitchen with my daughter was enough to send me staggering to my feet.

Caroline had made us a generous breakfast of eggs and thick cuts of bacon and toast slathered with homemade butter and honey from a hive Kit had found earlier in the summer. Landon complimented everything she put in front of him, reminding me of the boy who had sat in my mother's dining room, carefully praising every dish.

After breakfast, Kit announced that they were taking Adelaide fishing, and I packed the two of them some cold bacon sandwiches and rosehip tea and waved them off towards the river, breathing a sigh of relief.

Landon insisted on driving his mother and me into Orangeville in his car. I would have stayed home but, seeing the look on

Caroline's face, I went upstairs to change into something suitable for town. On the drive, Caroline sat up front and Landon talked to her the whole way, about the make and model of the car, who he had bought it from and other details I didn't bother to retain.

In town, Landon and Caroline wandered from shop to shop. He bought her a new hat, a box of chocolates and some new fall gloves. I trailed them, feeling totally off kilter. I couldn't remember the last time I had gone shopping for the sake of new things. Back in Montreal with Madeleine, I supposed. When Landon offered to buy me similar gifts, I refused, even though Caroline shot me a questioning glance. I left them to go to the bookstore and picked out a used copy of *Peter Duck* and *Le Petit Prince* to add to our collection, along with a spelling primer.

Landon and Caroline met me back at the car, Landon wheeling a shiny red child's bicycle.

"Absolutely not," I said.

"Oh come on. She'll love it. The kid needs a way to get around."

"It will be helpful for her to get to school, if nothing else," Caroline said, stroking the handlebars fondly.

"It's too much," I said. "You should be saving your money for—"

"You let me worry about that. If I want to spoil my niece, then what's the harm?"

I had no answer to that. In short order, the bike was loaded into the trunk, and we were rumbling back along the road to the farm.

Adelaide was overjoyed with Landon's gift. She bolted across the yard, leaving Kit to carry the string of fish. In moments, she was straddling the bike, and Landon was pushing her up and down the drive, her laughter carrying clearly in the air. We all watched them,

Caroline with a misty-eyed expression. "I wish Dermot could be here to see this," she said. Kit hugged her around the waist, leaning their chin on her shoulder. I took the fish inside.

Landon spent the rest of the afternoon touring the farm with Caroline, pointing out areas for improvement. I couldn't coax Adelaide into sitting down with her new books, she was so enthralled with the bike. Instead, I cleaned the fish, relieved that I was alone in the kitchen.

When Caroline came in to take over preparing supper, I went out to the barn for evening chores. As I came across the yard, I heard raised voices from the other side of the barn.

"Haven't you learned to keep your mouth shut?" Landon's voice was low and angry.

A muffled reply. I hurried around the corner of the barn, and found Kit and Landon face to face in the paddock, wearing identical furious expressions.

"It's none of your concern," Landon snapped. Neither of them saw me.

"So, what, you just knock her up and then disappear? You selfish bastard—"

"Still the same tune? I killed boys with more backbone than you, Kathleen."

Kit let out a snarl that was more animal than human and punched him in the face. Landon dove forward, catching Kit's sleeve and tearing it as he dragged them to the ground.

I was through the gate before I knew what I was doing. "Kit! Stop!"

They both froze, Kit kneeling on top of Landon, fist raised. "He left both of you with nothing. The bastard needs to—"

"I don't want you to hurt him," I said.

Landon was breathing hard, eyes furious through his mask of dirt. Kit got to their feet, stalked across the paddock and pushed past me without speaking. A moment later, I heard the kitchen door slam.

Landon lay for a few more moments in the dirt, panting. I walked over as he sat up, blood trickling from his nose. He took the handkerchief I offered.

"Damn, that was some left hook," he said, wiping his nose and then looking at the blood. "Where the fuck did Kath pick that up?"

"You wouldn't believe me if I told you," I said. "Can you walk?"

"I think so."

"Good. Then you can help me do the chores."

I turned and went into the barn, not bothering to look back. Landon caught up to me in the tack room as I filled a bucket with grain.

"You planning to tell me what that was about?"

Landon leaned against the doorway, the handkerchief to his nose. "The same thing it's always been about."

I glared at him. "I am not some fairground prize you can win."

"It's not about you." In response to my raised eyebrow, he added, "Or at least, it's not just about you."

I pushed past him into the main corridor of the stable. The animals shuffled and kicked in their stalls, eager for dinner. I went down the line, pouring grain into each trough.

Landon followed me. "It's always been like this, since the drowning."

I leaned the empty bucket on the edge of Daisy's stall door. "Kit has nothing to prove to anyone, least of all you."

"Look, for whatever I did, for everything, I'm sorry. To me the baby was just this abstract concept, not a little girl. Please believe me."

"I forgave you a long time ago. You don't owe us anything."

I took the water bucket from the nearest stall and walked past him into the yard. I filled the bucket and hauled it to the water troughs where I dumped the water. Landon remained where he was, carefully cleaning the blood from his nose. On my fourth trip, he waited until I had my back turned to him before clearing his throat.

"There's something else."

I turned, my arms beginning to ache from hauling water. He was staring at the ground, squeezing and twisting my handkerchief in his hand.

"I met someone else. Over there. A woman."

"Did you knock her up too?"

"What? No, of course not."

"You sure?"

"Very sure, and even if I had, it would be different because I— well, we . . ."

I stared him down. "You what, Landon?"

"I married her."

That night in the apartment, Landon's mouth next to my ear. *Marry me.*

I turned and left the barn. Landon chased after me. "Wait, Rebekah, let me explain. I hadn't heard from you in months and she, well, we met—"

"You didn't think to tell me you'd changed your mind? What's your excuse for never writing?"

"I did write! I wrote to Devil's Battery. Someone named Mathers replied, said you'd left months earlier. I had no idea where you'd gone."

"How could you just forget that you'd asked me to marry you and take up with the first piece of skirt that you—"

"No, it wasn't like that. We were stationed together for a while in Bristol. I . . . I didn't propose until after the war ended. After we got married, we stayed with her family. That's why we took so long getting back here. This wasn't some knee-jerk decision, Becca. I missed you, but . . . well, you weren't there."

"No, I wasn't. I was busy raising your child."

"I didn't mean—"

"Wait, why did you say 'we took so long'?"

Landon looked away, his cheeks reddening beneath the blood and dirt that smeared his face. "I was going to say something but, well, I didn't expect you to be here and it's not as though I could write and tell my wife to go back."

"Go back," I echoed. It was not a question.

"Sophie, of course. She boarded a ship a few days after I did. She's arriving here tomorrow. I was going to tell you, but then Kathleen heard me telling Ma and—"

I blinked at him. Everything fell into place now. His apology in the kitchen last night. The bike, the fight with Kit. Realizing I was still holding a full bucket, I slowly raised and upturned it over his head. He spluttered, coughing and spitting water everywhere. I dropped the bucket in the yard and walked away. I didn't remove my boots, just stomped into the kitchen and up the stairs. I pushed open the bedroom door.

Kit was inside, pulling a clean shirt over freshly rinsed hair. I leaned back against the door to shut it as they looked at me warily from beside the bed.

"If you're going to yell at me again, do you think you could do it quietly?"

I crossed the room in three quick steps and kissed them, wrapping my arms around their neck. When we broke apart, I cupped their face between my hands. "Teach me, so next time I can be the one to punch him."

"Of course. The secret is to—"

I kissed them again, smelling soap on their skin, water droplets from their hair running down our faces.

KIT

Landon and Caroline went to meet Sophie at the train station the next day, leaving the three of us to wander aimlessly around the house. Finally, Rebekah suggested we go swimming. By the time we arrived at the willow bend, we were sweaty and hot enough that we splashed straight into the water in our clothes. Adelaide whooped with excitement, scaring every fish for miles around. The water soothed my nerves and washed away the last of the dirt from the fight with Landon. Then Rebekah and I stretched out on the flat rocks while Adelaide explored up and down the bank.

"Not too far," Rebekah called after her.

The sun hot on my back, I turned my head to Rebekah. "Do you remember the last time we were here?" I asked.

A slow smile spread across her face. "I was scared half to death," she whispered.

"Me too." We both could hear Adelaide splashing a little farther up the bank, and Rebekah leaned over and kissed me, slow and sweet.

"Mumma! I found a crawfish!"

Rebekah sighed and heaved herself to her feet and I laughed as she waded out to her daughter.

We lingered until hunger drove us back to the farmhouse. We must have made quite a picture, tramping into the kitchen in our damp clothes, Adelaide carrying the crawfish in a bucket. Landon and Caroline and a blond woman were seated at the table, which was scattered with teacups and a box of chocolates.

"There you all are!" Caroline said. "I was beginning to think— well, here *we* all are."

Landon's wife stood up to greet us. She was neatly dressed in a travelling suit, with chapped, rosebud lips in a pretty, narrow face. Landon stood as well, looking nervous. "Sophie, this is Rebekah, my brother's widow. Rebekah, this is my wife, Sophie McNair."

Rebekah shook her hand politely. Sophie's face crinkled with concern. "I'm so sorry. From everything Landon's told me, Jep seemed just wonderful."

"Yes, he was," Rebekah said. I didn't look at Landon, for fear my expression would cause another scene.

Landon continued. "This is my niece, Adelaide, and this is my—"

"This is Kit," Rebekah interrupted.

Sophie shook my hand. "And you are?"

"Landon's my brother."

"Oh. I'm so sorry, he never mentioned that he had another— well, it's a pleasure to meet you."

There was an awkward silence, until Rebekah placed her hand on Adelaide's head. "You go and wash up. Caroline, shall I make more tea?"

I smiled to myself to see the aristocratic daughter reappear to take control of the room. We sat in the kitchen drinking tea and nibbling chocolate, and Rebekah engaged Sophie in a charming conversation about her family, her first impressions of Canada, her tour with the Women's Royal Navy Service in Bristol. Sophie looked relieved to be on familiar social ground. Landon sat, looking bemused. Clearly, Rebekah's gracious welcome was the very last thing he had expected.

After dinner, Rebekah announced that she would sleep in the attic, and let the newlyweds have the master bedroom. Sophie protested, until Adelaide announced that she wanted to sleep in the attic too, and in the end I spent a stuffy hour after dinner dusting and airing out the attic while Caroline changed the bedding. Shortly after the sun went down, our guests were installed in the largest bedroom and we all retired for the night.

I climbed the attic ladder to find Rebekah and Adelaide snuggled together, reading the first chapter of *Peter Duck* aloud. I had never understood the appeal of those books, but it was pleasant to listen to Rebekah's voice as I sifted through Jep's collections, handling each stone, feather and bit of wood, trying to see them as he would have seen them.

"Were those my father's?" Adelaide asked, after Rebekah had set the book aside and turned down the lamp.

"Yes," I said. "He loved to collect beautiful things."

"Can I see them?"

"In the morning," Rebekah said firmly, and drew the curtain closed around the bed that had once been Landon's. It was hot up here and the porthole windows let in very little air. One floor below, I heard Landon and Sophie talking as they got ready for bed, then silence.

I turned to Rebekah. "Want to go back to the river?" I whispered.

"What about Adelaide?"

"She'll be fine. Besides—" I lifted my chin towards the curtained corner, where tiny snores were already bubbling.

An hour later, we lay naked on the shale rocks, still faintly warm from the heat of the day. There was still no wind, but the air felt cool on my wet skin. Rebekah rested her head on my chest.

"She can hear them, you know."

"Hmm?"

"The voices," she murmured, half-dozing. "The ones in the water. Adelaide can hear them. She says they're like whispers, but from far away."

I lay still, listening to the crickets and the chuckle of the water close to my feet. The voices were there, at the edge of my awareness, laughing and coaxing. Gooseflesh rippled over my skin despite the hot night, as Rebekah sighed and her breathing deepened into sleep.

The weather only grew hotter as the days passed. By eight in the morning, the sun was already a scorching wave across the yard. The animals were restless and irritable when I went out to do the morning chores.

Inside the house it was hardly better. No one had the appetite or energy to consider any work beyond the minimum, all of us drifting listlessly from room to room. Landon listened to the new radio he had purchased, while Caroline let out a summer dress for Adelaide. I sat on the porch in the shade, listening as Rebekah and Sophie chatted, fanning themselves with folded newspapers. They were the same age, and Sophie's father had been a professor at a university; their shared love of books seemed to have sparked an unlikely friendship. I told myself I wasn't jealous, simply hot and tired, and went out to water the garden before the vegetables wilted.

The sky was hazy, as though rain was gathering somewhere beyond the horizon. I refilled the water troughs in the paddock and splashed my face and hands at the pump. As I headed back to the porch, Sophie and Rebekah were still in deep discussion.

"What's your favourite Dickens novel, Kit?" Sophie asked politely as I came up the steps.

"Never read him," I said, prompting an awkward silence from both of them. "I did read *Kitty Foyle* during my tour, though. I liked that one."

Rebekah looked up. "You never told me you liked Christopher Morley."

"You never asked," I said with a small smile, and I went into the house.

After a late, cold lunch that everyone picked at, Sophie went upstairs to read. Rebekah and Adelaide took books, lemonade and an old quilt out to the shade of the big maple tree beside the house. Landon asked Caroline and me to stay with him in the kitchen.

He was seated in Pa's old place at the table, a chair he regularly claimed. It was the hottest part of the afternoon, and the air indoors was stifling. Through the screen door, I could see the heat waves shimmering across the field.

Landon cleared his throat. "I think you both know what I want to discuss."

I shook my head and looked at my mother, who was nodding.

Landon caught my eye and looked away. "With Pa gone, I've inherited the farm." He reached over and placed his hand over my mother's. "I know the hardships you've endured while I was away. Things haven't been easy."

"Hold on," I said. "Pa left the farm to you?"

My mother sighed. "Your father died without a will. Now that Landon's returned, I am happy to give it over to his care." She patted his hand.

"But that's not—"

"I am not as young as I used to be," my mother went on. "I've worked every day of my life, trying to make this farm run and keep you all fed and clothed as best I could. But with your father gone, I am tired." She paused to collect herself and looked at me. "I want to enjoy the final years of my life with my grandchildren, not work myself into an early grave alongside Dermot."

"But what about—?"

"I believe that Landon and Sophie will be good stewards. They are young and they want to start a family soon. Landon told me his plans for this place and I think they are good ones."

"Rebekah has spent years here, working alongside you. How can you simply turn her out?"

"Rebekah and Adelaide are welcome to stay here until they find a place of their own," Landon said, though I noticed he refused to meet my eyes.

"Yes, I'm sure Rebekah will be thrilled to live here with you and Sophie and your future ten children—"

"As I said, she is welcome to stay."

I turned to my mother. "I've put time into this farm, too, spent years working—"

"If I left the farm to you, there is no guarantee that you would stay and do what was needed."

"You don't know that."

"Landon and Sophie are married, and more reliable than you."

Landon said quietly, "What's to stop you running away again and leaving our family's legacy to crumble?"

I looked from one to the other. They both had the same frown of concern, the same pinched lips. My eyes burned, though no tears formed in the heat.

"Where will I go?" I asked my mother, who looked away.

"Wherever you like," Landon said. "I have some money set aside. I could loan you enough to get you settled."

"I don't need money or anything else from you." I stood up and strode towards the door.

"Kathleen, be reasonable!" my mother called after me, but I slammed the screen door shut on her words.

My feet carried me blindly away from the house. With his love of machines and his desire to impress, Landon would bankrupt the place. We had only survived this long because of my parents' frugal ways and hard-headed practicality. With my brother in charge, I gave the farm a year at most, before it was foreclosed.

I kicked a patch of nettles clean off their stems and vaulted over the fence. The top rail gave way under my hands. I picked up the rotting cedar rail and hurled it into the forest alongside the field. It landed with a soft thud in the grass. I kept walking.

How convenient for Landon to be able to invent a clean, shining future for himself, free of any complications. As though Adelaide was a toy he could tuck away in the attic when it no longer suited him to play uncle. Rebekah had spent years here with my parents, putting food on the table and keeping a roof over their heads. I hadn't appreciated it before, but I saw it now, the way she had sacrificed to keep my family alive. What kind of repayment was this?

My feet had brought me across the river and up to the top of the ridge overlooking Harrichford, the place where Jep and Rebekah and I had eaten licorice so many years ago. The landscape shimmered in the heat. I snatched up a pebble at my feet and flung it out into the open air. It disappeared into the treetops below. I picked up another.

In those last years of the war, in the Pathfinders, during dozens of night ops dropping flares, I had comforted myself with the thought that at the end of it, when I was ready, I could come home. That no matter how long I stayed away, there would be a place for me here, that the forest would open its arms to me in welcome and I could sink back into the familiar embrace of the farm.

I threw another rock off the ridge, and another.

I had conjured home in my mind so many times, and with every recalling it had grown more my own, more my birthright: the smell of the wind from the lakes, fields of grass like ocean waves, my wild races to catch the train, the smallest violets growing under the willows beside the river, the feel of trout against my fingertips, the frogs peeping in the spring night. I'd pressed the ghosts of my crew between those memories like flowers in the pages of a book and carried them back with me across the Atlantic. And I thought—I thought if I could bring them here, and lay them down in this beautiful corner of the world, that it would be a kind of peace. That perhaps I had survived so that I could return here, with them. So that Laurie would be able to lie on the grass in the sunshine and finally be warm again. Matthew and Isaak could have eternity together in the cottage on the hill. And Jep—

I sank down on the clifftop, wrapped my arms around my knees and rested my head on my forearms. As long as I walked the same trails we had travelled together and sat here looking out at the view we'd shared, hearing his laugh in my head, then some part of my brother would live on.

But if I wasn't here, if this place wasn't mine to tend and love and keep, there was no point to any of it. I would be adrift again, along with all the others, as untethered as I'd ever been in the air, suspended between the void and oblivion. I'd failed to protect Jep, and Isaak and Laurie, and my crew. I couldn't afford to fail Rebekah and Adelaide as well.

A shadow passed across the sun, taking the heat with it. My skin prickled, the hair standing up along my arms. I raised my head. A wall of clouds had built along the horizon, piled into towering thunderheads. The base was dark grey-black, while the soft peaks, several miles up, were tipped gold and pink in the sunlight. The village and fields below me were swiftly falling into shadow as the storm crept farther up the western sky.

I lurched to my feet and hurried down the ridge and across the river. The forest was silent as I jogged back towards the farm—no birds calling, no click and buzz of insects. The whole world was flat and still, as though a giant had pressed a hot iron over the land.

As I rounded the edge of the barn, I saw the chickens huddled beside the coop, their feathers splayed as they crouched close to the ground. My mother was pulling washing from the line and tossing it into a basket at her feet.

"I don't like how this weather's turning," she said as I arrived.

"There's a storm coming up, and it looks like a bad one," I said.

My mother turned and hollered through the open kitchen window for Landon. When he appeared, she pointed towards the barn. "Get Jenny and Daisy inside, now. Then wake Sophie." My brother turned to go. "And get a lantern—we might need to head for the cellar."

I helped her pull the last of the clothes off the line. "Ma, I'm sorry about earlier. I shouldn't have run off like that."

"Never you mind," she said, handing me the basket, and heading towards the chicken coop. I followed.

"I know you think I'm unreliable, and I've given you every reason to believe it," I said, shooing a stray hen towards the coop with my foot. "But I know I can do this, if you'll just give me a chance."

My mother latched the coop door and turned to me, a hand planted on her hip. "Kathleen, it's not that—"

"Adelaide?" I turned to see Rebekah coming around the side of the house, quilt and books in her arms. "Have you seen her? We fell asleep under the tree, and when I woke up, she was gone."

My mother was already halfway to the kitchen door. "We'll check the house. Kathleen, you check the barn. She can't have gone far." Rebekah followed her inside.

I dropped the basket and ran to the barn. I looked in every stall, the pigsty, the hayloft, the tack room—all of Jep's childhood hiding places. Nothing. When I stepped outside, the clouds in the west had grown taller, rising and spilling across half the sky. I heard a distant growl of thunder. A shiver ran down my spine.

I looked among the tall raspberry canes in the garden, in the paddocks, under the front porch. Adelaide's bike was still where she had left it yesterday, leaning against the house under the kitchen window. Gordie followed me, a soft whine in the back of his throat.

The five of us met in the yard, next to the water pump. "She's not anywhere in the house," Sophie said.

Rebekah ran her fingers through her hair, looking wildly around. "She can't have just disappeared! One of you must have seen her."

The light faded, all colour draining from the grass and the fence posts and the buildings. There was a white flash of lightning from deep under the clouds.

"We should go to the cellar," my mother said, as the thunder rumbled. "Landon will—"

"No, I should—" Rebekah said, looking around wildly.

"I'll go," I said, and grabbed her shoulders, spun her to face me. "You need to stay here in case she comes back on her own." Rebekah's eyes were frantic. I tightened my grip. "I'll find her. I promise."

Landon was at the cellar doors, the hinges shrieking as he hauled them open. Sophie took Rebekah's arm and tugged her towards the house, my mother and Gordie following. I turned and started running.

There was only one place a bored child would go on a hot day— the same place I had been taking her all summer.

I ran past the barn, over the fences, along the back field. The wind found me halfway. First the tree canopy hissing in fear, then the fence posts groaning and creaking under strain, and then through the field as though some terrible, invisible animal was rushing up the hill towards me, flattening the grass in its wake. I ducked into the cover of the forest, and the wind crashed against the trees like a wave. I kept going, down towards the river.

I heard them before I reached the water. The rushing, murmuring water was loud over the sound of the wind. And louder still were the voices, hissing and whispering in my ears. I burst out onto the riverbank at the willow bend, where the trout lazed in the shadows. The voices were clamouring now, crowing and shrieking in triumph. And there, high over the river, cowering on the fallen willow tree, tiny hands clinging to the trunk, was Adelaide. The water beneath her was deep, up to my shoulders even in high summer. Plenty deep enough to drown a child.

"Adelaide!"

The wind whipped the branches overhead into a frenzy, sending leaves, twigs and branches pelting down onto us. She looked up and saw me on the bank. She raised her hand towards me, and overbalanced, sliding halfway down the log towards the water. One foot scrambled for purchase.

"Don't move! I'm coming!"

The first drops of rain began to fall as I plunged into the water, turned gunmetal grey in the approaching storm, and waded towards her.

"I'm coming for you, don't let go."

Adelaide was sobbing with fear, her whole body shaking with the effort of holding on to the tree. The water was colder than it had been all summer, and it was rising around me, sweeping me off my feet, the river running faster even as I swam towards the log.

"Hold on!" I kicked hard against the current, stretching my arms towards her as I drew closer. Her face was pale where it pressed against the bark.

"I'm coming, just don't—"

The water rose higher, then a single wave crested over the log, tearing her free and pulling her under.

I dove.

It was dark under the water, the current rushing past my face, pushing me back. The voices came from everywhere at once, mocking, snarling, pleading. I saw a blue-green glow from below me and swam down. It was deep here, too deep for this river, and the glow spread until I could see a small figure lying on the stones at the bottom. I fought the current, angling my body towards the light, the voices chasing me, hideous and raging. I pulled Adelaide into my arms. The current lashed me, pinned us to the stones, the voices screaming, the blue-green light flashing and blinding me. I held Adelaide close to my chest and closed my eyes. My lungs burned, my head pounded. Everything in me screamed for air. I opened my eyes.

They surrounded us, shadowy, elongated figures limned in green and brown. Long fingers stretching and bending in the current, eyes that burned like foxfire in the dark water. Their howling whispers resolving into a single demand.

"No," I said, silver bubbles rolling off my tongue. Their shrieks knifed through my ears, fingers clawing at my wrists, demanding that I let go. I held Adelaide tighter, braced my feet against the rocks and pushed with all my strength, rocketing us upwards, following the silver bubbles.

We broke the surface and I waded out of the river, carrying Adelaide onto the flat shale. For a long moment she was still and cold. I pounded her back and pushed her stomach, and then she was coughing and vomiting water and choking. And then crying, but alive and breathing. I gathered her into my arms, and we huddled for a moment as the rain fell on us. The river was flowing faster, the water churning and swollen by runoff upstream. The sky was a sickly green and black overhead. I rubbed my eyes. That couldn't be right.

Then I heard it, like the noise of a bomber swooping low in the night. A roar. Faint, but gaining strength. I lurched to my feet and gathered the child into my arms and started running back up the path. Hailstones began to fall, large as my fist. The roar drew closer.

As we broke out of the cover of the forest, the wind became a living creature, tearing branches from the treetops and hurling them around us. Thunder cracked overhead and the sky broke open, unleashing a torrent of rainfall. I stumbled towards the farm, the landscape disappearing in sheets of wind-driven water.

The wind seized my shirt, dragging me back, pulling me to the ground. I was back on *Friday's Girl*, the wind screaming past the torn edges of the metal, the force of it pushing me against the wall. I was tangled in my chute, I was holding someone, I had to get them to safety. A trail of blue-green light snaked across the ground. I followed it. The roar grew louder. The howling was inside me now, like an engine screaming in pain.

Overhead there was a sharp crack like machine gun fire and a huge branch plunged down, its jagged end driven several feet into the earth in front of me. I dodged the shower of earth and splinters and shrapnel, falling to the ground, shielding the bundle in my arms. My head was white-hot with pain, as though it might split open at any moment. I screamed. The wind swirled around me like a dust devil, snatching my voice and breaking it with easy fingers. The world flipped and the storm was inside my skin, blowing and buffeting me to the ground. My vision blurred and darkened on the left side, blue light rimming each blade of grass. There was water just below, like a deadly black mirror, and I was falling. I couldn't save them, couldn't save any of them. Laurie, Jep, Adelaide—bitter laughter among the trees, my own voice thrown back at me, only twisted and cruel.

A figure stumbled out of the rain and hail and branches. Landon, soaked to the bone, his face scratched and bloodied. He ran towards us and flung himself down next to me. The wind roiled around us, but in the space between Landon's shoulders and mine, we made a pocket of calm air. The scratch on his temple dripped blood down his neck.

Behind us, a small black tail unfurled from the edge of the clouds in the west, a snaking tendril reaching like a finger towards the earth.

I looked around, at the boiling sky and the branches whipping past us. The roar of the twister drew closer. The sound could have been an enemy squadron, engines fighting the wind. I drew a breath, conjuring the route that would carry us most quickly away from its path.

Landon threw his arm around my shoulders, and together we picked up the child and raced the twister back to the house, the wind pushing at our backs, billowing our shirts like sails. Foxlights danced in my eyes, under my feet. Hail pelted my shoulders, leaving bruises. We reached the house and nearly slammed against it, the wind clawing at our limbs, desperate to peel us from the earth. Landon crawled to the cellar door and pried it open, and I stumbled inside, my brother following, hauling on the door and slamming it shut above us with a sound like a gunshot. He threw the inside bolt, and I heard the wood vibrating in the wind. A cry. Rebekah, her arms around my neck, pulling Adelaide to her chest. Landon wrapped his arms around us all, and we knelt in a heap on the dirt floor, Rebekah sobbing, Landon shaking and gasping like a man pulled from the water. Our foreheads pressed together, Adelaide in the middle of us, trembling with fear, but safe and alive.

Overhead, the wind roared and shook the house, clawing at the foundations with vicious fingers. A howl in the sound now, like a lost ghost, and the slap of branches lashing the cellar door. There was a great crash like a tearing of the world itself, and we all shuddered to hear it.

I don't know how long we huddled there, in the dim light of the kerosene lamp, holding each other. At last Landon eased his grip on my shoulder, planted a soft kiss on Rebekah's temple, and stood up. He went over to Sophie, who was sitting with my mother, and gathered her into his arms. I coaxed Rebekah over to the wall and we sat together. I stroked Adelaide's hair and rested my forehead against Rebekah's shoulder. She was still trembling, but less so now. Soon, the two of them fell into an exhausted stupor.

My mother sat on a crate of preserves, Gordie huddled under her legs. She had her hands folded in her lap and was staring at the lamp. I went to sit beside her and put my arms around her waist. She was as still as stone, as though someone had replaced her flesh with granite. I held her for a long time, and we listened to the wind overhead grow quieter, and the roar diminish, until all I could hear was the light tap of rain on the cellar doors.

We waited until light shone through the cracks around the door. Then Landon cautiously threw the bolt, and we emerged one by one into the golden light of early evening.

The ground was littered with broken branches, ranging from the size of my thumb to larger than a full-grown man. Hailstones pockmarked the yard, melting into tiny puddles. The barn stood intact, a few of my new shingles stripped and lying useless in the paddock. The laundry I'd abandoned was flung across the paddock and up onto the roof of the barn.

The house was unrecognizable. The west wall was entirely torn away, revealing our rooms like a doll's house, our belongings scattered across the grass like children's toys. The tornado had picked up the maple tree and thrown it forty feet onto the roof, caving in the attic. The paddock fence was broken on both the west and east sides, where the tornado had driven right through. In the side field, I saw Daisy and Jenny wandering aimlessly. The chicken coop was unscathed, the white paint spotless.

The five of us stood in silence, surveying the damage. I put a hand on Landon's shoulder.

"You know what?" I said. "I've thought about it, and you're right. I think you should inherit the farm."

SEPTEMBER 1947

IN THE END, LANDON AND SOPHIE ELECTED TO PUT what was left of the place up for sale and move to Orangeville, where a navy friend of Landon's was starting a business and had offered him a job. No one was surprised when Caroline decided to move in with them. They found a buyer, a young architect from Toronto, who drove up from the city in his shiny Cadillac, surveyed the damaged farmhouse with his hands on his hips, and proclaimed that the land would do nicely for the house he wanted to build.

It took us a week to clean up the debris. Many of our belongings had been soaked or torn apart by the storm. I found my copy of *Kitty Foyle* ripped and scattered across the drive, while Adelaide's doll was discovered, unscathed, among the roots of the maple tree. Our clothing and papers lay tangled among the broken beams and shattered plaster. Meanwhile the black wood stove stood squat and square in the middle of the ruined kitchen, without so much as a scratch, though the stovepipe was a hundred yards away in the roadside ditch. Adelaide was the one to unearth Jep's photograph. The glass was smashed, but the picture intact.

Landon sold Jenny and Daisy to Sally Crochett, a childhood neighbour, now grown with three children of her own, and the pigs and the chickens went to market. Gordie, of course, would be going with Caroline to the new house in town.

We all slept in the hayloft and ate what vegetables we could salvage from the garden and cold sandwiches the neighbours brought by when they came to both offer sympathy and gawk at our misfortune. It was warm enough that we had little need for blankets, but I longed for the privacy to talk to Kit alone.

A week later, Landon and Sophie and Caroline sat on the undamaged side of the porch and discussed their future plans, the furniture that could be salvaged from the farm and what would need to be purchased. Kit was quiet, continuing to gather up pieces of wreckage and stack them in neat piles, scrupulously keeping a distance from the conference on the porch. I slipped the keys out of Landon's coat where it lay discarded over the far rail of the porch, and towed Kit and my daughter to the car. I settled Adelaide into the back seat and tossed the keys to Kit. They gave me a strange look as we climbed aboard.

"But you were in the Wrens," Kit said, reversing down the driveway at a slightly incautious speed.

"So?" I said.

"All of the RAF girls could drive."

"I did other things."

They gave me a sidelong look, but I focused on fixing my hair in the mirror. "How did you learn, anyway?"

As we took off down the road, Kit launched into a story involving a decommissioned Jeep, a dogsled team, and the flight training marshal's undergarments that was so far-fetched it was most likely true.

At the theatre in Orangeville, we ate popcorn, Kit's shoulder touching mine, and I smiled as Adelaide giggled along to *Fun and Fancy Free*. Afterwards, we walked through town, aimless and in no hurry to return to the farm. I bought us all ice creams, and we strolled through the park, where children screamed and ran in the playground and other families wandered the lawns just as we did.

"Have you given any thought to where we might go next?" I said, wiping a dribble of ice cream from the front of Adelaide's dress.

"I hadn't," Kit said, looking overhead at a plane that buzzed low in the sky. "You?"

"I always thought I would go back to Montreal, but I'm not sure I want that anymore."

Kit nodded. "Lincolnshire was nice, but it's a long way away."

We found a bench and sat while Adelaide ran back and forth clacking a stick against the nearby railings.

"Halifax?" Kit suggested.

"Too cold and too much . . ." I gestured vaguely.

Kit crossed their arms, stretched their legs out. "We could always stay here and find another farm."

I considered it. To stay and have the river and the forest and all the familiar faces and sights of Harrichford. I could see the appeal.

Adelaide plunked herself between us on the bench, the stick now a tool for stabbing the grass at our feet. I hadn't realized she'd been listening until she spoke up.

"I want to see the ocean," she said. Kit and I exchanged a look over her head.

"Halifax is awfully cold," Kit said.

I smiled. "Lucky for us, there's more than one ocean."

AUGUST 1953

ADELAIDE

"LAND HO!" I YELL.

"I have eyes," Kit grumbles from beside me, one hand on the tiller.

"But this is much more nautical," Mum replies. She is sprawled on the foredeck, a thick book open in front of her.

The island ahead of us is covered in forest and I can see boulders and cedars along the shoreline. A small crescent of sand marks the cove we're headed for.

"Addie, keep an eye out for deadheads," Kit says, leaning out to check the water depth.

"Aye aye, Skipper." I scramble ahead to the bow and look into the clear water. It's early evening and the sun is low in the sky, sending gold sparkles skimming over the surface. Mum shuts her book and climbs to her feet.

I spot a rock lurking underwater. "A little to port!" I call, and Kit nudges the sailboat to the left. Mum stands on the other side of the bow, the anchor chain in her hands. As we draw closer to the cove, I can see a trail leading from the beach up into the forest.

"Anchor away!" Kit calls, and there is a big splash as Mum tosses it overboard.

An hour later, we sit by the fire and eat the crab we'd caught earlier in the day. Kit makes skillet bread over the coals, studded with blueberries I'd gathered just up the trail, and we eat it slathered with butter. I give a big sigh and lie back on the sand, to stare at the sky, slowly turning from yellow to pink overhead.

"I wish we could live out here all the time," I say and sneak a glance at Mum. She gives me one of her looks. Kit takes the frying pan and goes down to the waterline to scrub it out with sand. No help from that quarter, I guess.

"You're going back to school next week, Adelaide."

"But I don't want to. I wish summer holidays would last forever."

Mum smiles a little to herself. "You'll have new books to read and things to learn."

"I could learn new things out here," I mutter, but the sulk is only half-hearted. Truthfully, I am looking forward to telling my friends back in Victoria about my summer adventures.

"Besides," Mum says, "I got a letter from Hatti. She's coming up from San Francisco in a couple weeks."

"You've never let me go to a show," I say.

"Well, this year you are grown-up enough, but if you'd rather stay here in the forest—"

"No, I want to go!"

"It's settled, then," Kit says, stowing the pan and tossing another log on the fire to build it up again. "Besides, I have to clear trails up Sooke Mountain next week. We'll be out here again soon. *Siobhan* isn't going anywhere."

Our sailboat is bobbing gently in the water a few dozen feet offshore, her green paint reflecting in the nearly waveless surface.

My parents start talking about work and house stuff, which is boring, so I get up and go searching for shells along the shore.

"Be careful!" Mum calls after me. I roll my eyes. I find a few that are nice, but I want a big one for my collection, large enough to hold the smaller shells my dad collected when he was my age.

The sun has set by the time I walk back, but the water reflects plenty of light to see by. Mum and Kit are lying on a blanket from the rucksack, and I can hear them talking as I approach.

"We could stay out here a little longer, you know," Kit says.

"Not you too. You know I have to be back at the college on Tuesday."

The fire has burned down to coals, and I poke it with a stick until it flames up again and then I add another piece of driftwood. The shore is dark, but the water is purple-grey and pink where it reflects the sky. I can just see our boat like a tall shadow on the water. The wind is cool off the ocean, but the sand feels warm under my palms.

"Will you tell the story?" I ask.

Kit groans. "Again? I told it just two nights ago."

"But I want to hear it again."

"Why don't you tell it this time?" Mum says, and I can tell she's stifling a yawn.

"Fine. Once upon a time and a long time ago . . ."

I look up at the stars as I'm talking, picking out Orion and Draco and the Big Dipper as they appear in the sky. I hold my fist up to Polaris and count the latitude down with my fingers, just as Kit taught me. Forty-eight degrees. The fire dwindles again, and I hear a splash offshore as a fish or a seal jumps in the water.

"Until one day Corin woke to find her gone." I glance over. They are fast asleep on the blanket, Mum's arm draped over Kit's waist.

I listen to the waves as they roll in and out from the shore. The voices are there, underneath the sound of the water, singing and laughing. I whisper the last bit of the story to them.

"Siobhan swam out to the ocean rocks. She sloughed off her human body—the thing she'd built of clay and seaweed—and left it there, an empty shell. There was no one to see, but if you had been there, you would have noticed something that might have been a shadow or a shaft of light, dive into the water and vanish, as boundless and untameable as a current. Because, after all, everyone knows that water spirits cannot drown."

Off in the distance, a seal barks in agreement.

AUTHOR'S NOTE

This book is, above all, a work of fiction. Whenever I had to choose between maintaining strict historical accuracy or risk overwhelming the narrative with detail, I chose to distill what was essential for the story and let the rest go. Thus, in this magical past, historical timelines have been ruthlessly shifted, a few things invented, and much of history ignored entirely.

The town of Harrichford is fictional, as is Harrichford County, though they would be located somewhere in the Dufferin-Simcoe region north of Toronto, Ontario. While Devil's Battery was a real coastal defence installation in Dartmouth, Nova Scotia, no WRCNS "huff-duff" operations occurred there. Kit's unnamed airbase in Lincolnshire is fictional, but it is similar to the dozens of RAF bases scattered across the UK at the time. The Bluebird nightclub in Halifax is also an invention, though there were similar nightclubs serving wartime personnel across Canada.

It was beyond the scope of this story to directly portray Jewish, queer, and Roma experiences in the Holocaust, or to explore the devastating impact of Allied Bomber Command's operations on European civilians and prisoners of war. I would encourage every reader to visit their local public library, or one of the many publicly available online war museum archives, to learn more.

ACKNOWLEDGEMENTS

All writing is, at its heart, a collaboration, and this book is no exception. I have so many people to thank for making this book come to life.

My grandmother Brenda, who supported my education and always believed this day would come. Anne Collins, unequivocally the best editor in the world. From our very first conversation, I knew you understood this story better than I did. Jennifer Griffiths for a gorgeous cover design, Tilman Lewis for a discerning and sensitive copy edit, Stacey Cameron for such a careful cold read. Lauren Park and Diyasha Sen, for such encouraging early reactions and useful comments, and the whole team at Penguin Random House Canada, for being so welcoming and supportive from day one. Meg Wheeler, literary agent extraordinaire, and Westwood Creative Artists, for guiding me through unknown waters. Annabel Lyon, the best adviser and mentor a student could ask for. Alison Acheson, Molly Cross-Blanchard, Jessica Johns, Keith Mallard, H.C. Phillips, Kiri Sawyer, Jasmine Sealy, Peter Takach, and Sara de Waal for your encouragement and critiques of early drafts. The University of British Columbia Department of Creative Writing and the Social Sciences and Humanities Research Council of Canada for generously providing funding for this project. The Canadian War Museum, the Halifax Military Heritage Preservation Society, Imperial War Museum, Royal Air Force Museum, and the Toronto Public Library, whose publicly available online archives proved invaluable during the global pandemic.

My parents, Clare and Reed, for being very understanding when I dropped out of an undergraduate pre-law track to meander around in creative writing and queer studies instead. My sisters, Rachael and Emily, whom I tortured with some truly abysmal writing in our early years and bossed around during living room theatre productions. Thanks for not killing me. Miriam, who was the first to encourage me to take my art seriously, and Kevin Chong, a generous mentor from day one. Rebekah, for cheerleading and hiking breaks, and Hermione, for owl post at just the right moment. Kayla, for texting me breathless updates in the wee hours—every writer dreams of having a reader like you. Morgan, for loving my characters the way I always hoped someone would and loving me more than I deserve. Mace, for confessing to staying up all night reading my story and assuring me that the sex scenes were, in fact, hot.

And finally, thank you to Michael, for everything. This book would not exist without you and neither, I suspect, would I.